Lucky
Bastard

Lucky Bastard

★ ★

CHARLES McCARRY

RANDOM HOUSE
NEW YORK

This is a work of fiction. Names, characters, places, and incidents are the products of the author's imagination. Where actual historical persons or incidents are mentioned, the contexts of such mentions are entirely fictional. Any resemblance to actual persons, living or dead, is entirely coincidental.

To the memory of Richard Condon

The
Talent
Spotter

One

1 The professor thought that I looked like Lenin. He often said so; he had said so the first time we met, years before in Cuba. Now, in a Chinese restaurant in Harlem, he was saying so again.

"The faintly—forgive me—Mephistophelean regard," he said. "The cheekbones, the forehead. Have you ever considered growing a beard?"

"No."

Unlike the professor, who cultivated the Che Guevara look— chestnut beard, green fatigues, romantic pallor—I was not trying to impersonate a terrorist. My goal was to look like a bourgeois intellectual who bought his clothes at Brooks Brothers, ate lunch in midtown restaurants where the headwaiters knew him by name, and lived on the Upper West Side with a highly intelligent wife and two cats. My speech was Eastern Establishment in tone and word choice. My personal English tutor, Princeton '31, a ruined asset who had fled to Moscow in 1956 after the arrest of his handler, the great Rudolf Ivanovich Abel, had even taught me to write by the Palmer method.

Studying me, the professor said, "It's the eyes, the epicanthic fold. Really, Dmitri, it's uncanny! You and Vladimir Ilyich could have a common ancestor."

Yes, I thought, *a rapist on horseback, absentee father of Holy Russia.*

The professor was babbling. Our meetings always excited him, but tonight he had other anxieties. He was a member of the underground, a spotter of talent at Columbia University. The last time we met, three months before—an eternity for an agent—I had reprimanded him. The young men and women he had recommended to me so far were of no possible interest—bourgeois neurotics who marched in demonstrations, thought in bumper stickers, took LSD, and spoke in tongues. Next time, I had said, bring me the real thing. Besides, he was not comfortable in these surroundings. The restaurant was noisy, smoke-filled, hot. We were the only whites in the place.

I will call him Arthur. From Arthur's point of view, this neighborhood was the heart of darkness. The truth was, my choice of meeting place was a punishment and a warning, and he understood this. He was afraid. He was ashamed of being afraid. He was a man of the Left. In the abstract he loved these loud, merry, downtrodden people. But in reality he was what he was, a nice bourgeois boy from the suburbs, and they terrified him.

The waiter, a dark-skinned Cantonese with wary eyes, gave us menus. In tone-deaf Mandarin (he had memorized one thousand ideograms as an undergraduate), Arthur quizzed him about the specialties of the house. The waiter clearly had no idea that Arthur was speaking Chinese. "Numbah six very spicy; Numbah five very good," he replied.

Arthur asked me what I preferred. I told him to choose whatever he liked. He smiled approvingly, thinking no doubt that I was too much the Soviet man to eat for pleasure. He ordered Number five, mu shu pork with extra hoisin sauce, and Number six, whole grilled fish in chili sauce, with fried rice. And Chinese beer.

Arthur chattered on about Lenin. He had written his doctoral dissertation on the great man's private life, so he knew many out-of-the-way details. Was I aware that Vladimir Ilyich may have had Kalmyk blood? That he sang baritone in family musicales? Arthur pronounced the Russian forename and patronymic perfectly, with easy familiarity, as if in some earlier life he had sung folk songs with Lenin on that sealed train to the Finland Station, as if he had been entrusted to deliver secret messages for the revolution: *Hang fifty kulaks a day as a demonstration to the peasants.* The real Lenin, hater of romantics, would have added a postscript: *Shoot the bearer.*

The food came. Arthur asked for chopsticks. The waiter handed them over and stayed for a moment to watch him take his first mouthfuls. Arthur nodded and spoke the Mandarin word for delicious. The waiter smiled; I wondered if he had spat into the food. I drank my beer, ate a little plain rice.

"Are you sure you don't want anything else?" Arthur asked.

"The MSG keeps me awake," I replied.

Actually I was afraid of diarrhea, the spy's complaint; I had had a lot of that in Shanghai, my last post, although bad food was not the only reason for loose bowels during the Cultural Revolution. My assignment in China had been to penetrate the Red Guards and baptize a few converts for the future, and also to make certain assurances to old friends who were being taunted and whipped through the streets and exiled to hard labor in mines and farming communes. I gave them what help I could—which is to say, none—and promised them that the true cause would be waiting for them after the madness passed or (same thing) Mao died. Not many of them lived that long, or ever wanted to see another Russian if they did. But some did, as we shall see.

After that, my target in America, the campus antiwar movement, should have been easy. It was a soft target, in no way frightening or difficult, but I had made little progress. After a year of close observation I had concluded that the counterculture was not composed of serious people. Their rallies were just another form of entertainment, their slogans another kind of cheerleading. Their movement had no ideological core, no vanguard elite, no discipline. It was make-believe, a game, a holiday, a new kind of fraternity party. Combat boots instead of white bucks, drugs instead of beer, but the objectives were the same—sex and intoxication. The true revolutionary makes revolution to escape from the inescapable. In America, nothing is inescapable. These children knew they could escape any time they wished simply by going home again, by acknowledging the reality of money and choosing it. American capitalism would roll over them like the irresistible ocean that it is. We, the real Left, the eternal Left, would be left holding a second mortgage on their idealism. They could not make revolution, but they could enable it when its moment came, when its leader emerged.

What I required, what I was looking for, was the leader. Once I had found him, history would make the moment. But first, the man. Revolutions almost always begin with one man. One man is all I ever hoped for. Arthur's job was to find him for me. He was not the only talent spotter we had recruited, of course; there were others like him on other campuses. But he was mine, and he was the one whose failures were freshest in my mind.

Arthur finished his food. He put down his chopsticks and said, "I think I've found someone for you."

I said, "Name?"

This was not the question Arthur expected. He had been trained never to utter names in the presence of strangers. I repeated the question. He cleared his throat and murmured a reply. Music played very loud—a woman saying goodbye to lust. The people at the next table were making a lot of jovial noise. Arthur's voice was weak. I could not hear him. I made an impatient gesture: *Louder.*

He paused, looking left and right for secret policemen.

"Speak up," I said in a loud voice. "It's quite safe. The FBI has very few black agents. That's why we're here."

Arthur leaned across the table and whispered a name.

I said, "Arthur, I can't hear you."

He tried again. His voice broke; the words came out as a squeak. I shook my head, made a disgusted face.

At the next table a beautiful fat woman in a low-cut dress—large sarcastic eyes, skin the color of aubergine—turned and gazed at us, head to one side like some huge curious bird.

His voice breaking with the effort, Arthur shouted, "*Jack Adams!*"

I said, "Jack Adams? How long have you known this Jack Adams?"

"Two years," Arthur replied.

"Two years? Two *years*? And this is the first time I hear his name?"

Arthur cleared his throat. "Sorry," he said. He was deeply agitated now—averted eyes, trembling voice.

The fat beauty, bright-eyed and knowing, stared harder at Arthur. What *were* we? It was plain to see what she thought we were. We are taught in the craft that sometimes the best way to divert attention is to draw attention. I lifted Arthur's inert hand from the table and kissed it.

The woman guffawed. Now she knew everything about us that she needed to know. She lost interest and turned back to her friends.

Arthur was sorely in need of reassurance. I poured him the last of the beer. "My dear comrade," I said, using a word I seldom speak even in a whisper, "tell me about this Jack Adams."

2 "First of all," Arthur said, "Jack is that rara avis among Ivy League radicals, a birthright member of the proletariat."

I said, "Meaning what?"

"He's poor. Working-class. Alone. No family, no connections, no influence. No future."

"So far, so good," I said. "Go on."

"He's an Ohio boy," Arthur said. "Alone in the world."

Jack Adams came from a long line of Ohio steelworkers. His forebears and their friends had been killed in fiery accidents in the mill or died of diseases caused by the superheated air they breathed. They had won World War II with prodigies of productivity and then been thrown onto the streets when the capitalists discovered they could buy steel cheaper from the defeated Japanese. Jack was an orphan, raised by his maternal grandparents in Tannery Falls, Ohio. He remembered the old days before the mills closed, the horizon glowing in the night from the blast furnaces, the smell of scorched air coming in the open windows of their little house, and the soft coal dust clinging to the wallpaper as it clung to the lining of the workers' lungs. His grandfather had lost his job like all the others, then died of drink. Jack was a child of the welfare system—social workers had bought his clothes, he had bought groceries with food stamps, the postman had delivered the monthly check with which his grandmother paid the endless mortgage on a house that had no market value. He had eaten free lunches at school, received free medical care. These details of lower-class life—the idea of losing everything, of having no recourse, of being glued to a certain fate, of being at the mercy of bureaucrats—fascinated Arthur, the son of a plastic surgeon, grandson of a banker. For at least four generations his family had lost nothing, had never considered it possible to do so.

In high school, Jack had been an honor student. His teachers loved him for his charming smile, for his eagerness to learn, and for his evident desire to grow up to be just like them. They had pushed him toward college, giving him better marks and better recommendations than perhaps he deserved. After making a high score on the standard college exams—Jack had an aptitude for aptitude tests, an aspect, no doubt, of his larger talent for giving answers that pleased his betters—he had been accepted at Columbia University with full financial aid. He was just as much of a success at Columbia as he had been at Tannery Falls High School, and for the same reasons. He paid rapt attention in class, he memorized, he regurgitated lectures without lapse or mistake. He was the best political science student Arthur had ever had—nimble in class, a good writer.

"There's more," Arthur said. "Jack is popular, very political—but a backstage person, not an up-front guy. He doesn't march with the troops. I think demonstrations scare him, actually—"

"Scare him?" I said.

"The unpredictability of the crowd, the idea of being arrested and handcuffed and dragged into the paddy wagon—"

"But it's all a game. Who has ever been injured at one of these things?"

"Lots of people," Arthur said. "That's beside the point. He's not a marcher, he's a thinker. He's close to the leaders of the movement. They listen to him. Most of the victories they get credit for are his ideas—defenestrating deans from first-floor windows, the defense of Harlem against callous capitalist exploitation by the university. A lot of the slogans. He's the invisible man of the Movement."

Arthur showed me a snapshot. Jack was quite presentable. An American boy. Curly hair, doughy young face, a brilliant smile: large square flashing teeth, eyes swimming with sincerity.

I said, "I am interested in his timidity."

"That may not be the right word for it," Arthur said. "Jack may not march on the Pentagon, but he's put his body on the line in other ways." He showed me another picture of Jack. In this one he was barely recognizable—an unsmiling near skeleton with unshaven cheeks. "This was taken on the last day of a forty-day water-only fast," Arthur said. "He lost seventy pounds."

"Why?"

"To beat the draft," Arthur replied. "An act of conscience. He refused to serve in an unjust war."

I said, "You mean he's a coward?"

Arthur flinched. This was not a word much used in the circles in which he traveled. He said, "Isn't everyone a coward in one way or another?"

"No. And cowards are always dangerous."

"Surely," Arthur said, "the truth is more complicated than that."

Was it really? I did not press the point. Arthur was a Freudian as well as a Marxist-Leninist. He did not wish to admit, ever, that things are what they seem. In his system of thought, the truth was always hidden, but discoverable by the enlightened, using approved methods of thought.

I said, "A question: What exactly is so special about this fellow?"

Arthur hesitated. "This will sound strange, coming from a good Marxist-Leninist like myself who believes so deeply in historical inevitability," he said at last. "But the answer is, Jack is lucky. In fact, he's the luckiest bastard I've ever met."

"Be serious."

Arthur said, "Dmitri, believe me, I've never been more serious in my life. He has a gift. Jack's a born politician. He's marginal in many other ways—IQ of 119, just like JFK—"

"Wait," I said. "How do you know what Kennedy's IQ was?"

Arthur blinked. "I taught at Choate for a year. That was Kennedy's school. It's in the files. The point is, it's a highly significant coincidence in Jack's mind."

"You told him about this coincidence?"

"Yes."

"An IQ of 119 says he is neither smart nor stupid. Surely he was not glad to know this."

"The coincidence made up for it. I mean, look where Kennedy ended up."

"Kennedy's father was not a steelworker."

"In Jack's opinion, neither was his, but we'll get to that," Arthur said.

"The fact remains, his is not an impressive score."

"You're right," Arthur conceded. "Jack's general intelligence is only a little better than average—not good enough, in theory, to get him into Columbia, even though he did well on the SATs. But I would like to suggest to you that this lack of a first-class mind is actually an advantage."

I said, "That you must explain to me."

"It makes him *seem* average to others when in fact he is not average at all," Arthur replied. "As I've said, he's extremely personable. People tend to think he's getting by on charm. They made the same mistake about Kennedy."

"In his case, money played a role."

"Okay, but for most of his life—right up to the day he died, if truth be told—his detractors thought they were smarter than him. Same thing with Jack Adams. That gives him a fantastic advantage. In the one respect that matters, political smarts, Jack is a brilliant, maybe even a unique, natural talent."

"How can you say this about a boy of twenty-one?"

Arthur was enjoying himself now. His IQ was much higher than 119, and he loved to show it.

"Trust me," he said. "Politics comes to him straight from the unconscious, in the same way that operas and symphonies came to Mozart. Whole concepts of how to use power just pop into his head, ready for orchestration. He doesn't even have to *think* about it. And he's never wrong. He's extraordinary in class, in his papers, in action. And unlike Mozart he has no Salieri. Jack doesn't have an enemy in the world. He's such a big dumb shit with such a dazzling smile that he excites no jealousy, no hostility. It doesn't matter what he does. It's uncanny. People will forgive him anything."

I interrupted. "What is there to forgive?"

"His sex drive," Arthur said. "He's mad for pussy. Tries to screw every female he meets, including the wives and girlfriends of his best friends."

"Does he succeed?"

"More often than not. It's puzzling in a way. The girls say he has absolutely no finesse—comes right at them, puts it in their hand. They say yes anyway. My wife says it's the way he smells."

"She's one of his conquests?"

"He made a pass," he replied. "Myra turned him down."

"Ah. But she noticed the way he smelled?"

Arthur smiled. He was not offended by my questions; he and his wife were people of their time and class—sexual revolutionaries who slept with whomever they wished. He reached into the little schoolboy knapsack he carried instead of a briefcase and handed over a thick brown envelope. Inside the envelope was Jack Adams's dossier, as compiled by Arthur's network of informants—at least one hundred pages of photocopied official records, together with neatly typed contact reports on Jack's background, behavior, apparent beliefs, and circle of friends. The contact reports—accounts of conversations with Jack—had been provided by student activists organized by Arthur to keep an eye on fellow radicals. These junior Chekists, all students of Arthur's, regarded themselves as a secret counterintelligence force whose work was necessary to protect the Movement from penetration by agents of the FBI, CIA, and other mostly nonexistent colonialist-imperialist enemies.

I put on my glasses and began to read. John Fitzgerald Adams— since birth called Jack and nothing but Jack—was the only child of a young woman named Betty Herzog. Betty herself had been an adored only child, pretty, smart, and lively. And—this is important—virtuous. In 1939, she was the Tannery Falls High School homecoming queen. This was the highest tribute to beauty an American village could pay, and in the period in question it could never have been bestowed on a girl who was not perceived to be a virgin. After high school, she became a registered nurse, and as soon as she was qualified, joined the U.S. Navy as an ensign. She was posted to a naval hospital in San Francisco. This was in 1943.

In her letters to her mother Betty seemed happy in her new life. She was promoted to lieutenant junior grade; her picture was in the Tannery Falls *Evening Journal.* Then, mysteriously, early in 1944, long before the war ended, she came home, discharged by the navy. A month later she married Homer Adams, a man ten years older than herself, a man too old for military service, a salesman of Hudson automobiles. On September 17, 1944, not quite six months after the wedding, Betty gave birth to Jack, a ten-pound baby.

It was Betty who insisted on naming the child John Fitzgerald, even though she had no relatives who bore either name. She gave no explanation. Her husband was angered and hurt. He wanted the boy to be named Homer, Jr., but Betty would not budge. "We'll call him Jack," she said. She corrected everyone who tried to call the child anything else—Jackie or Johnny or even John. "His name is Jack," she would say firmly. Jack remembered this vividly.

Betty and Homer Adams died five years later when a car driven by Homer, who was drunk at the time, crashed into a stone abutment at 70 mph. There were no skid marks at the scene. From his grandmother, Jack learned that Betty and Homer had had a terrible argument on the night of the accident—an argument so terrible that Betty had dropped Jack off at her parents' house, waking them at midnight. "Lock the doors, call the police if you have to, but don't let him touch my boy!" Betty had cried before running out into the night. This was the last time her mother saw her alive.

At his parents' funeral, five-year-old Jack had suffered a textbook trauma. The undertaker had done his best to put the smashed-up bodies back together. But to the terrified little boy, dangled over the open coffin by his weeping grandmother ("Kiss Mommy goodbye, Jack!"), the corpses, waxen and cold, looked like the stitched-together monsters in Frankenstein movies. Ever after, when Jack pictured death, his own or anyone else's, he pictured his parents in the funeral home.

Or so he told the people to whom he related this story—usually girls he was trying to seduce. Needless to say, Jack could not have seen very many Boris Karloff movies at the age of five, but he was never one to let facts stand in the way of a telling image. According to the reports, his voice broke as he summoned up the Frankenstein illustration; he covered his face with his hands and shuddered at the memory. Usually he was between the girl's legs moments later. Few objected afterward. Many reports mentioned that Jack was a single-minded, driving lover of amazing endurance. He bestowed orgasms on even the most disinterested partners.

"He does sex like in a dream, like he's in another state of consciousness," wrote one of his conquests. "Like he's on another planet. Like the woman is not there, or is somebody else. He just keeps going. And going. And going. Then he stops, gets up, and acts like nothing happened. This is weird but very sexy." The author of this report, who wrote on the basis of personal experience, was a psychology major. She thought that Jack's single-minded, blind copulations were an unconscious attempt to reenact his own conception over and over again. "Like he's trying to bring himself to life," she wrote.

Arthur watched me as I read. He saw that I was interested. He knew exactly where I was in the file, and what was coming next. I turned a page and came upon a brief report written by Arthur himself.

He said, "Heads up, Dmitri. The next part is the heart of the matter."

Indeed it was. As a teenager during the Kennedy presidency, Jack had discovered, hidden in the lining of his mother's naval uniform, several blurred photographs. One showed Betty in that same blue uniform, with her bright curly head on the shoulder of a scrawny young navy officer; other shots showed them together on a beach, or grinning at the camera from a convertible coupe. In one of these photographs, Betty, her young body obviously nude beneath the sheet that she held coquettishly beneath her chin, sat up in a rumpled hotel bed. In yet another, slim and naked, a truly lovely girl, she looked straight at the man behind the camera with the radiant smile of a woman in love. About that, there could be no doubt.

In the most important picture, the skinny young officer sat barechested in a hospital bed, grinning broadly, a bottle of beer in his hand and Betty's cap perched on his thick, tousled hair.

Arthur said, "Have you guessed?"

The answer was yes. But I replied, "Guessed what?"

"Jack's secret," Arthur said. "He thinks he's the love child of John F. Kennedy."

I took off my reading glasses and examined Arthur's face: a faint smile, a glimmer of triumph, but no sign of a joke.

"I kid you not," Arthur said.

I examined the pictures again. The quality was poor. They had been taken in feeble light with a cheap camera and inferior wartime film. These defects made them seem all the more authentic, of course.

I said, "Jack thinks this person in the snapshots is JFK?"

"He's certain of it," Arthur replied. "Read on."

The next item in the file was a magazine picture of the future president as he had looked in 1944 while recuperating from the injuries he received during the sinking of PT 109. This juvenile JFK was very thin, almost emaciated, but radiant with sexual glamour— just like the smiling young lover in Betty's snapshots.

Arthur said, "Jack thinks the snapshots were left to him by his mother as evidence that John F. Kennedy is his natural father."

"And you think that's possible?"

"The dates coincide. I researched it myself. PT 109 sank on August second, 1943. Kennedy spent some time in sick bay, then rode back to the States on an aircraft carrier. The carrier docked in San Francisco on January seventh, 1944. He stayed there until January eleventh. JFK being JFK, it's a fair assumption that he would have been looking for a piece of ass. He was in the navy; so was Betty. They were in the same town. Suppose he knocked her up the night before he left. Jack Adams was born 281 days later. Do the arithmetic."

"What would that prove?"

Arthur said, "Nothing, in itself. To Jack, it proves everything. The idea that he is a Kennedy bastard is the central obsession of this kid's life. True or not, that's the key to his being."

He went on. As a teenager, Jack had confirmed all the dates, all the coincidences. He had studied press photographs of JFK and the one surviving photograph of the lumpish Homer Adams. He had studied himself in the mirror. He looked nothing like his mother, nothing like Homer. He could not possibly be Homer's son. Betty had tricked Homer into marriage in order to legitimize the pregnancy that had gotten her kicked out of the Navy Nurse Corps—a pregnancy that she had wanted, a pregnancy that lifted her out of the drab and meaningless existence into which she had been born.

What could Betty's strange history possibly mean except that her fatal accident had been a murder-suicide perpetrated by Homer, the salesman of Hudson Hornets, who had somehow discovered the truth about Jack's paternity? The more Jack found out about JFK's frenetic sex life, the more likely the theory became.

I looked at the snapshots again. Even through my eyes, there was no question about it: At 107 pounds, smiling with those strong white teeth after years of practice in the mirror, Jack Adams the draft dodger looked very much like the handsome bag of bones who had been the post–PT 109 Jack Kennedy.

3 It was a moonless night in May, quite warm. The darkness was almost liquid; you hung in it as in a tepid sea, seeing glimmers of light far above your head. Perhaps one streetlight in six remained unbroken. The garbage had not been collected for days. The sweetish odor of rotting vegetation rose to the nostrils, as in a rain forest untouched by sunlight. We walked on between darkened tenements. Although we could not see them, people sat on stairways in the balmy weather, drinking. In inky shadow, bottles clinked on concrete. Men coughed and spat, women scolded: murmurs, bursts of laughter, profanity. Loud, angry music.

There was no possibility of finding a taxi in this neighborhood, at this hour. I took Arthur by the arm and walked him westward, toward the Hudson River.

Arthur resisted. "You're going the wrong way," he said. "The subway is back there."

"I know. We'll walk."

"You're crazy."

I said, lying, "I have a pistol."

Reassured, Arthur walked with a lighter step. He knew about pistols. I had recruited him in Cuba, where he had gone to cut sugar cane for Fidel Castro. In a training camp in the Sierra Maestra, he had fired Russian pistols into bags of slaughterhouse blood.

I said, "I'm interested in this boy's cowardice. Tell me more."

Arthur said, "Dmitri, please. Why do you keep using that word? It's so irrelevant. Does such a thing even exist?"

"It exists. And it's always relevant."

"Whatever you say. But look at the whole picture, Dmitri."

"The file does not give me the whole picture. For example, some of these girls he slept with seem to think that he is not in his heart of hearts a person of the Left, that he has no real political convictions."

"I disagree," Arthur said. "Appearances can be deceiving, especially to girls."

"So the only thing that *is* important is his delusion?"

Arthur stopped in his tracks. He was a picture of misery. He said, "Dmitri, what are you saying to me? That I've fucked up again?" His voice trembled.

I put a fatherly arm around his shoulders and squeezed.

I said, "No."

He had no idea how well he had done. At that moment, of course, neither had I. Another hug. How thin he was in spite of his appetites, how frail. How hard he tried. Like a father I smiled, a smile of real affection, of expectations fulfilled.

I said, "I see possibilities."

Arthur touched my hand, the one that gripped his shoulder, and smiled back, this time like a man.

By now we had walked many blocks downtown. We were out of Harlem, near the Columbia campus, where Arthur lived, apparatchik that he was, in an apartment that belonged to the university. The light was better, the sidewalks were all but empty except for husbands walking little dogs. We could hear the traffic signals changing, feel the subway trains passing beneath the pavement. The dangers Arthur had feared were miles behind us.

He gripped my arm, making his points after the need had passed.

He said, "The point is, Jack has a great natural gift. Since childhood, he has studied people, found out what they wanted, and made them believe he was giving it to them even when he wasn't. Without money, without influence, without connections, he has risen to the top every time. He has this uncanny gift for making others like him. Trust him. Want to help him. It's like a spell he can cast at will."

I said, "You're describing a born liar." My tone was encouraging.

Arthur swallowed the encouragement I offered like a sweet and cried out, "Yes! That's the point."

"Then why didn't you mention it before?"

"I didn't realize its importance until just now. Jack lies about everything, all the time. He always has. He's not even conscious that he is lying. He lies to please, to manipulate, to get what he wants. The amazing thing is, everyone knows that he lies all the time and about everything, but *nobody seems to mind*."

"So what does that make Jack?"

Arthur threw up his hands. "You tell me."

"A megalomaniac in the making," I said. "A driven man. Unpredictable. Mad. Biting the hand that feeds him."

Arthur laughed in delight. "An American Lenin," he said. "Just what Dr. Dmitri ordered."

"I think I had better take a closer look at this young man," I said.

"You want to meet him?"

"No. Observe him. In due course."

And that is how it all began.

Two

★ ★

1 Only a few days after Arthur told me about Jack Adams, my superior, by coincidence, arrived from Moscow. Everyone in this story will call this man Peter, a poetic choice of alias, because Peter was a fisher of men if ever there was one. Our intelligence service, founded by intellectuals and perpetuated by drudges, had an unfortunate tendency to assign excessively appropriate pseudonyms to secret operatives. This was a great weakness in our security because the entire basis of cryptanalysis is the discovery of context. If you call an agent Lothario because he is a compulsive seducer, you must expect that the enemy will work backward through a million females, if necessary, to discover his identity.

Peter had traveled to New York, where he was not welcome in his true identity, using a false name, as a specialist in fisheries attached to the Ukrainian delegation to a UN meeting on national rights to fishing grounds. Peter found this cover amusing. At the time in question, Soviet trawlers were indiscriminately vacuuming up huge quantities of fish off the coasts of North America, processing their catch using the most modern technology, and then unloading these frozen cargoes at Murmansk and other Barents Sea ports—where they thawed and rotted on the docks because there were no refrigerated trains or trucks to haul them to market. Or only enough to supply the Nomenklatura, as the higher-ranking circles of the Party and government officials were called, with the one fish in a million that made it to Moscow.

The real work of the trawlers, some of which were loaded with highly advanced electronic gear, was to eavesdrop on the U.S. Navy.

"This means," Peter told me over lunch at the Côte Basque, his favorite restaurant in New York, "that the price of each kilo of cod eaten by a member of the Politburo is about the same as that of a medium-range ballistic missile."

He spoke airily, as was his style, as if there was nothing unusual about a lieutenant general in the KGB describing a major espionage operation to a subordinate as a farce. You may think that he felt free to do so because I *was* his subordinate and could do him no harm without destroying myself, but he spoke just as recklessly to everyone. He was the son of one of the original Bolsheviks, now dead, who had begotten him on a famous ballerina. This alone gave him a license to be eccentric. Few outsiders knew this, but even under Stalin, Russia had a whole class of spoiled brats, the children of the mighty, who did and said pretty much as they liked—until their fathers disappeared. Peter's father had done him the inestimable favor of dying for the revolution, an act that placed both of them out of the reach of the secret police.

Peter looked like his mother, tall with a symmetrical European face and large, keen, nonepicanthic blue eyes. The ballerina had raised him as an old-fashioned gentleman, privately tutored in the old culture by men who had been saved from the camps by his father. He knew languages, literature, painting, music, delightful gossip about the famous, dead and alive. As an adult, Peter behaved like an English nobleman in a nineteenth-century novel: with a certain natural hauteur, but with a single manner for all mankind. He treated everyone the same, commissar or zik.

As children of heroes went, Peter was unusual in that he was talented, extravagantly so. He went straight into intelligence at a young age, placed in a favorable position by Lavrenti Beria, a devoted friend of his mother's. The boy was given opportunities to excel, and he worked hard and won golden opinions from the start. In Budapest during the uprising, the Soviet ambassador, Yuri Andropov, a future head of the KGB and of the Party itself, was so impressed by Peter's work in subverting the rebellion from within that he practically adopted him as a son.

Now, still in his forties, barely older than I was, he was head of a directorate that he himself had invented. Even inside the KGB no one was quite certain what this directorate did, or even what its targets were. With a very small headquarters staff that was absolutely loyal to him, Peter operated outside the usual chain of command, running strange operations for obscure purposes all over the world—but primarily in the United States. He reported directly to the Politburo through his mentor and protector, Andropov, by now the head of the KGB. Through Andropov's good offices and his own charm, Peter was also a favorite of the somewhat dimwitted general secretary of the time, Leonid Brezhnev. It was said in the KGB canteen that Peter could make Andropov laugh and Brezhnev think. This was enough to make anyone fear him.

That was Peter's advantage. Until those two turned on him or died, he was immune to the system. And even then, as we shall see, he was too much for his enemies. Peter could make anyone trust him, though few liked him. He also had a truly Napoleonic instinct for maneuver, timing, and choice of ground. And, of course, he was highly developed politically—utterly ruthless and without scruples or personal loyalty to anyone below him.

I had been working under him for ten years. He had chosen me, plucked me out of the squirrel cage of espionage operations, because he sensed that he and I were kindred souls. Sensed it? I blurted it out to him on first meeting. I came to his notice when he visited my language school and I was assigned as his guide. From the start we spoke American English together; his was perfect. Within an hour I was saying things to him for which I could have been shot.

Just before we met, I had been working in West Germany, my first major assignment abroad. I had arranged for the theft of several items of U.S. military technology. Over a period of months, these articles were removed, one by one, from an air base, dismantled, measured, and photographed, then returned. So far as I was able to tell, the Americans never knew that they had been missing. The cost of this operation in hard currency had been enormous, including huge bribes to all concerned and the subsequent murder, by poison, of the drunken American sergeant who had let us into the air base after I had covered him with a heap of boys and money. All the same it had been cheaper than developing the technology ourselves, so my superiors were pleased with me. I was decorated and promoted and selected for assignment to the target of targets, the USA.

Peter knew all this. As we walked together from one building to another, he asked me what I thought this operation had accomplished. I replied, "The same as all other thefts of American technology, Comrade General! An admission of inferiority!"

We were outside, fortunately. It was snowing—big wet theatrical flakes falling between us so that I saw him, an unreal figure to me anyway, as through a scrim.

I was seized—do not ask me why—by an irresistible impulse to tell the truth. I replied, knowing that I was probably writing my own death warrant, that the Soviet intelligence apparatus had spent trillions since 1917 to steal inventions from the West. Had we devoted the same sums to research and development, I said, we might have a modern state capable of doing its own science instead of one that stole and lied about everything to hide its weakness. A state that sought to steal everything rather than go to the trouble of making it itself would surely fall in the end because by its every act of espionage it conceded the superiority of its enemies—correctly, because such a state had no intellectual or moral core and therefore no reason to exist.

Peter listened intently to these wild words, smiling urbanely under his big snow-covered sable cap as though I had just told him a disarming bit of gossip that he, who knew everyone and everything, had somehow never heard before.

He said, "Then you believe, Comrade Captain, that all espionage is counterproductive?"

"In the terms of reference stated, yes, Comrade General."

Peter asked no more questions. On the rest of the tour he behaved as if nothing out of the ordinary had been said. I thought that my life was over. But instead of ordering my execution, which was in his power, he *hired* me—simply took me back to Moscow with him in his personal Ilyushin as if he needed no one's permission, as if there were no such thing as a bureaucracy that had been planning to send me to America to steal more hardware. On the airplane (we rode side by side) he turned to me and said, "This is our best transport plane, and as I'm sure you are aware, it is a copy of the American Lockheed Electra. A very bad copy. Never, Dmitri, speak to anyone else as you spoke to me earlier today. Unless, of course, you wish to order a Lubyanka breakfast."

A Lubyanka breakfast was a cigarette and a bullet. I had placed my life in his hands.

He preserved it because I suited one of his many secret purposes. He was always trolling for promising disciples. He certainly found one in me. Peter gave me something useful to do with my life. I understood, if only dimly in comparison to him, the opportunity that America represented. From the start—even when he was sending me to China as a means of making me useless to the rest of the KGB—he told me that my future was in America. He believed in America's future, in its potential for unlimited greatness, as fervently as any chairman of Merrill Lynch had ever done. He loved the United States—everything about it, even its defects—as another man might have loved an unattainable woman who could, if only she could be persuaded to yield, make all his dreams come true.

Wait a minute, you say. We are talking about a lieutenant general of the KGB. Let me explain.

To Peter, the Russian Revolution and all that had happened because of it was a mistake. This was not because he was not a true Marxist. On the contrary, he was the truest one I have ever known. He believed in the revolution of the proletariat. He believed in the establishment of socialism and its evolution into communism and in the sunlit era of equality, justice, and universal human happiness that would result from this inevitable historical process.

He was not, however, a Marxist-*Leninist.* Peter did not believe that the revolution had happened yet. Or, to put it another way, he thought that it had happened in the wrong country at the wrong time. In his opinion there had never been the slightest chance that a primitive state like Russia, which had always been ruled by criminals and, thanks to Peter the Great, had no culture of its own, could ever inspire the world, much less conquer it. The correct country for revolution in 1917 was Germany, an industrialized nation-state with a disciplined people and a great culture that could easily have become the world culture.

That opportunity had been lost forever, history had passed it by. And created the country of final revolution, America.

2 Peter had read Jack Adams's file that morning and committed it to memory, as was his way. He was interested in him, far more interested than I had expected him to be. Over gray sole Meunière, accompanied by a fifty-dollar bottle of Montrachet, Peter fired questions at me. Did I trust Arthur's judgment?

"He's new at the work," I said.

"You're not," Peter replied, drinking Montrachet with his eyes wide open above the rim of the glass. "What's your opinion?"

"That this boy may have possibilities, but also many negatives."

"Such as?"

"His extreme youth."

"He's twenty-one. Any older would be too old."

"His dementia."

"All great men are driven by a fixation."

"He's a boy from Ohio."

"Napoleon was once a boy from Corsica."

"Peter," I said, "he has possibilities. But I think we should go slowly. This boy is unstable."

Peter's fork, laden with gray sole, stopped midway to his mouth. This was not what he wanted to hear. I was spoiling his appetite.

"Dmitri, Dmitri," he said, "don't tell me reasons *not* to do things. Your job is to make it possible for me to do what everyone knows cannot be done. You do understand?"

"Yes."

He nodded and put the forkful of fish into his mouth. At that moment, while he chewed and cut himself another piece of sole that was exactly the right size and coated with exactly the right amount of sauce, I knew that we were off to the races. Some instinct told Peter that Jack Adams represented a golden opportunity, and he was determined to seize it. He had big things in mind for Jack before he even laid eyes on him. There is no way to explain this on the basis of the objective facts. Very likely Peter himself could not have explained it, because reason and logic were not involved. Peter made all decisions between his pelvis and his collarbone, and this was his great strength. He gave an outward impression of intellectual brilliance—his languages, his knowledge of power, his looks, his flashy methods, his devil-may-care way of speaking. But in fact, conscious thought played almost no part in his life. He operated almost entirely on impulse.

His impulse now was to see Jack for himself. This does not mean that he actually desired to meet him and talk to him, to show Jack his own face and let him hear his voice. No, that was a needless risk at this early stage. Peter wanted to observe Jack through the one-way mirror of surveillance. He wanted to see him in his natural state, see how he behaved with other people, see how they reacted to him. I told Peter that I had already instructed Arthur to arrange such an inspection.

"Make it tonight," Peter said. "Eight o'clock. A restaurant. I will be there."

"What kind of food?"

"Italian. Book me a table for two. You will sit alone."

My question about cuisine may seem odd to you, but Peter was going to be in the West for a few days only. He ate very little—at the Côte Basque no more than half his gray sole, one small potato, a single glass of wine, some raspberries. But he wanted to do as much business as possible while eating good food. Readers of thrillers written by English schoolmasters may have imagined that the KGB was composed of ascetics who met their agents in deserted warehouses or on fog-shrouded wharves. The secret archives tell a different story: These men came from a country where everyone was hungry and always had been. They had grown up on barley porridge, the manna of the revolution. Therefore, clandestine meetings usually happened in restaurants. Every great spymaster was also a glutton. According to Peter, who really was an ascetic, Stalin used to make Beria eat at secret banquets until his bowels moved.

I went immediately to the coin telephone at the back of the Côte Basque and called Arthur at home, where he spent most of his time, writing scholarly papers or tutoring Barnard girls in dialectics while his wife worked in a social agency. He taught only one class a week, which was why he had so much time for conspiracy. As a matter of basic procedure we did not discuss matters of substance on the telephone, but spoke to each other only in double-talk, so when I told him what I wanted in plain English, he panicked. In Cuba we had trained Arthur to assume that any telephone was tapped; he actually believed that his line *was* bugged, that the FBI and the CIA had been following him ever since he got back from the Sierra Maestra, that they regarded him as a threat to imperialism so serious that they had nothing better to do than listen in twenty-four hours a day while he argued over grades with students or planned orgies with colleagues at female schools: "We can get freshman girls!" (I *had* tapped his phone for a while before contacting him, as a routine precaution.)

Arthur was so frightened that I thought he might hang up on me, but instead he argued. The time was too short. He had other plans, a dinner party downtown; how could he explain this to his wife? He didn't know where Jack was.

"Find him," I said.

He protested, he wheedled. How could I place this impossible burden on him? It was bad, exposing him this way.

"Arthur, this is not a *request*," I said. "Are you refusing me?"

A silence. "No. Of course not."

"Good." I told him the name under which his table would be booked. "Eight o'clock exactly. Do not be late or early, not even by one minute."

"I'll do my best," Arthur said.

"You will do as I say. *Exactly* as I say."

My tone of voice left him with the impression that he had two choices: success or death. At the other end of the line he breathed deeply, as if hyperventilating. I told him where to go, Lombardia on West Fifty-fourth Street, a place frequented by publishers and their more successful writers at lunch but virtually deserted after dark.

"Soon after I sit down, I will order a glass of pinot grigio," I said. "That will be the all-clear signal. I will then go to the men's room. Follow me. Do you understand?"

In a small voice he said, "Yes."

After hanging up on Arthur, I called the restaurant and, posing as a hotel concierge, booked two tables for eight o'clock and a third for eight-fifteen.

Peter liked Lombardian food, Piedmont wines, and especially *tartufa*, the dark chocolate ice cream that was a specialty of the house even though it was not a northern Italian specialty. In

America, who knew the difference? This restaurant was quiet, no music, a well-lighted place in the Italian style. Peter hated Muzak and candlelight. He liked to see his food, liked to see the other faces in the room—and above all, he liked to hear what was being said.

3 Just before eight o'clock, as soon as it was dark enough, I took up a position in a deep doorway across the street to await Arthur's arrival. At a minute or two before eight o'clock he got out of a taxi with two young men. One of them, bony and nervous, was clearly Jack Adams. The other was a muscular fellow with short black hair. He wore a blazer and tie. He glowed with health, and one could tell from the lithe way in which he moved that he was an athlete. But he represented an unforgivable breach of security. Trailed by the boys, Arthur shambled into the restaurant.

I followed. They were seated in the back, against the wall, next to the kitchen, because Arthur was dressed in his usual tramp's costume, and had brought along two guests instead of the one I had mentioned when I called. The headwaiter started to seat me up front, far from these rowdies, but to his puzzlement I gave him ten dollars (he would have remembered a twenty) to seat me at a table from which I could see and hear what was going on at Arthur's table.

I ordered my pinot grigio in a loud voice, then headed for the men's room.

Arthur joined me.

"Who," I asked, "is the extra man?"

Arthur raised his hands in a gesture of apology. "Don't blame me," he said. "That's his old high school buddy Danny Miller, who just hitchhiked in from Ohio. Jack wouldn't come without him."

"Why?"

"Danny's been drafted, he leaves for basic training next week, so he drove to New York to say goodbye to Jack. It's his only night in town. He plans to get drunk."

"He's not a draft dodger like Jack?"

A sour grimace. Arthur said, "He's a jock. Glad to go if his country needs him."

This was interesting. "When was he drafted?" I asked.

Arthur sighed. Who cared? "Recently, I guess," he replied. "His number wasn't supposed to come up until later, but somehow it did."

"Where is Jack's draft board?"

"In his hometown. He went back to Ohio for his physical. They don't see as many starvation cases there as in New York."

"These two boys are from the same town, they're the same age?"

"Right. So what?"

"Then it's quite possible that Danny was drafted in Jack's place. Does he realize that?"

Arthur was incredulous. "Drafted in Jack's place?" he said. "Come on, Dmitri."

He changed the subject. "It's the end of the month," he said. "I don't have enough money to pay for this."

I handed him a wad of crumpled twenty-dollar bills. And made him sign a receipt with a thumbprint. Immediately afterward he rubbed his eye with his thumb and got ink in it. Crying "Ouch!" he splashed water on himself.

When he turned blindly from the sink, beard dripping, I handed him a towel.

"Remember the script," I said. "Have a lively conversation. Discuss everything from women to politics. Let Danny get drunk. Draw them out. And don't ask for the check until after I leave."

Back in the dining room, Peter had arrived. He, too, had demanded a table at the back of the restaurant, just across the narrow room from Jack and his friend Danny. Seated beside Peter on the banquette was a sloe-eyed girl wearing a white silk dress that clung to her body. As was then the fashion she wore no bra, and her erect nipples were discernible beneath the fabric. Like all of Peter's girls all over the world this one was striking, almost a model, with a crackling mane of dark hair in which she wore a large waxy tropical flower. She also wore a wedding ring, a broad gold band. In her shimmering sarong, cut at the knee, she looked like a Tahitian maiden in a Hollywood film. Even I, the enemy of impossible dreams, couldn't look at her without wanting to fuck her.

The effect she had on Jack was even more urgent. He couldn't take his eyes off her. She felt him looking at her, and in that slow self-aware way that good-looking women have, she turned her head to return his stare. If she expected Jack to look guiltily away like an ordinary male, she was disappointed. He stared boldly back. Their eyes locked. It became a staring contest. Neither would be the first to break off.

Jack's friend Danny watched in the mirror, grinning. Obviously he had seen this happen before, and he was looking for a familiar outcome.

He did not have long to wait. Suddenly, to my great surprise, the girl blushed. She turned away, hair tossing, and with an ostentatious laugh pretended that Peter had said something witty to distract her.

Danny laughed. "She had the vision!" he cried. His voice was distinct, flat, midwestern. Penetrating. The girl could hear every word he said even though his back was turned.

Arthur said, "The what?"

"She saw Bwana Devil," Danny said. "The one-eyed lion. Jack looks at a girl, and if she gives him a hard-on, he concentrates on that and looks deeeeep into her eyes. Nothing on his mind except Bwana Devil. After about two minutes, the girl sees it too. Like a vision of the future—the immediate future. No shit. I've had 'em admit it. Right, Jack?"

Jack shook his head, grinning: What a comedian.

The girl drank wine and lifted her eyes, looking at Jack again. He smiled at her, as if apologizing for his friend.

The smile was a sunburst—everything that Arthur and his spies had reported. The girl was startled, as if she had just realized that she knew Jack, that she had seen him before but could not quite place him. She studied him for a long moment, then shook her head, hair tossing, as if to tell herself that she was mistaken. But before she turned away she brushed Jack with a look that was like a tongue flickering across skin.

After that, for a while, they ignored each other. Waiters and sommeliers came and went. Danny got progressively more drunk. Jack did not drink at all. As instructed, Arthur drew Jack out, asking him questions, challenging his answers, making him talk, think, defend.

The boy was remarkably fluent, but always sincere and respectful. Humorous but never witty. Because of the girl, Jack was charming everyone in sight, which meant that he smiled frequently. And when he smiled, you saw what the girl had seen—something elusive but unmistakable.

The waiter, a sore-footed, gruff New York type who had seen it all, saw it, too. He hovered over Jack, explaining the menu, advising him to choose the cannelloni, followed by a nice porterhouse steak *alla fiorentina*. He liked Jack—it was obvious. And, effortlessly, Jack was making the waiter believe that he liked him.

The girl continued to stare at Jack. She was searching for something. A resemblance. He smiled. She saw it. I saw it myself. It was in the smile, which lasted just an instant too long. It was fleeting, not quite strong enough to be arresting, puzzling. And yet it made you stop and try to remember. You saw a face you could not quite summon up, a gesture you could not quite place, a charm that reminded you of someone. But who? And then Jack spoke in a staccato Kennedy tenor, Ohio-accented instead of Bostonian, and suddenly you got it, and black-and-white images from the past tumbled into your mind.

Between questions from Arthur, Jack took care of his friend Danny, who by now was at the point of passing out. There was nothing feigned about Jack's solicitude. These boys really were friends, in the unashamed way that only American boys can be friends. There was perfect trust and understanding between them. It was quite touching.

Toward the end of the evening, Danny had to go to the men's room. He could hardly stand up. Jack went with him.

Peter called for the check, and while he waited for it, his girl excused herself. We were the last customers. She was the only woman in the place. She was even more interesting to look at when she was standing up—high heels, long legs, no stockings, bottom like a peach, covered by narrow white panties that were visible through the thin white cloth of her dress. Even Peter seemed a little distracted, watching her walk away.

She was gone for less than fifteen minutes, but when she came back, though her hair was in perfect order and there was not a wrinkle in her dress, she was not the same woman as before. She moved with a certain unmistakable languor. The white flower was gone from her hair. Her eyes were different—no mascara, no makeup. She had washed her face.

Peter raised his eyebrows: Shall we go? She responded with a little nod, as if there was no more to his unspoken question than that. She took Peter's arm, swaying a little on her high heels, as if—I am not an imaginative man, I look for evidence—she was weak in the knees. Her back was to me. On her right buttock, through the thin cloth, one could see a tattoo and, looking more closely, identify it as a butterfly. This had not been visible when she walked away from the table. Was she wearing one less garment than before?

She felt my eyes on her and turned to confront me. In my case it was a quick inspection, a glint of contempt. But she showed me enough of her face for me to see that it had changed. The lips were a little swollen, and her dark wahine eyes looked inward, as if at a memory of pleasure.

She and Peter left. After a moment so did I, without waiting for Jack and Danny to reappear. To observe the departure of Jack and the others, I took up my post in the doorway across the street.

Quite soon the three of them emerged. While Arthur scouted for a taxi, Danny and Jack stood together on the sidewalk. Danny was laughing, pointing a finger at Jack, shouting, "Bwana Devil!" Less than half an hour before, in the restaurant, Danny had been so drunk he could hardly stand up. Now, strangely, he was no more than tipsy—a little loud, a little unsteady, but by no means helplessly intoxicated as he had seemed to be inside. There was no crosstown traffic. Their boisterous young voices were perfectly audible.

Jack said, "You owe me ten bucks, Miller."

Danny said, "That's your story. Let me see the evidence."

Jack shrugged. He reached into his pocket, then handed something white to Danny. Danny held this object up to the light, shaking it out. It was a pair of panties—the same ones that had formerly covered up the wahine's tattoo.

"You son of a bitch," Danny cried.

He dug into his own pocket, then handed Jack the ten dollars he had won.

Danny put the panties on his head like a hat, and he and Jack walked away, arms around each other's shoulders, Danny singing a tuneless song.

There is nothing one man admires in another so much as sexual luck. So it was with Danny and Jack. In my sour wisdom, earned by years of watching puppet shows, I knew that the girl had been under orders. But on the evidence of the look on her face after she carried out her assignment, she had enjoyed it.

Very impressive. I knew that Peter would think so, too.

4 As prearranged with Peter, I walked uptown along Fifth Avenue. Somewhere in the Sixties, Peter stepped out of the shadows of Central Park and joined me. By now it was past midnight, a dangerous hour. As usual Peter had no bodyguards; we were alone except for a few other pedestrians, scurrying and furtive and fearful of the dark—in other words, behaving far too suspiciously to be FBI men assigned to tail us.

I said, "I assume the girl was not an agent."

"No," Peter said. "A whore who specializes in fantasies. I told her my wife had been seduced by a stranger in a ladies' room, and I wished to reenact the humiliation."

Peter handed me a small tape recorder. We sat down together on a bench while I listened over an earphone. The prostitute's tone was matter-of-fact. Sex was her métier. She was used to speaking to men in language that would arouse them. She described her experience with Jack expertly, in the jargon of her trade.

Peter had told the girl exactly what to do and in what sequence: flirt with Jack, then break it off, then give him a sign, then follow him when he left the table. She was under orders not to make the first move. Jack must do that. It was part of the fantasy.

As she walked along the passage toward the ladies' room, she caught a glimpse of Jack, who was just disappearing into the men's room. She stared straight at him and, against orders, gave him a tiny sign—the tip of her tongue running sensuously over her lips.

Minutes later, as she stood before the mirror combing her hair, there came a tap on the door. She opened it, Jack was there. She let him in.

Here I will summarize: She had already removed her panties, which she held crumpled in her hand. She put them into Jack's hand. He grinned, lifted them to his nose for a moment. She stripped off her dress, but not her high heels. Wordlessly, smiling, Jack lifted one of her legs, put a finger between her legs, drew it out slowly, then put it into his mouth like a boy who had stuck his finger into a bowl of frosting.

Then he grasped her buttocks, spreading them as he picked her up—she was a small girl—and fitted her onto himself, sliding her, gasping, all the way onto his member in one deft effortless gesture.

The suddenness of this took her breath away. "It was absolutely the smoothest move I have ever seen," she said. "I was wet—this was a kinky situation—but he must have greased it. He's huge. My eyes were popping. My shoes fell off. He pumped about three times and came, and I thought, Shit! Already? But he kept on going as if nothing had happened, and even though he's just a kid he knew exactly what he was doing. I don't come with tricks, you just don't do that and usually it pisses me off if it happens by accident, but for once I wanted to.

"I came like I was turning inside out, about three different ways. I was dripping all over the place, I bit the shit out of his shoulder to keep from screaming, I pulled his hair, I said things. It was *so* kinky—like being raped in a wet dream. It was, like, unreal. Not that he was rough or weird in any way—all he wanted was an absolutely straight fuck. He was way, way inside himself, like hypnotized. His body would not quit. He kept it up forever, it was amazing. I began to cry. I *never* cry. I didn't even know I was crying at the time. But I heard myself sobbing, and with every sob, *wham-wham,* he was trying harder to tickle my backbone.

"Pretty soon he was getting off again, and I thought, this time it's over. So I put my hands on his chest and pushed a little—not hard, a friendly hint. My ass was on the sink, it was uncomfortable. Right away he stepped back, a perfect gentleman. Now, this is funny. All this time, all this going on, and he never tried to kiss me, never touched my breasts. I take his hand to put it on a tit and he pulls my hand down and puts it in my hand and it's still absolutely rigid, like nothing has happened.

"He smiles, asking permission, and puts the tips of his fingers, both hands, on my shoulders, and I think he wants a blowjob. But no. He says, 'May I?' He turns me around, and in the mirror I see my face, black with mascara, and he bends me over and slips it in again like it can see out of its eye. He's watching my face in the mirror, which is as close as he gets to intimacy. Not a word, not a hand on my tits, just in and out, in and out, touching everything, which in that position is quite a trick. I could see his face was in the mirror, all squinched up. He was loving it. This position is what makes him happy. I expected it elsewhere, but it was vagina only. He just liked coming at me from the back. I like it myself as an encore—there's less weight on you and if the guy is really hung you can tickle yourself at the same time, get a little bonus.

"I gave the kid some moves he maybe hadn't known before. He begins to breathe hard, finally, eyes squeezed shut. It was intense. I closed my eyes, too. Pretty soon I was coming like hiccups—I mean I couldn't stop if I wanted to—and so was he. I thought it would never end. But then it did. He stepped away. I'm half blind, holding on to the sink, gasping, limp as a wet rag, I can hardly stand up.

"And when I open my eyes again, he's gone. Vanished. Out the door. I think: *Oh shit! My purse, my dress!* I have this picture of myself walking back into the restaurant in my birthday suit and I think, a tablecloth, I'll grab a tablecloth! But everything was right where I left it. All he took was my panties. I looked at my watch, which was all I had on. Nine minutes by the clock, standing up and nonstop, and even then he probably had to throw cold water on it in order to get it back in his pants. I was staggering, trying to wash my face, wash the rest of me. I never saw anything like it."

I switched off the tape recorder and offered to hand it back to Peter. He waved it away. It was now part of my files.

Peter said, "She may be embroidering slightly, to give the old masochist the good time I paid for. But mainly, I think, she told the truth. Opinion?"

"That we go slowly. Learn more. Assess carefully."

"That's not an opinion, it's a recommendation."

"You want an assessment?"

"Yes, I do."

At this stage, I knew from experience, he wanted a devil's advocate. I said, "All right. Tonight I saw a boy of twenty-one who has charm, guile, and the gift of gab. Also a potentially disastrous case of Don Juan psychosis. And I think if we recruit him he will do to us what he did to your call girl."

Peter was amused—determined to be amused. "Steal our underwear?"

"No. Fuck us cross-eyed."

Peter did not like my answer. I had stepped out of character without permission: Flippancy was not one of the privileges he had granted to me.

I said, "May I ask what *you* see in this subject, Peter?"

"Yes," he replied. "I see talent in the raw. A cold heart. Boldness, contempt for the rights and feelings of others. Ruthlessness. He took the girl like a bandit because he wanted her, even though she wore a wedding ring and was accompanied by another man."

"She was a prostitute."

"He didn't know that. For all practical purposes he raped her. He created a diversion, made his friend act drunk for him, then paid him off with a pair of panties. And that smile, so American, so like the man he thinks is his father."

"*Thinks* is his father. An important point."

Peter shrugged. "Is it so impossible?"

Clearly Peter did not think so. That was all that mattered. Many times in the past I had seen him proven right when nearly everyone else thought that he was wrong. He was like Einstein: He saw the universe as a whole, he proposed the existence of things that other men could not see. The measurements, the mathematics, the proofs of his theory he left to others, who suffered the consequences of any small mistakes he might have made.

"I wish to proceed with this operation," he said.

"It will be a gamble."

"Yes. That's the beauty of it."

"If we win."

"Why shouldn't we win?" Peter said. "We will deal the cards. For the rest of his life."

My heart sank. Peter had long-term plans for this boy who lived in a dreamworld, to whom no one else was real, who did not even want to touch the women he fucked with any part of his body but his penis. He wanted to bind Jack to us, turn him into an agent of influence. He wanted to keep him as he was, but at the same time transform him into an operative who would live by subterfuge his whole life long.

"Are we sure we can do what we want in this case?" I asked.

Peter lifted a hand. My role as devil's advocate was over. What he expected now was acceptance, obedience.

"We are never sure," he said. "But it has been done before, with less promising material."

This was certainly true. We had taken many, many gambles on imperfect men, all over the world. Some had achieved success, even very great success, through the combination of our help and advice and what seemed, especially to the man himself, the exercise of in-born talent. The others were dead or in prison, and no further concern of ours.

As if reading my mind, Peter said, "I want you to put your heart into this case."

"Very well. What is the first step?"

"Get him to Germany."

"You mean, give him a ticket?"

"No. He would ask questions. He mustn't know we are helping him. And he must stay in Germany for several months."

"Perhaps a fellowship."

Peter considered this. "Good," he said. "By all means get him a fellowship."

"May I consider other countries?"

"No," Peter said. "It must be Germany, the American zone. But not Berlin."

"I'll do my best."

"You will succeed."

Peter looked at his watch, flicked a glance at a single set of head-lights approaching along Fifth Avenue, and changed languages. "I leave tomorrow," he said in English. "For Cuba. Shall I say hello to anyone for you?"

I shook my head. Peter smiled, looking into my eyes, expecting great things of me.

He said, "We'll discuss this again soon. After Cuba."

A limousine pulled up at the curb. Without another word, he strode across the sidewalk. He opened the door. I glimpsed a woman's legs, crossed at the ankles—not the legs I had admired in the Italian restaurant, but another pair, longer and even more shapely. This one must be an agent under discipline if Peter was allowing her to see me.

I said, "A clarification, please, Comrade General."

Peter closed the car door. The lady could look, but she could not listen.

I said, "This asset will be unwitting?"

"Of course. As you say, he is deeply unstable, committed to nothing. How can we trust him?"

In the jargon of espionage, an unwitting asset is a dupe who does not know (or may not wish to know) that he is working for a foreign intelligence service. Such an operative sometimes believes (or pretends to believe) that he is working for an entirely different secret entity from the one that actually controls him. He may never even meet the case officer who is handling him, but report instead to a third person who carries instructions to the unknowing agent and reports of his activities back to the case officer.

"There must be no one in his life but you and me," Peter said.

"Understood," I replied. "But I will need Arthur for the fellowship business."

"All right, but only that," Peter said. "When you're through with him, tell him goodbye. Tell him another man will work with him in the future. I will make some arrangements in Cuba."

"When will this happen?"

"As soon as you're through with him."

The conversation was over. Wordless departures were part of Peter's stage business. He whirled, got into his limousine, and drove away.

Alone, like a figure in a movie—which in a way I was—I walked downtown through the sleeping metropolis. In those days they still opened the hydrants to wash the streets in the early hours of the morning. The air smelled laundered, and where water gushed from the standpipes, creating mist that enveloped the street lamps, there were miniature rainbows.

5 By the Metropolitan Museum, where there were coin telephones on the sidewalk, I called Arthur. We met an hour later
inside the park. He arrived by cab, having directed the driver
straight to the place where I was waiting. This was a serious breach
of security, but I didn't have the heart to reprove him.

Arthur was sleepy-eyed but alert. He had brought me coffee in a
paper cup. The sun was just coming up. We sat on a bench, sipping
awful, acidic coffee while I told him what was required for Jack
Adams.

He said, "To Germany? This will be difficult."

"But not impossible, surely. What about a Fulbright?"

"You're joking. It's May. The Fulbrights have all been awarded for
next year."

"Can't someone be disqualified?"

"Not by sneaky means," Arthur said. "The system is designed to
prevent that. A committee of Americans and Germans bestows the
awards, so nobody but the committee can take them away. And
even if they did, they'd just award it to the applicant who came in
second."

I said, "Then get him some other kind of scholarship, as long
as it's genuine. He must believe that it's genuine. Do not discuss it
with him."

"Pennies from heaven," Arthur said. "You want him. That must
mean I've done a good job."

I said, "Better than you know. Can you do the thing I've just
asked you to do?"

"I think so, Dmitri."

"You must be sure."

"All right, I'm sure. An idea is forming in my mind."

He started to elucidate. I stopped him. "No need to tell me details," I said. "I'll count on you. Be quick."

"It may take several days. This will take organizing."

"All right. But, Arthur, there must be no failure. Do you understand?"

"Comrade," Arthur said, "I do not need to understand."

He thought he had earned the right to address me as *Comrade*.
And so he had. Now came the difficult part. I stood up, crumpling
my coffee cup.

"I'll take that," Arthur said.

"No."

Fingerprints. He could not be trusted. Arthur read my thought and flushed. But it was just procedure: No one can be trusted. I put a reassuring hand on his flaccid shoulder.

"This is our last meeting," I said.

He was startled. "Our last meeting? What's that supposed to mean?"

"It means we are entering a new phase. We must protect you."

Arthur gave me a reproachful look. "And that's the way it ends?"

"Arthur, it never ends."

I held out my hand. Arthur grasped it. "It has been a pleasure," I said. "We are very grateful. And now we must forget each other, forget everything."

"That will be difficult," Arthur said.

"For me, too, my friend."

I meant what I said.

6 A few days later Arthur delivered his report, as instructed. There is no denying that he had a certain flair.

A student of Arthur's—not connected in any way to the Movement, in fact a member of the ROTC—had won the Hoppert Fellowship to Heidelberg University. The Hoppert, endowed by a German immigrant who made a fortune manufacturing silk with child labor in the nineteenth century, wasn't a prestigious fellowship. But it paid all fees and travel costs and provided a stipend of five hundred dollars a month to the recipient.

The original recipient had been disqualified. The day after our meeting in the park, he was discovered to have plagiarized a paper on the Weimar Republic written for Arthur's honors course in political science. He had received an A for this paper—Arthur had graded it himself, but never returned it—and it had been an important factor in the award of the fellowship. Graduation was only two weeks away. The student protested his innocence, stating that his paper had been retyped by persons unknown who had erased his footnotes identifying long passages copied from an unpublished dissertation by an obscure academic named Markus Olshaker. Arthur asked the student if he really believed that he, Arthur, or anyone else could believe such a story.

Arthur told the young man he did not want to ruin his life, but a price must be paid. If he resigned his fellowship, Arthur would say nothing about the matter to anyone else. If, however, he insisted on his cock-and-bull story about forgery after the fact, Arthur would have no choice but to bring the whole matter to the attention of the dean. In that case the young man certainly would not graduate, he might very well lose his ROTC commission, and he would carry the burden of his mistake with him for the rest of his life.

The boy accepted Arthur's offer.

The vacated fellowship was awarded to a surprised Jack Adams, who graduated with high honors and won a prize for excellence in political science.

Under his yearbook picture an editorial wag inserted the words "Ruffles and Flourishes."

A portent.

7   Just after commencement, Arthur received a wake-up call from his new handler. To his delight, he was told that he was going back to Cuba for advanced training at his old secret camp in the Sierra Maestra. He would travel secretly this time, under a false passport, avoiding surveillance by the CIA and the FBI by means of a circuitous route through Santiago de Chile and Mexico City. He was instructed to tell his wife that he was going to Cuba to help with the sugar harvest once again.

He left in June. Early in July, his wife received through the mail an envelope containing Arthur's wedding ring and a brief note in his handwriting. He said in his letter that he had fallen deeply in love with another woman, and that he had decided to spend the rest of his life in Cuba. His decision was irrevocable. He hoped that Myra would someday know the happiness that he had found.

Love, Arthur.

No return address.

His handwriting, always untidy, was even harder to read than usual, as if he had scribbled this final letter while tired, or drunk, or under the stress that facing reality always induced in him. Myra thought Arthur would soon tire of monogamy and life among the masses and come back to New York, more full of himself than ever. But she never heard from him again.

2

★ ★

Seductions

One

1 An author I admire has written that "the great loves of men's lives are usually other men." He was not talking about homoerotic love, which like other passions of the flesh is haunted by suspicion and shame and is likely to end suddenly and badly, but about lifelong friendship, that exalted form of love—free of doubt, jealousy, and resentment—for which the currently fashionable term is male bonding. Friendship resembles other kinds of love in one respect only: As in all other couplings, there is always the one who loves and the one who permits himself to be loved.

In the case of Danny Miller and Jack Adams—the most extreme example of lifelong friendship I have ever encountered—it was Danny who chose Jack, and everyone who knew them as children agrees that this happened very early in life, even before the boys could talk. They met as infants living in adjoining houses. As a toddler, Danny gave Jack his toys. In grammar school he protected him from bullies. In high school, Danny, an athlete of breathtaking ability who was captain of every team, managed Jack's campaigns for class president and saw him elected four straight years. "A vote for Jack," said a classmate, "was a vote for Danny." Danny was elected Most Popular Boy in the graduating class. Jack was elected Most Likely to Succeed—with a parenthesis in the yearbook that read: "(as long as he sticks with Danny!)"

All his life, Danny had helped Jack to get girls. Half the adolescent females Jack seduced in backseats and on front porches and living room sofas began by having a crush on Danny.

"Jack would see that look in their eyes after Danny won the game with a touchdown or a homer or a layup in the last second, but he already had a girl, so he'd suggest a double date with his best friend," one of these girls remembered.* "As soon as Jack got her alone, he'd start talking and stroking. Jack was no Danny, but he wasn't bad, and he always smelled great—cologne, maybe. The girl would close her eyes and think of Danny in his basketball uni- form—he had this shock of black hair that kind of lifted and fell when he bounced a basketball, and smiling blue eyes and this amaz- ing buttermilk skin that every girl in town wanted to lick the sweat off of. She'd get real dreamy, and the next thing she knew, Jack had it up her kazoo. The son of a bitch carried Vaseline with him. He'd grease his thing with his spare hand, move the crotch of your panties to one side—I mean he was very deft—and before you had time to say *Hey!* he'd be in you up to his pubic hair. Never varied— Jack just kept running the same play on every down. 'Vaseline Jack,' the girls called him. But not until after the sexual revolution. We finally compared notes at, like, our tenth reunion. At the time he was doing his thing, nobody said a word because nobody wanted to look like a dope. I mean, back then before the Age of Aquarius, the wisdom was it was your own fault if you got, like, outwitted. And some of the girls must have enjoyed it. Jack was not exactly teeny-weeny. Funny thing is, he never came back for more. It was wham bam thank you ma'am and on to the next one."

Danny knew all about this. The seductions were a running joke between the friends, a feather in both their caps each time Jack added another conquest to his total. Amazingly, Jack never impreg- nated any of his partners. Danny attributed this to Jack's luck, in which he had mystical faith. He truly believed that Jack could get

---

Note on Methodology. This woman was interviewed early in Jack Adams's public life by an operative of ours posing as a tabloid journalist. He paid her a modest sum for her reminiscence, but her chief reward was the opportunity to betray secrets. An in- telligence report, the literary form with which I am most familiar, is seldom an eye- witness account, but rather a synthesis of one or many such accounts. So also in this narrative: I am not omniscient, but if I was not there, what I write is based on the firsthand reports of reliable witnesses who met the characters and heard the words they spoke with their own ears. It is not my plan, in this memoir, to keep anything I know from you. Of course, I didn't know everything, and it must be remembered that Jack lied to everyone about everything, and that some of our informants un- doubtedly lied about Jack's lies. In any case, I report what I know and all that I know and, like a good intelligence officer, do not guess at what I do not know. You are under no such restriction.

away with anything. So did Jack. A generation earlier or later, Jack's technique would have been called rape, and he probably would have gone to jail for a long time at an early age. But Jack's timing was good, as always. He ravished his maidens in a different moral epoch, after the Victorians had been overthrown and before feminist missionaries had codified the many varieties of rape that formerly were tolerated, even admired, under the heading of "all's fair in love."

Likewise, Danny's role in Jack's sex life did not seem as perverse at the time as perhaps it will seem now. As he saw it, he was just doing his buddy a favor and the girls weren't doing anything they didn't want to do. Danny's role was vicarious not because he couldn't have had the same girls himself, but because he was a monogamist by nature. Just as he had one true friend, he had one true love. Her name was Cindy Rogers, and Danny fell in love with her—and she with him—as a high school freshman. The difference was that Cindy was the one who loved, Danny the one who permitted himself to be loved.

Cindy was the prettiest girl in Tannery Falls, an all-American blonde with a lovely smile and a perfect body, head cheerleader to Danny's captain of the team. Apart from the physical match, they were an unsuitable couple. Cindy was the daughter of a local physician and therefore a member of the village aristocracy. Danny was the son of a manual laborer. Mutual passion swept away every objection. When Cindy, at fifteen, went to her father and asked for a birth-control device, he sent her to a female gynecologist in a neighboring town to be fitted with an intrauterine coil. Afterward the colleague reported to Dr. Rogers that his daughter's hymen was intact before the procedure. Cindy was a determined girl, but level-headed.

From sixth grade onward she despised Jack Adams. In high school she hated him. Danny told her everything, including the saga of Jack's conquests. "You're Jack's pimp?" she asked. "No, just his friend," Danny replied. But Cindy saw the arrangement as the corruption of Danny by Jack—and, in an odd way, as a case of Jack taking something that rightfully belonged to Danny, just like the class presidency. The real reason for her anger was the friendship. In effect she was Danny's bride, and like most brides she wanted to banish her mate's best friend. Jack was a threat to her authority; he stood between her and Danny, weakening her control of the relationship. It was Jack or her, she told Danny—choose. He laughed at her. Get rid of Jack? Nothing could dislodge him from his friend, and unfortunately for Cindy, she could not live without Danny. That meant finding room in her life for Jack, too.

When Jack went off to Columbia, Cindy thought their lives had separated at last. Although she had been accepted at Bryn Mawr and Wellesley, Cindy went to Kent State, just a few miles away from Tannery Falls, in order to be with Danny. He had been admitted on an athletic scholarship. At six-foot-one he was too short to play college basketball, but as a wide receiver in football he broke all existing school records for receptions and yardage gained. As a pitcher on the baseball team he mowed down the opposition with a 95 mph fastball and a slow curve that froze batters. He and Cindy lived together off-campus; she cooked, did the laundry, ran the errands, and helped Danny with his homework. In every sense but the legal one they were man and wife. They planned to remedy that as soon as they graduated—a big wedding in Tannery Falls, then a nice little house in Columbus while Cindy went to law school at Ohio State and Danny, who had been drafted by the Cleveland Indians, played baseball. Few doubted that he would end up pitching in the majors. In the off-season Danny would go to Ohio State, too, to work on a graduate degree in communications. He wanted to be a sportscaster when his playing days were over.

Then, a few days after they graduated, Danny was drafted into the army. It was the last thing they expected—Danny's number wasn't supposed to come up. But inexplicably, it did. He passed the preinduction physical and was ordered to report for induction in a month's time.

"I've got to see Jack," he told Cindy.

"Why? Because he dodged the draft by starving himself down to a skeleton and you're going in his place because your weight is normal?"

"Cindy, I'm not going in Jack's place. It's the luck of the draw."

"Yeah? Well, don't forget to frisk him for Vaseline."

Danny left almost immediately for New York.

When he came back three days later, he called off the wedding.

Cindy, controlling her anger, asked why. The church had been booked; they had bought the rings. Her parents had bought them a house in Columbus.

"What if I'm killed?" Danny said. "What if I'm wounded and come home no damn good for anything? Do you think I'd stick you with that, Cindy?"

"Simple," Cindy said. "If you're killed, I'll live alone for the rest of my life. If you come home in a coma, I'll sleep in the same room with you with the ball game on the radio. Anything less serious than that we can discuss when the time comes."

"You say that now," Danny said, "but I won't do it to you, Cindy. And that's final."

Because she was so much more intelligent than Danny, the emotion Cindy most often felt in his company, next to love and desire, was overwhelming exasperation.

Quietly, taking her lover's hand, she said, "Danny, listen. Whatever Jack Adams says—"

"Cindy, don't start. Jack didn't say anything."

Cindy retreated. "Okay, I'll rephrase. Whatever is going on in your mind, you don't have to go to Vietnam."

"Oh, really? Where should I go, Canada?"

"Danny, you're a college graduate. You can get a commission. You're a world-class athlete. The army is crazy about sports. All you have to do is tell them who you are. You can play on one of their teams. It will be a lot like going to college. I can delay law school for two or three years, whatever it takes, go with you. We can have a baby. By the time you get out, the kid will be big enough to go to nursery school while I go to law school."

Danny wouldn't listen. At Kent State, he had been disgusted by the antiwar protests, by the politicized kids who thought that sports were some sort of Nazi military drill, who burned flags and their draft cards.

"You think I'd go into the army and play ball while other guys got shot at?" he asked. "You think I'd sneak out of a war? Jesus, Cindy! What do you think I am?"

"I know what you are, Danny, and I love you for it," Cindy replied. "But, God forgive me, at this moment I wish you were a little more like Jack."

A week later, Danny went off to basic training. Cindy had been right: It wasn't so very different from football camp. He was an outstanding soldier. Cindy wrote him a letter a day, repeating her arguments. When he called collect every Sunday, she pleaded with him to tell his superiors about his athletic attainments. Danny refused to listen. He didn't want any special consideration.

Cindy knew that her last chance to save him from himself would come when he came home on furlough. Danny arrived at last—on embarkation leave. He had orders for Vietnam.

Cindy and Danny passed the first ten days of his furlough in a daze of lovemaking and argument. Cindy had researched the facts. Danny could be commissioned. He could play ball. He could even go to Vietnam if he wanted to—but not as a combat soldier. He'd be more valuable doing what he did best. Her father was willing to call his fraternity brother, the junior senator from Ohio. The senator would call the Pentagon and put in a word.

"I told you, Cindy," Danny said, "the answer is no."

She attacked him, fists flying, tears falling. "You son of a bitch, wanting to die for nothing!"

"For nothing? My country is nothing?"

"Danny, for God's sake don't leave me!"

"I have to."

"Like hell you do. Daddy will make that call whether you like it or not!"

Danny said, "Cindy, don't even think of it. I mean it."

Cindy said, "Oh Jesus, sweetheart! You're crazy."

Against her every instinct, because she was desperate, Cindy called Jack and asked him to come home and help her talk some sense into Danny.

"I have this terrible feeling, Jack," she said. "Something's going to happen to him over there. I know it."

"I'll be there Saturday," Jack replied.

"That's Danny's last day."

"It's the best I can do. I have to work."

Thanks to Arthur, who knew a trendy Leftist on the staff of one of New York's U.S. senators, Jack had a summer intern's job in the senator's Manhattan office. It paid no salary, but the contacts were good, and Jack was, you may be sure, making the most of them.

Cindy said, "What time can you get here?"

"I don't know. I'm broke. I'll have to hitchhike."

"For God's sake, Jack! I'll buy you a plane ticket."

"How? You're there. I'm here."

"Over the phone, with a credit card. You can pick up the ticket at the airport."

"Wow," said Jack. "A credit card? Amazing."

Was he really so naïve? With Jack you never knew. But as Cindy said, remembering this conversation later in life, nobody in Jack's family had ever had a credit card, or even a checking account. He was not only the first Adams to go to college, but also the first to ride on an airplane.

"And now look at him," she said. "No wonder Danny wanted to fight for America."

2   In those days Danny was the famous one. Everyone in Tannery Falls knew that Danny was leaving for the war, and they gave him no peace. He had come home a hero so many times that the people who had cheered him from the grandstand took it for granted that he would do so again.

On Danny's last night in town the three of them fled across the border of his celebrity to a roadhouse in a town twenty miles away. The roadhouse was small and dark. The four-piece band, dressed in powder-blue polka-dot dinner jackets, was led by a blind pianist who sang bouncy dance tunes of the 1940s in a foggy tenor.

"Hey, wow, merry-go-round music," Danny said.

He ordered a boilermaker and drank it down in a gulp, then swept Cindy onto the dance floor. The tune was "Puttin' on the Ritz." Danny was a terrific dancer. He held her close, whirling theatrically to the music. Fred and Ginger. It was all a joke—a signal, Cindy knew, that Danny did not want to get serious on his last night home.

As soon as they sat down, Danny called for another boilermaker. Cindy did not usually drink, but tonight she had two or three gin-and-Squirts—a lady's drink, the bartender said. Jack drank Coca-Cola as usual. Danny was soon quite drunk, and as the evening wore on he became steadily drunker.

Danny, doing imitations of friends and teachers, told stories about their high school days. He made them laugh.

Finally Cindy interrupted. "I don't want to talk about the past," she said.

Danny said, "Is that right? Well, let me tell you something, Cindy. I don't want to talk about the future."

"I know you don't. That's why Jack is here. Will you listen to him?"

"I *know* what Jack has to say," Danny said. "It's an immoral war. The U.S. Army, Navy, and Marines are just one big lynch mob, napalming the poor harmless Viet Cong who never did nobody no harm. It's my duty to oppose this war, not take part in it. We've got to oppose the system in order to change it. Right, Jack?"

Jack said, "You seem to understand the issues."

Danny reached across the table and grasped Jack's lapel, pulling him toward him. "What I understand, Jack, is that all that's just a bunch of bullshit," he said. "You and your pals don't give diddly-squat what happens to the Vietnamese or anybody else except yourselves. You don't want to go because you're afraid to go. You think you're too good to go. Too noble, too fine, too educated, too fucking valuable. Every time you open your mouths you tell the whole world how much better you are than everybody else. That's why you're so willing to let the niggers and the white trash die for you. 'This guy didn't even finish high school, so blow him up—it isn't like he's got a future anybody would want to live through anyway.'"

"Danny," Jack said, "that's fascist propaganda and you know it."

"Yeah? Well, I guess I've been brainwashed into a fascist by the army."

"You said it, not me. Let's talk sensibly for a minute, okay?"

"So you can tell me what?" Danny said. "That only a bonehead like me would go to a war like this? That I can get out of it just like you did, no sweat? All you have to do is lie, cheat, and let some other poor dumb son of a bitch be a war criminal on my behalf? No thanks."

"Danny, it's the government that's lying and cheating and sending young men to useless deaths. Why should you be one of them? You're worth your weight in moral gold. Don't let Nixon murder you."

"Nixon?" Danny said. "How about your old man? He started it, right?"

Jack jumped as if he had been struck. Color drained from his face. He said, "Thanks, Danny."

Cindy was puzzled by Jack's reaction. Danny had kept Jack's fantasy about his parentage a secret from her.

"Sorry, Jack," Danny said. "That was a low blow. But I just don't want to hear any more crap about this. I've been listening to it for four years at Kent State. Those fuckers aren't conscientious objectors who can't bring themselves to kill. They want the other side to win—that's what they really want. And I don't want to listen to it on my last night with you two."

"Danny," Jack said. "Nobody's asking you to join the Movement. Just don't get yourself killed for the wrong reasons. That's all Cindy is asking."

"I know what Cindy's asking. But I won't do it. I'm under orders. I'm going to Vietnam, and I *want* my country to win the war. I do, folks, I do. So let's drink, dance, and be merry, for tomorrow I'll be a mass murderer."

The band was playing a slow tune. Danny pulled Cindy onto the dance floor. She wept as they danced. Watching them—Danny gazing down into Cindy's sad face, Cindy smiling back—Jack felt a sob forming in his chest. By the time they came back to the table, he was wiping away tears.

Jack said, "Danny, listen. I wish I could go with you."

Danny gazed at him, wide-eyed. "No shit, Jack, do you? You want to go to war?"

"In a sense, yes."

Danny was grinning, that carefree smile that made Cindy's heart turn over. "But you're fighting temptation?" he said. "Jack, I know you. You wouldn't go to war if the other side was an all-girl orchestra."

The tension broke. Jack laughed. "Don't be so sure about that."

"The question is, does it work both ways? I don't care how many Communists you fuck, but will you still love me if I kill one?"

Jack said, "Danny, cut it out."

"No, you two started this. Let's let it all hang out. The difference between you and me is simple: You're afraid of getting hurt. You've been that way all your life. Isn't that right?"

Jack looked to Cindy, as if for help. She returned his look with a cold stare. But she intervened. "Danny," she said, "the subject of this conversation isn't Jack. It's you and me. If I could, I'd hide you in the attic till the war's over."

"I know," Danny said. "That's because you just don't get it, Cindy. There is no choice."

"But, Danny, there *is* a choice. You don't have to do this. Jack isn't doing it."

"I'm not Jack. I love Jack, no shit. I do, I always have. But I know him. Jack, you're a coward."

Cindy said, "Come on, Danny. Cowardice isn't the subject under discussion."

"It's not? What is—good old common sense?"

"Yes, for Christ's sake!"

Jack was fascinated. He said, "Wait. Let him finish."

"Thank you," Danny said. "To continue, Jack is yellow. He always has been. We all know it. Me especially. I've been fighting his battles all his life. But Jack can't help that. He was born the way he is, smart as a whip, backbone like a noodle. Me, I'm good at sports, fast as a striped-ass deer, brave as a fucking lion. Dumb as a stone. I'll crash into anything—three hundred pounds of doped-up motherfucker in football pads, stone wall, chain saw, doesn't matter. I don't give a shit about physical danger. I never have."

"Machine gunners and defensive linemen aren't the same thing," Cindy said.

"To me they are. I can't help *that.* I was born that way. Just like Jack was born the way he is. Get the point?"

"No," Cindy said.

"Then good luck to you both."

The blind tenor was singing "Good Night, Ladies."

Danny said, "One more boilermaker."

Danny sank his shot glass into the beer, steelworker style, and drank. In the singer's mirrored sunglasses, Cindy saw Danny's reflected image, drinking from his glass with one hand while playfully mussing up Jack's hair with the other.

The two boys were looking into each other's eyes, smiling faintly, as if they knew something that no one else could ever know. Cindy realized that she was out of the picture, that she had no place in this moment. These two really did love each other, and Jack was just as afraid of losing Danny as she was, and for the same reason: Danny was his other half. Nothing could possibly be the same without him.

Danny said, "Don't misunderstand me. I don't think there's any difference between you and me, Jack. Your fear is no different from my guts. It's what God gave us when he made us. Maybe there's some mysterious purpose that's about to be revealed. Like I said, there's no choice, because God has already made the choices for us. Jack, Cindy—I *want* to go to Vietnam. It's just the way I am."

Cindy said, "Okay. Then go."

Danny said, "Don't worry, Jack. I'm not going to get killed."

He was telling *Jack* not to worry. He'd come back and fight his battles for him, just as he always had done.

Cindy realized that she was never going to get Jack out of Danny's life, or out of her own. Never.

3 Danny was too drunk to make love to Cindy on their last night together, and he slept on in the morning long after Cindy was awake, so they had no time to themselves before Jack came for them in Cindy's car. It was a brand-new Ford, a graduation present from Cindy's parents. Jack had driven it home the night before, after dropping them off in front of her parents' house.

Danny's plane left in the late afternoon. He insisted that Jack drive him and Cindy to the airport, fifty miles away over twisting back roads. He himself was too hungover to drive, and though Cindy wanted to spend their last hours alone together, he told her no. He did not want her to come home alone in the dark. Especially not in a state of emotion after saying goodbye to him. What if she had an accident, alone on those dark and lonely roads?

"God knows what might happen," he said.

In order to fly on the cheaper military fare, Danny wore his uniform. He had come home from camp wearing civilian clothes. Cindy gasped when he came downstairs in his green trousers and blouse, his khaki shirt and black tie, his clumsy, thick-soled patent-leather shoes, an expert rifleman's badge on his chest.

This was reality. Cindy bit her fist and ran upstairs, fending him off when he tried to stop her, and locked herself in her room.

She did not come out again until Jack rang the doorbell. In the car, there was silence between the lovers. Jack kept quiet, too, driving while Danny and Cindy sat in the backseat staring out the windows, not even holding hands. Jack stopped the car once or twice so that Danny could get out and vomit. He was a beer drinker; whiskey made him sick, and he had drunk a lot of it the night before.

The plane was several hours late. They waited in the restaurant, where Danny, still silent, had several beers to cure his hangover. Cindy, made reckless by anger and anxiety, matched his silence with one of her own and also matched him drink for drink— gin-and-Squirt against Budweiser. Jack drank Coca-Cola.

When at last Danny's flight was called, he stood up, slung his bag over his shoulder, and shook hands with Jack. Danny gathered him into a bear hug.

"Be careful crossing the street," he said.

"You too," Jack replied, eyes brimming.

"No sweat," Danny said. He pulled him closer and whispered into his ear. "But take care of Cindy. She's pissed off and she's loaded. So watch it."

Jack nodded.

Cindy glared at him. He said, "Cindy, I'll be out front in the car."

At last Danny put his arm around her and they walked together to the gate. Cindy tried to kiss him, but he drew back. Danny said, "No kisses. I don't want the taste of puke to be the last thing you remember about me." He patted her on the cheek and turned away. She knew him, she read his meaning in his eyes: That's all you get, baby.

He was punishing her for locking herself in her room. She understood this, and as he disappeared into the plane, a stranger to her in his uniform, she was overwhelmed by anger, pain, unspeakable love, and—most of all, just as Danny had intended, the son of a bitch!—guilt.

4 Cindy was weeping unashamedly when she came out of the terminal. Jack opened the door for her, but she slammed it shut and got into the backseat. She curled up in the fetal position, her back to Jack, her body wracked by sobs. Jack put the car in motion. After a while she fell asleep, one hand falling to the floor, one long leg extended, blond hair tumbling.

When they were about halfway home, Cindy woke up and shouted, "Stop the car."

She was choking, hand clapped over her mouth. Jack pulled over. Cindy burst out of the car, retching violently.

"Shit, oh shit!" she moaned. She fell to her knees, vomiting helplessly, then dropped to all fours. Her unbound hair swung in the path of the vomit. She tried to sweep it out of the way with one hand, but the gesture was hopeless. Jack gathered up her hair. She pushed him away.

"Fuck you, Jack!" she said. "You're no friend of mine."

She staggered toward the car, lost her balance, and fell onto the blacktop on her knees. She howled in pain, beating her fists on the pavement.

A car went by at high speed in the opposite direction, rocking their parked vehicle on its springs. A few moments later another car approached, then slowed down almost to a stop, with Cindy in its headlights. The passenger, a middle-aged woman, rolled down her window and looked out at Jack, memorizing his face.

"What's the problem here?" she said.

The driver, pad and pencil in hand, was writing down the license number. Jack felt a stab of panic. All his life he suffered from an irrational, poor boy's fear of policemen. He felt like a fugitive in America, as if old Joe Kennedy might find out at any moment who he really was and send the cops to put him away on some trumped-up charge so he wouldn't embarrass the family.

Cindy got to her feet and waved drunkenly at the woman. "It's okay," she said. "Keep going."

"Are you sure?"

Cindy responded with another tipsy wave.

"Beautiful girl like you!" the woman said. The car drove on.

Jack said, "Come on, Cindy. Time to go home."

"No," Cindy said. "Got to sober up."

"Cindy, let's go home. Really."

" '*Really*,' " Cindy said, mocking his new Eastern accent. "It's my fucking car, and I say no. My mother hates Danny enough already."

Cindy got into the backseat again and immediately fell asleep, or seemed to. Cars roared by on the narrow road, blowing their horns. Sooner or later a sheriff's cruiser or the Ohio State Patrol would come along. The Patrol were bastards; there was no telling what they might do. Jack started the car and drove on until he saw a strip-mine entrance he recognized. It led into a labyrinth of old roads and mines. He had taken girls there before. He turned in, drove to a spot he remembered, and switched off the engine.

The moon had come up. Cindy, sleeping on her side on the back-seat, lay in its buttery light like an odalisque. Even drunk, even smelling of vomit, even unconscious, she was as pretty as a picture. She was snoring.

Jack lay down on the front seat and went to sleep himself.

How much later he did not know, he jerked awake. In the back-seat Cindy was fighting herself awake, arms flying, hands clawing. Her eyes were tightly closed.

"Cindy!"

She stared wildly at Jack.

He said, "Cindy, it's okay. It's me."

"Jack," she said, "I dreamed he was dead."

"It was a dream. You're okay. Danny's okay. Everything's okay."

Cindy didn't seem to hear. She wailed, "Oh Jesus! What am I going to do? What am I going to do?"

Jack did not know what to say to her, so he smiled, always his best weapon. Eyes streaming, Cindy climbed over the front seat and sat down beside Jack.

She was trembling violently. She said, "Jack, hold on to me. I feel like I'm falling apart."

Gingerly, Jack put his arms around her. She hugged him back, shaking, Jack thought, as if she were freezing and only the warmth of another body could save her. He imagined she was thinking of Danny. After a few moments she relaxed, then fell asleep.

Almost immediately she woke with a start, crying, "Don't let me fall asleep. I don't want to be in that dream again."

Jack said, "Okay, I'll turn on the radio."

They listened to music for a while. Cindy made no attempt to move away from him. Finally, intending to push her gently away from him and start the car, he kissed her lightly on the forehead. She looked at him for a long moment, as if trying to understand who he was and what he wanted.

Then she kissed him, chastely, on the lips. Jack kissed her back, lightly. She responded. Up to this moment Jack had not had a sexual thought, at least not one he felt he could act on. But the kiss triggered the essential Jack. He was overcome by desire. He kissed Cindy lingeringly; she accepted his tongue, then turned her head violently aside, as if she were the one who tasted vomit.

But, as Cindy was to remember in years to come, she did not say *Stop*; she did not push him away.

Jack was moving her body, arranging their positions. And then, yes, he did what he had done so many times before in similar situations.

Cindy said, "Oh my God!"

But Jack had gone too far to stop, so he continued to the end, and through the haze of alcohol and grief, Cindy felt her body responding. She tried to make it stop. She was as limp as a rag doll; she felt incapable of movement. Nevertheless she was moving, responding. She fought against this. Owing to Jack's peculiar method of approach, Cindy was still wearing her panties. They had been twisted into a sort of tourniquet, shutting off the circulation in her left thigh. This was painful. She concentrated on the pain, tried to fill her mind with it. But her body took over, and though it was the last thing in the world she wanted to happen, she was taken by the wave.

5 Cindy had realized that Danny's furlough would coincide with her cycle of fertility. Before he came home, before she ovulated, she went to a gynecologist who removed the intrauterine birth-control device she had worn since adolescence. Cindy told Danny nothing about this, and as they made love every day, several times a day, he supposed that nothing could come of all this copulation except pleasure.

A week after Danny left for Vietnam, she missed her first period. Ordinarily this would not have upset her. Her cycle was irregular and she had been late many times in the past. When this had happened in the past, she and Danny always renewed their promise to each other that if she really was pregnant they would marry and have the child.

However, this child might very well be Jack's—and if it was, she realized that she was capable of killing it with no more thought than was required to crush an insect. There was no way to know which man was the father—the one she loved or the one she hated. Even after the child was born she could never be sure. How could she ever love it if she could never know for certain to whom it really belonged?

The desire for control was very strong in Cindy; it was her real religion. She had learned in Sunday school that good actions produced pleasant consequences and bad actions, unpleasant ones. All her life she had avoided unpleasant consequences by behaving herself, by planning ahead, by making things come out the way she wished. Now she was losing control of everything at the same time—her own body, her own life.

Cindy longed to hear from Danny. He had not called her from California before his plane took off for Vietnam. He had never written a letter in his life. The rational part of Cindy's mind told her that he had not called because he had not been able to get to a telephone; the other part of her mind told her that it was because he was still angry at her—that he might die in a state of anger. On television every day she saw American boys wounded, dying, dead in their body bags. Danny's fate and the fate of the child she had wanted to have—but whose existence, whose chance of life, she feared as much as she feared the possibility of Danny's death—joined in her mind, got mixed up in her dreams.

She waited, checking for menstrual blood ten times a day, trying not to think about consequences.

She had never been so alone in her life.

Cindy loaded her car with clothes, books, her electric typewriter, the unwashed bedding that still smelled of Danny, and drove to Columbus. She moved into her new little house—almost a doll's cottage—and started her new life as a law student.

Most of her professors and nearly all of her fellow law students were opposed to the war. In one of her classes the professor humiliated a student who had fought in Vietnam, asking him questions on legal ethics and turning his answers into an argument about the morality of a modern technological society using its machines to slaughter the population of a defenseless primitive society. On the faces of her classmates Cindy saw a certain look of triumph when the veteran, who limped from his wounds, was stricken dumb by the eloquence and ardor of the professor.

By the first of October, Danny still had not written or called. Cindy watched the evening news on CBS at seven o'clock and ABC at eleven, then woke up early to watch the news segments on the *Today* show on NBC. By covering all three networks, Cindy hoped to catch a glimpse of Danny, but she was afraid that this would actually happen and the Danny she would see would be the tormented, dying Danny she had seen in her dream. She could not sleep. At night she studied until she could no longer comprehend what she was reading, and then wrote Danny long, half-coherent letters.

The letters never caught up to Danny, but Cindy had had her telephone in Columbus connected before he left, so he knew the number. On October tenth, a week after her second period had been due, he called her collect from Saigon. She covered the mouthpiece and sobbed when she heard his voice.

Danny told her how bad the chow was, what lousy movies he had seen. Half the army in Vietnam was smoking dope, the other half was drunk. It was a lot like going to Kent State except that everybody had a short haircut and a gun. The officers were like coaches, full of shit about discipline and game plans and team spirit, and living off other people's sweat and reputation.

Cindy said, "Are you in the fighting?"

"Not especially. What we do is go for long walks with guns and grenades hanging off us and try to make friends with the natives. Scares the crap out of them, but you know me—just old John Wayne who wouldn't hurt a fly."

"Where in Vietnam are you, exactly?"

"Military secret. But watch out for me on TV. I wrote you a let—"

The line crackled; he was gone. They had been cut off by a timer. Into the dead connection Cindy said, "I love you," forming the words, not speaking them aloud.

A week later she received Danny's letter. After class that same day she caught up with the limping veteran and showed him the return address: I & R Plt., 1st Bn., 26th Inf., 1st Inf. Div.

He read it. "So?"

"It's my boyfriend's address. What does it mean?"

"It means he's got his ass in the grass."

"This is a combat outfit?"

He snorted. "You could say that."

Cindy said, "Look, I just show up for class with that jerk, just like you. Give me a break."

The man shrugged. "What Intelligence and Reconnaissance platoons do is, they go out on patrol all by themselves and try to locate the enemy. Draw fire. Then they radio back to the battalion and wait for everybody else to move up."

"It sounds dangerous."

He was still unsure of her motives. After a pause he said, "It is. The First Division operates in War Zone C, which runs from Saigon all the way to the Cambodian border. That's where all the best gook outfits hide out—just across the border in Cambodia. The First Division goes in after them. Your boyfriend is probably walking point."

Cindy knew from television what that term meant. It meant that Danny was the first American soldier the enemy would see as they lay in ambush in the jungle.

She said, "I see. Thanks."

Her voice trembled. For the first time, the vet showed some human feeling. He said, "What's your name?"

"Cindy."

"Hang in there, Cindy," he said. "He's got a good reason to be careful."

6 As soon as the conversation ended, Cindy drove to a clinic off campus and took a pregnancy test. A woman called with the results a couple of days later, early in the morning.

She was pregnant.

Cindy had been studying all night in her nightgown and robe, and after hanging up the phone she stripped these off and looked at herself in the full-length mirror. She was absolutely beautiful.

Better than anyone, she knew how perfect her own body was. She had always loved it. Now she thought of what might be growing inside it, and for the first time since she and Jack Adams had done what they had done and spoiled the pleasure she had always taken in looking at herself, she met her own eyes in the mirror. If the child was Danny's, Danny would never die, and she and Danny would never be separated. The child would carry Danny's genes and her genes into the future, and it was possible that the right combination of egg and sperm might someday, maybe centuries from now, come together and result in another Danny—black hair, blue eyes, mirthful smile, amazing grace. And memories he did not even know he had.

But if this fetus belonged to Jack Adams, it too would perpetuate something—the shameful memory of the betrayal she had visited on Danny in her weakness and folly. Like a shudder, dark and unbidden, guilt and shame and hatred ran through her flesh one after the other, like the orgasms that Jack had given her.

She brushed her teeth, showered, dressed, and went directly to the abortion clinic.

In the recovery room, Cindy was awakened by a nurse—the same one who had helped with what they called the procedure.

"Which was it?" she asked.

The nurse said, "It was an embryo, Cindy."

Cindy sat up on the gurney. "*What was it?*"

"We're not permitted to say."

"I want to know."

"It really is better not to assign human characteristics to it."

After a moment of silence, eyes locked on the nurse's, Cindy said, "I insist."

"Okay." The nurse looked at a chart. "First trimester male embryo," she said.

"Hair color?"

"We don't make a note of that. How are you feeling?"

Cindy didn't answer.

"A little woozy?" the nurse said. "That's normal."

She took Cindy's blood pressure, then her pulse, and, after she was through, held on to her wrist for a moment. She looked down with a practiced, smilingly sincere expression of—what?

"Cindy, listen to me," the nurse said. "Nothing happened here that you need to feel anything but good about."

"You may be half right about that," Cindy replied.

Two

1 Off a clown-white Haitian beach, while suspended from an inflated plastic ring in surf that was the exact temperature of saliva, Peter revealed the outline of his plan for Jack Adams.

First, he was going to bind Jack to us for the rest of his life. Then he was going to manage his future in minute detail. And then Jack was going to be elected president of the United States.

"Legitimately, in an honest election," Peter said. He named the year. "It is perfectly possible."

I said, "You're going to turn the president of the United States into an agent of influence?"

"No, Dmitri," he replied, "you and I are going to turn Jack Adams into an agent of influence, and then with our help and advice and moral support, Jack is going to transform himself into the president of the United States."

"Are you going to tell Jack why we are doing all this for him?"

"Of course not," Peter replied. "He will be unwitting."

You blink? You wonder if Peter was mad? Resist the impulse to disbelieve. Peter was not mad. He was something even more unsettling, an original thinker. To Peter, the student of the American psyche, this plan to make the ultimate dream of the KGB come true was not a grandiose objective. It was an obvious operational objective that needed only the right plan, the right touch, and above all, the right asset to succeed.

"Let's swim out a little farther," Peter said.

As before, he spoke in a conversational voice, but with his back to the shore so that his words would be carried out to sea. Useless precautions are the silent prayers of espionage. Between us and the beach, half a mile away, several swimmers approached, round dark heads bobbing in the swell: the same smiling boys and girls who had driven us into the water earlier by shadowing us, offering delights, as we walked along the sand. These children were no threat to our secrets. All they were interested in was money. But Peter had ordered me to meet him here, at a resort hotel on a remote point of land, so that we would be absolutely alone. He had imagined that we would be undisturbed. And as always, he insisted on having precisely what he had imagined.

Farther out, the surf was higher. We rose and fell several meters each time a sluggish wave rolled in from the open sea. We swam clumsily in our plastic doughnuts. It was quite unsafe to be so far from the grip of the land. Even the little prostitutes, who swam like fishes, thought so; they turned back. I am not at ease in tropical waters. I wonder about sharks, barracuda, treacherous undertows that might sweep one out to sea.

Oblivious to exterior realities, Peter resumed his monologue. He had been thinking about this project for years, looking for the right man, waiting for the right moment. Now the Vietnam War, combined with pathological fear and loathing for that nemesis of the faithful, Richard Nixon, had provided the moment. History had turned America upside down. Golden opportunities were falling out of its pockets.

Jack Adams was just the man to snatch these opportunities; Peter was sure of it.

I said, "The fact that he seems to be a born liar doesn't bother you?"

"Lies are the truth of the Left," Peter said, flicking my question off the table like a crumb. "The revolution has always lied about everything for its own reasons. So does Jack for *his* own reasons. We will make the reasons the same."

Peter continued with his main line of reasoning. Jack's humble origins were precisely the thing that made him the ideal lump of clay. With rare exceptions, American presidents came from exactly such origins. Truman, Eisenhower, Johnson, Nixon, Carter—all were nobodies from nowhere, poor boys like Jack who escaped from obscurity as a result of highly unlikely combinations of circumstances.

"Almost always they are from families that are not merely humble, but scorned," Peter said. "Religious fanatics, bankrupts, outcasts. There is always a deus ex machina involved: The unlettered Truman catches the eye of a political boss, the charming athlete Eisenhower is appointed to West Point, the resentful lone wolf Nixon answers a want ad and is elected to Congress. Only in America."

Jack Adams's deus ex machina would be us—or, rather, Peter.

No one must ever know about our hidden hand. Not even Jack. And especially not Moscow. We would run this operation outside the apparatus. To the rest of the KGB, Jack would be just another ineffectual American asset, another of Peter's wild gambles, a waste of time and money.

I said, "A question. This is going to cost a lot of money. If Moscow knows nothing about this operation, how will we pay for it?"

"Certain arrangements have been made," Peter said.

That was all he told me, then or later. It was all I needed to know. I assumed he had devised some way to bury the expenses of this operation in the labyrinthine budget of his directorate—called "Peter's Follies" by the rest of the KGB. He pounded into my head the absolute necessity of compartmenting Jack from the espionage directorates. They must never know how important Jack was, they must never be able to touch him, never be able to demand their money's worth, because they would destroy him with their stupidity, just as they had destroyed Alger Hiss.

I said, "Alger Hiss? I thought he belonged to the neighbors."

The neighbors is slang for the GRU, Soviet military intelligence, to whose Washington network Hiss, an American diplomat, was said to have belonged in the 1930s and 1940s.

"He did," Peter replied, "but they are all alike. All they can think about is stealing secrets. They destroyed an asset who was in a position to give history a shove by sabotaging U.S. foreign policy— blew their own agent. And why? So that he could rifle wastebaskets in his spare time. They would do it again."

This Hiss story, said Peter, was a political Passion play, a triumph of faith over reality. Hiss may have been convicted in a court of law on the basis of secrets copied down in his own hand and handed over to the Russians, but the progressive element in the United States adamantly—furiously—refused to believe in his guilt. For half a century—and this was the part that Peter loved because it was such an inspired diversion—they defended Hiss's innocence as if it were their own, which of course it was, since this fallen angel was the archetype of the good liberal. By admitting that he was something other than he seemed to be, they would be admitting that they also had something to hide. They wore his clothes, spoke in his vocabulary, thought his thoughts. To those who were so much like him, Hiss was not a traitor but a prophet sent from the twentieth-century version of heaven—the socialist motherland—only to be condemned before his work was done by an ignorant mob controlled by a corrupt priesthood of reactionaries, the Republican Party.

"It's the Jesus story all over again," Peter said, "with Marx as the father, Alger as the son, Whittaker Chambers as Judas, the FBI as the Romans, Nixon as Pontius Pilate, and the liberals as the disciples, preaching the word, proclaiming the holiness of the martyr. Do you understand the opportunity, the *power* this puts in our hands? The holy spirit is in them unto the third generation. They are an unconscious underground, demanding no support, requiring no instruction, driven by blind faith and the thirst for revenge. All we have to do is give them another Messiah who reminds them of Alger and this time they will kidnap him from the cross. Alive."

Gulls circled and cried overhead, as if summoned by Peter's wisdom. He treaded water until they went away. Then he returned to his parable.

"The same people who beatified Alger will discover and love Jack—the Jack we are going to design for them," Peter said. "They will invest every kopeck of their moral and political capital in him as soon as they hear him speak in parables. To them, Jack's weaknesses will be strengths, his lies truths, his crimes miracles."

"His masters invisible?"

"Not entirely. We must give them signs. Everything depends on their understanding exactly how this rabbit was pulled out of the hat."

Peter's contempt for those Americans who loved us was breathtaking, but that is the revolutionary's way. All that mattered to him was the outcome. He would gladly use fools to gain his ends—in fact he could hardly attain his ends without their help. And then he would shoot them before they did to him what they had done to their own country. He would no more let such weaklings survive than he would marry another man's worn-out widow after screwing her for twenty years of secret afternoons in her late husband's bed.

Unlike Hiss, who was never more than the bureaucratic equivalent of a gentleman's gentleman, a valet to the Old Guard, Jack would fight the good fight in the open, proud of his beliefs, always on camera, eager to answer any question, his whole being written on his face. Talking the talk, smiling the smile.

"But first we must bind him to us," Peter said. "I have made certain arrangements in Heidelberg."

"Who do we have in Heidelberg?"

"An old friend named Manfred," Peter said. "He arrives tomorrow, to meet you. Manfred loves beaches."

Manfred was a lecturer in political philosophy at Heidelberg University, a talent spotter like Arthur, but a more serious person, with more serious resources. Every August he was rewarded for his difficult and valuable work with an all-expenses-paid holiday at a beach. These were working holidays; he always spent a day or two with Peter or one of his men, who gave him his next assignment. Sometimes Manfred went to Tunisia, sometimes to Greece, once to an island in the Indian Ocean—wherever skies were blue and skins were dark.

This year he was recreating himself in Haiti, and I would give him his instructions. To prepare me for this task, Peter sketched in the Heidelberg phase of his plan for Jack Adams. He mentioned individuals, wild young vandals who called themselves terrorists. Their cases were familiar to me.

"Give them latitude," Peter said. "They're very creative. And they're expendable, as long as Jack is protected."

I said, "You see the risks. These kids are mad, unpredictable."

"That will help Jack remember his adventures all the more vividly," Peter said.

That evening by the swimming pool he introduced me to Manfred.

"You can have absolute confidence in Dmitri," Peter said. "He is my opposable thumb."

Manfred, the screwdriver Peter had just handed to me, smiled in quiet satisfaction at the subtlety of the image: revolutionaries as the users of tools, all others as apes.

We made our arrangements. Then I left Manfred among the urchins.

2 Heidelberg, a living postcard, was the first foreign city Jack had ever seen. Arriving by train from Frankfurt, he thought it looked like a set for a Hollywood musical about a prince in disguise—his favorite story line. Manfred met him at the Hauptbahnhof, claiming to be an old friend of Arthur's, who by this time was moldering in a Cuban grave and was in no position to deny it. Manfred took him to lunch in a student hangout, then drove him to the old quarter, where garret rooms had been engaged for Jack. The dormer windows looked out on a narrow cobbled street. All very picturesque: heraldic Teutonic shields carved into the ancient stones, leaning eaves all but touching so as to admit only a thread of light. As if on cue, zither music drifted through a window: the *Third Man* theme, issuing from a television.

As Jack soon discovered, this romantic medieval exterior concealed a bloated capitalistic Heidelberg, awash in the new money of the German economic miracle and drenched in counterculture sex and politics that were far more intense, far darker than anything he had known in the United States. On his second night in town, a Saturday, Manfred invited him to dinner at a cellar restaurant in the old town. Like the city itself, the rathskeller was a peep show into a vanished Germany. Oompah Muzak played in the background. Waitresses in dirndls and white knee socks rushed about serving mugs of beer and having their bottoms patted by hearty fat men who stuffed enormous tips into their aprons.

Most of the girls were pretty in the smooth-skinned German fashion. Jack was immediately alert. A waitress bustled up to the table. Manfred ordered a Pilsner, Jack his usual Coca-Cola.

"No, no. You must have beer," Manfred said.

Jack held up a hand in firm refusal. "No thanks. I don't drink alcohol."

"But beer is not alcohol! It is—"

Jack interrupted. "Liquid bread. I know. But I don't want any."

Jack waited for Manfred to ask him why. This was an opportunity to establish a bond with this new acquaintance by revealing that he had grown up in a house with an alcoholic. However, Manfred's attention was directed elsewhere. Ignoring Jack, he stood up and waved. A red-haired girl, standing on the stairway at the other end of the long, low room, saw him and returned his greeting with a sullen gesture.

She headed toward their table, striding purposefully past parties of old men who gazed at her in astonishment as she passed. The girl wore boots, a miniskirt, a Bundeswehr camouflage field jacket, and a long student scarf. An ancient green rucksack was slung over her shoulder by its one remaining strap. Her red hair was wild, curly, uncombed. She marched as if in uniform—which in a way she was. She could hardly have caused a greater stir if the year had been 1930, and memories of the Kaiser were as fresh in customers' minds as Hitler was now, and she was the first storm trooper any of these people had ever seen.

"Here comes someone I want you to meet," Manfred said.

Jack pushed back his chair, legs squealing on the stone floor, and stood up.

The girl arrived, a scowling pale face inside a mare's nest of Titian curls.

Up to then, Manfred and Jack had been speaking German—slow, textbook German to accommodate Jack's unpracticed ear and tongue, but German nevertheless. Manfred made the introductions in English. "Greta Fürst, please meet Jack Adams from the United States."

Greta said, "An Ami? For God's sake, Manfred, why?"

Jack held out his hand. Greta ignored it. In slurred, barely enunciated German, the worldwide accents of youthful scorn, she said, "Don't tell me he can't even speak German?"

Her eyes, heavily made up, were green, intelligent, and icy with contempt.

Jack said, "I like your voice, Greta. You sound like Marlene Dietrich in *The Blue Angel*."

Greta stared at him in disbelief. "God!" she said.

"Just the voice," Jack said. "You're much thinner than she was then."

Manfred said, "Sit down, Greta. Join us for some supper."

"No thanks. I'm not hungry."

"Something to drink, then."

"I'm not thirsty."

"Then at least sit down." Greta sat down. To the waitress Manfred said, "Bring her a lager, please. And three mixed sausages."

Eyes fixed on Jack, Greta dug a package of Gauloises out of her rucksack and lit one. She picked a fleck of tobacco off the end of her tongue, inhaled deeply, and blew a cloud of acrid smoke across the table.

Jack coughed, then smiled apologetically. Greta, refusing to look at him, feigned interest in the ceiling and took another drag from her poisonous caporal.

Greta caught Jack's smile and made a sour face. Manfred watched, waiting to see what might happen next.

In his slow, annoying German, Jack said, "So, Greta, do you go to the university?"

Greta did not respond. The food came. Cigarette burning in her right hand, she cut up her sausages into little pieces and ate them with her fingers. She ate her fried potatoes, even her salad, in the same way. Jack recognized the style: He knew a lot of bourgeois Movement girls who had adopted infantile table manners along with round heels as a means of semaphoring radical political beliefs. He himself used a knife and fork in the American manner—cutting a morsel of sausage, putting down his knife, shifting his fork from left hand to right, spearing the food, lifting it to his mouth, chewing thirty-two times before swallowing. This unmistakable evidence of Jack's revolting nationality further disgusted Greta.

While they ate, Manfred carried on a dialectical discussion with Jack. The subject, inescapably, was politics—American politics as seen from the Left. At first, Manfred's questions were condescending, and he only half-listened to Jack's replies. But before long he began to realize that these answers were subtle, deeply informed, and, most surprising, free of cant. Jack was no fervent youth, unsure of his opinions and eager for approval. He did not protest the correctness of his own beliefs, or even bother to describe them. Nevertheless the listener felt that Jack's political convictions were so pure, so deep, so genuinely held, that he felt no need to announce them, even on first meeting. He seemed to assume, while offering no bona fides that this was the case, that Manfred would take it for granted that he believed in all the right things. This was an amazing trick of the mind.

Quite soon Jack turned what had started out to be a Socratic dialogue with himself as the learner into a tutorial on American realities—a monologue that rushed along like a river in flood, swelling as it went, picking up all sorts of strange debris. Jack was calm, collected, good-humored—impervious, apparently, to the stimuli that drove most people his age, and many older men and women, into frenzies of resentment and anger. Drowning, Manfred seized an uprooted oak—Richard Nixon—in the hope that his weight would cause it to snag on the mud of Jack's rhetoric and give him a chance to scramble ashore onto the terra firma of Marxist-Leninist principle.

But Jack was dispassionate, even about Richard Nixon.

"By any rational standard of judgment," he said, barely pausing for breath, "Nixon has been a very effective president. An enemy, yes, and a dangerous one. He'll end the war as soon as he can, on whatever terms he can get."

"What about his constituency, the warmongers?"

"There are no warmongers," Jack said. "Just people who want the whole thing to be over. If he gets peace on any terms he'll be re-elected in a landslide."

"And then what?"

"And then Armageddon. Nixon will have so much power that his enemies will either have to destroy him or be destroyed by him."

"Which will happen?"

"Both, in the end."

Up to then, Greta had shown no sign that she understood a word of the conversation. Suddenly she said, "What a load of shit."

Jack said, "Interesting point. Would you like to elaborate?"

"No." Greta ground out the stub of her third Gauloise.

Manfred smiled indulgently, then, as if remembering something, looked at his watch. "Oh dear," he said, in English. "I'm late. Greta, will you see that Jack finds his way home?"

She replied in German. "What is he, blind?"

"No, darling, not blind. Jack is our guest, a stranger in Heidelberg, and he doesn't know the town yet. And you are his first experience of German womanhood, which is famous for submission and kindness to strangers. So walk him home, please."

Greta shrugged. She stood up. "Come, Jack," she said. "Time for your walk."

She spun on her heels and marched toward the exit.

Manfred said, "Take my advice. Go with her. She's not so bad when you get to know her."

Greta had reached the stairs. She stood at the top, glaring.

Jack smiled at her, the full Kennedy display.

"I'll bet," he said.

3 Outside the rathskeller it was raining. Glistening in the dim glow of the streetlights, the city itself was the color of rain— roofs, steeples, cobblestones, parked cars, even the whey-faced people hurrying by in wet raincoats, holding wet umbrellas. The only splashes of color were the bedraggled flags and banners, wrapped around their poles in watershot floodlight.

This dismal scene seemed beautiful to Jack. He said so, invoking the name of Ingmar Bergman because everything he had so far seen in Heidelberg reminded him of foreign films. The city was black and white, badly lit, hokily mysterious, so filled with solemn meaning that it would be ridiculous if filmed in a language you could understand.

"Beautiful?" Greta said. "You think this is beautiful?"

Greta, raised in sunless northern Europe, stared at him in pitiless disbelief, then pulled a collapsible umbrella out of her book bag and popped it open. One of the ribs was broken. A dimple in the cloth filled with water, which ran over the edge of the umbrella in a tiny cascade. Greta darted into the traffic. Jack, who had no umbrella or hat or raincoat, stayed where he was in the doorway of the rathskeller.

Greta, realizing after a few emphatic steps that Jack was not following her, stopped in the middle of the street and looked back.

"What are you waiting for?" she called in English.

"For this to let up," Jack replied.

"*What?*"

"The rain. I'm waiting for it to stop."

"Stop? It will never stop. You are in Germany. Come."

Jack shrugged and stepped out in the downpour.

Greta said, "You have no umbrella?"

"Afraid not."

"Ach! Use this!" She pulled a copy of *Bild Zeitung* out of her book bag and handed it to him.

Jack held the newspaper over his head. "'Ach!'" he repeated. "Vunderful!"

"It won't be so wonderful for you in Germany if you have no umbrella," Greta replied. "Come!"

Greta really did pronounce her *w*'s as *v*'s. It was the only flaw in her English. Jack said, "Just like Marlene."

"*What?*"

In Dietrich's throaty diction Jack sang, "'Falling in luff again, never vanted to . . .'"

Again Greta stared at him, again pointedly unamused. "Unbelievable," she said. "Come, quickly."

She strode away under her tiny broken umbrella, red curls bouncing, combat boots splashing decisively through puddles. Jack hurried to catch up, then skipped a stride when he was beside her in order to walk in step.

Unspeaking, she led the way into a steep, narrow street, then through several turnings into other medieval passages. Most were dark, but at length they turned into a particularly picturesque alley lined with luxury shops. Jewels, crystal, silks, were tastefully displayed in tiny windows.

"Beautiful stuff," Jack said admiringly.

"Garbage," Greta said. "For ersatz Americans. Look."

They were standing in front of a shop window. Inside, a clerk hovered, smiling, as an expensively dressed man considered buying a bracelet for an expensively dressed woman. Both were middle-aged, smiling, overweight. The woman smiled adoringly at the man.

"His mistress?" Jack said.

"That sausage?" Greta said. "Never. She's his wife. His mistress would be skinny. They make you vomit."

"Who?"

In the reflected light, Greta's face twisted with disgust. She looked up at Jack, her umbrella tilting so that rainwater spilled from the dimple in its fabric.

Vehemently she said, "What do you mean, 'Who?' Them." She pointed at the fat couple in the shop. "The class enemy."

"Oh," Jack said. "Is that what fat people are?"

"How do you think they got fat?"

"Gosh. Just like in those German expressionist pictures. But better—pictures can't fart."

Greta's lip twitched. Jack thought that she was going to smile, but she stopped herself in time and attacked instead.

"You are very, very clever," she said. "But you are not serious."

"Really? How do you know?"

Greta spun on her heel and led him onward past more glittering shops. "I know because you are an American," she said. "You see these people, all alike, all looking at jewels and clothes and all these beautiful things, all with full bellies while half the world starves or dies from American bombs? They are what America has made in Germany."

Under streaming umbrellas, well-fed men and women in matching trench coats, mostly Burberrys, window-shopped like sleepwalkers.

"*Look at them!*" Greta said.

Jack looked. "Okay, what's the point?" he asked. "Ersatz Americans have nice raincoats and umbrellas, and real ones hold newspapers over their heads?"

"The point is," she said, squinting fiercely, as if Jack's smiling American face were a page she could not read without her glasses, "the *point* is that they are blind. America, your country, has blinded the world to reality, to the suffering of others, to hunger, to everything that is wrong in life."

"Okay. So?"

"So this is the result. They are hypnotized by baubles, they are under a spell, they are oblivious. They are lost."

She was speaking German now, a torrent.

"*Verloren,*" Jack said, repeating the only word of hers that he had really understood. "Can you maybe talk a little slower?"

"No." Greta switched back to her fluent, comical English.

"All that shit you were speaking to Manfred," she said. "As if politics as usual will change things, as if clever maneuvers will satisfy history. You are all alike, you Americans. You march, you scream like babies who have pissed in their diapers, you burn little pieces of paper and a shitty piece of fascist cloth that is red, white, and blue, and you call yourselves revolutionaries."

The rain was falling harder now. Water spurted from downspouts and swirled down cobbled gutters into storm drains. Jack could hear it rushing through the sewers, he could feel it running underground through the worn-out soles of his soaked shoes. The shoppers took shelter in doorways or hurried away. Greta paid the downpour no attention.

"In Germany, we know what fascism really is," she said. "We have seen it up close, and we fight it with a million fists."

"You do?" Jack said. He made a gesture at the shoppers, women clinging to the arms of the men and smiling through the trivial misery of this cloudburst, all of them seemingly happy after a good supper, a show, taking a stroll before conjugal sex. "These people don't seem to have any black eyes."

Greta was stung. "You think not? That is because they are blind. So are you, my friend! You ask what antifascists do in Germany? I will tell you what they do—things that a spoiled American brat could not possibly imagine. They *act*. They don't just whine and play guitars and piss their pants. They make bombs, they rob banks, they attack American military bases with rockets! They hijack airplanes! They take fascist prisoners of war and try them in people's courts and execute them with people's justice. Even if they are their own mothers and fathers. I have friends who have arrested their own fascist parents, their fat capitalist uncles, and delivered them into the custody of people's tribunals."

"Wow," said Jack. "Very impressive."

He was wet, miserable, but also fascinated. This girl was serious, a true believer—a real psychotic, not just the usual Movement chick reciting this season's radical boilerplate in the same way and for the same reasons that she wore her hair long and dressed in bib overalls and work boots, because it was what all the other girls were doing this semester.

He said, "Greta, what can I say? Good for you and your friends."

"Don't condescend! Our fighters have died."

"I know. I'm impressed, but maybe you guys are a little hard on your parents—"

"Hard on them? It all begins with them! Destroy the enemy closest to you! That is the first rule."

"Okay. Maybe I'm a little soft because I'm an orphan—"

"Then you are lucky! They died before they could fuck you up!"

She was glaring up at Jack again, water pouring off her broken umbrella. She was at least ten inches shorter than he was, he outweighed her by fifty pounds, and yet her whole posture suggested that she was the wolf, he the sheep. How could anyone so small be so ferocious?

Shivering, Jack said, "I'm beginning to understand why there are so many exclamation points in German."

"*What?*"

Jack said, "Greta, you're the one who's full of shit. The methods you're talking about won't work. They just give your enemies an excuse to hunt you down and liquidate you. Just like Hitler liquidated the Communists in the thirties. They were asking for it, and so are you."

As always, Jack's tone was reasonable, friendly, gentle. But Greta was stung by his words. "*Ach so?* Then if we do not confront, what do we do?"

"You get inside the beast, capture its nerve centers, and give it orders."

"And then it takes a laxative and shits you out. *Ach, du Lieber!*"

Jack laughed, a great irrepressible snort. He could not help himself; he had read this most Germanic of exclamations in so many comic books that it was deeply amusing to hear it spoken aloud by an actual German who was no less fanatical than the cartoon Krauts in *G.I. Combat* comics.

Greta said, "Something is funny?"

"No, of course not," Jack said. "Everything you've said makes perfect sense. Blow the bastards up. It's the interim solution."

"You are laughing at me."

Jack said nothing. Greta was beginning to frighten him. He thought it possible that she might pull a pistol out of the bag that had produced the Gauloises, the umbrella, the *Bild Zeitung,* and shoot out the windows of the luxury shops that so offended her.

"Explain me why you think it's so funny," Greta said, making a rare mistake in English.

"Greta, you win. It's too fucking wet out to argue. Just show me how to get home."

"Home? Not yet. First I'll show you something," Greta said.

She threw her umbrella to the ground. Then her bag. Then her jacket.

"Look at them," she said, pointing at the ersatz Americans in their Burberry coats, standing in the doorways motionless as dummies. "They're blind."

Greta seized her sweater, already wet, by its hem. She peeled it off and threw it, too, onto the wet cobblestones. She stood in the rain, bare-breasted. The shoppers paid no attention.

"You laugh," Greta said. "But where is your courage? Would you do what I am doing?"

"Not in the rain," Jack replied.

"Why not? There is no danger. They will not see."

She did a little dance, whirling her long scarf. Her small breasts lifted and peeped out from behind the scarf. She covered her breasts, exposed them, covered them again.

"Come on," she cried. "Be brave, Jack!"

Cold as he was, wet and miserable as he was—and above all, for this was Jack, nervous as he was—he was aroused by the half-naked Greta, dancing in the rain. Yet what if a shopkeeper called the police? What if the fat woman came out of the store, saw Greta doing her cooch dance, and screamed? And what if, after the police came, Greta cried rape as a crazy joke, as a blow against American imperialism?

Greta whirled the scarf. Her wet skin shone as if oiled.

Snapping the scarf like a whip, she skipped across the pavement toward Jack. The scarf, heavy with water, wrapped itself around Jack's waist. Greta ran around and around him, winding him up in the scarf and, when she was close, pressing against him, groping him with her free hand. She pinched him hard.

"My, what a big American boy," she said in German. "Are you going to do something with that? Do you have the guts?"

Jack said, "Not here."

"Here or not at all. Make love, not war."

Before Jack realized what was happening, Greta unzipped his trousers and reached inside. Her fingers were cold.

Without warning she leaped, supple as a monkey, one arm around his neck, legs around his waist, her free hand guiding him below.

It all happened in an instant. She was as slippery as an open mouth. After placing him inside herself she was silent, staring, tight-lipped. She uttered a tiny *Aaaah,* as if a demon had escaped from her mouth to make way for Jack.

Jack could not believe what was happening to him. Fear ran through him like a current. And lust, too—a weird pornographic thrill, to have a girl take him by utter surprise, to do to him what he had done to so many girls. He responded as most of the girls had done, and submitted. Greta heaved against him as if she were the man, not speaking, but pulling aside his shirt collar with her teeth and then biting him fiercely on the neck. Over her shoulder, through a red mist of pain and fear, he could see the shoppers standing in their doorways like mannequins, faces averted, umbrellas shining.

Greta clung to him with teeth, fingers, calves, heels, more. "Aaaah," she gasped, "aaah, aaah, *aaaaaaaaaaaaaah-h-h-H.*"

Then, again without a word of warning, she let go. She said, "Get my things."

Jack did as she ordered, chasing Greta's windblown umbrella a long way downstreet. The shoppers in the doorways ignored him.

Greta put her clothes back on. "Look at them," she said. "I told you. They saw nothing."

Jack said, "Are you absolutely sure of that?"

"*Look at them.* Where are the police? Why are they not stoning me for public fornication?"

"It's a mystery to me."

"Everything is a mystery to Americans," Greta said. "But now that changes. This was your first lesson in reality, Jack. This make-believe America all these people live in is the kingdom of the blind. We can do in this kingdom of the blind anything we have the courage to do. Freely. Absolutely in the open. No one will stop us, because they cannot see us. *We* are the real mystery. Do you understand what I am teaching you?"

"You bet I do," Jack said. "Now come on home with me."

Greta, under her umbrella again, pointed. "That's your street. Good night."

"Come inside."

"The experiment is over."

Greta walked away.

4 Late the following morning, Greta woke Jack with a phone call. His body still smelled of her; her secretions were the first odors he apprehended as he turned over to reach for the phone, releasing trapped air from beneath the bedcovers.

Her throaty voice said, "It is now eleven-forty-two. Meet me at the end of your street in exactly one hour."

The voice excited him. Jack realized that he wanted Greta again. Half awake, half remembering the bizarre encounter of the night before, he wondered what was the matter with him. Never before had he been tempted by the same woman twice. It was the act itself, the ritual of seduction, that counted for Jack. He had never been interested in performing many different sexual acts with one particular woman. The woman had to be new every time.

He said, "Which end of the street?"

"Where you raped me last night," Greta replied.

"I raped *you*?"

"Turn left when you go out the door," Greta said. "One minute late and it will be the police who will be waiting for you, not me."

She hung up. The events of the night before tumbled through Jack's memory. What a maniac he had been! He felt the familiar symptoms of fear: shortness of breath, a tingling of the scalp at the back of his head, a wave of nausea, an impulse to curse. Through it all, he also felt desire.

As is often the case with cowards, Jack was also a hypochondriac. He feared death by disease as much as by gunfire or bayonet. In his imagination the air he breathed was dark with flights of migrating germs, all looking for a place to breed in the hidden waters of his body. In his foolishness he had got soaked by rain last night; this morning he expected to have symptoms of pneumonia. Before the mirror above the washstand he felt his forehead, expecting to be feverish; he took a deep breath, expecting chest congestion. Greta's teeth had left a huge bruise on his neck. Had she broken the skin? He touched the bruise and flinched at the pain, but there was no abrasion. He seemed to be all right. *So far,* he thought. But human bites were worse than animal bites, more septic. You could die in hours.

His clothes lay in a heap on the floor. They were still wet. He put on his only spare garments, jeans and a sweatshirt, but had to wear the wet shoes. On his way downstairs he sneezed. He felt another pang of anxiety. All he needed was a cold, the flu. What would he do if he developed diarrhea? The toilet was at the end of the hall, and he had already found out that it was always occupied by an old woman who shouted angrily through the door if you asked her to hurry up, then glared when she emerged.

Outside, a pale sun shone in a milky sky. It was Sunday; the city was deserted. Church bells rang, setting up peculiar quivering echoes, as if the sound was being captured and twisted before being released again by the stones of the ancient town.

Jack's street was closed to cars, but a large black shiny automobile with smoked windows stood in front of the jewelry store. Its motor was running and its radio turned up to the maximum. The car looked like a 1930s model, but it had up-to-date speakers. The whole vehicle throbbed with the beat of a rock song.

The moment Jack came into view, the horn blew, a long, rude blast. A window went down. Jack caught a glimpse of Greta.

Greta said, "Ah, the rapist returns. Get in."

In the half-light inside the car, Greta looked scrubbed and combed. No eye shadow this time, only a touch of pink girlish lipstick. Amazingly, given the color of her hair, she had no freckles. She wore glasses: steel frames, round lenses, like a schoolteacher. Her mop of curls, formerly wild, was gathered in a ribbon; she wore crocodile loafers with silver buckles, a fawn-colored cashmere sweater. Her tweed blazer with leather elbow patches must have cost a thousand marks, much, much less than the gold Rolex on her fragile left wrist. The only wanton note was a pleated skirt pulled up to her thighs, revealing shiny black stockings.

Jack said, "You look different in daylight."

Greta smiled at him with the perfectly regular, straightened teeth that had gnawed his neck black and blue the night before. It was a brilliant, fixed smile, like the one Jeanne Moreau gave her French lover before her demented character drove the car off a bridge in *Jules et Jim.* Years later, when Jack was forced to remember Greta— he never thought about her otherwise—he would sometimes wonder aloud why he had so often seen her in his mind's eye as an actress. This is not, as you will soon realize, an unanswerable question, but it remained a puzzle to Jack.

The car smelled of cigar smoke, old leather, varnish, and for some reason, shoe polish. Also, surprisingly, a delicate perfume, apparently Greta's. The front seat was drawn up close to the steering wheel so that she could reach the pedals. Jack's knees were under his chin.

"Nice old Mercedes," Jack said.

"It's a Daimler. It used to belong to Göring."

"You're joking."

"You think so? Then why does it have such a big backseat?"

"I'll bite. Why?"

"Because Göring had such a big belly. To make room for it he always had midgets for drivers. Like me. Hold on."

Shifting gears expertly, steering with one hand, Greta drove the antique car at high speed through the narrow streets, tires squealing on the cobblestones, bulbous fenders missing stone walls and pedestrians by millimeters.

"Slow down!" Jack cried, hands fluttering as he searched for something to hold on to.

Greta turned her head, stepped on the gas, and gave him another glassy smile. They crossed the Neckar River, climbed hills covered with vineyards, and arrived finally at a high iron gate that opened when Greta sounded the horn. The Daimler rolled up a drive lined with cropped plane trees. At the end they came to a large cream-colored stucco villa, aglow despite the season with flowering shrubs and bristling with chimneys. At the end of the drive, a dozen Mercedes and BMWs of the largest and most expensive models were lined up on the gravel near the door.

Greta got out. Jack followed. He saw that the flowers grew in tubs that had been sunk into the flower beds. Through the broad spotless windows of the villa, Jack could see a room filled with very tall Germans, all dressed like Greta in the best tweeds and cashmeres that Deutschemarks could buy. The men were beautifully barbered; the women wore their hair combed back from high, flawless foreheads. Jewels and precious metals glittered at their wrists, throats, and fingers. They smiled easily at one other; their lips moved in relaxed conversation.

"Come," Greta said.

Jack said, "You want me to go in there?"

"You don't want to meet my mom and dad?"

"Look at me."

"Why? They won't."

She led him inside. Last night, Greta may have been a revolutionary practicing free love on a public street. Today, in her own house, she was a gay, smiling mignonette, a favorite of the guests. Like fond aunts and uncles they held her hands, kissed the air beside her cheeks, exclaimed over her prettiness.

Greta did not really introduce Jack, just indicated his presence as he followed along behind her by saying, in English: "This is my American friend."

The guests shook hands with Jack, smiling and inquiring politely what brought him to Heidelberg, listening courteously to his answers. They all spoke English, too. He had just graduated from Columbia? How splendid. They had friends in New York. Did Jack know the Osborns? No? But he must; their daughter Lydia had just finished up at Barnard: beautiful girl, very musical. For all the notice they took of Jack's jeans and sweatshirt and wet misshapen penny loafers, he might as well have been wearing one of their blazers from Savile Row and hand-stitched calfskin oxfords. Their own grown-up children dressed in rags; it was a sign of the times.

"I like your American," said one of the women, a tall gaunt blonde like most of the others, but still a beauty. "He has a wonderful smile."

"He's very shy," Greta said.

They were speaking German. Jack was looking straight at the woman, who coolly returned the gaze. "Are you quite sure?" she said.

"Mother!" said Greta.

A short curly-headed man joined them.

"My husband," Frau Fürst said. "Bruno, this is Greta's American."

Herr Fürst looked up at Jack with the cold intelligent eyes of a man who has made a lot of money and plans to make a lot more. He shook hands, up-down-away. He smiled, he spoke English like all the others, but he took no interest in Jack. He asked no questions, made no pleasantries. He spoke only one word directly to Jack, when a waiter came by with a tray filled with glasses.

"Champagne?"

"No, thank you."

"He drinks only Coca-Cola," Greta said.

Her father turned away. So, with a final calculating look at smiling Jack, did her mother.

"You see?" Greta said. "Nothing to worry about. You're the invisible man."

The party was a buffet lunch. Greta filled two plates with food and, carrying them, led Jack toward the back of the house, down a corridor into a room filled with soft light that fell through high narrow windows of beveled glass. The panes were so thick that, like glasses that did not fit, they distorted the magnificent view of the Neckar valley. The room was paneled in dark, carved wood; the furniture was leather; hundreds of leather-bound books stood on shelves in perfect order. Photographs in silver frames crowded the vast leather top of a library table. Jack examined them: men in German uniforms. The largest was a study of a hawk-faced officer, knight's cross at his throat, swastika badge on his breast, one gloved hand on the collar of a large Alsatian dog.

Jack asked, "Is this a general?"

"Only a colonel. My grandfather, fallen at Kursk."

"What's Kursk?"

"A place in Russia where there was a tank battle. So many tanks were destroyed on both sides that Americans saw the rust spot from the moon twenty-five years later. Their usual distance from history."

The room smelled like the inside of the Daimler, waxed, oiled, dustless, with a lingering underscent of expensive smoke. Jack traced the pattern of the rug with the toe of his ruined shoe.

"Do you know what is the name of this rug?" Greta asked.

"No."

"You have no education. It is a Heriz. Repeat."

Jack said, "It's scratchy as hell."

"Do not comment. Repeat the name."

"Heriz."

"Good. Now eat."

The food was cold, unfamiliar, delicious. This time Greta ate it daintily, with a knife and fork, and drank a glass of mineral water. They ate in prim silence, Jack because he was intimidated by such a blatant display of wealth, Greta for reasons of her own.

As soon as they were finished, Greta removed her clothes, except for the black stockings. Taking him by the hand, she led him behind a huge leather sofa and fell to her knees in front of him. She pinched him in the same place as she had done the night before—hard.

"Ouch."

"No remarks," Greta said. "Actions only. I will do everything. You will respond. Understand?"

She began.

"Jesus, Greta," Jack said.

"Shut up," Greta said, lifting her head. "Think only about what is happening."

While it happened the party went on at the other end of the house, murmurous, punctuated by the ring of china and crystal. Over the noise of his own rushing bloodstream, Jack heard rippling laughter—soprano, tenor, and bass-baritone guffawing in unison, as if a choir had just been told a joke by a bishop.

Greta took Jack through a sexual act the likes of which he had never imagined, much less experienced. Seconds before it should have ended, she bit him.

Jack said, "Don't stop, for God's sake!"

"You sign a blank check? You will pay me anything? Yes?"

"Yes."

Afterward, Jack sank to the floor, exhausted. In the hall, the guests were saying goodbye. German words of parting drifted down the corridor. Outside the open front door, powerful engines started; tires crunched on gravel.

Wearing nothing but her black stockings, Greta stood up and glanced round the room. "Ah," she said. "Somebody cleared the dishes for us."

5 Greta drove Jack back to Heidelberg in a different car, her own Mercedes roadster.

"About the blank check," she said, "this is my price. You and I must be an absolute secret. No one must know about us. No one must know that we even know each other."

"Manfred knows. So does everybody at the party we just went to."

"Manfred thinks I hate you. The ones at the party are blind. You understand the bargain? Yes or no?"

"If you put it that way, yes."

"Good. 'No' would have meant death."

Greta smiled her glittering sidewise smile and turned up the music. Jack saw no sign that she was joking. The car, faster and more nimble than the antique Daimler, hurtled down the steep road like a stone released from a slingshot.

After that, the sex games continued. Greta always came to him; by the rules of their affair he was forbidden to approach her, even to call her. Each encounter was comprised of one act only, never more. Jack was always left in a state of arousal.

"Next time, something better," she would whisper, then slip away.

Jack could never imagine anything better than what had just happened, but Greta always kept her promise. Jack lived in a world of continual erotic surprise. They had sex constantly, always feverishly, always in risky situations: on park benches, in cars, in cinemas, in darkened churches, in bathrooms at parties after ignoring each other all evening, on trains and buses, outdoors in darkness and light, in rain and snow. Greta was perverse, wild, beautiful, hot as a firecracker, insatiable. Often Greta would pounce on him in disguise. She wore wigs, costumes, walked on crutches, dressed as an old woman or a little boy. Jack was obsessed by her and by this game of sex that had no limits and never ended.

As a result of such conditioning, Jack's sexual personality altered.

From an amateur rapist who remembered nothing and imagined nothing, he was transformed into a sex object who reimagined the hours he spent with his lover and attempted, always in vain, to guess what oriental delight was coming next. As Greta put it in one of her reports, "He is losing his power to fuck and forget."

Greta was an expert. She had been trained in these matters by a technician Peter had sent to her two years before, when she was seventeen. This man, a German who had been brought to Moscow by Communist parents who escaped from the Nazis and later died in the gulag, looked like he had stepped out of an SS recruiting poster. During a summer holiday in Majorca, he had taught Greta the entire manual for Swallows, as girls and boys who provide operational sex were called by our organization. Usually such youngsters have the temperament for this work to begin with; Greta certainly did, which made her subsequent recruitment quite easy. And usually they fall in love, as Greta did, with their teachers. Alas, back in Russia this virtuoso of the bedstead was as unhappily married as anyone else, so he and Greta met only when he had an assignment for her. And afterward, when she collected her reward.

Our original interest in Greta was not herself but her father, who was an important figure in the Christian Democratic Party. Most of the glossy people Jack encountered at the Fürsts' villa were leading political figures of the German Federal Republic. But Greta was so revolutionary, so highly sexed, and so wild, that we soon realized that we could not get to her father through her. Herr Fürst was a practical man who knew that his daughter was an uncontrollable psychopath and would thank us most sincerely if we got rid of her for him.

So Greta became a time bomb, and her psychosis became a fuse for Peter to light and walk away from. If she blew a finger or two from her father's hand when she went off, so much the better.

6 The fuse was quite long. Sometime in March, after five months of operant conditioning—certain behavior by the organism earns certain rewards from the operator—the time came for Greta to lead Jack onto more dangerous ground.

The ground chosen was a low-grade operation run by Manfred, who was a station-keeper on an underground railroad for American deserters. Manfred's method was to entrap lonely GIs with young German girls, who would then turn them against the Vietnam War and persuade them to desert. Heidelberg, location of the head-quarters of the U.S. Army in Europe, was an excellent place to do this work. Once the soldiers had deserted they were smuggled into Sweden, where—after denouncing America and its colonialist-imperialist war in Southeast Asia—they were granted political asylum and granted stipends, university scholarships, and other benefits arranged by members of the Swedish antiwar movement. After that, their sex lives, like the other parts of their lives, were over. Most turned themselves in to the American embassy after a few months of loneliness, and went home to be court-martialed and dishonorably discharged.

As these trivial results suggest, this was meaningless work except as a training exercise for youths who would later be asked to perform more serious missions. It was virtually free of risk be-cause the U.S. Army had no police powers in Germany and the German police did not care how many American soldiers escaped to Sweden.

It was the no-risk factor that made it attractive as a way to pro-voke a predictable response in Jack. He would, we knew, be terri-fied at the prospect of being involved in such an operation. Realizing that he could not be drawn into such an activity gradually, or be talked into it, we instructed Greta to entrap him, then com-promise him. The obvious means were already in place: yet another sexual ambush. We waited until he was firmly in Greta's power, then sprang our surprise.

This time Greta, driving her Mercedes roadster, picked Jack up as he walked along a busy street on his way home after class. It was late afternoon. As usual Greta offered no explanation, made no small talk. She wore her rich-girl costume, cashmere and tweed, crocodile and gold.

With Jack beside her, she drove out of town, north on the auto-bahn. At first Jack saw nothing unusual about this; they sometimes rode a long way before arriving at whatever destination Greta had in mind. This time, however, they drove on for hours, listening to music, saying little, because every time Jack tried to speak, Greta ordered him back into silence by laying a finger across her lips.

When they did talk, Greta insisted that they speak German. By now Jack spoke the language like a precocious twelve-year-old. Around nine o'clock, as they left Hamburg behind, Jack asked Greta what she had in mind.

"For a while," he said, "I thought maybe we were going to get out of the car and tear off a piece on the autobahn."

"Not a bad idea," Greta replied. She turned her head and smiled. The smile lasted a long time. They were traveling at more than 100 mph. In his anxiety, for which no one could blame him, Jack took a deep breath filled with the sound of saliva, extended his palms, and pressed his body against the back of his seat.

"Good move, Jack," Greta said. "You are now five centimeters farther away from the next car we crash into."

She accelerated to 120 mph, flicked the wheel to the right, crossed five lanes of high-speed traffic, and plunged with shrieking tires down an exit ramp.

Jack covered his eyes with his hands. When he uncovered them, he saw that the car was speeding along a two-lane road that ran straight north across a marshy, featureless plain. Greta was still driving at the same tremendous rate of speed she had maintained on the autobahn.

Jack said, "I have to pee."

"Soon," Greta said.

Jack saw a sign: CUSTOMS AHEAD. PREPARE TO STOP.

He said, "Denmark?"

With a squeal of brakes, Greta pulled into a rest area where several cars with German and Danish tags and many large trucks were already parked. The frontier was in sight now, a glow of lights from the customs posts clearly visible about a kilometer away.

Greta said, "You can piss now. I'll join you."

Jack jerked his head, indicating the parked trucks.

"They're asleep," Greta said, squatting behind the Mercedes, lifting her cashmere skirt.

Jack felt a stab of anxiety; in spite of the delights it produced, Greta's exhibitionism still made him nervous. He turned his back and emptied his bladder.

This took a long time. Behind him he heard Greta opening the trunk. Its light went on.

Jack, still pissing, turned his head. Greta was looking into the trunk. He heard her say, in English, "Almost there. Would you like to pee-pee?"

A second voice replied, "No thanks, I used the bottle."

Jack whirled, zipping up, and saw an American soldier curled up in the trunk.

Greta handed Jack a bottle filled with the soldier's urine. She said, in German, "Empty this."

The soldier, sleepy-eyed, was staring straight at Jack. Jack dropped the bottle. It smashed on the pavement, releasing the odor of its contents.

Jack stared wildly at Greta. "You're crazy," he said.

Greta said, "Time to go." She closed the trunk. "Your turn to drive."

"Across the frontier?"

Greta said, "What's the matter? Don't you want to get fucked in Denmark?"

"I won't do it."

She held up the car keys and shook them. "Then I'll fuck the soldier right in front of your eyes and leave you here. How much money have you got on you?"

A wave of nausea took hold of Jack. He never had more than ten marks in his pocket.

"I said no, Greta, and I mean it," he said. But his voice wavered.

"Then you'll want to ask somebody for a ride back to Heidelberg," she said. "Do you know how to say that in German?"

She reached inside the car and blew the horn. Truck drivers woke up and looked out the windows of their cabs.

Greta opened the trunk. She said, "I'll count to ten. *Eins, zwei, drei, vier, fünf—*"

Jack said, "I can't do it, Greta."

"Fine."

She reached under her skirt and wriggled out of her panties. To the soldier in the trunk she said, "What's your name, sweetheart?"

"Duane," the soldier said.

She lifted her skirt. "Would you like a little going-away present, Duane?"

The soldier's eyes opened wide. Jack slammed the trunk lid closed. "Give me the keys."

She slid the key into the trunk lock. "First you get into the car."

When Jack was behind the wheel, Greta put the keys in the ignition and started the engine.

Jack's hands trembled on the wheel. He said, "I'll have to show them my passport."

"That's the whole idea," Greta said. "Duane doesn't have one."

He put his forehead on the steering wheel. "I can't do this."

"Choose, Jack! Lust or fear!" She held a wetted forefinger under his nose.

Jack put the car in gear and drove toward the lights of the Danish customs post.

When the guard saw the cover of Jack's passport, he waved them through without inspection.

7 After the Danish adventure, Greta told Jack that they would be together one more time—and only one. She would choose the moment and the place.

"It vill be vonderful," Greta whispered, Dietriching *w*'s into *v*'s as Jack liked her to do. "I vill give you vot you've always vanted."

"Vot vill that be?"

"Silly boy! Vot else? A maiden's dearest possession."

And then she broke contact.

Jack did not see Greta again or have another woman (for she really had spoiled him for his old pleasures) for seven weeks. Then, on a rare sunny morning in May, Jack, who had gotten plump again, was out for his morning run along the Neckar embankment when the antique Daimler pulled up beside him.

The windows of the Daimler were down. A Strauss waltz blared from the speakers; cars behind it sounded their horns. Greta smiled at him through the open window. She wore a blond wig with two long braids. She pulled over to the curb, then slid across the front seat, reached into the back, and flung open the door.

"Get in," she said. She was dressed in a puffy dirndl, petticoats billowing above her bare, dimpled knees.

Gasping with laughter, Jack got into the backseat. Greta slammed the door, rolled up the front window, and put the car in motion to a fanfare of klaxons. She looked at Jack in the rearview mirror.

"Take off those clothes," she said.

He wore a sweat-soaked T-shirt and running shorts.

"I'm going to get perspiration all over the leather," he said.

"Never mind. No one will ever know you've been here."

No one could see him through the smoked windows. He did as she ordered. Greta drove on, shooting glances at him in the rearview mirror. In moments he was naked except for his running shoes and socks.

"The shoes and socks, too."

Greta's rucksack lay beside Jack on the backseat. He took hold of its strap, intending to move it to the floor.

"Don't touch that!" Greta cried. "Don't touch anything!"

She handed something to him, folded into a wad: surgical gloves.

"Put them on."

Jack said, "On what?"

"No boasting. Your hands."

"Why?"

They stopped at a red light. Greta reached over the back of the seat and scooped up Jack's T-shirt and shorts and jockstrap. She rolled her window down a hand's breadth.

"Put on the gloves or I'll throw these out the window."

She was in a state of high excitement, sexual and otherwise. Jack did as she ordered; rules of the game. Greta slid across the seat.

"Climb over and drive," she said.

With some difficulty because of the state he was in, Jack clambered into the front seat and got behind the wheel.

"Put the seat all the way back." Jack did as he was told. His toes barely touched the pedals. "Where to?"

"Straight on," Greta said.

In addition to the dirndl, Greta wore white kneesocks and laced brown oxfords—the entire Rhine maiden costume. She took off her wig and tossed it into the backseat, along with Jack's clothes. The wig was stiff, like a helmet; it rolled back and forth on the seat.

While Jack drove through heavy traffic, Greta worked on him with hands and tongue, bringing him repeatedly to the point of ejaculation, then preventing it with a fingertip applied with clinical precision to exactly the correct pressure point.

"Greta, for God's sake! That's *agonizing*."

"*Nicht war?*" She lifted her head and gazed through the windshield. "Turn right at the next street. Park on the right, in the middle of the block, in front of the shop with the red dress in the window."

Groaning, Jack did precisely as ordered. They were in a no-parking zone, across from a bank. Cars flowed by in a steady unending stream; the smell of exhaust leaked into the Daimler through its open vents.

Greta, still fully dressed, reached into her bodice and brought something out.

"Look, Jack, for you! All the way from America!"

Greta waved a brand-new tube of Vaseline in front of Jack's eyes. She unscrewed the cap and passed the open tube under his nose.

She said, "Have you guessed?"

Jack shook his head. All this was happening on a public street at eight-thirty in the morning in the midst of rush-hour traffic, in a car that stuck out like a sore thumb even when it was not illegally parked. He was stark naked.

"Now you get the one thing I would never give you," Greta said. "I'm all ready. Do you want some, too?"

For once, Jack knew exactly what she meant. He couldn't believe his luck. He nodded, paralyzed by a mixture of fear and desire. Greta squeezed half the tube into the palm of her hand and showed it to him.

Whispering, Greta said, "This is the last way I am a virgin. Sit back from the wheel."

Jack obeyed. She lifted her skirt, then tulips within snowy tulips of scalloped petticoats. With her back to his chest, she straddled his body. Gripping him like the hilt of a sword, she lowered herself with brutal force, free arm out-thrown, screaming at the top of her voice.

"*Aaaaaaaaaaah!*"

She sobbed, apparently in real pain, as she repeated the movement, producing in Jack an ecstasy so intense, a realization of fantasy so complete, that he feared, even as it was occurring, that he would never be able to duplicate it.

It lasted only seconds, but when it was over, Jack was helpless, nearly senseless. His heart pounded. He was, for the first time ever after such a moment, limp. Greta got off him, more gently than she had got on.

Jack lay with his eyes closed, in a state of trust and satiety. While his mind drifted, Greta placed his hands on the steering wheel, bent his fingers around it. He heard a tiny noise: *click.* And then another *click.*

His eyes sprang open. His hands in their transparent gloves were handcuffed to the steering wheel.

Jack said, "Jesus, Greta—"

Greta knelt on the seat beside him. She said, "And now, our first kiss."

Never before had they kissed; Swallow customs were not so different in this regard from those observed by other prostitutes. And Jack, who liked his sensations localized, did not really care for kissing. But now Greta grasped his head with both hands, and covered his open mouth with hers. He felt her tongue on his, then something else.

The key to the handcuffs.

"Don't swallow it, Liebchen."

Greta put on her Jeanne Moreau glasses and smiled her mad smile. She leaned over the back of the seat, her sweet round dirndled behind sticking up, and wrestled her rucksack into the front seat.

She opened the rucksack, unbuckled and unlaced its puckered top, and removed an Uzi machine pistol and a magazine.

Jack leaped in his skin. Voice cracking, he cried, "What the fuck is that?"

Greta said, "Quiet. You'll swallow the key. And then what?"

Greta put the loaded Uzi back into the rucksack and put on her wig, smiling sweetly, tucking rufous curls up under the blond helmet.

Jack's heart was pounding. He rattled the chain of his handcuffs. He said, "Unlock these." He stuck out his tongue, key balanced on the tip.

Greta shook her head no and, with a stiff forefinger, pushed Jack's tongue back into his mouth, tucking the key beneath it. He tasted Vaseline.

Wild-eyed, Jack said, "You belong in a fucking concentration camp."

"And you're *in* one, piglet. Now listen to me."

Jack's eyes still popped from his head. He could hardly breathe. He threw himself violently toward Greta. The cuffs cut into his wrists with all the force generated by this sudden movement of his two-hundred-pound body.

Greta said, "Jack, be calm. See the bank across the street? It opens in three minutes. I am going to go in. I will be followed by others you will recognize. We will make a great victory for the people."

Realization, followed by overwhelming sensations of dread and fear, flooded into every cell of Jack's body. *"You're going to rob the bank!"*

"No," Greta said. "We are going to collect the people's taxes."

"Greta, don't do this."

Greta said, "You will stay here and watch, lucky boy, until I come out and get into another car. Then you will drive away. You can shift with your foot, so." She demonstrated. "When I come out of the bank," she said. "But not sooner. If you try to go sooner, this car will explode. Someone is watching. He will press a button and Goodbye, Jack. Do you understand?"

"No!" Jack screamed. "I *don't* understand, you fucking maniac!"

"Good, then you will learn something," Greta said. She looked intently at her Rolex, counting the minutes.

Then she turned the key in the ignition and started the Daimler. When she opened the door, Jack could hear its exhaust, regular and soft as the respiration of a sleeping human.

She said, "Goodbye, Jack. Find yourself a wonderful American girl and have lots of little Jacks and Jills. But never forget Greta!"

Jack was too terrified to reply. She gave him no last smile. Greta saved that for the old bank guard, who watched with unconcealed pleasure as she waited obediently for the light to change, then crossed the street, dirndl swinging with every stride of her shapely calves in their snow-white kneesocks, blond cap shining in the morning sunshine, the very picture of German girlhood. When she added a virginal smile to all this, the guard exclaimed, *"Wunderschön!"*

Greta disappeared into the shadowy interior of the bank. Moments later she was followed by three other young people. All carried rucksacks.

Suddenly the air was split by police hooters—many of them, approaching at high speed. Traffic scattered as cars got out of the way. Half a dozen police cars arrived, strobe lights flashing. Policemen wearing bulletproof vests and steel helmets with transparent visors leaped out, assault rifles at the ready.

At this moment, inside the bank, gunfire erupted. A squad of policemen rushed the front door. Two of them were knocked down by a burst of gunfire from within. The others flattened themselves against the wall on either side of the entrance. The old guard pulled his pistol and charged the door. He was killed before he could fire his weapon; bullets exiting his body stitched a line of bloody pockmarks across his back.

Greta's three friends came out the door abreast, crouching and firing Uzis. The remaining policemen, using their cars as breastworks, fired back, killing them all. One of them, a painfully skinny boy, jerked upright and did a crazy final dance, spewing bullets from his Uzi and splintering upstairs windows as he went down.

Greta had emerged while this was happening, and was now running down the sidewalk, concealing the Uzi against her dirndl. She had lost her wig. Her own wild red hair stood out around her head as if electrified. Guns at the ready, the police watched her, puzzled. Was she one of the terrorists, or was she what she was dressed to look like?

A BMW waiting at the end of the block threw open its door. Greta made for it, and as she turned, the police saw her gun. She raised it, but before she could shoot, they fired on her in unison with twenty automatic weapons. These sounded like the enraged snarl of so many animals. Greta's body spun as if gripped by the terrible fangs of an invisible wolf pack, blood whipping like long red tresses from dozens of puncture wounds.

Sobbing with fear, Jack put the Daimler into gear with his foot, let out the clutch, and drove slowly away. In the rearview mirror he saw the BMW being torn apart by police bullets as it sped in the opposite direction. He expected to be followed by the police cars, to be pulled over, to be told to put up his hands, to be unable to obey because his hands were chained to the wheel, to be killed in indescribable pain by a hundred rounds of ammunition. He prayed, shouting: "Save me, save me, let me live, I'll do anything you say!"

But nothing happened. Absolutely nothing. Two blocks away from the battle, the world went on in the bright May sunshine as if death and madness had never been invented by a deaf supreme being, as if Jack could not smell Greta on his own fouled body with every breath he drew.

He drove into the old city and parked the Daimler near the castle. He spat the key to the handcuffs into his palm and freed himself. Then he put on his clothes. They were cold, wet with sweat.

Trembling violently, Jack got out of the Daimler, locked all the doors, and began to run again, the car keys in his hand. A few blocks from the car, as he passed a storm drain, he let the keys drop from his hand and kicked them down the sewer.

Following some instinct he had not known he possessed, he ran in a long circle, to protect the secret of his den. Home at last, he ran up the stairs and went directly to the toilet. He closed the door behind him and vomited. Minutes later, when he threw the key to the handcuffs into the bowl, he realized that he was still wearing the surgical gloves. He stripped them off and threw them in, too, but then fished them out again, afraid that they would stop the drain and regurgitate the only evidence against him.

And then he realized that the gloves were not the only evidence. There was more, if the police looked in the right place for it during the autopsy.

Greta! Obeying her last instruction, he remembered her as she was in their last game together, shrieking and twisting in pain or pleasure—who could know which?—in the final, unforgettable moment of what neither of them had ever called love. But was.

Three

★ ★

1 Jack's only class that day began at eleven o'clock. By noon, television crews were set up outside the gates, interviewing students who might have known Greta and her fellow terrorists. One of these was an NBC crew, whose director was calling out in English, "Americans over here! Americans over here!" A woman reporter holding a microphone stood on tiptoe, searching the crowd for American faces.

Jack looked for an escape route, but he was pushed forward toward the cameras by the jostling crowd. One long-haired German boy kicked over a light stand, crying, "Shitty imperialist television!" On camera, a policeman seized the boy, shook him roughly, shouted in his face, then let him go with a violent push that sent him staggering halfway across the street. Jack watched him run away, hair flying.

"He was lucky," the American cameraman said. "Two cops were killed in this thing."

"Plus five terrorists," said the woman with the microphone. "The driver of the BMW just croaked in hospital." British style, she left out the *the* before the noun. She added, "So it's five to two in favor of the *Polizei.*"

"They got them all?"

"That's the word."

Heart pounding at this good news—he was not a suspect!—Jack walked briskly past the camera, face averted, concentrating hard so as not to run. He got past and hurried on toward home, a dozen different plans of escape forming in his mind: escape from the TV cameras, escape from Heidelberg, escape from the police if he found them waiting in his room as surely he would. But where could he go? All the money he had in the world was in his pocket. He had counted it during the lecture: 13 marks, 43 pfennigs.

Behind him, where the policeman had been, he heard firm footsteps hurrying to catch up. Jack's hair prickled on his scalp. He walked on. Then a male German voice—therefore loud and commanding—said, "Jack Adams."

Jack twitched and halted, sure that a gun, or at least a camera, must be pointing at his back. His hands trembled. He plunged them into his trousers pockets; the palms were wet with sweat. He began to hyperventilate. He took a deep breath, held it, and turned around.

It was Manfred, Arthur's friend, the lecturer in political philosophy. Jack let out his breath through his nostrils and took another mighty breath. Manfred stared at him, flicked a glance at the sweat that shone on Jack's face.

He said, "Are you all right?"

"Fine," Jack replied. "Long time no see."

Since the night in the rathskeller, Jack had seen Manfred only in the lecture hall. For his part, Manfred had read Greta's reports before passing them on to us, so he knew a great deal about Jack.

Solemn-faced, Manfred said, "You've heard?"

Jack said, "Heard what?"

"Greta Fürst was shot dead by the police this morning."

Jack stared back. He thought he saw a sardonic light in Manfred's eyes. Did he know? *How could he know?* God knew what Greta had told him, or what she had told the world. For all Jack knew, she might have kept a diary and sent it to the newspapers. Or written a farewell manifesto. Better than anyone, he knew that she was capable of anything. Jack tasted the metal of the handcuff key he had spat out while Greta bled her last. Suddenly, with a lurch of the heart, he remembered that he had left the handcuffs in the Daimler. He remembered himself saying, *I'm going to get perspiration all over the leather.* What else had been left on the leather by his last coupling with Greta, and what would the police make of it? His stomach heaved; he tasted bile. He smelled Greta as she had smelled on his own body. *He had not washed his running shorts! They could be matched to the evidence in the Daimler!*

Jack said a silent prayer, his second that day, on which he had had his first thoughts of his Maker since childhood: *Get me out of this.*

He was answered by what seemed to be a miracle: Jack's nature took over. He lied.

"Greta who?" he said.

"The girl I introduced you to at the rathskeller," Manfred said. "The redhead. Smoked Gauloises. Walked you home."

"Oh yeah," Jack said. "The nutcase. Actually she just walked away. I wandered around in the rain for hours."

Manfred, who knew in graphic detail what had happened that night, and on every other meeting between Greta and Jack, opened his eyes wider in feigned surprise. "Really? What bad manners. You never saw her again?"

"I wasn't exactly keeping an eye out." Jack smiled.

"So you don't remember her?"

"The bad manners I remember. What happened?"

The lies had relaxed Jack. He took his hands out of his pockets. He gazed frankly into Manfred's eyes, feigning interest, registering innocent ignorance. Lost in his favorite role, Smiling Jack.

Manfred said, "It's big news. She and some friends tried to rob a bank. The police killed them all."

"Wow. Were they terrorists, or what?"

"The Red Army Faction has claimed responsibility."

"What's that?"

"The Baader-Meinhof Gang. Serious people."

"Good God. What a mess."

The Baader-Meinhof Gang? Jack's breathing was back to normal now. He struggled to keep it that way. The pores opened along his spine, releasing a rivulet of sweat. Manfred watched him very closely, with something that could easily be called suspicion in his eyes.

Manfred said, "The talk around here is that they must have been betrayed. The cops were waiting for them right around the corner."

Jack said, "What do you mean, betrayed?"

Manfred shrugged.

Jack was seized by a sickening realization: The police *knew.* How else could they have known the precise moment of the bank robbery, how else could they have arrived so quickly, in such overwhelming force? Why else would they have used so much firepower, been so intent on killing with such merciless brutality, if they had not been sure they were dealing with terrorists—people who deserved to die, people of whom they wished to make a bloody example?

Jack regained control of himself. In an even voice, holding on to the character he was playing, he said, "I wouldn't want to be the guy who called the cops."

"Whoever did will be in a nutcracker," Manfred said. "Police on one side, Baader-Meinhof on the other."

What was Manfred saying to him? That Greta had been marked for death? That she had been betrayed to the police? *That she had been an object of suspicion? That Jack was also under suspicion?* If she had been watched by someone, how could that someone *not know about Jack?*

Jack inhaled, shook his head. Manfred's eyes, still fixed on his open, smiling face, opened a little wider and his lips twitched. He was not smiling, exactly, but once again Jack had the feeling that he was aware of the truth, that he saw through Jack's lies, that this casual meeting was no accident.

Don't be paranoid, Jack told himself. *Be cool.* He said, "Too bad about the girl. She seemed like a nice enough person, underneath the politics."

Manfred laughed aloud. "Greta? A nice enough person? She was a psychopath who came from a gene pool swimming with Nazis. And if she didn't have syphilis it was a miracle."

Syphilis? Jack held on to himself. He made what he hoped was a wry face.

Manfred said, "You're lucky she walked away."

Manfred laughed at his own joke. Jack snorted appreciatively. But another terrible thought was racing through his mind— through his bloodstream: *If they do an autopsy, they'll match my semen to the semen they find in Greta's body.*

Jack thought, *Of course they'll look there; they'll look for semen. They'll look for everything. They're Germans.* He was doomed; he knew it. He wanted to get away from this German. He lifted a casual hand and said, "Well, good seeing you."

But Manfred was gripping his arm, preventing him from going. Manfred said, "Anyway, rest in peace. On to the next thing."

Hand on Jack's biceps, Manfred walked him down the street, speaking into his face: German intimacy.

"Actually, I wanted to talk to you for an entirely different reason," Manfred said. "An opportunity has come up. There's a student peace conference in Stockholm, starting tomorrow, and the Swedes need an American to give a little speech about the U.S. antiwar movement. I thought of you."

Paranoia, Jack's close companion, returned in a rush. "Why me?" he asked.

"Because I've been impressed by your papers, by the way you've improved your German," Manfred said. "And I understand from Arthur that you're a good speaker."

"Not in Swedish," Jack said.

"You'll be speaking in English. Even the Swedes don't talk Swedish."

Jack's heart was leaping. Escape! Luck! But his voice was calm. He said, "When would I have to leave?"

"Tonight, I'm afraid, change trains in Frankfurt. I have your tickets with me."

"Why such short notice?"

"As I said, there was a no-show."

Manfred had said no such thing, but Jack did not argue. He was remembering the American soldier in the trunk of Greta's roadster, and the Swedes who had been waiting on the other side of the Danish frontier. They had been parked beside the highway, in a misting rain. The whole experience had been like a page from a thriller: three short blinks of the headlights followed by two long. Greta walking Duane to the Swedish car. Duane, stiff from his long ride in the fetal position, limping in the glow of the headlights. Were the Swedes Manfred knew the same Swedes Greta knew? Terrorists? Allies of the Baader-Meinhof Gang? Jack's blood ran cold.

"I don't know," Jack said. "I have studying to do."

Manfred said, "Jack, no one has to study for the courses you're taking. Take the tickets. Go to Sweden for a few days. There is even an allowance for expenses." He smiled. "When was the last time you got laid?"

"I can hardly remember," Jack replied.

"All right, then!" Manfred said. "The sun is out, so the Swedes will be fucking."

Jack gave him a sharp look. But Manfred himself was the picture of guilelessness. He was holding out a plain, sealed envelope. Jack took it.

"Okay," he said. "Why not?"

Manfred shook his arm, gave him a little salute, two fingers and a thumb touching an imaginary hat brim. *"Wiederschön!"*

In his room, Jack opened the envelope. Anonymous second-class train tickets, couchette, to Copenhagen and return.

Copenhagen?

A sheaf of hundred-deutsche-mark notes was paperclipped to a file card on which were typed instructions for taking the ferry from Denmark to Sweden. "Buy your tickets when you get to Copenhagen," said his instructions. At the bottom of the card was a typed name and phone number: "Your host in Sweden; call on arrival."

Jack counted the money: one thousand deutsche marks, worth over five hundred dollars—more money than he had ever held in his hand before.

Our money, of course. He suspected it might be, even then. But it was money—angel's wings—and at the moment that was all that mattered.

2 Manfred's underground railroad had more than one set of tracks. In fact, the GI-smuggling operation was nothing more than a branch line, a temporary scheme designed to take advantage of a passing opportunity.

The main line, a much older and much more useful enterprise, catered to a different class of passengers altogether: sympathetic graduate students, usually but not always Americans, who were on Peter's short list for recruitment. It ran through Stockholm, where the semifinal selection was made by our agents, then on to Moscow. Inside the Soviet Union, the final, very serious assessment would be made by professionals. Very few were recruited in Moscow. The final act of the drama was quite often staged in Prague, where the various youth organizations financed and controlled by Soviet intelligence were located.

Although sex was the usual bait—you can't make a revolution without free love—few candidates required the sort of conditioning that Greta administered to Jack. For one thing, there was only one

Greta—and, more to the point, only one Jack. Not many young men would have stayed the course with a psychopath like Greta no matter what the epoch or the sexual rewards.

In this, as in so many other ways, Jack Adams was the exception. If Greta proved nothing else before she went to meet her Maker, she confirmed that Jack would follow his appetites wherever they led him. He really would do anything for pussy. In nearly all other respects he may have been as fearful as a lamb. But lust made him brave. This is an important thing to know for certain about a human being whom you propose to manipulate on a lifetime basis.

Jack's case was unique. In the first place, Peter was managing it personally. In the second, as I have mentioned, it was Peter's aim to shield Jack from the curiosity of the rest of the Soviet intelligence apparatus. And finally, after Jack's experiences in Heidelberg, Peter felt that he already knew as much about this particular handful of clay as it was necessary to know. Jack Adams was ready for recruitment if ever anyone was.

Nevertheless, Jack won high praise from our people in Sweden. He acquitted himself well at the youth rally. Without ever actually uttering such terms, he gave a rousing speech about the struggle by American youth against the Nixonites and their evil war against the Vietnamese patriots. Even so early in life, Jack was a gifted orator who connected instantly with his audience. This was not a matter of substance: Then, as later, Jack hardly ever said anything that anyone could disagree with, and dealt in the tiniest of concepts. No, what worked the miracle was technique—tone, body language, facial expressions, an entire demeanor that was Jack's alone, inimitable and endearing. The audience listened to Jack as if hearing their own thoughts. Of course they agreed with everything he said. Strangely, they were unable to remember, after the speech was over, exactly what he had said. Jack was good with audiences because to him a speech was just an elaborately developed lie, with all questions forbidden until the end, when it was too late. He loved to speak and his exhilaration showed, bonding him even more firmly to the audience.

He connected best with his fellow Americans, of course, but his appeal was the same even when the people in the audience were Swedes and other Europeans. The applause at Stockholm was tumultuous, the questions friendly, and if Peter had not given strict instructions to Jack's nannies in Stockholm that he was not, under any circumstances, to have any sexual contact, he could have been in bed with half the girls in the audience before the sun rose.

Jack's host, a lawyer under Party discipline, hustled him off afterward to a dinner party. Greta, the freshest heroine of the cause, and her heroic death were the chief topics of conversation over the smoked salmon, roast duck, and apple tart. She had become famous. One or two had actually met Greta—such an intelligent girl, burning with idealism. Like her, they were all against the war, against capitalism, against American imperialism in all its forms. They explained to Jack, as if teaching him some cabalistic alphabet in which he, as a naïve American, could not hope to read or write, who Greta was and what she stood for. In modest silence, Jack listened, empathized, agreed with everyone, made a good impression. One or two of the guests pressed cards on him before they left.

By then, as a result of his long uncharacteristic silence, Jack was in a pent-up state. As soon as the guests were out the door, the lawyer found himself listening to an embroidered story of Jack's life, leaving out JFK and the bank robbery.

During his two days in Stockholm, Jack bought the German newspapers both mornings; the Greta story was still very much on page 1, the police were still following up clues and leads, arrests were imminent. No mention was made of the Daimler. In his secret panic, Jack took this as a certain sign that the police had, in fact, found the Daimler, that its contents had been analyzed by German science, and that one of the imminent arrests referred to would be his own; Jack panicked. Could they have him extradited from Sweden? Would the American embassy protect him? Could he hide out somewhere, somehow? Claim asylum like the GIs?

Asylum! Jack went to the lawyer for advice as if to his only friend in the world. By now you know Jack well enough to understand that he breathed not a single word to this dangerous stranger that might connect him to Greta. His aim was absolution, not confession. Consequently he discussed, in a steady voice with a steady eye, his fears about the draft, his hatred of the American system, his moral inability to do harm to a fellow proletarian in Vietnam or anywhere else. Why, his best boyhood friend, the son of workers like himself, was in Vietnam at this very moment, in who knew what danger, perhaps even dead, and so brainwashed by the culture that he imagined that it was his duty to be killed or maimed in defense of the profit system. This friend did not even know that it cost the U.S. Army twenty-five thousand dollars in expended ammunition to kill every single Viet Cong, and that at least twenty thousand dollars of that went into the pocket of some bloated capitalist! Or that the real reason for the war was to gain control of offshore oil fields for the benefit of Nixon's right-wing friends!

Every bit of the genuine emotion Jack was feeling about his part in the bank robbery spilled over into this false confession.

When the lawyer's sympathies seemed to be fully engaged, Jack asked him about the possibility of asking for political asylum in Sweden. The lawyer, no amateur actor himself, feigned surprise and shock, but this was the opening he had been hoping for.

"Political asylum is not for you, who can be a great revolutionary," he said, placing a manly hand on Jack's trembling shoulder. "No, Jack. That is for people of a different order of abilities—soldiers who can only offer their bodies to the cause. Your battleground is America—its mind, its soul, its future. With your eloquence, your sense of honor, you can do so much for history."

As if inspired by a sudden thought, the lawyer offered a suggestion. Obviously Jack needed time to think. How would he like to join an international delegation of student leaders on a visit to Moscow for a friendly unofficial get-together with student leaders from the USSR and Eastern European countries? It was a wonderful opportunity to see the Soviet Union for himself, and to be among like-minded people. Then, afterward, if he still wanted to move to Sweden, perhaps something could be arranged. Political asylum might not be necessary. Perhaps a grant for a graduate degree could be arranged at some Swedish university; the course could be as long as necessary, it could last longer than the war. All wars end; the one in Vietnam would also end.

"You have more friends than you know, Jack," said the lawyer with great sincerity. "Friends who believe as you do, friends who will help."

Jack had a moment of deep relief, which was almost immediately obliterated by a flash of anxiety. What about his passport? If it had a Soviet visa in it, Soviet customs stamps in it, he would be questioned when he got back to the United States.

Never mind. The lawyer went to his desk, opened a drawer, and returned with a Canadian passport. "Have a look at this," he said. "It belongs to a delegate who had to cancel out. Poor fellow was run down by a taxi. He'll be in the hospital for weeks."

This unfortunate Canadian was about Jack's age and size—and he even looked a little like Jack. Not only that, he had the same first name, so Jack could still be called Jack by his new Russian friends. How remarkable. What luck.

Jack looked at the passport. The picture did resemble him.

"Won't this fellow mind my using his passport?" he asked.

The lawyer waved an avuncular hand. "Nonsense," he said. "It will make him happy to do something for a man he would certainly admire."

The lawyer studied Jack with warm affection. "So what do you think?"

Jack was desperate. "I'll do it," he said.

"Splendid," the lawyer cried. He held out his hand. "Now you must give me *your* passport."

Jack looked at him in shocked surprise, his first unguarded facial expression of the evening. "Give you my passport?"

"For safekeeping," the lawyer said. "It would hardly do to carry two different ones into Russia. The Soviets are very thorough at the frontier."

Jack swallowed, gazed at the window filled with blackness, felt sweat on his palms.

"Come, Jack," said the lawyer. "You must learn to trust your friends."

Jack smiled sunnily; he had just realized that he could always go to the American embassy in Moscow and tell them that his passport had been stolen.

Pictures formed in his mind. His pocket had been picked in the subway! A drunk bumped into him! He hadn't suspected anything until he got back to the hotel, and then he discovered that the pickpocket had taken not just his passport but his wallet. He heard himself: *I have no family. What do you advise?*

Jack handed over his passport and tucked the Canadian passport into his pocket.

"Good," said the lawyer. "Very sensible. And this"—he tapped Jack's U.S. passport against the tabletop—"will be waiting for you safe and sound when you come back."

"You would never guess, to look at him in his disguise as a typical American bourgeois, that underneath is such a fierce and implacable enemy of everything the U.S. stands for," wrote the lawyer in his final report to Moscow. "This is no half-baked student playing radical games because that is the passing fashion; this is a serious revolutionary."

The lawyer was deceived, of course. You can imagine how much that pleased Peter.

3 Jack traveled by ferry to Leningrad. Like so many Soviet products, this vessel, top-heavy and rusty, looked as though it had been built by guesswork before the invention of measurement. In the Gulf of Finland, it sliced clumsily through thin, almost invisible sheets of ice, sometimes upending them. When this happened the morning sun shone through the ice, creating dull rainbows that the steel prow with its Cyrillic lettering immediately shattered.

On arrival in the USSR an expressionless official opened Jack's false passport, glanced at his face, stamped and scribbled, and then waved him across the most closely guarded frontier in the world and onto the train for Moscow. Like so many sympathetic pilgrims before him who had expected more romantic scenes, Jack was surprised by what he saw through the windows of the train: the vast threshold to the steppes and budding birch forests in hazy impressionist hues, yes, but also godforsaken villages marooned in a bleak patchwork of mud and unmelted snow. The occasional onion dome, beautiful and symmetrical, suggested the work of a vanished race that had been overrun by barbarians; everything else was ugly. When he smiled at the Russians on the train, they broke eye contact convulsively, as though someone had jerked on an invisible fishhook in their lips.

At the station in Moscow, Jack was met by two very proper members of Komsomol, who escorted him to his hotel and gave him literature in English about the youth conference. It was Friday; the conference would not start until Monday. After a tasteless dinner served by sullen waiters, Jack wandered through the lobby, trying to strike up a conversation, but once again no one would speak to him. He was afraid to go for a walk with the false Canadian passport in his pocket. What if he was arrested and fingerprinted? He went upstairs and read the copy of *Soviet Life* that he found in his room.

At about ten o'clock the phone rang. "Hi, my name is Igor," said a voice speaking rapid English with Slavic phonetics. "We are waiting for you downstairs. There's a party, for the conference."

Igor turned out to be a smiling youth with a broken nose, a little older than Jack. He looked like a boxer. He was muscular, jovial, slightly contemptuous.

He led Jack outside. A large black car was parked at the curb. Jack piled into the back with four or five other boys, all Russians as far as he could tell. They ate pickles and drank vodka from a bottle, and when they emptied the first bottle, another was produced. Igor, the driver, peppered Jack with questions as the black car sped over unlighted roads pocked with potholes. What is the population of Ottawa? Who is the best Canadian hockey player? Is it true what they said about Canadian girls?

"I don't know," Jack said. "What do they say?"

"That they're really hot. Especially when they go abroad."

"That's a new one on me," Jack said.

Their destination was a dacha, glowing with lights in the heart of a forest. Inside, Jack entered the world of the privileged Soviet youth—vodka, strange food, and beautiful girls from all parts of the Soviet Union. At that time Coca-Cola did not exist in Russia, at least not at this level of society. He was offered whiskey, hashish, red pills; he refused them all and drank mineral water.

It was the girls who interested him, but none of them would talk to him.

"They're not allowed to fuck foreigners for pleasure," Igor said, steering him away from a slender, swan-necked girl who held herself like a ballerina.

Igor's friends guffawed. They were very drunk. In fact, Jack and Igor seemed to be the only sober males at the party.

To Jack's amazement, the talk in the dacha was not so very different from what he had heard many times before at student parties in America. It was cocksure political talk, directed against the ruling order, against people over thirty, but in this case, against the Soviet Union, against the Communist Party. His friends at Columbia would have been shocked, but these kids sounded just like their American counterparts discussing the older generation, the Establishment, the Republicans. And as in America the most fluent talkers were the children of privilege, the indolent, well-fed, well-dressed, pleasure-seeking sons and daughters of the Nomenklatura—the highest circles of the Party, the government bureaucracy, the military, the arts, and the media. Igor, someone whispered, was the nephew of a general of the KGB. He was untouchable.

The youths talked incessantly about this uncle of Igor's, a Russian who seemed to be a mentor to all of them and also to be the lover of most of the beautiful girls. In any case he was a man of mystery. No one knew his true name, or where he was from, or what he did. Only that he was an important figure, close to the top. They were all bound to him, the girls by sex, the boys by awe. They called him Peter.

Where was Peter now? He was supposed to be at this party.

Out of the country, said someone. That's how amazing he is, he's fucking the Nomenklatura from within, and they let him travel anywhere!

The party lasted all weekend. Jack could not get near the girls, though others did; Igor was always in between, apologetic but firm. On Monday the conference began—dull meetings during the day, more wild parties in Moscow apartments at night.

On Jack's last night in town, at an especially crowded party, he fell into conversation with an elegantly dressed, perfectly behaved man in his forties. The man spoke idiomatic American English in a prep-school drawl. There had been talk at the conference of CIA agents provocateurs, of impostors and spies; here, as in America, listening devices, hidden cameras, all the underhanded tools of the class enemy, were assumed to be omnipresent.

The man with whom Jack was conversing was friendly, relaxed; he asked no personal questions. Nevertheless, Jack was overcome by panicky suspicion. Was this a CIA man, someone sent out to catch him up, shanghai him back to be drafted? Or perhaps KGB, trained to impersonate an American. Why was he interested in Jack? Had he sniffed out his false passport? Or worse?

Jack blurted a question. "Are you an American?"

The man smiled, as if he had been expecting this question because it had been asked so many times before.

"No, alas," he replied. "Are you?"

"No, Canadian," Jack said.

"Ah. I had a feeling that we might be of the same nationality."

"You're Canadian, too?"

"No."

"What are you, then?"

The man smiled, almost as charmingly as Jack. "I'm Peter," he said.

Jack realized that this was *the* Peter, the hero of the Russian counterculture. He held out his hand. "Jack."

"A pleasure," Peter said. "We must talk about this nationality question. I want to hear your opinions. Where are you staying?"

Jack told him.

"Tomorrow night, then. A very small dinner party, quite informal. Six o'clock."

Without waiting for Jack to accept and with no word of goodbye, Peter turned on his heels and left. The crowd parted as he walked across the room and vanished out the door.

The girl with the swan neck gave Jack a long look. She lit a cigarette and exhaled smoke through lips drawn into a perfect O. And then she, too, went through the door, smiling tremulously at someone who waited for her in the hall.

4 Another large black car came for Jack at his hotel and drove him through Moscow streets to Peter's house. He expected to find a party attended by the usual crowd, but he and Peter were alone. The table was already laid with a spartan meal of black bread and a sour red soup that Jack took to be borscht. No alcohol was offered, nor any dessert. They ate in silence.

When they were finished, Peter spoke.

"When we met last night," he said, "I said I thought we were of the same nationality."

"I remember."

Peter said, "Good. Let me explain what I meant. In every country, there are people like us—a supernumerary nationality to whom patriotism is a shoddy product, to whom ideology means nothing, to whom the people and only the people mean everything. There are others like us everywhere. Even in Russia. Even in China. Even in America. Do you consider such a thing possible?"

Jack doubted quite strongly the possibility of such a high-minded, world-embracing fraternity; in his experience, most people who hated the United States automatically loved Russia and China and all others who did likewise. But he gave the answer that was expected of him. "Sure. Why not?"

"All right," Peter said. "Though we are few, we represent great power. We have been given a great historic opportunity. If we recognize each other for what we are, if we join together now, if we work together in the future, we can defeat the bastards who now run the world. They do not know we exist, we will never tell them we exist, but we can bring them down. We can take it all away from them, we can make a new world. Do you believe in that possibility?"

Wondering where all this was leading, but eager as always to please someone who might be able to do something for him, Jack replied, "Yes. Certainly. With work, with luck, in the right circumstances." His gift of gab clicked into gear. "For example—"

"Good," said Peter, cutting him off. "Now I must ask you one question. Depending on your answer, we will either say good night and goodbye or our conversation will continue—I mean exactly what I say—for the rest of our lives. This is the question: Do you love your country?"

Jack thought, *What?* But he composed his features into a look of deep thoughtfulness, as though he had been taken by surprise by Peter's question and was struggling to come up with a completely honest answer. His antennae were up and quivering. Something was going on here. He sensed that this was a vital moment in his life, that this was a chance that might never come again.

Once again the right answer was obvious. He said, "No. I don't. I never have."

And then something very odd happened. Jack realized that for once in his life he was speaking the truth. In fact, he did not love America. He did not love anything that America expected her native sons to love—not his grandparents, not his town, not his school, not Columbia, not any of the dozens of American girls he had fucked, not anyone he had ever known. Not even Danny Miller. Not even his dead mother, who had taken the secret of his identity to the grave with her, denying him his right to be a Kennedy, a member of the most godlike family in American history.

For the first time in years, Jack thought of his mother in her coffin. Images of Greta, dying by mutilation just like his mother, flashed on the screen of his memory. He remembered what he felt for her at the moment of her death. It was the same thing he felt for her at the moments of her innumerable orgasms: nothing. In both cases he had been concentrating on himself, the only thing that mattered. What he felt for everything in life except the only important thing in life, himself, was . . . nothing.

He said, "The truth is, Peter, I have absolutely no feeling for my country. I mean, none. Not one iota. No connection. I was born an alien."

Peter was watching him closely. Jack met his eyes with all the frankness at his command. He said, "That's how I feel, really—like an alien in my own country, as if I came from another planet. I always have. And I don't see that changing, ever."

He meant it. Peter saw this. He said, "Good," answering Jack's candor—rewarding it—with deep approval.

Jack, who was so much like Peter, was on the same wavelength as Peter now, and he understood that Peter was approving nothing but the answer to his question, which was exactly what he had expected to hear.

Now Peter smiled. He said, "Your alien days are over, Jack. From now on, for the rest of your life, you will always be among friends. Friends who will work for your success, who will never let you want for anything. Who will protect you. Who will never forget you. Do you like that idea?"

Friends? Jack thought. What was that a code word for? Was it possible that this discussion was not really about politics and the long, long thoughts of youth? Was it conceivable that he was alone with well-spoken, well-dressed Peter for another reason? No. Impossible. Not in Moscow.

"Yes, I like that idea," Jack replied. "Who wouldn't? But—"

Peter held up a hand. "Will you accept friendship? Remember, this is a lifetime commitment. It is irrevocable. Once in, never out."

"You mean friendship with other members of this supernumerary nationality you were talking about? In order to change the world by political means?"

"Yes. Exactly."

"I understand the concept," Jack said. "How will this friendship work in practice?"

Impatience kindled in Peter's eyes. "I have already explained that," he said. "Your friends will always be with you even though you may not be able to see them, even though you may not even guess who they are. They are with you already, and have been for a long time, or we wouldn't be talking as we are now. This is the final moment, the turning point. Come with us. Or go your own way. There will be no second chance."

Jack's face was a study in high seriousness. Still, he made a show of hesitation. He said, "I'm a little puzzled, frankly. Why exactly do all these people want to be my friends?"

"You have been noticed," Peter replied. "You have been studied. You have won favorable opinions. You have a talent, a political talent. With the right help and advice, we think you can rise to extraordinary heights."

"Like what?"

"I see no limits."

As if embarrassed by his own skepticism, Jack looked aside for a moment. Then he said, "Where I come from, rising to extraordinary heights takes money. Lots of it."

Peter smiled; he waved a dismissive hand. "Don't worry about money. You will have all you need. Much, much more than you can make by robbing banks."

Robbing banks? What does this man know?

Somehow, even though he felt that a fist had just smashed into it, Jack kept control of his face. Peter was watching him very carefully; Jack could see that. He kept his composure, but in the panic that washed over him he could scarcely breathe. Jack said, voice steady despite his pounding blood, "What is that supposed to mean?"

Peter placed an attaché case on the table and opened it with a snapping of locks; he pulled out a flat cardboard box and placed it on the table between them. Jack stared at it, but left it where it lay.

Softly, Peter said, "Open it."

Still Jack did not move.

Peter said, "Please open the box, Jack."

Jack did as he was told. The box was filled with photographs of Jack and Greta engaged in sexual acts. Every one of their meetings, even the first, was depicted, in sequence, time and date in the lower right-hand corner of every print. Jack turned over about half the pictures, then raised his eyes to meet Peter's.

"A veritable kaleidoscope of young love," Peter said.

Jack shoved the box across the table. Peter turned it over, squared the stack of photographs, and then dealt them out like playing cards. This sequence showed Jack in the Daimler outside the bank, naked alone, naked with Greta, naked in handcuffs watching as bullets macerated Greta. With a fingertip, perfectly manicured, Peter separated one picture from the rest. It was a shot of Greta on Jack's lap. Her mouth was open in the scream he re-membered. Apart from the open mouth, there was absolutely no expression on her face. Now, as at the moment of Greta's death, Jack felt nothing for her, terror for himself.

Peter said, "Enough?"

Jack nodded.

Peter said, "As I was saying, Jack, we know a great deal about you. As you can see, some of it is quite embarrassing, potentially. But we never betray our friends, as long as they remain our friends. Do you understand what I'm saying to you?"

Jack, mute and frightened to the marrow, truly did not under-stand. How could he? A tear escaped his eye and ran down his cheek. He shook his head no.

"Then I will explain," Peter said. "If you say yes to the friendship I am offering you, we will be friends for life. No ifs, ands, or buts. No going back. No limits. You can never change your mind. Neither can we. And if your answer is yes, we will never do anything to harm you. Now, do you understand?"

Jack nodded.

"Then what is your answer? Speak the word out loud."

In a strong unquavering voice that surprised Jack himself but merely confirmed Peter's good opinion of his essential character, Jack said, "Yes."

"Good," Peter said. "Now pick up the pictures and put them back in the box."

Jack did as he was told. He realized he was carrying out his first order under discipline.

Peter held out a peremptory hand. Jack placed the box in it. It was quite heavy. Peter put it back into his attaché case.

He said, "For safekeeping. While our friendship lasts, you need never worry that anyone but the two of us will ever see these items. Or even know of their existence." He then removed an envelope from his attaché case and shoved it across the table. "Please open it."

Jack did as he was told automatically. The envelope was full of money—crisp fifty-dollar bills smelling of ink. Peter handed Jack a pen and a blank sheet of paper.

"Sign, please," Peter said. "At the bottom. It's just a receipt."

Without hesitation—what would have been the point?—Jack signed his name at the bottom of the blank page.

That did not end the ritual. Peter produced an ink pad and directed Jack to add his thumbprint to his signature. Jack complied, asking for no explanation. He understood the situation perfectly.

"One last thing," Peter said, in the same pleasant tone in which he had uttered every word he had so far spoken to Jack. "The Canadian passport. I will keep that for you, too."

Jack handed it over.

"Thank you," Peter said, unsmiling now. "That's enough for tonight. You will sleep here. In the morning we will talk again."

A door opened. Igor came through it, wearing a sweatsuit, a costume that made him look more than ever like a middleweight contender.

"Igor will see to your needs," Peter said. "Sleep well."

5 Igor, tremendously strong, shook Jack awake at six in the morning and told him to hurry; he was wanted. It was like being shaken by a machine. In the next room, Peter awaited, still as a reptile, in a massive leather wingback chair. He was reading that day's Paris *Herald-Tribune,* half-moon glasses perched on his nose, silk-socked ankle crossed over pinstriped knee. Peter folded the newspaper and gestured Jack into a matching chair. They sat knee to knee, gray worsted to faded denim.

"We won't be seeing each other again for a long time," Peter said. "So pay close attention to the instructions I'm about to give you. They're very important. You must take every step exactly as instructed. This is vital. Do you understand?"

Jack said, "Can I take notes?"

"Absolutely not. You must never commit anything having to do with me or your other friends to writing. Never. This is a confidential relationship and it is permanently binding. Is that clear?"

"Perfectly."

Peter's every question seemed to cast doubt on Jack's intelligence. Jack did not mind; in fact, he provided opportunities for Peter to condescend to him. If Peter wanted to feel that he was smarter than Jack, that was fine with Jack. All he wanted was to get out of this situation, out of Moscow, get out of the Soviet Union. But to go where? Not Germany, certainly.

Peter said, "The most important instruction is this: Lead a normal life. Do exactly what is expected of you by the world. The key to your future is—listen carefully, Jack—the key to your future is to be yourself. Doors will open for you. My job is to make that happen and tell you which doors to go through. Is that clear?"

"Yes. Thank you."

"Good," Peter said, "Now we will start turning keys. I have a few more instructions for you. They are very simple. Listen. Memorize. Are you ready?"

Jack nodded.

Holding up a thumb, European style, for number one, Peter said, "First, go back to Heidelberg."

"But, Peter, my God—"

Peter cut him off. "You will not object. You will not interrupt. You will not substitute your judgment for that of your friends. Go back to Heidelberg. There is no danger. Believe me. Write your paper. Take the exams. Finish your course. Do what is normal."

Peter held up his index finger. "Second, go home."

Jack said, "To the States?"

"Yes, where else? Third, withdraw from the antiwar movement. Isolate yourself from radicals. Their day is over. But do not alienate them. Someday you will need them. They will always be activists, so they will always be useful."

Jack nodded, as if Peter had provided him with a profound insight. In fact, he had. Jack was beginning to see a pattern.

"Fourth," Peter said, raising his ring finger, "do some sort of military service."

Jack cried, "Military service? Go to *Vietnam*?"

"Of course not Vietnam," Peter replied. "Join the reserves, the National Guard. The war will soon be over. Go to drill, wear a uniform once a week."

"What if the unit is called to active service?"

"It won't be. America has lost the war. Fifth, get a temporary job with your senator. Write to him from Heidelberg. He'll be glad to have you back."

"Are you sure of that?"

"Yes," Peter said. "I'm sure." He lifted his other thumb. "Sixth, apply to law school."

This astonished Jack. The last thing he wanted to be was a lawyer. He said, "Law school? Wait a minute. I can't afford it even if I wanted to go, and I don't."

Peter said, "All that is irrelevant. The U.S. government is run by lawyers. You must be their equal; it is a matter of credentials. Study. Take the exam. You will do well. Apply to Yale, Harvard, Cornell, Georgetown. Not to Columbia. You will be accepted by one of those schools with a full grant."

"Which one?"

"You'll know when it happens."

"And then what?"

"Then, obviously, you go to law school," Peter said.

"For three years?"

"Yes. Just like a normal person," Peter said. "One more thing. At a certain moment—this may happen any day or it may not happen for years, but it will happen—a person chosen by me and your other friends will come to you. That person will speak the following words: 'Welcome to the country of the blind.' "

Jack said, "Ouch."

"Yes, I realize that phrase has certain personal associations," Peter said. "But that's why it was chosen, to ring a bell. When you hear those words you will know that the person who speaks them comes directly from me. This person will be your friend, and you must do as he or she suggests as if it were I myself who made the suggestion. You must comply, cooperate with this person always, without fail, no matter what the suggestion is. This is the price of friendship."

Jack, himself a born actor, recognized Peter's behavior for what it was, a performance. He (or so he said later) was offended by it. He himself, after all, was a virtuoso of untruth. Suffering through Peter's deceptions was, for Jack, what watching a spy movie would have been for Peter—a confection that was laughable in its technique, preposterous in its assumptions. To Jack, this spelled weakness.

Peter said, "Do you understand?"

Jack thought, *Better than you know.* He said, "I understand everything you've said to me, Peter, and I appreciate everything you're trying to do for me."

" 'Try' has nothing to do with it. We will succeed, not try."

"I believe you. But you left things out. Who exactly are these friends you keep talking about? The KGB?"

Peter's handsome face darkened. He was silent for several heartbeats—eight; Jack counted them.

"That's a stupid and insulting question," he said at last. "You know what I am, who I am, and what I stand for. I have explained everything. You have accepted."

"Yes, I have," Jack said. "It's a deal. On the terms stated. But I'm not sure you're telling me everything, Peter. You can see how difficult that makes things for me. Whatever my opinion of the United States may be, and I told you truly what it is, I'm an American citizen, subject to American laws. My whole future is at stake. I hardly know you. We're in Moscow. And you've made it obvious that I'm at your mercy. All I'm asking is the truth."

Peter folded his fingers into a fist and gazed at it for a long moment. Then he opened his hand again and said, "Jack, listen carefully. I never lie. The KGB has a name. But what I am, what you are, what we all are together, has no name. It will never have a name.

But together, in our lifetimes, we will change the name of everything. Are you now telling me you don't want to be part of that?"

Jack was just as unsmiling as Peter. This was serious business. There was no spark of sympathy in Peter's eye. Jack felt a chill. He *was* in Moscow, under a false identity. All he had with him to prove who he was were his fingerprints. He realized that he could die—now, quickly, in this room, or, if Peter chose to make it slow, elsewhere. But he also realized that he had something that Peter wanted, and wanted badly, or all this would not be happening. Otherwise, Peter would not be dangling carrots and asking him for promises.

Jack said, "I'm not saying I don't want to be part of what you describe. What I want to do, Peter, is trust you. Bear with me. This is a new experience for me."

"I know that," Peter said. "As you say, we are in Moscow. I could be shot for talking to you as I have done. But I have talked to you anyway. That was an act of trust. Do you agree?"

"Yes, certainly."

"I'm glad to hear you say that. Now the question is, Will you reciprocate? For your own good as well as for the good of the work we can do together?"

Jack locked eyes with Peter. After a long moment he said, "Yes. I will."

"In that case you'll have a wonderful life," said Peter.

Jack knew that his answer was the equivalent of taking a final vow before joining this secret order that Peter kept talking about but never actually described. The answer had pleased Peter and he let Jack see this. But he did not let Jack see what had pleased him even more: Jack's behavior under stress. It was not only appetite that drove Jack. He had the courage of a lion and the cunning of a Jesuit when his own interests were at stake. He had just forced Peter to admit that he needed Jack more than Jack needed him.

Peter stood up. "Now I'll say goodbye. Your train leaves in two hours. Igor will drive you to the station. KGB flatfoots will follow you. This will be obvious. You are intended to see them. Don't be concerned."

Peter opened his attaché case and removed Jack's Canadian passport. He handed it to him.

"Use this to leave the Soviet Union and to enter Sweden and Germany. Do not alter it in any way."

He gave Jack a meaningful look. He gripped his hand. "Jack. We *will* meet again."

"I hope so," Jack said.

"In happier circumstances," Peter said.

He tapped a story on the front page of the *Herald-Tribune.* Jack glanced at it. Manfred's bespectacled face, harshly lit, gazed out of the identity-card photo that accompanied the article. Jack scanned the text: The corpse of a lecturer at Heidelberg University had been found floating in the Neckar River. Police said that there were one hundred bullet wounds in the victim's body, apparently inflicted by a nine-millimeter machine pistol used as a weapon of torture. Every joint of bone had been shattered before a fatal burst was fired into the heart. The Red Army Faction claimed responsibility for what it called the execution of a traitor. Police were investigating possible links between the murder and last week's attempted robbery of a Heidelberg bank by terrorists connected to the Red Army Faction.

By the time Jack finished reading and lifted his eyes, Peter had vanished. The house was deeply silent. Jack thought about Heidelberg, thought about America. He could not picture them; they were things he had read in a book that he had outgrown.

But this! The silence, the absence of clocks, the cold that no furnace could heat, the absence of sensations. He smelled the hand that had held the American money Peter had given him. It was the only thing in this room that had aroma. He breathed the dead air, which seemed incapable of transporting odor, sound, even light.

He rose to his feet and took the first soundless step of his return journey to America.

3

★ ★

Peter's Gift

One

1 Just as Peter had promised, doors began opening for Jack Adams soon after he got back to America. Following instructions to the letter, he landed a menial but paying job on the staff of a subcommittee chaired by his senator. Soon afterward, with help of the same sympathetic staff director who had recommended his reemployment, Jack joined a field hospital unit of the U.S. Army reserves as a laboratory technician trainee. Next to leading the riderless horse in a dead president's funeral, this military occupational specialty was the least likely job in the army to require his presence on a battlefield. The only combat soldiers he would ever see would already be wounded and evacuated back to America.

It was summer, and ordinarily Jack would have gone off to an army camp for an abbreviated period of basic training, but because his senator was an important member of committees that approved the Pentagon's budget, this formality was waived. Instead, Jack reported every other Thursday night to Walter Reed Army Hospital, just outside Washington. There he changed out of the jungle-camouflage fatigues he had been issued, put on the pastel pajamas of a technician, and learned how to draw blood and prepare it for laboratory analysis. Most of his teachers were female soldiers who knew exactly why Jack was in the reserves. They treated him coolly, and he quickly understood that sleeping with a draft dodger was, in their culture, as loathsome an act as servicing a GI would be for a Movement chick. Jack regretted this exceedingly. These were working-class girls looking for love. They reminded him of his high school dates, and he felt that, given the opportunity, his old methods would work well with them.

To everyone's surprise, including his own, it turned out that Jack was good at drawing blood. The sequence—sterilizing the skin, wrapping the rubber tourniquet, finding the vein, inserting the needle—required total concentration combined with a deft touch and the ability to regard the arm from which the blood was being drawn as an abstract object rather than a living limb attached to a human being. Jack possessed all of these qualifications, especially the last, in abundance. At first he worked on outpatients who came into the lab, but his natural skill was soon noticed, and he was sent into the wards with a long list of patients who needed blood tests.

Walter Reed was the army's top hospital, where its best doctors worked on its worst cases. Most of the surgical patients were soldiers who had been wounded in particularly dreadful ways. Jack's superiors had not told him what to expect; the horrifying shock of walking into a room filled with amputees, burn cases, blind men, and men whose faces had been obliterated was a rite of initiation. Jack took one look at this gallery of suffering and fled.

Back in the lab, the man in charge of the night shift was depositing drops of blood from a pipette into a tray of tiny glass receptacles.

Jack said, "Motley, I'm sorry, but I can't do this."

Motley went on with what he was doing. Without looking up, he said, "Can't do what?"

"Draw blood from those guys."

"What guys?"

"The ones on the surgical floor."

"Really? Why not?"

"I can't look at them."

Motley—a kind of sergeant, Jack thought—continued to work steadily with his tray of blood. He did not look at Jack. He said, "I'm not surprised, you yellow-bellied, draft-dodging piece of shit." Motley had a slight lisp, so the sibilants were quite noticeable.

Jack said, "*What?*"

"You heard me."

"Okay. But why are you talking to me like this?"

"You want to know why? I'll tell you why. Those men are the way they are because they defended the United States of America against its enemies foreign and domestic and whatsoever. They paid the price you would not pay. They bled for the country while you pissed on the flag. Is that not the situation, Private?"

"Whatever you say."

Lisp notwithstanding, Motley was enormous, black, and angry. He said, "Glad you agree. Now get your sorry pink ass back up to the ward and carry out your legal orders, or I will personally take you into the latrine and beat that selfsame sorry pink ass into dog meat. *Do you understand?*"

Jack nodded.

"Good," said Motley. "Now get of my sight, dogshit. If you had the balls to look those men in the eye, you wouldn't have to look at their stumps and burns and shot-off faces. *Do you understand?*"

"Yes, Sergeant."

"Don't call me Sergeant. I am not a sergeant. And don't even talk to me no more. Move it!"

Jack went back to the ward and began to draw blood, moving from bed to bed. The first man was unconscious, bleeding through the bandages that covered his face. The next, who had lost both legs, watched with disinterest as Jack stuck the needle into his arm and filled the several vials that were required by the lab.

He said, "You new around here?"

Jack said, "Sort of."

"When you came in the first time, you looked like a queer in the girls' locker room, man. Left in a hurry."

No one laughed. The soldier said, "Where was you headed?"

Jack scratched his head, looked straight into the soldier's eyes, and said, "To buy some rubbers."

It was a feeble joke, but the legless soldier laughed, one bark. To the man in the next bed he said, "You hear what the man said, Harper?"

Harper nodded; he was watching television.

The first soldier said, "You ever see anybody get shot, man?"

The death of Greta flashed in Jack's mind, a gory nickelodeon. "No, I haven't," he lied.

"Don't sweat it, man," the soldier said. "Ain't fuck-all to it. Hello, bang, you're dead, who gives a shit."

That described it, all right. Jack realized that this man, who would be better off dead and knew it, was being kind to him. He said, "I can't believe that, but thanks."

After that, it wasn't so bad. If Jack could talk, he was all right. He had the touch. He asked questions, he made jokes, he charmed and entertained and talked about sports. Soon guys in the next bed were listening in, telling him he was full of shit if he thought Carlton Fisk was in the same class as Johnny Bench, that gook pussy *squeaked,* man. Jack began to enjoy himself. He stopped seeing the horror. Ignoring the wounds, pretending he and the wounded had something in common, was just another form of white lie. He was good at both the things he was doing—drawing blood and blowing smoke. He was, in a strange way, happy.

Jack worked his way down one side of the ward and was about halfway back on the other side when he came to a bed in which a soldier lay rigid and unmoving, face covered by the sheet. Was he dead? Jack started to back away. Then the man spoke from beneath the sheet.

"Other side of the bed," he said.

He stuck his left arm out. Jack thought he understood: There was no right arm. He went around the bed, swabbed the soldier's arm, applied the rubber band, found the vein, inserted the needle.

In a falsetto, the man said, "Ooh! That hurt."

Jack said, "Sorry."

"Sorry doesn't help. You're supposed to be an angel of mercy, motherfucker."

The voice was black. The arm was white. Jack said nothing.

Face still covered, the soldier fluted, "You always were a clumsy lout."

This time Jack recognized the voice and looked up, startled. The man in the bed uncovered his face. It was Danny.

2 On night patrol inside Cambodia, Danny's squad had been advancing along a jungle trail in pitch darkness, each man tethered to the man ahead of him by two bootlaces tied end to end and fastened to their belt loops by a quick-release slipknot.

Danny was walking point, several meters ahead of the other

men. It was so dark that he sometimes had to fall on his hands and knees to locate the path by sense of touch. The talcumlike red dirt of the trail had been pounded into chalk by the feet of the enemy. He was worried about mines. The thought of stepping on a mine in the dark was a particularly horrible one to Danny; the idea of losing his legs, of dying in the dark, of bleeding to death while not being able to see a thing, made him shudder.

Right now he had a feeling that he was almost on top of a mine, that the next step he took would detonate it. He drew his bayonet and slid its point gently into the dirt, probing for metal. He thought he heard a click, but it came from somewhere down the trail. He paused, crouched in the darkness, and listened hard. He immediately heard the unmistakable *spoing* of the spring-steel safety lever flying off a captured American hand grenade. Four seconds later a phosphorus grenade exploded behind him. It went off at the feet of the first man in the file, almost certainly because he had stumbled over a trip wire that detonated the device. This meant that enemy soldiers lying in ambush beside the trail had let Danny go by, and had then tightened the wire across the path so that the first man behind him would trigger the booby trap.

"Shit!" Danny cried, spinning around.

He saw the explosion as a blinding blue-white fountain of burning phosphorus that threw off droplets of burning liquid in all directions, just as a real fountain releases a mist of water.

Danny was out of range, but the squad leader and the man behind him were burned alive when the phosphorus set their clothes and then their flesh on fire. A third man was burned, too, when two or three globs of liquid fire landed on his shirt. He ran down the trail toward Danny, screaming and shedding equipment. The wind created by his movement fanned the flames, and in a matter of seconds he was on fire, too. Danny dropped his rifle and tackled the man. He then attempted to put out the flames by rolling him in the dirt. It was too late for this, so Danny attempted to smother the flames with his own body. His own fatigues caught fire, enveloping the entire right side of his body from ankle to shoulder. As he rolled on the ground trying to put out the flames that were igniting his own body fat, the dead man's ammunition started to go off. Danny threw off the bandolier he was carrying and pressed the burning half of his body into the ground. The flames died—but not before they had consumed most of the skin and about 20 percent of the muscle of his right arm and leg.

Down the trail, Vietnamese soldiers were firing assault rifles and a machine gun at the surviving members of the squad, who had deployed into the trees on the opposite side of the trail and were returning fire. Danny was in shock, so he felt very little pain. He had lost his rifle, and when he found it again by sense of touch and tried to lift it to his right shoulder, he discovered that his right hand and arm no longer functioned. He found his discarded bandolier and grenades and crawled in among the trees, intending to attack the enemy from the flank, but he lost consciousness before he could reach them.

When he woke, the sun had risen. He made his way back to the trail. Three charred corpses lay on the path. He found blood and scattered brass among the trees on both sides of the trail, but no other bodies or equipment, either American or Vietnamese. By now he was out of shock and in agonizing pain. He lost consciousness again. An hour or two later another American patrol found him lying in the path and carried him out to a landing zone. None of the missing members of his squad were ever heard from again.

Jack said, "You tackled a guy who was on fire?"

"Saved my life," Danny replied.

He was right, of course. With the sheet pulled up to his chin, Danny looked the same: thick blue-black hair, dancing blue eyes watching for an opening, twisted grin. The eternal optimist.

Jack said, "What about Cindy?"

"I haven't exactly been communicating with Cindy."

Jack said, "Not communicating with Cindy? Since when?"

Danny's face lost all expression. "Since when do you think, Jack?"

An electric shock ran through Jack's body. He was a stranger to guilt, but dread was his constant companion. Getting caught is the liar's greatest fear, and like all liars Jack lived with it every day. Danny was staring into his eyes. Did he *know*?

He said, "What are you saying to me, Danny?"

"You figure it out," Danny replied.

Good God, he *did* know. Jack hadn't thought about his hour with

Cindy since it happened. But suppose she had told Danny? He could hear her sweet, flat, Ohio voice saying, *I wish it hadn't happened, honey, but it did. With your best friend.* For a long moment Danny stared brightly at Jack. Then tears filled his eyes. He closed his lids. The tears squeezed out between them like a child's tears, great beads of water appearing one by one and then bursting.

"Shit," Danny said, his eyes still closed. He wiped his eyes with the sheet. Jack handed him a box of tissues, and—touched to the heart, Cindy forgotten—he reached under the sheet and took his friend's good hand. Danny returned the pressure.

Jack said, "Danny, I don't know what to say. Things happen—"

Danny grinned again, painfully. "That's what I mean," he said. "She must be pretty horny by now. The minute I tell her, she'll be down here with the wedding rings and a bouquet. I'd never get rid of her."

Relief flooded through Jack's whole being. Danny didn't know what had happened between him and Cindy. He had no suspicion, no idea. And now how could Cindy ever confess? She couldn't, not ever, not to this victim of fate. Jack was safe.

Jack said, "So she comes down in a wedding dress. Would that be so bad?"

"Being married to Florence Nightingale for the rest of my life? It would be terrific."

"How long have you been back?"

"A month."

Jack said, "And she doesn't know you're here? Danny, let's go. There's a phone in the hall."

"I can't."

"Like hell you can't."

Danny tightened his grip, but Jack wrenched his hand free and ran out into the hall and grabbed a wheelchair. When he returned with it, Danny waved him away.

Jack said, "Danny, get in the fucking chair."

The men in the other beds, those who were conscious, were watching and listening. Who were these guys?

Danny said, "No fucking way. Get your ass out of here, Jack."

"Get in the chair or I'll call her myself."

Danny was angry now—a good sign, in Jack's experience of him.

When he got mad on the gridiron or the diamond, he usually did something amazing.

"*You*'ll call her?" Danny said. "She'd hang up."

"Not before I told her what's going on."

"You'd do that to me?"

Jack said, "You have no fucking idea. Believe me." Then, softly: "Come on, Dan. Pick up the phone. Please."

Danny closed his eyes. Then he said, "I haven't got the balls."

"Yes, you have. And that's the whole point. Come on, Dan. Get in the chair."

Danny thought hard, eyes vacant, remembering his life: a landscape with three figures: Jack, Cindy, Danny.

He said, "I'll need a hand."

Jack thought he meant that he wanted him to break the news, prepare Cindy before Danny came on the line. But then Danny threw back the sheet and Jack saw what had happened to him, and he understood what kind of help Danny really needed. Half of his body—the body that had been such a wonder, such a gift—was frozen, scarred, numb to commands from Danny's brain.

Jack helped Danny into the chair and wheeled him out to the pay phone by the elevators. Jack placed a collect call and handed the phone to Danny.

Jack heard Cindy's voice shrieking, "Yes! I accept!" And then shouting, "Danny! Danny!"

Danny held the mouthpiece against his chest. His eyes were fixed on the pay-phone box. Jack knew that he wanted to hang up, but he was too far below the phone to be able to reach the hook, and he could not get up on his own.

He said, "Jack, help me out."

Jack shook his head, then locked the wheels on Danny's chair and walked away, out of earshot.

Danny said, "End of the fucking world." Then he put the phone to his ear and said, "Hi. It's me."

He talked to Cindy for more than an hour, weeping most of the time. At the end of it, he waved the phone at Jack, asking for help. Jack walked over and hung up the phone.

Danny said, "Thanks a lot, buddy. You just dropped me on the flypaper. She's coming tomorrow."

Jack wheeled Danny back to his bed and helped him in. He covered him up. He said, "I'll be back."

"When?"

"Soon. Maybe not tomorrow, though."

"Good thinking."

"You mean she didn't send me her love?"

"I told her you got here first," Danny said. "The rest was silence."

"Does this mean I don't get to be best man?"

"Don't ask," Danny said. "At least the two of you were right about the one thing you ever agreed on. I never should have gone to 'Nam. Wrong man in the wrong place at the wrong time." He grinned. "Lost at least ninety miles off my fastball."

Jack's eyes filled with tears. He said, "Danny, I'm so sorry."

"Why?" Danny said. "You weren't there."

3 One Thursday evening, Jack, finishing a long Jesus joke, failed to notice that the floor of the ward had just been mopped. Syringe in hand, he slipped, fell down, and impaled his hand on the needle.

Sitting on the floor, staring at the blood on his palm, he said, "That's what I get for trying to walk on water."

After that the men called him Jesus.

When they caught their first glimpse of Cindy, they were stunned by her beauty and her love for Danny. After she left, the loud soldier on the other side of the ward said, "Hey, Miller, is that the chick Jesus forced you to call up on the telephone?"

"That's her," Danny said.

"What a friend you have in Jesus," said the man. "Holy Jesus, what a friend."

Cindy and Jack took care not to meet. She drove to Bethesda every weekend, bringing books and magazines and a picnic cooler full of Ohio treats: ham loaf sandwiches, makings for sloppy joes in a wide-mouth thermos, double-sweetened apple pie, jam made from her father's red raspberries. She and Danny picnicked on the grounds of the hospital. She pushed his wheelchair for miles along suburban streets where magnolia and azalea and oleander bloomed in the soft spring sunshine. She made friends with the nurses, who showed her an empty room where she and Danny could find privacy. Gently, against his will, she drew him back to lovemaking. His beautiful tawny skin was now the color of entrails, dead-white, butcher-red, bruise-blue. If she wept over what had happened to him, she did it after she left. As far as Danny could tell, his injuries made no difference to her; what was left of Danny's body was still Danny's body.

Three or four nights a week, when Cindy was attending her law-school classes in Columbus, Jack came to see his friend. He, too, brought treats—pizza, mostly, and sometimes take-out food from Chinese restaurants. Soon he was bringing food and other items for the other men. His nickname, which began in derision, took on another meaning. He gave his office phone number to the men, and if they called with a request—"Hey, Jesus, bring us out two buckets of fried chicken from the Colonel!"—he would do as they asked without fail.

Where the wounded were concerned, he developed an almost otherworldly kindness. Danny had many operations, and while he recovered Jack was always by his bedside in the evenings. While Danny slept, Jack would read to the illiterate, write letters, make phone calls to straighten out matters of the heart that were a worry to one man or another. He would run errands. All this he did on his own time, after he had completed his eight hours of duty on Thursday, or on other days when he came to see Danny.

Danny said, "How come all these corporal acts of charity, Jack? You got something on your conscience?"

"No, it's déjà vu," Jack replied.

"What's that supposed to mean? You were Walt Whitman in an earlier life, bandaging wounds and kissing the boys good night?"

"Not really. I got my start in a place like this."

"You did? When was that?"

"When Mom met Dad."

Danny cocked his head, eyes alert and skeptical. After all these years, did Jack still believe that JFK had boffed his mother in a navy hospital and he was the result? Looking into Jack's face, as Irish as his own, Danny grinned. "Oh, yeah, almost forgot," he said. "The Camelot Kid."

Everybody on the floor knew that Jack was a draft dodger, but as time went on, few held it against him. "You done the right thing, Jesus," they told him. "'Nam was no place for a fuckup like you." But they liked him—his humanness, his sense of his own ridiculousness, the way he chattered all the time. And as in so many other instances, this had something to do with Danny. He was the captain of the surgical floor just as he had been captain of the team. There were many reasons to admire him: his good looks, his good humor, Cindy.

Also, his deeds in Vietnam had surfaced—not because Jack had betrayed his confidence, but because Danny had been overheard telling Jack the details by a man in the next bed who knew a truthful battlefield story when he heard one. Jack did make sure that everyone knew that Danny had been a great athlete who had had a shot at pitching in the major leagues. That Danny had not been decorated, or even thanked, for actions that should have won him the Medal of Honor confirmed every sardonic lesson that war had taught the other men. To Jack, it made the pathetic consequences of Danny's wounds even more poignant. The plastic surgeons were aware of Danny's legend—Jack made sure of that, too—and they did their best work for him.

But something more than his friendship with Danny was involved in Jack's popularity on the floor. This was his extraordinary gift for making people like him—for insisting that they like him because he simply could not live with disapproval. As with Danny, so with the whole world: No matter what the situation, Jack made himself lovable so as to have the option of letting himself be loved. It was not necessary for him to love in return. He got everything he needed from being loved.

They liked his friendship with Danny. Most of them never had visitors, but Jack came to see his friend almost every day. To pass the time, the two of them studied for the law-school admissions exams together, Danny asking Jack questions, then Jack asking Danny. Jack said Danny was helping him, but they saw through that: What Jack was really doing was getting Danny ready to take the exam, too. And when the time came, he did take it, right in the hospital, with Danny telling a volunteer the answers and the old lady marking them down for him.

Not only that, they knew that Jack was a swordsman. At first they were skeptical. Success with women was the last thing they would have suspected about him. Danny told them about Jack's conquests in high school; he told the story of the girl in the New York restaurant. "You telling us Jesus just followed her down the hall and she handed him her panties and he whomped her just like that in the ladies' room?"

"While her husband finished his coffee."

"Any witnesses, man?"

"Afterward Jesus had the panties and she had a big smile. What can I say?"

There were resentments: "Fuckin' draft dodger just the same."

But Danny said, "That's right, and look what he missed."

Nobody contested the point. Jack himself never referred to the war. He knew that the distance between the two sides was too great ever to be crossed. He knew, too, that if it weren't for Danny not one of the wounded men would ever have spoken to him. But they did speak to him, and Jack found ways to respond without giving offense. He talked sports, a subject in which he had almost no interest. From Capitol Hill he brought them brand-new dirty jokes and racy stories about the famous. He invented for their amusement a comic Tannery Falls, Ohio, a one-man Punch-and-Judy soap opera in which Jack played three thousand roles, every one of them in a different voice.

"Speak in tongues, Jesus!" the men would cry when he got going. And afterward they would say, "That Jesus oughta be on TV. He's running for Savior!"

Before Jack parted from them, he wrote down every single name and address, along with other details. And then he forgot them until he needed them. Years later, on TV, he remembered everything about them and talked to them in the same old way, no matter how much things had changed. They were flattered, but it was a politician's trick. Jack had a liar's memory; he stored every word he spoke because he could not afford to forget it, and had no more trouble remembering it than truthful people experience in recalling the truth. It, too, is sometimes elusive.

"Same old Jesus!" the men said when he wheeled them out into the klieg lights long afterward and, holding back the tears, told the

world how they had taught him the meaning of sacrifice and forgiveness.

They knew better, but that made no difference. They could see
that Jack believed it was the truth, and in a way they were sorry
that it wasn't, now that he was famous.

Two

1 The next winter, a few weeks after he entered Harvard Law School, Jack's Grandmother Herzog died, leaving him alone in the world—at least on the Tannery Falls side of the family. She was buried from the same funeral home in which Jack's mother and Homer Adams had been laid out side by side twenty years before. Looking down on the blue-haired, rouged old woman who wore her rhinestoned eyeglasses even in death, Jack realized that he had no memories of her whatsoever except for the kissing of his mother's corpse. All the years he had lived in her house as a lost princeling had vanished from his mind; he had never belonged there. The house remained, long since sold to pay for Mrs. Herzog's nursing-home care, but Jack did not go by for one last look.

Danny, now living with Cindy in the little house in Columbus, came to the funeral. It was a graveside service. Apart from the minister, a stranger to Jack, the two friends were alone with the coffin at the cemetery. Danny walked with difficulty over the frozen ground. After a year of surgery he had been discharged from the army. He was able to get around without help, but his right hand was a claw and he walked with the aid of an aluminum crutch. He was learning to write with his left hand, against the day, a few months in the future, when he would enter law school at Ohio State.

They ate lunch together in the diner where they had hung out as boys. Danny ate clumsily with his left hand; Jack had to put the ketchup on Danny's hamburger. Townspeople—men and women who had lived for the Friday nights in autumn when Danny Miller carried the ball against the prettier, more prosperous towns that surrounded Tannery Falls—watched in funereal silence from their stools at the counter. One woman, unknown to either boy, ran weeping from the diner.

Danny still went to twice-weekly physical therapy sessions at a veterans' hospital. He had machines at home on which to exercise; he lifted weights, swam, stretched. After a while he would have more surgery. He had no complaints; he had trained all his life, commanding his body to do more than it was designed to do. Therapy was just another form of training.

Jack said, "Do you think about the baseball thing?"

"What might have been?" Danny replied. "No. Cindy's the athlete now. She plays tennis three times a week. Against a girlfriend, she says, but she comes home pretty sweaty."

"Maybe she's playing a lesbian."

Danny snapped his good fingers. "That's it. What a relief."

Danny and Cindy had been married in the chapel at Walter Reed with two patients from the floor as witnesses. Except for the army chaplain, a Baptist who refused a plastic champagne glass of the cold duck Cindy had brought for the celebration, no one else was present—especially not Jack. They had gone to a motel in Bethesda for the night. Cindy had insisted on making love with the lights on. *I'll do all the work,* she had said. *Like hell you will,* said Danny. But she had.

Danny told Jack nothing of this. He asked what Harvard was like.

"About what you'd expect," Jack said. "I'm the only dumb one there."

"Don't worry," Danny said. "You'll fake 'em out."

"The funny thing is, half the law school will never actually practice law," Jack said. "I'm not sure I will."

"Sure you will, for a while," Danny said. "Win a famous case, run for governor. Maybe we can be partners."

"Now you're talking."

"I'm serious," Danny said. "You'll be the courtroom guy, saving the widows and orphans. I'll chase the ambulances." He mimed a man on crutches, moving at top speed.

Keeping it light, Jack said, "Where does Cindy fit into this plan?"

"She'll back me up with a paycheck from another firm."

"Sounds good to me."

"In that case," Danny said, "don't get yourself kicked out of Harvard for porking the dean's daughter. We'll need that Ivy League diploma on the wall."

Was Danny serious? Jack did not know and Danny gave no sign.

The people of Tannery Falls had taken up a collection and given Danny a brand-new Chevrolet with hand controls as a coming-home present. He drove Jack to the airport. He was still a fast driver.

"Been down this road before," Danny said as they passed the abandoned strip mines.

2 We had friends in the circles in which Jack now traveled, and Peter was very pleased with the reports we received from them. Jack was turning out to be every bit the chameleon that Peter's intuition had suggested he could be. His brains, his personality, and his dazzling mendacity carried him from triumph to triumph. Perhaps these were small triumphs, but they were triumphs nonetheless.

This was as true at Harvard Law School as at any of his previous way stations. Our friends had helped him in the beginning, but before long he had several perfectly legitimate mentors on the faculty. Although he was not among the leading scholars in his class, their influence won him a place on the *Harvard Law Review*. They took him to their clubs, invited him home, introduced him to visiting legal celebrities. The Harvard establishment liked Jack; it was as simple as that. By the middle of his second year he had become one of them.

This, in particular, pleased Peter. Gazing at a glossy photograph of the staff of the *Law Review*, Jack smiling in the front row, he exclaimed, "Just like Alger! He was a member of the Cane Club at Johns Hopkins; he also was elected to the *Review* at Harvard Law. The photos are remarkably alike, everyone in a suit, a row of snobs, with Jack and Alger blending right in and standing out at the same time." Peter was quite carried away. "They even *stand* alike—look!" he said. "Entirely at home yet entirely out of their element." I wanted to say, *Jack should be warned about this resemblance.* I said nothing.

Apart from watching him in a loose sort of way—we did not want to draw attention to him among our American friends, either—we left Jack to his own devices. That, too, was part of the plan. The fundamental idea when manufacturing an agent of influence is (forgive me if I repeat myself) to let him live a normal life—establishing credentials, making friends, establishing not cover but face value. We gave him no money, no advice, no help. At least not overtly or at first hand. There was no need to instruct our friends in the unconscious underground to do what they could for him. They had already adopted him as one of their own and designated him Deserving Poor Boy of the Year. The price of their patronage was moral guidance. Gently but in many different ways they reminded Jack where his good fortune came from and what was expected from him in return. Just as every good Swiss keeps his rifle at home, ready to spring into action at any hour of the day or night to repel an attack on the *Heimat,* so every good progressive must be prepared at a moment's notice to transform himself into a white corpuscle and rush to the point of infection to attack any germ of heresy or doubt that infiltrates the body of the revolution.

As in all other outward things, Jack was obedient to Peter's injunction to separate himself from the radical left. The antiwar movement died the moment American troops were removed from Vietnam and the draft ceased to be a threat to radicals, so it was not so very difficult for Jack to keep his distance.

The problem was, the sexual revolution seemed to be dying, too. Nearly four years had passed since Heidelberg. Though she still invaded his dreams, Jack never thought of Greta now, and the sexual tricks that she had taught him were all but useless at Harvard and in Washington. The women he met now were ex–Movement chicks who had been transformed by feminism into lobbyists, journalists, congressional staffers, advocates of one kind or another, environmental activists. All were attempting to live the life of the raised consciousness, in which political virtue was everything, intimacy a vestige of slavery. Sex to them was what it had been to Jack before Greta—pleasurable but soon over and disconnected from such absorbing questions (impenetrable to Jack) as boycotting Nestlé products because that company's baby formulas discouraged breast-feeding in Africa. Jack did not live the life of a monk, but his couplings were infrequent, unpredictable, and perfunctory, as if his partners had developed a troubling symptom, diagnosed it as sexual desire, and ordered an orgasm from the pharmacopoeia of radicalism.

"Jesus," said a naked lawyer, grimacing as she stripped the sheets off her bed minutes after howling through a hysterical climax, "I'll be glad when a girl can get this done by taking a pill."

Jack said, " 'Girl'? Watch those four-letter words, honey."

His bedmate whirled to confront him. "Get lost, pig," she snarled.

"It's a *joke.*"

"All male jokes are chauvinist insults. Out. Now."

3 During the full moon in February, Jack was invited by one of his professors to a sliding party at the teacher's farm outside Cambridge. Jack did not know what a sliding party was. He discovered that it consisted of drinking a good deal of hot buttered rum (Coca-Cola for Jack) and eating charred hot dogs and hamburgers while standing in trampled snow around a bonfire, in between rides on a child's sled down steep, snow-covered hills.

For the sled rides, Jack was paired off by his hostess with a young woman named Morgan Weatherby. Morgan was in the final year of her Harvard MBA. She was, their hostess murmured, first in her class, a tremendous distinction, for B-School students were notoriously smart and competitive. "But she's *fine,*" said the hostess, meaning, *She's one of us, a good person, a believer.*

Making conversation after they were introduced, Jack said, "The B School, eh?"

"What's that supposed to mean?" asked Morgan, bristling.

"I don't know. At first glance it seems a little out of character."

After a long angry stare, Morgan said, "Thanks for noticing. The idea is to use the techniques of capitalism against the capitalists."

They talked some more, Jack slipping back into the vocabulary of the Movement as though a switch had been thrown in a long-dormant part of his brain—which was exactly what had happened. Morgan was cerebral, humorless, withdrawn. She wore steel-rimmed glasses, army boots, bib overalls, a knit cap with a peace symbol under which she had tucked every strand of hair. She insisted on steering. On their fourth descent, Jack, behind her on the

Flexible Flyer, put his hands on her breasts. Morgan kicked the steering bar hard to the right and overturned them.

They rolled down the hill. Morgan leaped to her feet and stood over Jack, sprawled in the snow and laughing.

"Very funny," she said. "Next time you'll get a combat boot in the balls."

Jack believed her. But she had lost her cap and her glasses in the spill, and when Jack found them and handed them back, he saw that the hair she had hidden inside her cap was a regulation Movement mane, parted in the middle and falling nearly to her waist. It seemed to be blond, bounteous but nondescript. She wound it into a knot and, holding this on top of her skull, covered it again with the knitted cap Jack had recovered from the snow. Jack grinned; she still glared. He thought, *Nice tits just the same.* Reading his thought as if the words were inscribed in the air between them, she sneered, turned around, and strode back up the hill. She was tall, slender, but somewhat heavy-hipped. Jack followed, pulling the sled.

Later, standing by the campfire, tongue loosened by the many cups of rum Jack had fetched her, Morgan answered more questions about herself. Earlier in the radical epoch, as a Smith College undergraduate, she had been a front-line campus militant. She had screamed obscenities and squirted urine from a Baggie at the cops in Chicago; she was the girl waving the Viet Cong flag in the front rank of the march on the Pentagon. She had been nearby when the protester immolated himself like a Buddhist monk under McNamara's windows.

"McNamara was watching from behind his bulletproof glass," Morgan said. "I saw his face. A rat in bifocals."

"Really?" Jack said. He didn't believe this could be so. But he said, "Amazing."

"I didn't see you there."

"Nope, but I was into all that at Columbia."

Morgan shot him a look of deep suspicion. "You were? Then why don't I know you?"

"I wasn't up front like you," Jack replied.

"Why am I not surprised?" she asked. "Who did you hang out with at Columbia?"

Jack furnished a list of names famous in the Movement.

"Oh," she said. But he could see the doubt in her eyes. She was a Movement activist, surrounded by enemies of the people. Everyone was a liar, an infiltrator, until proven otherwise.

Nevertheless, Morgan finished telling him the story of her life. In her sophomore year at Smith, she had broken with her parents, believing like Greta that the overthrow of the bourgeois family was the first, indispensable step toward total revolution against the entire bourgeois capitalist-imperialist Establishment.

She had rooms in a slum in South Boston, devoting the income from the trust fund set up for her by her right-wing parents to the support of the PLO, the Black Panthers, the Angela Davis Defense Fund, and similar political causes. She walked through this dangerous neighborhood without fear because the people knew she was one of them and therefore she could come to no harm.

"That's great," Jack said.

Hearing this personal history of a Movement pilgrim, Jack was strangely moved. He had heard it so many times before, from so many girls with trust funds. She was, like her many counterparts, deeply deluded about almost everything, a state of being that left her convinced that she was one of the few sane people on Earth, and that her beliefs would keep her that way as long as she lived by them.

It was a passionate conversation. In the past, a confession like Morgan's had usually been followed by sex. Jack was aroused, a Pavlovian effect produced by the vocabulary, the intonations, the leitmotif of paranoia. Morgan reminded him of sweaty grapplings, unwashed hair, unshaved legs, furry armpits.

The bonfire had burned down while they talked. They realized that they were alone. Cars were starting in the distance and switching on their headlights.

They heard a female voice hallooing. It was their hostess, trudging toward them through the snow, waving a flashlight.

"You two!" she said, pleased to think she had made a match of true minds. "We almost left without you."

But when Jack asked Morgan for her phone number, she turned away as if she had not heard the question.

4 A few days later, Jack was strolling across Harvard Square with a classmate named Whitlow, a very tall man with a preppy accent.

Whitlow, who could see over the crowd, said, "Look what's coming. The Morg."

Jack said, "The what?"

"The Morg. The queen of the B School."

He jerked his head, directing Jack's gaze. Morgan Weatherby was striding toward him through the noonday crowd. He did not recognize her at once, but then he remembered her woolen ski cap with the peace symbol. She wore bib overalls under a strange long coat that hung down to the tops of her yellow, high-topped work shoes.

Jack said, "You know her?"

"Only by reputation. She's said to be extremely smart."

Morgan planted herself in front of Jack. It was a cold day; the tip of her nose was red. She sniffled once, coughed twice. According to the label stenciled in white paint inside its upturned collar, Morgan's dark blue coat, made of rough wool, was Canadian navy surplus.

"I've checked you out," she said. "The people at Columbia say you're for real."

In a mock-hearty voice, Jack said, "Wow, that's a relief. So what's next?"

"We can talk. How about tonight? My place, eight o'clock."

"Where do you live?"

She gave the address in Roxbury.

Jack said, "Sure. But let's do it in Cambridge—take in a movie, have a pizza afterward."

Morgan said, "What are you saying? You're afraid to come into my neighborhood?"

Jack nodded.

"Why is that, exactly?"

"I don't have a trust fund, so my contributions to the Black Panthers are in arrears."

"That's a racist remark."

Jack said, "*The Battle of Algiers* is playing."

Maintaining eye contact, Morgan considered this information

for several seconds. "Okay," she said. "You're on. Seven o'clock show."

She turned away and strode into the crowd.

"*The Battle of Algiers*?" Whitlow said. "Talk about your aphrodisiacs. You're going to need all the help you can get."

Jack said, "Oh? Why's that, Whitlow?"

Watching Morgan make her way through the crowd, Whitlow's eyes filled with merriment. "She's a dyke, Jacko."

"Ten bucks, Whitlow."

"You actually want to bet you can score?"

"Ten bucks."

"Against what deadline?"

"Commencement Day."

"You're on," Whitlow said. "But I'm not taking your word for it, Adams."

"There'll be corroborative evidence," Jack said.

"Like what, teethmarks on your dick?"

Morgan had seen *The Battle of Algiers* many times before, but each viewing yielded new details and insights. She watched the screen intently, elbows on knees, chin in hand, as Algerian terrorists murdered French policemen and French paratroopers tortured Algerian terrorists. From Morgan's point of view, sympathetic to the heroic terrorists, it was a two-hankie movie, and when it was over her eyes were wet and wounded and she had difficulty speaking.

"Every time I see that movie it leaves me more pissed off than the last time," said Jack, who had never seen it before.

Morgan said, "You have to go to the movies to get pissed off?"

"I'm not sure I understand the question."

"It's pretty basic. If you're what you say you are, a committed person, you should be pissed off by injustice all the time. Every minute of every day."

"I try," Jack said. "But sometimes I get distracted."

They were standing at a bus stop. Jack put a hand on Morgan's cheek, then took off her glasses. She said nothing, but gave him an unblinking, teacherish stare. *You have just done something wrong. Think for a moment, then tell me exactly what that was.*

Tentatively, even deferentially, Jack kissed her. Morgan kept her eyes open, watching for the bus, but parted her lips slightly and did not move away. However, that was her only response. When the bus arrived she stepped back, took her glasses out of Jack's hand, and got aboard. When he made as if to follow, Morgan held up a hand like a traffic cop.

For the next three months, in the interstices of Morgan's interminable revolutionary monologues, Jack made many attempts to nuzzle, fondle, and undress her. None of his moves succeeded. She always wore trousers over pantyhose, a new kind of female undergarment that would have made Jack's adolescent sex life impossible unless he carried scissors. By the middle of May, with commencement fast approaching, Jack had still not touched skin on any part of her body except her hands and face. When he tried, she intercepted his hand and held it off. She was extremely strong for a woman.

Jack did not lie about his progress to Whitlow or to the many others Whitlow had told about the bet. He knew that he would not be believed.

"How's the foreplay coming, Jack?" Whitlow would ask at editorial meetings of the Review staff.

"We've done all the positions in Mao's Little Red Book, up to page fifty-six."

"Give up?"

"I've still got fourteen days."

Oddly, Jack had the idea that Morgan loved him. In every respect but physical response, her behavior displayed the hallmarks of passion—of obsession, even. Morgan gazed at Jack as if she desired him—tenderly, as if she wanted desperately to take his body into hers and repeat over and over again the burlesque of procreation that was the calisthenics of the Movement. But this hadn't happened. If Jack had not known better, he might have thought that Morgan really and truly did not know about sex, that she was some sort of cryogenic virgin, a woman of twenty-seven who had been frozen and stored at absolute zero since the age of five. She was awake now, but in a state of puzzlement about the breasts and pubic hair she had grown in her sleep.

Rejection is a powerful aphrodisiac, and Jack was half in love himself. This weird absence of sexual awareness was, in its way, as exciting as the wild, cold-hearted couplings with Greta. Even more so, in a way. Having never before experienced the unattainable, Jack was beginning to understand why so much poetry had been written about it through the ages. Two days before commencement, he was still unsuccessful. Whitlow asked him how such a thing could be.

Only half lying, Jack replied, "The Morg is my Beatrice."

"You mean, as in Dante?" said Whitlow, eyebrows climbing.

"You mistake virtue for perversion, you fucking cynic."

Whitlow gave Jack a look of mock sympathy. "You need help," he said. He looked left and right, then reached into an inside pocket and produced a twisted marijuana cigarette in a plastic bag. "Tijuana gold," Whitlow said. "A graduation present. Get her to smoke it. And may it rid you of this hag."

5 Because she hated Ma Bell—believing, like Greta, that the CIA was one of its wholly owned subsidiaries—Morgan did not have a phone. Therefore, later that evening, Jack knocked without forewarning on the door of her apartment. It was his first visit to Roxbury. Morgan had been right: Merely imagining this neighborhood filled him with fear. Seeing the reality terrified him.

She lived in a fourth-floor walk-up. Stepping over children both sleeping and waking who perched on the steps as if waiting for something to end or begin, Jack made his way upward. Morgan's door stood at the end of a cluttered dark hallway that reeked of milk, urine, scorched food. Through the door, a brand-new one, sheathed in steel, he heard the sound of very fast typing. He knocked. The typewriter keys ceased to rattle; he heard a page being ripped from the platen. Morgan's green eye appeared in the peephole, wary even though disembodied. The peephole closed. He heard the sound of many chains and locks being undone.

Morgan did not seem to be surprised by Jack's arrival—or particularly pleased by it, either. In silence, she refastened the various chains, deadbolts, and bars. A blackjack hung by its thong on a hook beside the door.

She wore a long T-shirt but no other garment. Jack watched appreciatively as she worked on the locks, bending and stretching, putting her whole body into the effort. Her bottom was harp-shaped, womanly, and pleasing, like a nymph's bottom in a painting by Bouguereau. Jack had never seen her legs before. They were long, as he already knew, and shapely and strongly muscled, as he had suspected, but the remarkable thing about them was that they did not match. The left one was much thinner than the right one. Each in its own way was normal, even pretty. But they were not a pair.

That was why she always wore pants. Her bib overalls hung from a hook by their straps. He expected her to grab them and put them on, but instead she sat down in a kitchen chair and hid her legs under the table.

She still had not spoken. The apartment consisted of one big room with the table in the middle, a Murphy bed folded up against the wall, an old-fashioned wardrobe trunk, and an alcove kitchen with sink, hot plate, and tiny refrigerator. Through an open door Jack could see a bathtub and toilet. The table was piled high with books, but otherwise the place was spotlessly clean. A tumbler of apple juice stood beside the typewriter.

Morgan wasn't wearing her glasses. Her eyes were large, green, slightly tilted. Suddenly she swept her hair over one shoulder and held on to it with both hands as if to keep from falling off the chair. It was the most maidenly gesture Jack had ever seen her make, and certainly the most unexpected.

Jack said, "Do you always type without your glasses?"

"Always. I only wear them for distance."

Jack looked more closely at her swimming, slightly-out-of-focus eyes and realized that Morgan was wearing contact lenses—the only woman in the world, he thought, who wore glasses in public and contacts when she was alone.

Morgan said, "Why are you here, Jack?"

"To celebrate," Jack replied.

"Celebrate what?"

"Tomorrow. The big day. How about a pizza?"

"Jack, tomorrow doesn't mean a thing. I'm busy."

"Doing what—writing a paper on the night before graduation? Give me a break."

Expressionless as usual in the face of innuendo, Morgan said, "What kind of a break did you have in mind?"

In return, Jack smiled at full wattage.

Morgan stared. Quizzical and very nearly smiling herself, she said, "I'm sure you don't realize it, but you look kind of like a Kennedy when you smile."

Jack said, "No kidding? Is that a point in my favor?"

Morgan was still holding on to her hair, and she was still wearing nothing but a T-shirt. Her legs were not crossed, nor were her arms. She had just said something to Jack that could be construed as a compliment. He was beginning to think that this might, after all, be his lucky night.

Jack produced Whitlow's marijuana cigarette.

Morgan said, "What's that supposed to be?"

"A graduation present."

"I thought you didn't do drugs."

"I don't. It's for you."

"How sweet." Her voice dripped sarcasm. "What, as an aid to se-duction?"

Jack said, "Jesus, Morgan, lighten up. You've got your blackjack."

This seemed to amuse her. She said, "Okay. There are matches in the kitchen."

Jack fetched a kitchen match and lit the joint for Morgan. She in-haled deeply, doing something she had obviously done many times before. Her chest expanded, breasts stretching the T-shirt. Eyes squinting, she passed the joint to Jack. He waved it away.

She exhaled. "None of that shit, Jack," she said. "You brought it, you help smoke it."

"I have no idea how."

"Like this."

She inhaled again, then passed him the joint. Jack took a mouth-ful of smoke and held it. He hated the taste. Smoke leaked from his nostrils. He opened his mouth and the smoke rolled out.

"Again," Morgan said. "Inhale."

Jack dragged inexpertly on the cigarette.

"Oh, for Christ's sake," Morgan said.

She got up out of her chair. Static electricity had pasted the tail of her T-shirt to her bottom. Morgan leaned over him, breasts swinging freely beneath the gray cloth, and clapped one hand over his mouth. She pinched his nostrils shut with the thumb and forefinger of her other hand. Jack's eyes rolled. He swallowed the smoke and coughed, then retched.

Morgan said, "Give me that fucking thing."

Sitting in the kitchen chair, drawn out from the table now, she smoked the joint down to the last half inch. Jack looked at her legs. She put them on the table, ankles crossed.

"They never matched," she said. "One was always smaller than the other. What's your secret?"

Jack pointed at his lap.

"Ah," Morgan said. "Omar the tentmaker."

Conditioned by Morgan's frigidity, Jack was taken unaware by this remark. He realized that he was a little shocked that she had it in her to say such a thing.

She pulled the Murphy bed down from the wall and stripped off her T-shirt. She had endearing cockeyed breasts: one pink areola stared straight at Jack while the other glanced shyly to the side.

Jack took off his own clothes—speedily, lest she change her mind. Reclining on the bed with one ankle crossed over the other, Morgan watched, unblinking, silent.

Jack had never felt such intense sexual desire. Except once, in the Daimler. He was afraid it might be over for him before he could make it to the bed.

6 Jack soon found that Morgan unclothed was no more responsive than Morgan in bib overalls. As soon as he joined her on the bed she wound her smaller leg around the larger, tight as a tropical vine. As if performing some perverse yoga exercise, she then hooked her left foot around her right ankle. This utterly defeated Jack's tried-and-true technique with girls whom he wished to spare the trouble of saying no. Try as he might, he could not get Morgan's legs uncrossed, much less slip between them, Vaseline at the ready. Jack was trapped in the portcullis of desire with no way out and no way in. Morgan did not resist his fondling her breasts, but even more than most men, Jack had no interest in foreplay sans aftermath. His urgency was great, but when he tried to guide her own hand onto his body, Morgan clenched her fist and resisted. He pressed himself against her and groaned. She watched his twisted face with clinical interest, neither resisting nor assisting.

Panting, Jack said, "What in the name of God is the matter with you, Morgan?"

"In the name of who? Nothing that I know of."

"Well, at least tell me this much: Is it just me, or are you always like this?"

Morgan said, "It's not just you."

"What is it then, men as a class?"

"No."

"Are you sure about that?"

"Jack, listen," Morgan said. "I'm not the one who just came all over you, so I don't owe you any explanations."

She got out of bed and went into the bathroom, closing the door behind her. After a moment Jack heard water running in the tub. Stealthily, he tried the bathroom door. It was locked. He went back to the bed, covered up and closed his eyes, feigning sleep. Perhaps Morgan, thinking him asleep, would drift off after her bath. Unless she tied her ankles together, he could wake her up with a big surprise. The key to Jack's plan was to stay awake. But, exhausted by the struggle and by the marijuana, he soon fell asleep in spite of himself.

Much later, he woke shivering with cold, to find himself alone in the bed. He groped for the covers; they were gone. He tried the bathroom door; it was locked. Morgan had taken the blankets and locked herself inside.

"Hey, Morg," he said, knocking.

No reply.

Jack covered up with Morgan's naval coat and fell into a deep sleep.

He opened his eyes and saw Morgan, completely naked, crouching at the foot of the bed, legs apart, fur showing. The room was filled with morning sunlight. Morgan stood up on the bed and threw back her hair with a practiced shake of her head; it swirled away in a ripple of light, thousands of individual hairs moving as one. But, amazingly, it was dyed: the roots, like her pubic hair, were dark.

With an incandescent smile—it *was* his lucky morning!—Jack sat up and reached for her. His hands were jerked to a stop. He felt sharp pain in both his wrists. His wrists were handcuffed to the bed. His hands, fingers curled, were encased in surgical gloves.

Morgan said, "Don't struggle. You are completely in my power."

"Jesus Christ, Morgan!"

"Relax."

She moved between his legs. He realized that he was tied by the ankles to the foot of the bed. Did she have implements of torture? Her blackjack still dangled from its hook by the door. There was no sign of anything sharp. She seemed to be empty-handed. But what might be under the bed? He began to hyperventilate.

Morgan said, "Be calm, Jack. It's only a game. Just cooperate."

She was expert, practiced. Though still fearful—what was going to happen afterward?—he was soon in a state of almost terminal excitement. Adroitly, Morgan pressed the underside of his penis with a thumb, preventing ejaculation. He writhed in agony. She continued the pressure until the spasm passed, gazing sympathetically into his wild, pleading eyes. She was not wearing her contact lenses, and the glitter of anger had vanished from her eyes, which now swam with the dreamily vacant look of the very myopic. Jack smelled shampoo, perfume, female musk. Morgan's legs gleamed from the razor; her armpits, too, were shaved. Apparently she had prepared for this pornographic encounter with a ritual bath.

Jack started to speak. Morgan, straddling his thighs, drew an *X* across his mouth with a slippery fingertip. He tasted Vaseline. She showed him her palm, on which a gob of petroleum jelly glistened. She greased him, deft and quick. And then with a brilliant smile— she had beautiful teeth all the way back to her throat—she turned her back, seized him, fitted him.

Jack thought, *The Daimler!*

He had suppressed, banished, forgotten the details of his last terrifying moments with Greta. But now they came flooding back as Morgan, as if playing a role for which Greta's ghost had rehearsed her, descended on him in some sort of reenactment of the last sexual act performed on him in Germany. He heard Morgan screaming, the same long shriek that Greta had uttered. Just as before, he was seized by an uncontrollable spasm of fear and remembrance, as if he was remembering his own death as it had happened in a former life. In mid-orgasm—the first time he had ever had a conscious thought at such a moment—he realized that, figuratively speaking, that was exactly what was happening.

He lay for a long time with his eyes closed. When he opened them, he found Morgan waiting. She was wearing her glasses; nothing else. He was too frightened to laugh.

"Hi," Morgan said in a clear Junior League voice he had never heard her use before. "Welcome to the country of the blind."

6 What followed, to Jack's surprise, was a week of impulsive lovemaking. Afterward Morgan sometimes had the face of a woman in love—of a woman long deprived of love and starved for it. She fucked, Jack told Whitlow when they settled their bet on Commencement Day, like a widow who lived with her mother.

Tender passion was not the only surprise Morgan had in store for Jack. The day after commencement, they were married in Boston by a perfunctory Unitarian minister. The old church was empty and stony cold, and the taxi driver and the church janitor stood up as witnesses. The clergyman said nothing about the holiness of matrimony. Instead he quoted Nietzsche on the subject: "The best friend is likely to acquire the best wife, because a good marriage is based on the talent for friendship." Though he depended on memory for everything else, the minister read these words from an index card. At the center of his stunned yet racing mind, Jack was sure that Peter, the broker of supernumerary friendship, had chosen these words and passed them to the clergyman via Morgan, his messenger.

Morgan wore a pantsuit, pearls at her ears and throat. She had cut her thick hair and dyed it back to its original dark-brown color; lustrous crow's wings now curled upward to touch her cheekbones. She was wearing her contacts. In the dim light of the church, falling through stained-glass windows, she looked quite beautiful, and as dreamy-eyed and sweetly victorious as any bride who ever took vows.

Three

1 Immediately after the wedding, Jack and Morgan flew to New York and thence to Barcelona. Morgan was thoughtful and silent on the night flight across the Atlantic. Jack did not ask questions. Below the wings of the plane, the Atlantic heaved in phosphorescent moonlight like some vast and stormy Styx. He was being delivered to his fate, and Morgan was Peter's Charon. It was as simple as that. He felt quite calm about this, quite resigned. After the cabin lights were turned off, Morgan covered Jack with a blanket, then put her head under the blanket. When, many minutes later, he groaned aloud, she kept on with what she was doing, but reached up blindly and covered his mouth with her hand.

They spent the day in Barcelona, lunching on the Ramblas, visiting the cathedral, wandering down twisted streets, before taking an afternoon flight to Palma de Mallorca. They took a taxi from the airport, Morgan giving the driver directions in fluent Spanish. Dark was beginning to fall when the taxi stopped at the gate to a white stucco villa. From the outside the house seemed as small as an American tract house, but once they were inside—Morgan opened the front door with a key—Jack saw that it was built into the face of a cliff, and that it was very large. They stood on a balcony overlooking a huge, two-story room that took up the entire reception floor of the house. Through a wall of glass, they saw the sun setting over the Mediterranean. The figure of a man, tall and slender, was silhouetted against the sunset.

The luggage Jack had carried down the path still dangled from his shoulders. "Ah, Jack," Peter said. "Already the overburdened husband."

He clapped his hands. A silent, unsmiling manservant material- ized and relieved Jack of the bags.

Peter said, "Ramón will show you to your quarters. Freshen up, but hurry back. We have a lot to talk about."

The bedrooms were on a lower floor, separate rooms at opposite ends of a long hall. Morgan seemed to expect this. Jack was sur- prised by nothing. He opened the window and saw that the wall of the villa dropped thirty feet to a heap of boulders. He could smell the sea, iodine and brine. He felt vaguely nauseated; his palms were sweaty. Though a brisk salt breeze poured through the window, whipping the curtains, he had difficulty breathing.

The reality of his situation overwhelmed him. Everything that he had willed himself to forget about Greta, about Peter, and now about Morgan, his lawful wife, poured back into his mind as if the sound of the waves had released him from a hypnotist's command to remember nothing. He was a prisoner, gazing helplessly out the window of a castle. He would never escape. His imprisonment was his own fault, all of it. Jack pounded the windowsill and said, "Stu- pid son of a bitch!"

He tried the door. It was unlocked. He tiptoed down the corridor to the door of Morgan's room and softly knocked. No reply. He tried the knob. The door was locked. He whispered Morgan's name. She did not answer.

2 They dined late, at a table laid with crystal and silver. Ramón appeared out of the darkness with a silver tray: cold soup, a large fish with the head still attached from which he dexterously cut and served portions with a large silver spoon and fork held in one hand. He wore anachronistic white gloves, buttoned at the wrist; there was a small hole in the index finger of the left glove. The food smelled and tasted of garlic and scorched olive oil. Jack did not like it but he ate everything, even the salad, which came last.

Morgan wore a long skirt and a scoop-neck silk blouse that re- vealed an inch or two of cleavage. Her table manners, formerly those of a motherless Stakhanovite, were now exquisite. In Peter's presence she was quiet, attentive, even submissive. Peter had per- mitted candles to be lit, and these burned in an ornate silver candelabrum. In the dark glass wall, as in a Velázquez come to life, Jack could see their animated images dreamily lifting forks and goblets. Morgan's reflection was eerily beautiful because her newly dyed mahogany hair was absorbed into the surrounding darkness. Her disembodied face seemed to float in midair, green eyes glowing in buttery medieval light.

Like an uncle taking an interest in things that he already knew, Peter asked questions about Jack's life in the years since their last encounter. Jack answered every one factually, sparsely, spinning no tales. His instincts told him to be very, very careful, but to show no fear.

"You've done extremely well," Peter said. "You've followed instructions to the letter. I'm pleased. So are we all." He nodded benevolently to Morgan, including her in the circle of his praise. "But all that was Stage One. Now you're no longer alone. Now the real work begins. The plan takes hold."

Peter paused, raised a finger. "This is very important," he said. "Your trust in Morgan is your trust in us. If that trust is weakened by doubt, the whole plan will fail. Do you understand?"

Jack nodded.

Peter said, "Aloud, please."

"I understand," Jack said. "But I have questions."

"Ask them." Peter sipped his wine, eyes alert over the rim of the glass.

Jack said, "What exactly *is* the plan?"

"I thought I had answered that question the last time we met," Peter replied. "A life for you in politics."

"With what goal?"

"I have already told you that. There are no limits."

Jack said, "Meaning what in the end, if all goes well?"

Peter said, "The White House, of course."

Peter delivered these words casually, as if this were the most natural answer in the world. Jack looked at Morgan. A look of serene belief, of calm confidence, had taken possession of her face.

Jack said, "You think this is possible, Morgan?"

"Yes, of course I do," Morgan said. "Why else would I be here?"

"You don't think we're going to have a lot of competition for this particular job?"

"Yes. But that's irrelevant."

"What is relevant is this," Peter said. "You want this. Am I correct?"

Jack shrugged.

Peter said, "Don't shrug in my presence, please. Answer yes or no."

"Yes," Jack said.

"Good. That's the starting point. You are electable. Not the slightest doubt about that. What you didn't have until now was the rest of the package—money and, above all, a powerful figure in the background who can make things happen for your benefit, who can make things come out right in your life."

Methodically, as if reading from a checklist, Peter outlined the life that Jack and Morgan would live. First, move to Columbus, Ohio. Morgan opens a business as a financial adviser and gets involved in liberal causes. Jack passes the bar examination and opens a law practice. He makes liberal noises but stays clear of liberal causes. After establishing a name for himself on the basis of Morgan's instructions, he runs for the first available public office, then for a higher one, followed by an even higher one.

"Timetable, twenty years," Peter said.

Jack blinked. "That's quick."

"You're twenty-six," Peter said. "Your father was elected at the age of forty-three."

Jack said, "You're serious, aren't you?"

"Absolutely serious."

"You do understand how much money this is going to cost?"

"Money is not a problem."

Jack smiled his full, charming, dead-eyed smile. "Okay," he said, "then let's get going."

Peter's expression changed. Jack, a student of faces, saw something in Peter's face that surprised him: relief. It came to him, as if written in the air by the spectral finger of his dead father, that he, Jack, had nothing whatsoever to fear or worry about. Peter needed Jack more than Jack needed him. And if Peter's plan actually did succeed and Jack did by some miracle become president, Peter's power to reveal how he got there would cease to exist. No one in the world would believe him, no matter what proof he offered.

Ramón poured champagne from a bottle wrapped in a napkin.

Peter raised his glass again. "To all our fathers," he said. "May we surpass them." Jack touched the rim of his glass to his lips but did not drink, but even so tiny an evasion did not escape Peter's notice. "Come, Jack," he said. "Be a little more filial. You must at least wet your tongue."

Jack drank. Peter watched him, as if the sparkling wine contained some secret ingredient that enabled him to see into Jack's mind. And as if reassuring a doubt he had read there, Peter said, "I mentioned your father for a reason."

"Which was?"

"To tell you I take this possibility seriously. And to remind you of certain historical facts. John F. Kennedy is a legendary figure now, a King Arthur, an Alexander, a figure for the ages. But that was not always so. For all his money, for all his charm, for all his genius, there was a time when he was regarded by the world as an upstart, as a lightweight with nothing to recommend him except a rich and powerful and laughably ambitious father. No one thought he could be elected to any office, let alone president, or be any good if he were. His own party laughed at him. Harry Truman ridiculed him and advised him to get out of the way of his elders until he grew up. He was his own father's second choice for a Kennedy president."

Jack said, "Who was *your* first choice, Peter?"

Peter never settled for a second choice. Morgan looked downward. Jack had stepped over the line. Peter smiled faintly, one eyebrow lifted. Finally he laughed, a wintry sound. "Jack," he said, "you're quite a fellow. Genes, I suppose."

Silence.

"Now," Peter said. "There's something I want to say to both of you about this marriage of yours."

Jack and Morgan waited.

"You understand that it must be absolutely platonic."

Jack said, "Absolutely *what*?"

"Free of sex. A sexual relationship would interfere with good judgment."

Jack glanced at Morgan. Her cheekbones were flushed. She stared into her dessert plate. She had known this all along. No wonder she had been screwing Jack cross-eyed for a week; it was her last chance. Jack gave her a long, slow, conspiratorial smile.

He said, "When do we stop?"

"Immediately," Peter said. "Morgan is your handler, you see. Being your wife is just a cover, a way to explain her presence in your life."

"My handler?" Jack said. "What exactly is that supposed to mean?"

"Let me answer that question in language that cannot possibly be misunderstood," Peter said. "You will do as your wife says in every circumstance of your life. Morgan's role is to act as the messenger between you and me. She is the link, the liaison, the go-between. For all intents and purposes, she is me. She speaks for me. She acts for me. She instructs for me. Money, advice, everything you need to succeed in your mission, will flow through Morgan."

Jack said, "Really? Then why do you need me?"

"You know why," Peter said. "You are the prime asset. Morgan's role is to protect you. You must stay clean, never handle money, never get involved in the details of getting elected, and never, *never* have contact with anyone, including me, who might compromise you. All plans, all benefits, all advice, will come through Morgan."

"Including women?"

"I'm glad you asked," Peter said. "The answer is yes. As you know, we are aware how strong your sex drive is and what it can lead to. You can have as much variety as you want, with one proviso: We provide the women. No outsiders. Is that absolutely clear, Jack?"

Jack said, "What do I do in case of emergency?"

He was grinning and shaking his head in disbelief. Morgan would not meet the merry glances he was sending her way.

Peter sighed. "Jack, I advise you to take this seriously."

Jack said, "I'm trying, Peter. But—"

Peter's urbanity vanished. "Enough. We have a long experience of professional marriages. They do not succeed if sex is involved. Their psychological consequences can never be anticipated or controlled. So it is forbidden between you. Absolutely, forever, and under all circumstances. You two are handler and agent. That is all."

"Fascinating," Jack said. "But it's hard to break a habit. What if we sleepwalk?"

Peter said, "Have you ever heard of János Kádár?"

"Yes. The Hungarian president."

"Prime minister, after the uprising in '55. In Moscow you seemed to be interested in the KGB and its Oriental mentality. Let me answer your question by telling you a true story about this famous organization. After the Red Army put down the Hungarian Revolution, the Russians made Kádár premier. But he was a ladies' man and he was inclined to question his instructions. So to make sure he concentrated on the job, and to make sure that he knew that they were serious, the KGB castrated him—completely. It was done by a surgeon, naturally, under anesthesia. When he woke up, he pissed through a plastic tube into a plastic bag for the rest of his life and never made any more difficulties. In fact, he seemed to love the people who had done this to him more than he ever loved his women. Do you understand what I am saying to you?"

Eyes locked, the boy and the man were silent for a while. It was Jack who broke eye contact; he felt it was expected of him. He nodded, completing the surrender.

Peter said, "Aloud, please."

"I understand."

Suddenly, Peter's face lit up in a brilliant smile. "Ah, Hedi!" he cried with real pleasure. "What perfect timing!"

In the glass wall, Jack saw the reflected figure of a tall, blond woman in a dramatic white dress. Light flashed from what seemed to be a diamond necklace. Jack rose to his feet and turned to look at this newcomer. She was young, voluptuous, perfumed. Morgan stared at her as if examining a cow that had wandered into the dining room. The woman ignored them both and floated toward Peter, arms outstretched.

"Peter, darling," she cried, kissing air.

Peter introduced her. Hedi was a Dane, an actress, a dear friend. As if meeting the man of her dreams, she clung to Jack's hand and gazed with swimming blue eyes into his face.

Peter looked at his watch. "My goodness," he said. "It's late, and Morgan and I have an engagement."

Hedi pouted.

"I'll make it up to you," Peter said. "I promise."

He put a fatherly hand on Jack's forearm and squeezed, a paternal gesture. "Jack," he said, "I wonder if I could ask you to see Hedi home. These sex-starved Spaniards do so annoy blond women who go out alone."

Hedi was smiling. Waves of scent rose from her hair, her skin. She was as perfect as a doll. Her ears, her nose, her every feature, were small and perfectly formed and impossibly smooth and white, as if her flawless maquillage had turned her face to porcelain.

"Will you see me home, Jack?" Hedi asked, saucer-eyed. "I'm terrified to go out alone. Peter is so right!"

Jack said, "My pleasure."

Morgan's face was a mask.

3 Villa la Nicha was, as you will have surmised, the very house in which the nymphet Greta had received her training as a Swallow. Morgan had been here before, too, but for more serious purposes. A couple of years before, she had cooled off in Majorca after killing a man in South America. This man, a psychopath whose idol was the Cambodian madman Pol Pot, opposed a certain plan of Peter's on ideological grounds.

This plan will play a certain role in the story of Jack Adams, so I will describe it here as briefly as possible. Ever since his days in Southeast Asia, Peter had seen drugs as a way to undermine, even destroy, the capitalists in America. He also saw it as a practically inexhaustible supply of funds for his more unconventional operations. The rise of the cocaine industry came at the same historical moment in which guerrilla movements—mostly inspired and financed by Peter through Fidel Castro's intelligence service—were ceasing to be effective. In Peter's fertile mind, this fork in the path of history presented a golden opportunity. At a remote location in Amazonia, he brought together the bosses of certain drug cartels and the leaders of certain guerrilla movements and proposed that they join forces. Peter's logic was irresistible. The cartels were already paying "taxes" to the guerrillas who agreed in return not to attack them. But what if the guerrillas went a step further and actively *protected* the cartels from attack by the army and police? This would benefit both sides. The guerrillas would go on kidnapping, assassinating, bombing as before, but now the cartels could designate targets of interest to themselves. Instead of killing indiscriminately, the freedom fighters could kill selectively, eliminating each threat to the cartels' business interests as it arose. The guerrillas, after all, did not care which enemies of the people they murdered, as long as they were enemies of the people.

Seeing realities and opportunities that were invisible to others was Peter's specialty. All present except one of the guerrilla leaders were in favor of Peter's visionary plan. The drug dealers might be inadvertent enemies of the United States, he argued, but they were also capitalists like any other. He would not pollute his movement by going into business with them. His opposition discouraged others, who knew that it was impossible to know what he might do if his advice was ignored. To him, a Marxist-Leninist was a Social Democrat with a gun. He would kill them as readily as he would kill an American tourist or a policeman. He himself was so closely guarded by his fanatical followers that he was regarded as being invulnerable.

In anticipation of this complication, Peter had arranged for the guerrilla chieftain to meet Morgan. His weakness, Peter knew, was turning left-wing American girls into sex slaves. In no time at all, Morgan won his confidence with jargon and his besotted gratitude for the astonishing skills that later made such an impression on Jack. On Peter's signal, Morgan removed this man from the picture, brusquely and permanently. After a tumult of passion, while he slept, she administered a certain poison in a most artistic way. This poison, made from castor beans and sulfuric acid, was then quite new to the secret pharmacopoeia. It produced death by inducing dozens of simultaneous ruptures in the vascular system, and was untraceable by any laboratory test then known to medicine. So imaginative was her method that there was not the slightest suspicion that the man's death was anything but a heart attack. Nobody even tried to blame it on the CIA.

With the ideologue out of the way, the rest of the freedom fighters agreed to Peter's plan. Morgan's deed had assured the financial future of his entire worldwide enterprise. Although she was only a beginner, Peter immediately promoted her to the rank of honorary captain in the KGB and bestowed a decoration on her.

When Jack Adams came along, she was the obvious choice as handler, conscience, and protector. Morgan accepted the assignment without demur. It was she who suggested the methodology: the impersonation of an aging Movement chick, the ambush at Harvard. She had already been accepted by the Harvard Business School, and her purposes in attending were precisely as she described them to Jack: penetrate the Establishment, capture its guns from the rear, and turn them inward against the defenders. She was the Trojan horse, Peter was Odysseus.

For all this I bear some responsibility. Morgan and I were old friends. She was one of the young Americans—like Arthur, like so many others—that I harvested out of the Venceremos brigade. From the beginning she showed promise. This was something of a surprise. Because the highly intelligent are usually also highly imaginative, a dizzying IQ is not regarded as a desirable quality in an agent destined for dangerous work. Someone like Jack, just bright enough, is the preferred material. Morgan was the exception. She was in every way an exception—that rarest of beings, an operative who was both imaginative and almost uncannily brave. She believed in her own intelligence and assumed that it would keep her alive in any situation. And unlike most brainy people, she took to discipline as a duck to water. We were exactly what she was looking for, and she already knew this when she came to us. In another time and context one would have said that she had the monastic temperament, and indeed she had certain saintly characteristics, including the psychotic impulse to repress, deny, and if possible kill her own powerful sexuality. Child of privilege and permissiveness that she was (her father was the head of a famous investment bank), she had been looking for certitude all her life. We provided it.

Morgan was, in fact, such a perfect fulfillment of our notion of the perfect agent that some suspected for a time that she was a CIA plant. Not I; she was too unreal not to be real. I saw in her not only a talent for tradecraft that was as great as Jack's talent for politics, but also that rarest of all qualities in Americans: seriousness and staying power and a belief that the benefits of discipline were in direct proportion to the incomprehensibility of its purposes. One example: In Cuba she had been permitted to take a lover, a Georgian who was an instructor of Swallows. She surprised him by her intensity, by her control. He could not break through to her. However, she broke through to him. After a few months, the Georgian told me that he feared that he was—he could barely speak the words— almost in love with her. This was a man who was irresistible to women, who had used them all his life, who had had no idea that any female could reach him sexually. Morgan showed him otherwise; like the good Communist he was, he reported this immediately. Abruptly, without explanation, they were separated. Morgan accepted this decision, which meant traveling in an hour from ecstasy to chastity, in exactly the way that a nun in hope of beatification might have accepted an order from her mother superior to give up all food except bread and water in the name of the Lord—obediently, humbly, happily.

4 After the dinner with Peter and Jack, and after Jack and Hedi had left, I switched off the monitor on which I had been watching their encounter over closed-circuit television and came downstairs to greet Morgan in the great room of Villa la Nicha. We kissed cheeks three times, Russian style.

I said, "Well, Morgan. What is your opinion of our Jack?"

The image of Hedi still lingered in her memory, so perhaps she answered more candidly than she might otherwise have done in Peter's presence. She said, "He's a hollow fool. A liar. An egomaniac. A child at sex, a child at everything. Except talk and politics, at which he is a genius."

"How nice he has a good side."

"All sides of him are good, considering the purposes Peter wants him to serve," she said. "He's the most likeable person I have ever met. *I* like him. Even knowing all that I know, even knowing that he means nothing he says, I like him. When he throws an arm around you, you believe that he's your friend. You love him. Afterward, but only afterward, you wonder why. But the feeling doesn't go away. You keep wondering but you also keep liking him. Everyone reacts to him in the same way—anarchists, Republicans, men, women, rich, poor, smart and stupid, straight and homosexual. Men whose wives he's seduced. Everyone likes him. It's amazing."

Peter said, "I take it, Comrade Captain, that you think that this operation can succeed."

Morgan said, "I believe that we can make this man president. But that he will be difficult to control."

"And you, Comrade Major," he said to me. "What are *your* expectations?"

Peter already knew my answer to his question, but I stepped up to my mark just the same and delivered my line: "Comrade General, with some reservations I accept the assessment of the comrade captain."

"State your reservations."

"I agree there is a very great danger, Comrade General, that this asset will prove to be uncontrollable. No matter who is handler."

"Why?"

"Because of his unstable character. And because of the historical precedents. He thinks it is his destiny to rule. If he becomes what you think he can become, he will thank his destiny, not us."

"An interesting thesis, Comrade Major." Peter turned to Morgan. "Your comments?"

"A question, Comrade General?"

Peter nodded benevolently.

She said, "Is there a fallback plan? Have you a lesser objective in mind as an acceptable final result—such as the Senate?"

Spacing his words, Peter said, "Understand me well, Comrade: Absolutely not."

"Good," Morgan said. "Because with what he has to hide and what he has to fear, he wouldn't last for a year in the fishbowl of Washington. Except for one place. The only place Jack can operate with impunity is in the best hideout in America—the White House." She paused. "May I speak frankly?"

Peter nodded.

"I just hope," Morgan said, "that your reference to the fate of Kádár will be enough to keep him in his own bed."

Peter did not smile. This was no joking matter. He said, "If you awake to find him in *your* bed, Comrade Captain, you will remove him. Then you will punish him. Your function is to provide the things that are lacking in Jack's character: judgment and conscience. You must be his superior. This will not be the case if you open your legs to him. Such a lapse of discipline would be unforgivable."

"I understand."

"Then be a wife," Peter said. "Keep an eye on him. Regard him like any other American husband, a creature that exists and labors and succeeds for the benefit of the wife who spends his money, manipulates his appetites, and controls his every action, word, and thought."

Morgan did not reward Peter with the laugh he had expected. Instead, just for a moment, she looked stricken to the soul. I thought I knew why, and I still think so even though she has denied it. What Peter was describing to her as her duty to the Party was exactly what she had joined the Party to escape: a bourgeois American life in which nothing was real, in which there was no passion, a life built on ruthless promotion of self-interest and the pretense of love and respect. In the name of all she believed to be holy, Peter had sentenced her to be what she was born to be and had sworn she never would be.

4

★ ★

The Cover Mechanism

One

1 During the years Jack Adams was completing his education and Morgan was passing through the various tests of piety and stages of betrothal that ended in her becoming a bride of Lenin and then the sister-wife of Jack, I kept busy providing for their future. Like most young couples with a well-defined goal in life, they required two extra advantages: money and influence.

Peter had promised money; it was my job to deliver it. This was no simple matter. Funding is the Achilles' heel of covert operations. There is good reason why *Follow the money and find the traitor* is an adage of counterintelligence. As Jack kept reminding Peter, the making of an American president requires huge amounts of cash. It is one thing to hand Jack Adams, the obscure student, five thousand dollars in fifties in a safe house in Moscow and have him sign for the cash with a thumbprint. It is another matter altogether to explain where Jack Adams the presidential candidate got the mountain of gold required to be elected to an office that pays $200,000 a year in salary in return for an investment in campaign costs of at least $150 million. This cost-to-earnings ratio helps explain why politicians in the world's greatest democracy have been reluctant to pass laws that require close scrutiny of the sources of one another's pocket money. But there are rules. For example, you must be able to present a balance sheet that does not arouse undue suspicion. I worried about this from the start. People take money seriously at the grass roots. The lower the office, the greater the scrutiny. Jack's career was far more likely to be destroyed at an early stage, when questions were asked about the $100,000 he would need to run for mayor or the $1 million that a gubernatorial campaign costs, than later on, when one could suppose that legitimate donations would be large enough to mask clandestine funds.

It all came down to mechanisms. Money had to be passed through bank accounts; there had to be an explanation for it. You will remember that Morgan had told Jack that she had a trust fund. This was an accurate statement as far as it went, but the trust fund did not come from her estranged parents, heartbroken Republicans who lived in discreet retirement in Arizona and never mentioned their lost daughter to the people with whom they played bridge and golf and drank martinis. It was I, Dmitri of the KGB, using a million dollars in cash provided by Peter, who set up the fund in Morgan's name, converting Peter's million into many small cashier's checks, which were then invested piecemeal in bonds and equities. In approved medium-risk Wall Street style, the million was split five ways and managed by three separate brokers: One fourth was invested in good old U.S. Treasury bonds, one fourth in large company stocks, one fourth in small company stocks, and the rest in foreign equities and cash. Then the fictitious but well-documented "owner" of these equities, a recluse who had been "living" in an apartment in Manhattan, converted them into a trust in Morgan's favor, vacated his lease, moved out his furniture, and vanished. So he was a little odd, but this was America. What he did with his money was nobody's business but his own.

In the early 1970s, before Jack and Morgan were joined together, the trust produced a so-so average annual yield of 12 percent, or roughly $120,000 a year. This was much more than Morgan needed to live on—she did not really give away money to the PLO and the Panthers, much as she might have wished to do so. I reinvested the surplus in good solid equities, and by the time Jack and Morgan set up housekeeping the capital amounted to a little more than $1.25 million. I was proud of my accomplishment. Morgan felt somewhat polluted by all this wealth. After all, she had divorced her parents and turned her back on her country precisely to escape from the power of money. "Maggots!" she said, expressing her opinion of dollars. I counseled her to regard our success as investors as yet another proof of Karl Marx's famous remark about money feeding on its own body; *yech*. After the marriage, Morgan took over management of the fund herself and, thanks to the things she had learned

at Harvard, quickly increased the yield. True as always to his instructions, Jack never touched this or any other money of ours, or
even asked about it. Morgan wrote all the checks for their house-
hold and provided him with pocket money.

As far as influence was concerned, Jack had an inexhaustible
trust fund of his own: that community of right-thinkers that Peter
called the Unconscious Underground. Such people manned the
junction boxes of influence and opinion in America. It was only
necessary to whisper in a dozen ears that a young progressive was
a comer to establish his credentials as one of the elect. Once he had
this toehold, Jack's talent for ingratiation kicked in. Everyone liked
him—or liked the personage Jack represented himself to be. He
never gave offense. His deep dislike of confrontation of any kind
was seen by many as just another sign of his inborn cowardice, but
the fact is, it is a quality that he shared with most men who rose
high in American politics. For example, both FDR and Nixon, non-
pareils of partisanship, were famous for it. It stood Jack in good
stead, and never more so than in the first week after he and Morgan returned from Majorca.

They went immediately to Washington, where Jack was faced
with a situation fraught with the possibility of serious, even career-
threatening embarrassment. As you know, Peter had instructed him
to go back to Ohio and establish a law practice. At once; no delay;
he had only twenty years to win the White House. However, there
was a complication. Jack had already accepted a position as an associate in a famous Washington law firm. The senior partner who
had hired him was a famous man, a man accustomed to getting his
way. A journalist with an indulgent editor had described him as "the
chambered nautilus of the Washington establishment—a ninety-
tentacled, night-feeding organism inside an impenetrable pearly
labyrinth." Jack's interview had been brief. He won the old man's
heart with his usual combination of eloquence, nuanced confession, and dazzling conversational improvisation. And, of course, the
haunting smile that his heredity had bestowed on him. The inter-
viewer saw in Jack a younger version of himself and hired him on
the spot at a starting salary higher than usual. "We're going to be
close, Jack," he had said in parting. "I want you right in the huddle
with me."

Jack had been recommended for this job by two of his law professors, and the nomination had been seconded by his senator. Jack had thanked his new boss and his mentors profusely and made promises of future hard work and fidelity. Now he had no choice but to inform the old man and his various sponsors who had put their reputations on the line for him that he had changed his mind. Another youngster might have made lifelong enemies of them all. Not Jack. He knew that all he needed was a reason based on the pretense of unselfishness that all these old men practiced as an article of political faith.

With the utmost sincerity, in person or over the telephone, Jack told them all the same story. At the last moment at Harvard, he said, he had found love with Morgan, and in finding it he had also found the courage to do the thing he knew was right.

First, he had to put aside the glittering prizes that his Harvard degree had won for him and go back to Ohio to start a law practice with his childhood friend Danny Miller. He told them the story of his friendship with Danny—how Danny had shared with him, stood by him, protected him, helped him since sandbox days. He described what had happened to Danny in Vietnam, described the meeting that fate had arranged at Walter Reed, described what Danny and the other horribly wounded men on the surgical floor had taught him about courage, sacrifice, and patriotism.

"I avoided the draft," Jack told them. "I thought the war was wrong and I thought resistance was the right thing to do and I'll never apologize for it. But Danny went, and he lost everything for this country that we love. I'm sorry, sir, but I owe my friend a greater debt than I owe anyone else in the world, and I just can't . . ." Here Jack would start to smile, then be stopped by the solemnity of his own words and thoughts, shake his head, and go on: "Sorry, but I just can't dodge the draft on this one."

Listening and watching Jack's performance, imagining a jury in Jack's hands, the old lawyer coughed into his handkerchief with real emotion. He said, "I admire you, son. But your gifts may be a little large for Columbus, Ohio. Don't you think you owe the rest of mankind something, too?"

"I guess in a way, that's part two of the story," Jack replied. "My wife wants me to go into politics. She says I might be able to help others who think the way that we do to change things so that what happened to Danny is less likely to happen in the future. I guess it's a forlorn hope, but what I'm giving up is nothing compared to what my friend had taken away from him. So I think I should try. I may even get elected to something."

The old lawyer shook Jack's hand. "Wouldn't surprise me in the least," he said. "Sorry to lose you."

"It would have been an honor, sir. I can't thank you enough."

"Nothing to thank me for," the old man said. "You say your wife's got an MBA from Harvard. Does that means she's a Republican?"

Now Jack did smile. "Far, far from it, sir. I've always tried to stay out of bed with Republicans."

A nod of the old white head. "Good luck to you then." The lawyer walked Jack to the door and shook his hand. "I've got a friend or two in Ohio," he said. "I'll give 'em a call. And godspeed to you, young fellow."

All the others to whom Jack delivered his news said the same.

2 Having completed law school in two calendar years by dint of attending night and summer classes in addition to the two regular academic semesters, Danny Miller had graduated from the Ohio State Law School at the same time Jack finished at Harvard. Neither he nor Jack had ever talked to each other again about the partnership Danny had proposed after Grandmother Herzog's funeral. Nevertheless, Jack called Danny from a pay phone as soon as he had bid the old lawyer farewell. In a matter of minutes the two friends agreed to open the firm of Miller & Adams in downtown Columbus. Jack would handle trial work, Danny civil cases. They would study for the Ohio bar examination together, just as they had studied for the law school admission test in the hospital ward.

Jack presented all this to Morgan as a fait accompli—and as an improvement on Peter's plan.

"Putting a Vietnam baby-killer between us is an *improvement?*" Morgan cried, heart pounding in her surprise. "It's a disaster."

Jack said, "What a way you have with words, Morgan."

"Call him back. Call it off."

"No."

"*No?* I said, get rid of him. That's final."

"Morgan, I need him. Danny's the key to the whole thing."

"I don't want to hear it."

"The answer is still no," Jack said.

The next day, on a park bench on the Mall in Washington, Morgan reported all this to me. It was a July day of equatorial heat. Morgan's face was pink because of that, and because of something coming from within her which closely resembled female fury with male disobedience. Defiance was the last thing she had expected from obsequious Jack.

"Not a word of warning, not a hint of discussion," Morgan said. "Can you imagine?"

Yes, I could imagine, early though it was in my life with Jack Adams. But I did not answer at once because I had my mouth full of food. I was eating one of the plump local hot dogs called a half-smoke, purchased for the occasion from a street vendor. The sausage was the all-clear signal: If I took a bite as Morgan approached, she could make contact in safety. As usual it was impossible to know if it was, indeed, safe. The Mall teemed with half-naked civil servants out for a jog in the midday sun. For all I knew, half of them were FBI agents. Many of the girls, bare-legged and sweaty in their T-shirts and shorts, were lovely. In China a naked girl, lying in a strip of golden sunlight, had quoted a line of poetry to me. *There is a maid for every honest civil servant:* Li Shang-yin, T'ang dynasty. It is a touching sentiment in Mandarin; not bad in English, either. For years I had thought the Chinese girl was dead, but then, by chance, I discovered that she was not, so perhaps the poet was right.

This was not the moment—supposing there ever could be such a moment—to share poignant memories with Morgan. I said, "This partnership was a sudden idea of Jack's?"

"No, that's the thing. It's a secret he kept from us. The two of them hatched the idea three years ago, at his grandmother's funeral. Or so he says. He didn't report that, either."

"He had no one to report it to."

"You're defending him."

"Merely pointing out the reality."

"Nevertheless he has blindsided us."

"True, but this way of life is new to him. He has no training. Tell me, what's the real problem? Are you angry over what he did, or over the fact that he did it without asking your permission?"

"Both."

"Choose the worse of the two."

I was stern—an actor playing the demanding father. This was necessary. Morgan was being emotional. Jack had been calculating. It was important that she understand which, in our work, was preferable.

Morgan flushed; she knew what I was suggesting. "That he did not ask permission," she said at last, a little short of breath.

"Ah. He has insulted your authority. So you are angry with him."

"No," she said. "That's not it."

"Then what *is* the problem?" I was demanding a confession. *Fuck you,* said Morgan's eyes, before she bowed her head. But she obliged: a matter of discipline.

"I've failed to control him," she said. "I'm angry at myself. Because I've failed."

Crumpling the paper in which the half-smoke had been wrapped, I said, "Let's look rationally at what Jack has done. And why he thought it was the proper thing to do."

Morgan said, "Isn't it obvious? He's putting an outsider between him and us. He has put the operation in danger."

"Is it? Has he? Yesterday Jack was a Harvard boy who dodged the draft. Today he is the partner of a wounded war hero who was one of the most admired athletes in Ohio. An American tragedy, a golden boy cut down by cruel fate, his greatest races never to be run."

Morgan, still the seething daughter, said, "He was a baseball player."

I was glad I hadn't shared my lost love's poetry with her. Morgan's single-mindedness, her literalness, her need to correct, to control, were formidable obstacles to sentiment. I had often told her so.

I said, "Morgan, try not to be so paranoid. Jack has done us a great favor."

"He has?" Morgan said. "I guess I must be too literal-minded to see that."

I said, "Comrade Captain, cut the girlish shit. React like an offi-cer, not like a child."

She flinched. Then she nodded, accepting the rebuke, and awaited further correction. Unlike Jack, she knew the rules. Longed for them.

I continued. "Let me explain. By joining up with Danny he has protected himself and therefore protected us. No one can hold his war record against him if Danny doesn't. He has made a very clever move. Danny *is* the key to the situation."

This was hard for Morgan to take. But she was not stupid, and at length she saw my point and accepted it. "You're right," she said. "On all counts. Thank you for your patience."

"And you were right, too," I replied. "He should have told you beforehand, consulted you. Why didn't he do so?"

Morgan—contrition never lasted long with her—looked me full in the face with a sarcastic smile that twisted her lips. Kindly, un-derstanding Dmitri, the smile said, leading a promising young offi-cer toward self-knowledge. But this was still a self-criticism session just the same.

She said, "Because he was afraid I'd say no. That I would not un-derstand his purpose. That I would get in his way."

"Very likely true," I said. "There's a lesson in this. As a handler, whenever you can, you must reward, not punish. You must make this asset want to please you."

"I understand."

Again the ironic smile. By making a nun of her, Peter had taken away nine tenths of her power to reward, and we both knew this. Even if he had not, the facts of this case might not have changed. Praise and reward, let alone apology, did not come easily to her. In-telligence and high energy did, and a love of results. Also anger, which was what she was feeling now despite the smiles. She was in love with anger. Even at this early stage I feared the conse-quences of these qualities in her more than I feared Jack's weak-nesses.

"It is not me but Jack you must strive to understand," I said. "Otherwise you haven't a hope of staying ahead of him."

"I'll do my best," she said. "But you said it first. He's essentially uncontrollable."

"That's why you must understand him in every way. If you cannot control, you must anticipate."

Morgan said, "Forgive me, but that's easier said than done. He doesn't think, so how can you anticipate? This guy is one hundred percent instinct. Hungry, eat. Horny, fuck. Talk, lie."

"That's what Peter likes about him—his intense humanity."

"Peter sees things that are invisible to ordinary mortals."

"Quite true," I said. "Remember that. And remember, too, that your job is to make what Peter sees in his dreams come true."

"I understand. But that will be difficult."

"True but irrelevant," I said. "You were chosen for this assignment for good reasons. Your strength. Your intelligence. Your loyalty. Your patience. Now go to Ohio, make friends with Danny, and carry out this mission."

There was nothing more to say. Morgan inhaled, exhaled, saluted again with one of her brisk nods. Then she leaped to her feet and with determined stride set out westward toward the Washington Monument, as if she were going to walk all the way to Ohio.

3 At a used car lot in Alexandria, Morgan bought, for cash, a two-year-old Volkswagen bus emblazoned with peace symbols and plastered with bumper stickers, the haiku of the Movement. She and Jack drove this underpowered death trap to Columbus. Within a week of arrival they had secured a mortgage on a modest bungalow near the Ohio State campus. It closely resembled the little house in which Danny and Cindy lived nearby.

With a certain sense of dread—remember, at this time we knew nothing of the tensions between Jack and Cindy, let alone the shameful reason for them—Morgan had anticipated a social life with the Millers. What she already knew about Cindy appalled her: a cute blonde who dressed like Barbie, stood by her man, went to church, made her own clothes, was an active Republican who worked for a law firm that represented banks, insurance companies, and every other kind of capitalist mechanism for repressing the masses. Not exactly Morgan's cup of tea. The fact that Cindy had graduated in the top 2 percent of her law school class did not impress her. Ohio State?

However, the couples did not get together. Steeling herself, Morgan called Cindy twice at her office to suggest dinner, but on both occasions Cindy said tersely that she'd have to call her back. She never did, and when Morgan tried again, leaving word with a secretary, Cindy did not return her calls.

Morgan asked Jack for an explanation of Cindy's behavior. "My guess would be that she doesn't expect to like you any more than she likes me," Jack said. "Let sleeping dogs lie."

"Sleeping dogs?" Morgan said. "What's between you two?"

"Danny."

"Is that all? Jack, are you keeping something from me?"

"On the contrary, I'm being as frank as I know how. Cindy hates me. She always has."

"Why?"

"I told you—Danny. She's a girl. She wants her man all to herself. Just one of those things, Morg."

He would say no more. In any case, Morgan had little time for social life. With her usual efficiency she had found a suitably seedy office on the edge of the inner city and opened her own business as a consultant to, and manager of, good causes. Through Movement contacts—nothing to do with us—she was soon deeply involved in political, feminist, and civil rights, consumer advocacy, and other activist groups. Chartering all these self-absorbed sects and orchestrating their obsessions kept Morgan busy seeing clients in the day and attending meetings at night, so Jack was left to his own devices most of the time.

Just the same, like the insecure and watchful bride that she was, Morgan called Jack many times a day at unpredictable times. In business hours she found him always with Danny. From nine to five, the friends studied together for the bar examination. Danny knew the law cold. He had found in it something that was almost as natural to him as sports had been. He loved the language of the law, its precision, its simplicity, its magisterial finality. Besides, memorizing codes and references had provided Danny with an escape from memories of combat.

In their bar exam study sessions, Danny was the tutor, Jack the learner. Jack, who had never wanted to be a lawyer, had learned only enough at Harvard to get him through exams that were generally graded by professors who wanted him to succeed. But Jack was nothing if not a quick study, and when the friends took the bar exam it was Jack who got the much higher mark, just as he had done on the law school admission exam and every other exam they had ever taken together. This outcome confirmed what Danny had always believed, that Jack was the smart one. And the lucky one.

He said, "Last week you didn't know shit, and now you finish in the top five percent?"

"Jes' lucky, I guess," Jack replied. "I've already forgotten half the answers. But I've got you, pal."

In high school, if Jack aced a math test after strenuous studying, he would forget all the theorems and equations soon afterward. There is no algebra in real life, he would tell Danny. No chemistry, no geometry. Just the green and the pink, moola and pussy, the more you had the more you got. Now, in their last hours as students, they sat around between study sessions, eating a large combo pizza for lunch and drinking Coca-Cola and Budweiser and recalling these good old jokes. Laughing. Danny had not been so happy in years.

In the evening, Morgan found Jack at home less often. He went to the movies, he told her. Walked around. Through his senator he was in touch with the local political establishment. He was getting to know them: drinks after work, gossip, skull sessions, sometimes dinner in a steak house with hundred-dollar bills flashing. But was that really all he was up to after dark? Morgan could never be sure. No sexual partners had yet been lined up for him in Columbus, and he never approached Morgan for relief. They slept in separate rooms, and he had never so much as tried the doorknob in the night—grounds for suspicion in itself, as she herself was often tempted to slip down the hall. Jack could not live without sex. Jack being Jack, that could mean only one thing: He was providing for his own needs.

Sex was not the only thing missing from their domestic life. Morgan would not cook as a matter of feminist principle and probably could not have learned how even if Yuri Vladimirovich Andropov himself had ordered her to report to the Cordon Bleu in Paris in the name of the Party to master the omelet and *tripe à la mode de Caen.*

The bungalow was a shambles of unmade beds, unwashed clothes; the refrigerator was empty. When Morgan did come home, she would bring a pizza—plain cheese or with mushrooms. Then as afterward she and Jack lived on pizza except at breakfast. Jack ate jelly donuts in the morning; Morgan, nothing but coffee.

Morgan and Danny saw little of each other. Even limited to glimpses, she recognized his charm. This made her even more wary of falling into the tiger trap of an incorrect friendship. When sitting down, as she usually saw him, Danny looked quite normal. But when he stood up and reached for his crutch, gripping the edge of the table with whitened knuckles, Morgan saw him as she imagined him to have been in Vietnam, reaching for his diabolical M-16 before firing a burst of tumbling bullets designed to mutilate and dismember freedom fighters.

Cindy's name was never uttered by either of the men. In her preoccupation with a growing circle of post-Barbie women, Morgan had all but forgotten that she even existed.

4 At home, however, Danny discussed Jack with Cindy. The conversations were always marked by anger. In Cindy's mind, the partnership between Jack and Danny represented betrayal, and the way in which they had planned it, deceit.

"How could you have done this behind my back?" she demanded.

"I didn't do it behind your back," Danny replied. "Ten minutes after his phone call, I told you the whole deal."

"*After* the phone call, without asking my opinion. When did you two first talk about going into practice together?"

"After his grandmother's funeral."

"That was three years ago. Why didn't you tell me then?"

"Why upset you?"

"Then you knew it would upset me?"

"Cindy, it was just talk. Why would Jack want to practice law in Ohio with me if he had a degree from Harvard? He could write his own ticket in New York or Washington. I was as surprised as you when he went through with it."

"That I doubt," Cindy said. "But let's just look at this for a minute.

When exactly did Jack accept this offer from Whiplash, Kickback, and Backscratch?"

Cindy was not trying to be funny; this play on words was her real opinion of the practices of the famous Washington firm, run by liberals for liberals, that Jack had been invited to join. Danny did not smile. He said, "I didn't ask."

"Recently, would you say? Like maybe in the last three or four months when the big-time firms usually visit the law schools looking for the real shits in the class?"

"Sounds about right."

"Okay. So at the time Jack didn't want to practice law in Ohio with his old pal Danny. Is that a reasonable assumption?"

"I guess so."

"And then he changed his mind and all of a sudden he can't wait to move to Columbus and hang out his shingle with his old high school buddy. So what happened?"

"He changed his mind."

"So he turns down a starting salary of thirty-five, forty thousand dollars in a Washington firm for the chance to earn nothing in Columbus, Ohio. Why?"

"Maybe he doesn't care about money."

"Ha!"

"Cin, what difference does it make?"

"A lot of difference. Maybe he told one too many lies and they got wise to him in the nick of time and passed the word, and he's out in the cold."

"Got wise to what? Come on, Cindy, this is a law firm we're talking about. What do they care about his veracity? Jack's imagination would've been an asset to them. Just consider the possibility that he's keeping a promise to me."

"You said there was no promise."

"Okay, an act of friendship."

"Altruism? *Jack?* Okay, let's go to scenario number two: Jack isn't keeping a promise to you but wiggling out of a promise he made to someone else and using you as his excuse. Would you agree that that's at least a possibility?"

"Come on, Cin."

"'Come on, Cin,' my eye. I repeat the question: Is it a possibility?"

"Yeah, it's possible," Danny replied. "But that's Jack."

"It sure is," Cindy said. "I don't know anyone else who'd stoop so low as to trade on somebody else's war wounds to get whatever it is he wants this time."

"Low blow, baby."

"*That's* a low blow? Let me ask you another question. Is there anything—anything—Jack could do to you that would wake you up to what a slime bag he really is and always has been and always will be?"

Danny said, "Was he a slime bag when he came to see me every day in the hospital?"

Cindy said, "Oh, Danny! Open your eyes."

Danny said, "Cindy, I know all about Jack."

"Are you absolutely sure of that?"

She was on the point of tears.

She lifted a hand, opened her mouth to speak, then let the hand fall helplessly to her side.

Danny said, "Cindy, what's really the matter?"

"Nothing," Cindy said, using a Kleenex. "Forget it."

"Jeez, Cin," Danny said, "That's a relief. For a minute there I thought you were going to tell me he raped you or something."

She paused, Kleenex at the corner of her eye. "No, Danny," she said. "I'm not going to tell you that."

5 On the Saturday night after the results of the bar exam were published, Danny invited Morgan and Jack to dinner.

Jack said, "Does Cindy know about this?"

"She'll be tied to her chair," Danny said. "Try not to notice."

Cindy was everything that Morgan had expected: Doris Day in her Rock Hudson period, without the sunny smile. The women made no eye contact when Danny introduced them. Cindy did not even look at Jack before she led them into the dining room. Their places were marked with name cards in Cindy's round, perfect penmanship.

In frigid silence, dashing back and forth to the kitchen, Cindy served zucchini soup with a touch of curry powder, eggplant parmigiana, tossed iceberg salad with halved cherry tomatoes and blue cheese dressing, and a frozen lemon dessert she had made in an ice-cube tray.

"Somebody must have told you I was a vegetarian," Morgan said. "Everything was delicious. Especially the eggplant parmigiana."

Cindy did not break her silence. She poured more coffee, then rose from her chair, cleared the dishes, and disappeared into the kitchen. Morgan put down her napkin and followed. With a bright smile, Cindy took the plates from her hands and slid them into the dishwater.

Morgan said, "It was a delicious dinner, but I think we'd better be going. Good night."

Cindy, washing the dishes, did not look up from her task.

Back in their own apartment, Morgan said, "Jack, tell me what this is all about."

"I already have," Jack replied. "The girl hates me. Always has."

"Why?"

"Competition for Danny? Penis envy? Morg, I don't think about it. It's been going on for years."

"Don't call me Morg. You're telling me this is nothing more serious than a case of a bride being jealous of her husband's best friend from high school? Bullshit, Jack. Tell me the whole truth."

"For what purpose?"

"You know the answer to that. This ridiculous situation is a threat to the plan. What happened between you two, Jack?"

"Okay. We had a little fling while Danny was in the army. I suppose she thinks it might happen again if we're living next door."

"A little fling?" Morgan said. "You fucked your best friend's lonely little wife while he was fighting for his country?"

"Girlfriend," Jack said. "At that time."

"Oh. That would make all the difference."

Under her relentless questioning, Jack told Morgan about the evening of Danny's departure. With each answer—she dragged the entire episode out of him detail by detail, as I have already de-scribed it to you—Morgan's eyes widened. At last she said, "And to you this was just another one-night stand?"

Jack said, "More like a one-hour stand."

"Jack, you raped her."

He was shocked. "Raped her?" he said. "She dug her heels in my back and came like a fire engine."

"She was drunk."

"That was her own doing. Just like what happened later. She started it. These things happen."

"And it was just that one time?"

"That's right. This is the first time I've seen her since the fateful night. As far as I was concerned, it was over the minute it was over."

"For you, maybe. Not for her."

"I can't help that," Jack said. "The moving finger writes."

Morgan said, "Jack, you really are a piece of work. Don't you ever touch her again. Do you understand?"

6 The next morning when Cindy arrived at her office building, Morgan was waiting for her in the lobby. Cindy tried to walk on by, but Morgan seized her by the arm.

Looking downward, Cindy said, "Let go. Right now."

Morgan held on for a moment, then did as she was told. She said, "You're not a deaf-mute after all. Good, because we have things to talk about."

"Like what?"

"The whole fucking situation."

Cindy said, "I don't like that adjective."

"That's a start," Morgan said. "We've just agreed on our first ground rule. No dirty words. Here's the second: If we can't talk in private, we'll talk in public."

"Why would I want to talk to you anywhere, about anything?"

"Because," Morgan said, "I know what Jack did to you."

They went across the street and sat down together on a bench by a parking lot. The conversation was surreal. Nearly everyone who parked in this lot seemed to know Cindy, and as they passed by, they smiled friendly Ohio smiles and said hello. Meanwhile, Morgan was describing the episode in the strip mine minute by minute, checking Jack's version.

"And then you got in front with him?"

"Hi, Cin!"

"He kissed you and you accepted it?"

"Hi, Cin!"

"He lifted your skirt, got between your legs?"

"Hi, Cin!"

"Even then you didn't say no?"

Cindy answered none of these interrogatories, but listened without expression, eyes steady, perfectly manicured hands folded around the handle of the briefcase she held in her lap.

"You didn't think you *had* to say no. You'd had a lot to drink. Maybe you didn't really want to say no. You were mad at Danny. And then Jack banged you, his best friend's girl. And it was different and you liked it in spite of yourself, and in the morning you just wanted to die."

A white-haired gentleman lifted his hat and said good morning to Cindy. She replied, "Good morning, Your Honor."

To Morgan, Cindy said, "Okay, now we know what the defense's cross-examination would be like. Is that all?"

Morgan said, "Not quite. No matter how it would sound in court, you were raped. We both know that. And I promise you, if he ever tries it again, we'll kill the son of a bitch together. I mean exactly what I say."

Cindy nodded. "Fine with me. And in the meantime, what?"

"I'm going to forget what I know."

Cindy said, "I sincerely doubt that."

"I mean what I say," Morgan said.

"Then you'd better get him out of town before you have to keep the promise you just made to me."

"Leaving town is not an option. That's why we have to understand each other."

"Then we'd better get to the other ground rules," Cindy said. "Bearing in mind that you've made the point you really came here to make."

"Which is?"

"That one way or another you can ruin my life, and it's up to me to choose the method."

Morgan did not contradict her. She said, "Suit yourself." She stood up. So did Cindy: every hair, every seam, every expression in place. Morgan said, "You're fucking immaculate."

Cindy turned on her heels. Morgan caught her arm again. Cindy said, "Under Ohio law, what you're doing to my arm is assault and battery."

"So call a cop," Morgan said. "But first, a word of advice. Get help. Deal with it. I know some good therapists."

Cindy said, "Lucky you. You'll need them."

Two

★ ★

1 The law firm of Miller & Adams prospered from the start. This had little to do, in the early stages, with us or our friends in the Unconscious Underground. It was Danny's admirers who jump-started the practice. As Jack had foreseen, the community was eager to give Danny a helping hand. The local establishment sent business his way—real estate closings, wills, divorces, minor lawsuits, juveniles in trouble, a steady supply of public defender work.

Morgan's one-woman office was located next door to the law firm, with a connecting door to Jack's office. She handled finances for Miller & Adams, which in return handled all the legal work for Morgan's growing list of eccentric clients. This involved a good deal of litigation, because her radical women were always suing corporations and societies and institutions of government on the theory that such lawsuits were revolutionary acts that, like a guerrilla war, simultaneously sapped the energy of the oppressor and opened the eyes of the people to the Establishment's crimes and to its essential and fatal weakness.

Morgan's people usually won these skirmishes. Danny was a meticulous researcher of the law, and Jack was every bit as good in a courtroom as his law school mentors had anticipated. He won or settled case after case, some of them all but hopeless on the face of the evidence. Jack was by nature undismayed by facts. He had an instinct for the telling human detail, for the confusing diversion, for the subtle distortion that seemed to reveal a lurking possibility of chicanery. Witnesses trusted him. Juries liked him. His powers of negotiation in out-of-court settlements were impressive; those whom he bested went away wishing he had been on their side. Meanwhile, Danny, who never made a promise he could not keep, was building up for the firm an aura of reliability and trustworthiness. For his part, Jack attached himself to the political powers in the community and state, and as his usefulness to them increased he too began to bring in a fair amount of business.

By the end of the second year of practice the partners were taking annual salaries of forty thousand dollars apiece. In those days that was an impressive wage for a young lawyer just starting out in Middle America. Added to Cindy's growing earnings from her own job, it was enough to enable the Millers to buy a nicer house in a suburban development. Morgan and Jack remained where they were, in their modest bungalow within a stone's throw of the slums, and within walking distance of the law offices of Miller & Adams.

Jack always walked to work, chatting with friends and introducing himself to strangers as he went. Jack walked everywhere, in fact, or took buses and taxis. For a time this had the effect of lulling Morgan's anxieties about unsuitable female companions. What chance for tomfoolery did a man on foot have in this possessions-driven society in which the only truly private space was the interior of an automobile? Jack's sex life, or the lack of one, preoccupied her from the start.

Peter's airy supposition that we could provide a man of Jack's insatiable appetite with women who could be trusted was based on Russian, not American, realities. Swallows abounded in the USSR, even in Western Europe, but in America the choice was limited to prostitutes and political hysterics, neither of whom were suitable for our purposes. Morgan could not scout for Jack without jeopardizing her own cover, and I was too far away to be useful on a day-to-day basis. Besides, I had my own cover to think about. Jack was not supposed to know of my existence, and at this stage of his career, he certainly did not know of it. I had no wish to weave a daisy chain between us for the future convenience of U.S. counterintelligence or, worse, the media. From the start I anticipated great difficulties in satisfying Jack's pathological appetite for women, but Peter's dispensations, like God's, did not take into account the convenience of his priests or acknowledge original design flaws. Lust is an excellent way to breed up a new species or a revolutionary type, but difficult to extinguish later on with a commandment.

At first, Morgan's periodic reports on Jack's private life were reassuring. He seemed to spend almost all his free time within a circle of about a dozen young professional males, doctors and lawyers, bankers and stockbrokers, executives and entrepreneurs. All were close to local politicians, all were Ohio-born; many, like Jack, had gone east to college and flirted with mock revolution and value-free fornication. None had served in Vietnam. Now that the war was over they had put revolution behind them and were devoting themselves to the accumulation of wealth. Danny was not a member.

They got together for a roundtable lunch at a downtown restaurant every day that they could make it, played racquet games with one another, met for a low-stakes poker game every second Thursday. They pooled their money to buy blocks of season tickets to the Cincinnati Bengals and Cincinnati Reds games, attending in groups of five according to a schedule decided by lot. They stayed overnight in Cincinnati if it was a night game. Their good-fellowship was a continuation of fraternity life, but with even greater exclusivity and secrecy. No one but the members, only twenty in number, and their wives even knew that the group had a name and dues, an oath and rules. They called themselves the Gruesome. Their ironic motto was Omertà: the silence of brotherhood.

Most, like Jack, were married to wives who were also members of the professional caste, so they had time on their hands. Four times a year, rotating houses, they got together as couples—bring-your-own-bottle barbecues and tag football in summer, Ohio State football games and tailgate parties in fall, potluck dinners and card games in winter. At these two-gender parties men talked to men in one room, women to women in another. Pot was smoked, the joint passing from hand to hand round a circle, and a great deal of white wine and beer was consumed. Jack, living as a celibate as far as Morgan could discover, seemed content, even glowing. This in itself was a cause for suspicion.

Morgan, playing the role of naïve pilgrim from the East, questioned the other wives about the real purposes of the Gruesome.

"It's Tom Sawyer's gang," one therapist-wife explained. "They look at centerfolds and drink beer and chew steaks and holler hoo-hah, but they're always in a group. It's when a man's alone with no witnesses that you'd better start worrying."

Morgan was not so sure. Gradually she had come to suspect the Gruesome, to believe that its outward camaraderie was a cover for hidden purposes—another of Jack's bewildering diversions designed to get him what he wanted behind a screen of co-conspirators. These friends of Jack had lived through the sexual revolution, the drug culture, the whole hedonistic street fair of the sixties. Every one of them had lied systematically to the United States government as a means of evading the draft and was proud of it. Why should anyone trust them now?

Reporting all this to me, Morgan said that she was deeply worried. "Character does not change," she explained. "Jack is a sex maniac for the first twenty-five years of his life and then becomes a monk? I don't think so."

"And if he's satisfying his needs in secret like half the husbands in America," I asked, "what then?"

"*You* ask *me* that question? It means he's vulnerable to influence, to blackmail, to control by others, and the operation is vulnerable to penetration. That's what it means. That's what Peter wanted above all to avoid."

The Gruesome also meant, if Morgan was right, that Jack was setting up his own networks, binding other men to him, building private loyalties, moving up on the basis of his own talents. Likewise what Peter wanted to happen.

I said, "On this, watch and wait. Let it develop."

"Is that wise?"

"Wiser," I said mildly, "than smothering the Gruesome in its cradle and having Jack replace it with something we don't know about and therefore have no hope of controlling."

This was a first principle of our craft: Better the enemy you know than the one you do not know exists. Morgan understood the reference.

"Very well," she said. But she was not happy.

This conversation took place in the Keystone Motel, beside a secondary road off the Pennsylvania Turnpike. We met in such places as opportunity offered. Her business with her splinter groups often took her to Washington, the Mecca of activists. As a demonstration of virtuous poverty she always drove to the capital in her Volkswagen bus and stayed overnight with a co-believer, usually in a sleeping bag on the floor of a cluttered, triple-locked flat on Capitol Hill or some other benighted neighborhood of Washington. On the way down or the way back we would rendezvous in Maryland or Pennsylvania or West Virginia, checking into separate motels in adjoining towns to avoid the giveaway of parking my nondescript, little-gray-man's car and Morgan's rolling billboard of McGovernism side by side in a motel lot.

I was not surprised by her fixation on Jack's sex life or by the way in which she rationalized her conflicted emotions as professional vigilance. Just as a real wife will regard adultery as a menace to the marriage, a destroyer of trust, a threat to the financial and social safety that are her rights, so did Morgan regard Jack's hidden sex life—whose existence she could not prove—as a danger to the operation. And the operation was everything to her.

She told me this over and over. For all the subliminal reasons just stated, I believed her. But I also thought that Peter had made a great mistake in not providing for Morgan's sexual needs, and a worse one in supposing that we, or anyone except the late Greta Fürst, could keep up with Jack's. Those who do not marry for desire will fear desire as an enemy. If that is not a Russian proverb, it ought to be.

For the moment, there was nothing to be done about this, but as I observed Morgan's agitated state, which so closely resembled that of a neglected and suspicious wife, I knew that the error must somehow be corrected. That would take time. Not to mention the most sensitive approaches to Peter. Meanwhile the best course for Morgan was to push onward along the path of her suspicions. Even if this Gruesome was not the adulterers' workshop Morgan thought it was, it was worth looking into. Besides, her suspicions were taking up too much of her time and energy. I sought, therefore, to channel them.

"I see your point," I said, after listening to her report. "We can't have Jack belonging to a secret society, compartmenting himself from us. Look into this more deeply. Bring me a list of names of Gruesome members with the usual biographical details and personality sketches, credit ratings, debts, habits, addictions, allegiances, anything that might be buried in the past. Photographs."

Most of this information would be easy enough for Morgan to obtain. Her business gave her access to credit ratings, academic records, applications with their recommendations and evaluations, goods purchased, magazines subscribed to, insurance policies and medical records pertinent thereto. Police records, court records, licenses, were all public records. The life history of every American is thrown, bit by bit, into this great whirlpool of information. The process is disjointed, inadvertent, but most secret police agencies elsewhere in the world would salivate over such a treasury of disjointed gossip from which they could assemble the scarecrows so dear to their imaginations. She could take snapshots at the next barbecue. Still, it was a daunting assignment for a busy person.

"There are twenty members of the Gruesome, Dmitri," Morgan said. "And just one me."

"And twenty wives," I replied. "Some of the other girls must share your doubts. Make friends with a suspicious wife, strengthen the suspicion, and you're halfway home."

"That will take time. I haven't made an effort with the women."

"Then make one. Go slowly; stay in character. Some of your clients must know some of the Gruesomes and their wives. Mine every source. I'm prepared to be patient. This is important, not just for the present but for the future."

There was a touch of exaggeration in this, but basically, as always, I was telling Morgan the truth. Her demeanor changed. Now she was alert, professional, with a head full of schemes. She had been given permission to do what she wanted to do—ferret out that which she already knew in her heart must surely exist, evidence of Jack's shenanigans. This would keep her busy and happy for months. And who knew? It might produce something useful; the friends Jack was making now would, like Danny, be with him for the remainder of his life.

But at bottom it was only jujitsu, a trick of balance, a way of seizing control of Morgan's emotional momentum and propelling her in the direction in which she wanted to go. It was clear that she was inexorably becoming what she was pretending to be, a wife. Even after the metamorphosis she would still be a fanatic. And for that condition there was no remedy in Peter's philosophy—or yet discovered in the history of the world.

2 Jack, an early riser, was always the first to arrive at work, and on the morning after my meeting with Morgan, while she was driving westward in her Volkswagen toward Columbus, he arrived at Miller & Adams to find a young woman waiting for him in front of the locked office door. She was a little too plump for her best dress and there were fresh signs of motherhood on her person—a yellowish stain on the shoulder of her peach-colored jacket, the sweetish aroma of regurgitated milk. But behind all this, as in a yearbook photo, Jack visualized the small-town beauty she must have been not so long ago.

She smiled, the American curtsy, and said, "Are you Attorney John Fitzgerald Adams?"

Jack had started using all three of his names as soon as he entered practice, but in private he was the same informal Ohioan as before. "I'm Jack Adams," he said with a brief grin.

"I recognize you from TV," said the young woman. "I'm Mrs. Phil Gallagher. Teresa."

"Ah," said Jack.

Phil Gallagher, a police lieutenant, had been arrested the night before by his own men, who had discovered him in the backseat of his cruiser with a fifteen-year-old girl in his lap. The cruiser was parked in a secluded spot. The girl was naked. The media had taken pictures of the arrest.

Teresa Gallagher said, "You've seen the news this morning?"

"I have," Jack said, "and I'm sorry for your trouble."

"Thanks," Teresa said. "Can we talk?"

He unlocked the door and showed her into his office, arranged by Morgan to impress clients like Mrs. Gallagher: Harvard diploma, handsome old desk that might be mistaken for an heirloom, well-worn leather furniture, oriental throw rugs, soft-focus picture of a most photogenic Morgan, reproduction of a Matthew Brady portrait of Abraham Lincoln, group portrait of the *Harvard Law Review* staff with Jack front and center, framed replica of the Bill of Rights, campus towers in the single window. This client was slightly ill at ease, alone with a strange man in a deserted office suite. Jack put the desk between them and left the door open.

"If you've seen the news," said Teresa, "I guess I don't have to describe the problem to you, thanks to those sons of bitches."

Nodding as if he, too, knew the sons of bitches well, Jack said, "Have you talked to Phil since he was arrested?"

"Finally, over the phone about an hour ago. I called before when he didn't come home at the usual time. They said they had him in a cell, that was it."

"They wouldn't let you speak to him?"

"They said he was too doped up to talk. That's when I knew what was happening. The bastards had got to him, just like they always said they would," she replied.

"Who exactly are the bastards?"

"The wops and the dirty cops, who else?"

"I understand," Jack said. "But, Teresa, let's not use those words again. Even between ourselves."

"Whatever you say, but that's who it is," Teresa said. "And what Phil told me was, he doesn't have a chance."

Jack looked at her for a long moment, and then he said, "We'll see about that."

Teresa never forgot these words, spoken with an easy confidence that reassured her to the heart. In years to come she would quote them to the world in many interviews and campaign ads. "And after he told me that," she would go on, "Jack Adams put his arm around me like a brother and gave me that wonderful smile, and I knew that there was hope." And then she would go on to say that Jack's words and the way he said them made her think that he had been just waiting for the chance to save her innocent husband from life in prison and their children from a lifetime of poverty and shame.

In a way Jack had been doing exactly that, because as soon as he heard about the Gallagher case on the morning news he realized that it was the chance of a lifetime. It was the breakthrough case he needed. It would make his name, provide him with an image, give him an issue that would leapfrog him into public office. If he could win Gallagher's acquittal, and he was sure he could.

The facts were stark. When the arresting officers arrived on the scene, they found Gallagher with his pants around his ankles. He was out of his mind after taking LSD, and more LSD of a particularly potent variety was found in the pocket of his uniform. His service revolver lay on the floor of the cruiser. The girl said she had been raped and sodomized at gunpoint by Gallagher after he arrested her on a dark road for driving without a license. Footage of the terrified girl being placed in an ambulance and of the stupefied lieutenant, babbling and thrashing in the throes of his bad LSD trip, being handcuffed by his own men had been the lead story on the morning news.

In Jack's office, Teresa Gallagher said, "They did it up brown. I told Phil they'd get him sooner or later. You can't fight city hall."

Several years before, as an idealistic young patrolman just out of college, Phil Gallagher had spied on corrupt cops by pretending to be one of them. He had provided evidence to a grand jury that led to the indictment and conviction of several policemen on charges of consorting with and accepting what amounted to a salary from a local Mafia figure called Fats Corso.

A few months after the rogue cops went to jail and Fats Corso went free on a hung jury, a reform mayor was elected, largely on the strength of promises to clean up the police force and put Corso behind bars. He immediately ordered Patrolman Gallagher's promotion to lieutenant over the heads of many senior men, an action that provided the new mayor with a front-page picture of the hero cop, but assured Gallagher of the undying hatred of most of the rest of the police force. As long as the reform mayor was in office, Gallagher was untouchable. Unfortunately, the mayor had been defeated for a second term.

Jack said, "Did Phil give you any details about what happened last night?"

"What little he remembers," Teresa said. "He said he pulled into the school yard to drink coffee from his thermos. All of a sudden this girl raps on his window. She's got no clothes on except white tennis shoes."

"He remembered that detail?"

"Wouldn't you? Phil puts down his coffee and gets out of the car. The girl runs away screaming. He thinks she's probably on drugs. Naturally he chases her. It's very dark in the school yard, and as he goes around the corner of the school somebody trips him."

"Who?"

"Not the girl. She's way ahead of him, running like a deer."

"And?"

"That's all he remembers, falling ass over teakettle."

"He was knocked out by the fall?"

Teresa said, "Come on, Jack. How could he be? Somebody whacked him on the head."

Her voice was firm and, with its hard-edged Ohio diction, absolutely clear. No tears, no sign of nervousness. Yet her face was a mask of desperation. A jury, Jack thought, would believe every word if she took off ten pounds.

Jack said, "Let me ask you this, Teresa. Do you believe what your husband has told you?"

"Every word."

"Do you always believe every word he tells you?"

"No." Teresa's intelligent blue eyes snapped with anger. "But let me ask *you* a question," she said. "Do you believe a man who was smart enough to fool them all for two long years and then send them to jail like they deserved would be stupid enough to let himself be caught in a situation like this? Knowing what enemies he has? Knowing they've sworn to get him?"

"Not really," Jack said. "I'm sorry if I upset you, but—"

"It's not you I'm upset with," Teresa said. "Now I ask you, will you take the case?"

For the moment, Jack did not answer. This was not because he had not made up his mind, but because he was already, in his mind, addressing the jury. He got up and looked out the window, as if pondering his decision.

"I have to tell you we have no money," Teresa said to his back. "I mean, none whatsoever. No savings. All we have is Phil's paycheck. We rent. The car is eight years old. We've got three kids under school age and I just missed a period. They'll stop Phil's pay. God knows how much the bail will be."

"Forget about money," Jack said.

"What does that mean?"

"It means I'll take no fee and we'll find the money for expenses elsewhere. Put money out of your mind."

"Then you'll do it?"

Jack was the picture of sincerity. He said, "I'll do my best for you, Teresa."

Now tears did appear in Teresa's eyes. She wiped them away with the back of her hand.

Jack said, "Did Phil know when the preliminary hearing is going to be?"

"Tomorrow morning at ten," Teresa said. "They slipped him too much dope for him to appear sooner."

"I'll see you there," Jack said. "Don't talk to the cops. Be nice to the media if they call, but don't discuss any of the details of the case or repeat anything Phil told you. Just say you know your husband is completely innocent of any wrongdoing and let it go at that. No accusations of a frame. No wops and cops. Count to ten before every word. Don't let them see anger. Let others be angry for you."

"Who, for instance?" Teresa said.

"You'll be surprised," Jack said. "Now go home to the kids, and I'll go talk to Phil. I'll see you tomorrow morning at the hearing."

3 After Teresa left, Jack called a reporter friend who had been at the scene of the arrest and had written the lead story about it for his paper.

"One question about the Gallagher business," Jack said. "Where did they find the girl's clothes?"

"Let me check," said the reporter. After a moment he came back on the line. "In the girl's car," he said. "Are you taking this case?"

"One more question. Did you happen to look at the knees of Gallagher's pants?"

"Before or after he put them back on?"

"After."

"No, but I've got some pictures here." He looked at the photos, Jack could hear him slapping them down on the desk one after the other. Finally he said, "Here it is. The pants were torn at the knees."

"Like he fell down on pavement? If you blew the picture up, could you see if his knees are scraped?"

"Maybe. Are you taking this case?"

"Yes."

"What's the gimmick?"

"Gimmick?" Jack said. "There's no gimmick. Phil Gallagher's an innocent man."

The reporter said, "Sure he is. All the signs point that way. Especially the fact that he had a hard-on the size of a three-cell flashlight."

"You have pictures of that?"

"This is a family newspaper. But that's what the other cops said."

"'That's what the other cops said,'" Jack repeated. He said, "Let me ask you a question, Glenn. Do you think an honest man like Phil Gallagher, a hero cop who has laid his life on the line for what's right, a guy who has powerful enemies, bad cops and notorious criminals who will stop at nothing, would be stupid enough to rape and sodomize a fifteen-year-old girl at gunpoint in the back of a police cruiser, on a public street, while under the influence of LSD? And if he did, that he'd still have it up after all that?"

"Good line, but the question is, will a jury believe Gallagher's enemies would be stupid enough to set him up in such a crude and obvious way? A lot of people would say the situation is so unbelievable that it can't be anything but the truth."

"That contingency is not covered by the rules of evidence," Jack said. "Juries know the truth when they hear it."

"That must be why they fuck up as often as they do," said the reporter. "They hear it so seldom. You're going to have to prove this guy's innocence, Jack. Reasonable doubt won't be enough."

"My client will be acquitted because he is innocent," Jack said.

"Oh yeah," said the reporter, typing away. "Good luck, counselor."

He hung up without saying goodbye. But he was pleased that Jack, a Harvard man, wanted to hear his opinion, and he was betting on Jack to win and hoping that the dirty cops who hated Gallagher would lose and be humiliated, and all that came through in the story that he wrote for the next day's edition.

Every news organization in town, plus the wire services, sent a reporter to Phil Gallagher's preliminary hearing. The defendant, now wearing county jail coveralls instead of his blue uniform, was an upright, handsome man, but he was disoriented by the drugs he had taken, and he had not shaved in two days. The day before, Jack had talked to him for about an hour but had learned little more than Teresa had told him. Gallagher remembered falling, remembered pain. His knees and hands were skinned like those of a child who has taken a fall on a sidewalk. He remembered not being able to breathe.

Jack showed no curiosity about this detail. He said, "When was the last time you fired your service revolver?"

"Last Monday, on the range."

"When did you last clean it?"

"Same day."

"Has it been out of the holster since?"

"No. Because of the kids I lock up my whole harness in the hall closet as soon as I get home."

"What about the LSD?"

"The only thing I can figure," Gallagher said, "is someone slipped it into my thermos."

Jack said, "Like a police officer who had just confiscated LSD while making an arrest?"

The judge disallowed the question, but it was already on the record with the media, which was all that counted. Gallagher was charged with rape and forcible sodomy of a minor, resisting arrest, assault with a deadly weapon (the arresting officers said that the drug-crazed Gallagher had fired his pistol at them before they wrestled it away from him), and several other felonies and misdemeanors. If convicted on all counts he faced life in prison, almost certainly without possibility of parole. Gallagher pleaded not guilty to all charges. The prosecutor asked that bail be set at $200,000, but after a conference at the bench he did not press the point when the judge, at Jack's suggestion, released Gallagher without cash bail but confined him to his own home under what amounted to house arrest.

Jack asked for certain tests to be carried out on Gallagher by the crime lab unit of the Ohio State Patrol, and not by the local police. These included saliva, urine, and blood tests, close-up photographs of the accused's knees and elbows and palms and forearms, a wax test to determine if he had recently fired a pistol, and a complete medical examination, including physical and X-ray examination of the skull and a search for recent bruises or punctures of the skin on any other part of the body. He also asked that the court forthwith take custody of and place under seal all evidence so far gathered in the case, including any blood or urine samples already taken, and all of Gallagher's personal belongings, especially his uniform, his thermos, and his service revolver. The judge granted all these requests.

These unexplained requests made excellent copy and raised many questions in the minds of journalists; as Jack knew, their questions would soon become the questions of their readers and viewers.

Outside the courthouse, Jack told the cameras and microphones, "The truth will be discovered in this case. I promise you that. And the truth is, Phil Gallagher is a hero in war and peace who can stand on his own two feet in any court in the world. The truth is his friend just as the forces of darkness are his sworn enemies. Phil Gallagher is an innocent man. Phil Gallagher will be free. Justice will be done by the great state of Ohio and its people. That's all we have to say at this time, ladies and gentlemen."

Phil Gallagher, standing beside him, shaved now and dressed in blue jeans and a winter jacket, said nothing. As Jack had earlier instructed him to do, he put an arm around his wife, as if afraid for her safety.

4 Morgan arrived home from our meeting in the Keystone Motel in time to watch Jack's statement on the noon television news. She was outraged. Jack had taken the case, devised his strategy, and splashed himself all over the media without consulting her.

In her agitation, short of breath, she looked out the window. Down below was Jack, bantering on the sidewalk with a little pack of pencil reporters who had walked back from the courthouse with him. As he talked, they scribbled in their notebooks. Because of her training, because of her true auspices and secret purposes, Morgan felt a pang of anxiety. She feared the press, feared its curiosity, its stupidity, its moralism. Below her window a perfectly relaxed Jack smiled, looked serious, joked, insinuated, charmed. She thought it was folly to let journalists come so close.

One of the reporters was a thin young female with a soft-lipped vulnerable face. Morgan knew the type: Ten years ago she had gone to demonstrations, a copy of Che's memoirs held title outward against her chest, not to fight for the cause but to meet boys and sniff tear gas from afar. To outward appearances, Jack paid no more attention to her than to the others, but Morgan knew Jack. His eyes were on this female, and she knew it. The interview ended. The reporters scattered. She stood on tiptoes—miniskirt, skinny legs, windblown hair—and hailed a cab. As she got in with flashing thighs, she gave Jack a shy smile.

"Jesus!" Morgan cried, closing the door of Jack's office behind the two of them.

Jack said, "Hi, Morg. How was your trip?"

Morgan said, "You're all over the goddamned television."

She never swore among strangers anymore, but now she was swearing at Jack in the harsh half-whisper she used when talking to him in the office. Danny sat on the other side of a thin partition, working on his wills and trusts and torts.

Jack said, "Practicing law."

"Oh, is that what you call this sideshow? You didn't think you should consult me on something as public as this?"

"You think lawyering is too public?" Jack said. "What do you think the future's going to be like?"

Morgan said, "This is now. You've exceeded your instructions. Behind my back. This is very serious, Jack."

"Well, gee, Morgan," Jack said. "I'm sorry I slipped the leash, but I wasn't exactly in control of the timing. You were on the road, no phone number. It was an opportunity to be seized."

"A rapist cop? Take on the Mafia and the police?"

Jack said, "Wops and cops."

Morgan said, "This is not a joke."

"No, it's a breakthrough case. I'm going to defend this guy, and I'm going to get him off, and we're going to reap great benefits from that."

"Jack, for Christ's sake. He's a pig. An enemy of the people. You're going to save a cop? A cop that raped a child?"

"Why not?"

"What planet are you living on? You can't fulfill this mission by fighting for the wrong side."

Morgan was close to Jack, still whispering, waving her arms. Jack seldom touched her, but now he captured one of her flying hands and held it between both his own hands.

He said, "Morgan, honey, I'm sure you're absolutely right about everything and I've made a terrible mistake, but it's too late to do anything about it. No matter how badly I've fucked up the plan, I've got no choice now but to win this case. If I lose it, I'll never recover. So give me a break, okay?"

"And if you do win it?"

"It will cut five years off the schedule."

"Oh, really?" Morgan tugged at her hand.

Jack held on for an instant. He said, "Really. When you're calmer, I'll explain."

Accusation still smoldering in her eyes, Morgan drew a long deep breath. She said, "Okay. What do you want from me?"

"Two things," Jack replied. "Money—"

"What a surprise."

"—and the support of your loonies."

"My *what*?"

"Just kidding," Jack said. "The support of the good people— how's that?—for a good cop, unjustly accused by the forces of evil, whose acquittal would do more damage to the image and power of the corrupt police than anything since Attica."

"Come on."

"Think about it. Yesterday, before he was framed, Gallagher was a hero cop. Save a hero, be a hero."

Morgan was calmer now—oddly, Jack had that effect on her when he talked political realities—and theoretician that she was, she suddenly saw the same possibilities he saw, and even greater possibilities beyond those. Peter was right about this guy; Peter was always right.

She said, "Okay. It's a go. How much money will you need?"

"About twenty grand for an investigation by private detectives, expert witnesses, and so forth. I'm forgoing a fee."

"So I heard on the tube. And what kind of support do you need from my loonies?"

Her lips compressed in a sardonic quarter-smile. Jack grinned; he had won. He was relaxed now, big oxblood wingtip shoes on the desk, hands clasped behind his head. "Demonstrations, plac- ards, pressure on the press, posters, pamphlets, speeches, phone campaigns, a woman at every meeting in the city demanding jus- tice and an end to the link between the Mob and the cops, until the trial."

"That's easy."

"I don't mean zealots' meetings. I mean PTAs, missionary societies, the mainstream."

"That can be done. I'll write a check."

"No. It has to be raised from the people. Quarters, crumpled dollar bills, small checks from fearful widows." Jack smiled. "I even thought of a name for the fund-raising operation." He wrote it on a slip of paper.

Morgan smiled, shook her head. Giggled. "I love it," she said.

"Atta girl," Jack said. "And I've got another idea. Phil and Teresa Gallagher are all alone with their kids in the house. Who will protect them? The Mafia is out there, also fascist cops. What if you organized a round-the-clock vigil, a circle of women around the house, protecting a sister?"

Morgan's eyes widened in admiration. She said, "You are a once-in-a-lifetime motherfucker, Jack. Really you are."

That same day an organization calling itself the Greater Ohio Oversight Defense Coalition Opposed to Police Corruption (GOOD-COP) posted four women sentinels, the first of hundreds who would keep watch day and night outside the Gallaghers' modest rented home. With more exposure in the media, GOODCOP collected about thirty thousand dollars in the first week of its appeal. This was enough to disguise the additional twenty thousand that I later passed to Morgan in cash.

"If ever there was a case that should be fought pro bono publico—for the public good—this is it," Jack told the reporters who walked to work with him almost every morning now. "And compared to what Phil Gallagher did for the taxpayers a few years ago, forgoing a legal fee is nothing."

5 It was months before Gallagher's trial began, but by seeding the media Jack kept the case alive in the public mind. On opening day, hundreds of the curious waited in line for the handful of available seats that had not already been allocated to journalists, including network camera crews from as far away as New York City. Jack did not disappoint them. In a courtroom filled with lambent April light, he turned the trial into a replay of the David and Goliath story.

"Ladies and gentlemen of the jury," said Jack in his opening statement, "Fats Corso is the man in the shadows who lurks outside every decent home in our community, looking for men, women, and children to corrupt and victimize with his drugs, his gambling, his prostitution, his whole portfolio of crime and evil. Fats Corso is the man in the shadows who is trying to trick his neighbors into sending a clean cop, a hero cop, a cop who is one of us, to prison because he exposed Fats Corso's connections to dirty cops."

Jack said all this, and much more, in a tone of calm reason. As he spoke, he positioned himself in a diagonal beam of sunlight. Speaking without notes, head thrown back, perfectly at ease, he seemed to be breathing in golden words from the very sunshine and then breathing them out again for the spellbound jury. The David and Goliath image was magnified by the physical appearance of the prosecutor, a big clumsy Republican named F. Merriwether Street who was six feet six inches tall. Street introduced a parade of policemen and expert witnesses who established, item by item, the seemingly damning evidence against Gallagher. On cross-examination, Jack showed that the officers who arrested Gallagher were not responding to a call but had "happened" on the scene, which was several miles from their assigned patrol area. A witness had noticed Gallagher's thermos lying on the front seat of his cruiser, whose door was open. When Jack showed the witness, a plainclothes nun who worked in the inner city, three similar thermos bottles, she chose the correct one.

Jack's exchange with one of the arresting officers, Patrolman Randy Sebring, was the keystone of his defense:

JACK: Officer Sebring, you have testified that Phil Gallagher was in the backseat of the cruiser when you arrived at the scene, that he had a naked young lady on his lap, and that his service revolver was on the floor of the backseat. Is all that correct?

WITNESS: Yes.

JACK: Was the back door or any door of the cruiser open?

WITNESS: No.

JACK: All four windows rolled up and locked? All four doors, too?

WITNESS: Yes.

JACK: The door opens from the outside but not the inside? Cannot be opened from the inside, standard police cruiser without inside door handles, designed to make sure dangerous criminals can't just open the door and escape? Got a screen between the front seat and back so the perpetrator can't get out that way?

WITNESS: Yes.

JACK: Officer Sebring, I find that fascinating. Let me ask you this: Why do you suppose Lieutenant Gallagher would get into the backseat of his own cruiser with a naked young lady, knowing that he couldn't get out?

WITNESS: I don't know.

JACK: Was Lieutenant Gallagher wearing his hat?

WITNESS: What?

JACK: You have testified that Lieutenant Gallagher resisted arrest and was subdued by you and your partner after a violent struggle in which he fired his revolver. Is that correct?

WITNESS: Yes.

JACK: I show you a photograph made by a news cameraman at the scene of this incident on the night in question. What is happening in the picture?

WITNESS: It looks like we're putting the cuffs on the subject.

JACK: What is that on Lieutenant Gallagher's head?

WITNESS: A cap.

JACK: Is it standard police procedure, after subduing a suspect in a violent struggle, to put his hat back on his head before handcuffing him?

WITNESS: No.

JACK: Officer Sebring, isn't it a fact that there was no struggle to get Lieutenant Gallagher out of the cruiser? And isn't it a fact that you and your partner picked an unconscious Phil Gallagher up off the ground where he had fallen after being tripped? And didn't he fall several yards away from his cruiser, near the school building? And isn't it also a fact that you or your partner, or both of you, then searched in the darkness until you found his cap, which had fallen off when he was tripped, and that you then jammed his cap back on his head and carried him, limp and unconscious, back to his cruiser, where you hastily handcuffed him as you observed the approach of the news media?

WITNESS (glaring in anger): No!

JACK (after a silence): Tell me, Randy, did you two fellows slip LSD into his mouth then, or was the LSD somebody put in his thermos of coffee enough to do the trick?

PROSECUTOR: Objection—

JACK: I withdraw the question.

An expert witness confirmed Gallagher's story from scientific evidence. There were traces of LSD in Gallagher's thermos bottle. Gallagher's fingerprints were not on the packets of LSD found in his pocket.

WITNESS: There were no fingerprints of any kind on Gallagher's service revolver.

JACK: What does that suggest to you, Dr. Garrett?

WITNESS: The possibility that the weapon had been wiped clean of fingerprints.

The wax test on Gallagher's right hand and arm, designed to show whether he had recently fired a handgun, was negative. There was a bruise on the back of Gallagher's head that was consistent with a blow from a nightstick or blackjack. Fragments of asphalt and slag removed from scrapes on his knees, elbows, and palms matched similar material from the school yard.

Jack then called the head of the vice squad, who testified that the mother of the fifteen-year-old girl, a woman named Whisper Fisk, had been arrested twenty-three times in the past ten years for prostitution. She worked as an exotic dancer and hostess in the Blue Grotto, a bar and restaurant where Fats Corso spent most of his evenings. Although the Blue Grotto was legally owned by Corso's two sisters, it was widely believed that Fats was the real owner.

JACK: Lieutenant Karp, I will ask you this: To your official knowledge, has the name Domenico D. Corso, also known as Fats Corso, ever been linked in any police investigation to the illegal practice of prostitution in this city?

WITNESS: Yes, sir. Fifteen times from 1933 to 1945.

JACK: How many times did these charges lead to trial and conviction?

WITNESS: Never.

JACK: Why was that, Lieutenant?

WITNESS: Insufficient proof.

JACK: Isn't it a fact, Lieutenant, that Mr. Corso runs prostitution in this town?

WITNESS: I couldn't swear to that, sir.

JACK: Will you swear now, before this jury, that Mr. Corso does *not* run prostitution in this town, and was not running it every time Whisper Fisk was arrested for soliciting for prostitution?

WITNESS: I couldn't swear to that, either.

JACK: Was Whisper Fisk ever released on bail after being arrested for soliciting for prostitution?

WITNESS: Yes.

JACK: I hand you an abstract of the records of the Municipal Court in regard to all such charges against one Eleanor R. Fisk, also known as Whisper Fisk. Will you read the name of the person who furnished bond in each and every case?

WITNESS: It was always the same person, Domenico D. Corso.

The jury deliberated for forty-two minutes before acquitting Lieutenant Phil Gallagher on all counts. Jack immediately filed a $50 million civil lawsuit against Fats Corso on the Gallaghers' behalf.

6 Walking to work the following morning with a large retinue of reporters, Jack was asked by a writer if he was going to forgo his share of the judgment if he won.

"The money is meaningless," Jack said. "I just want to get Fats Corso under oath."

The writer was from New York. His profile of Jack, "Young Man with a Future," ran the following week in a national magazine. Jack was interviewed on *Good Morning America* and on two network magazine shows. Jack was completely at his ease in a television studio. The camera liked him: It was at this point that it began to be noticed that Jack had the quality, common to stars, of looking better in pictures than in life. Jack knew that the media's attention span was fleeting, and that hot as he was, he would soon be replaced by

someone hotter. But he had become part of the media's consciousness, which meant that they would revisit him in the future. In
commercial breaks he made friends with the producers, who would
remember him. He was unfailingly polite to the smiling, overdressed interviewers, all of whom asked him the same five questions, usually in exactly the same words, as if they were all wired to
some invisible mothership that was whispering into their earpieces.

Through Gruesome contacts, Jack had already made friends with
the governor of Ohio. A week after the Gallagher trial, he was appointed counsel to a new Governor's Task Force on Organized
Crime. He immediately called for an all-out investigation of Corso.
His position gave him access to most of the state's files on Corso.
Jack leaked selected bits of this confidential data to investigative reporters. The material, like most raw investigative files, was mostly
gossip and hearsay and the rancorous accusations of enemies who
believed that their identities, if not their words, would remain secret, and for that reason it made excellent newspaper copy. Although Jack was never identified as a source, his name and picture
popped up in the stories.

So notable was this burst of notoriety and its consequences that
Peter himself attended my first post-trial meeting with Morgan, at a
picnic table in a roadside park in West Virginia. We lunched on Kentucky Fried Chicken, for which Peter, epicure though he was, had a
secret taste—as did the vicious, tiny blackflies that plagued us.

"Jack," said Morgan, "wants to change the plan."

Peter never registered surprise, but Morgan's words caused him
to close his eyes in momentary displeasure. Finally he said, "In what
way?"

"In almost every important way," Morgan said.

"Continue," Peter said.

Morgan did so, in her most neutral voice. Jack had never accepted the slow, rung-by-rung climb up the political ladder that
Peter had envisaged for him. Local offices, being close to the people,
were not stepping-stones but stumbling blocks; most people elected
to city councils or even to mayoralties never rose higher. That was
because petty officials had a duty to resolve petty disputes, and
there was no better way to make political enemies. Jack's plan was
different: make a splash with a big early success, claim an issue that

lets you pursue an enemy of the people, and as soon as your name is big enough, run for an office that seems to be out of your reach. Jack had attorney general of Ohio in mind, then lieutenant governor, then governor.

"This will take less than ten years," Morgan said.

"He can do it?"

"He thinks so," said Morgan. "And he may be right. Look at the record. He's made a big splash; he's a media figure. He has his issue, Jack Adams, Nemesis of the Mob. And he has an enemy the whole world loves to hate, Fats Corso. The personification of evil, the demon who wants to make every child a dope addict, every little girl a hooker, every father a helpless slave to gambling."

"Is that an issue that will make a president?" Peter asked.

"Issues don't make presidents," Morgan replied. "Publicity does."

"Brilliant!" Peter's eyes welled with sudden admiration. "Is that your phrase?" he asked.

"No, it's pure Jack."

The blackflies were swarming around our heads. With frantic gesticulations we batted them away, slapping one another to kill them; had the FBI been watching from a distance, we would have looked like three deaf people having a violent argument. I did not want to prolong the conversation, but I felt that a devil's advocate was needed.

I said, "I join in the admiration. Jack is clever. Jack is good. But what this shows is, he is beginning to think he doesn't need us. He is putting himself in a position to succeed without us. It would be a mistake to let him have what he wants in this case."

"Even if what he wants is to our advantage?"

"That's the question. Is it? Or is it his way of slipping the leash? This is a serious issue of handling."

To my surprise, Peter immediately agreed, although it took him a long time to respond because he was deep in thought. "Very well, he has played leapfrog with us," he said at last, with a slight excess of English idiom. "And now we must show him that turnabout is fair play."

He then described how Jack was to be taught a lesson. Reminded of the leash. For the first time since Majorca, Morgan looked her original radiant self. This was the work that she liked: action, deception, violent shocks to the system. Secret results that were mistaken for something they were not.

7 By football season, when the Ohio consciousness focused on the gridiron, Jack had turned Fats Corso's life into a living hell. The remorseless publicity that had enlivened the slow-news summer months had forced a police investigation. Bored detectives and sheriff's deputies in parked Fords, not to mention an occasional team of dapper FBI agents in somewhat better cars, joined the media shock troops who swarmed around the Mafia chieftain. He seldom ventured outside without being pursued by shouting reporters.

Fats rarely stepped out onto the pavement without sending a scout in advance. Georgie Angels, Corso's driver, usually played this role. If the coast was clear, Georgie would go back and knock on the door. Corso would then emerge, white fedora pulled down over his eyes, and walk with leisurely step toward his snow-white Cadillac Brougham, which was always parked at the curb. It was evident to onlookers that this nonchalant, unhurried pace was an effort, that Fats's nervous system was ordering his body to scuttle for cover while his street smarts were commanding it to remember who it was and not show anxiety. There was something perversely sad about this spectacle of a hit man terrorized like a moth by klieg lights, and something mysteriously American about it, too. Fats's nickname was a cruel joke: He was and always had been painfully skinny, with knobby knees and elbows and a large spherical skull, and when he was chased down the street by shouting reporters, his great pumpkin head bobbed heavily on its fragile stalk of a neck.

The Cadillac was equipped with a special remote-control device that permitted Corso to start the engine from a distance of several yards. Instantaneously, in response to a radio signal, the powerful motor would fire, the radio would switch on, and, if it was night, the car's headlamps and interior lights would come on, too. When all this happened a look of pride and happiness would flash across Fats's skull-like face. He loved this gadget.

One morning just before dawn, an hour when Corso was seldom bothered by journalists and the cops tended to be asleep in their parked cars, Georgie Angels conducted his usual surveillance. He failed to note a freelance television cameraman who was shooting with a long lens from the roof of the building across the street. Believing himself unobserved, Georgie knocked on the door of the club as usual. Fats Corso immediately emerged, remote control in hand. When he pointed it at the parked Cadillac, it blew up in a huge fireball, sending parts of the car spinning above the rooftops and shattering every windowpane in the deserted block.

The shock wave blew Georgie Angels backward into Fats. The fall broke Fats's left leg and dislocated vertebrae in his neck. Georgie Angels suffered a scalp wound that transformed his coarse but handsome movie-mobster face into a mask of blood. This made a page 1 newspaper photograph that was even more dramatic than the footage of the actual explosion that the cameraman sold to every station in Ohio, and many others across the country.

How did the cameraman happen to be there at such a dramatic moment? "I just had a feeling," he said. "So I threw a couple of cameras in the car and went on down to the Blue Grotto."

Actually he had been tipped off by an anonymous caller, but because he was, at least technically, a journalist, his improbable explanation was accepted without question by the rest of the media.

Naturally Jack was asked, during his morning walk the following day, for an opinion. He said, "Maybe the rest of the boys are getting a little nervous about Fats Corso."

"How about you, Jack? Does this make you nervous?"

"Why should it? Nobody has sent *me* any flowers."

The reporters laughed. This was a reference to a page 1 picture in that morning's newspaper, showing Corso in his hospital bed, long meager leg in traction, neck in a brace, surrounded by banks of floral tributes and baskets of Italian delicacies whose combined cost was estimated by the newspaper at not less than two thousand dollars.

Jack's quip made the noontime news and went out over the wires. That evening, when he arrived home, he found a large horseshoe of white lilies on his front porch. The gilt lettering on the red ribbon read, *Good Luck, Jack.*

Jack's viscera leapt and twisted; as always in moments of extreme fright, he tasted vomit. And as always he kept his composure in front of the newspeople. He posed for pictures with the wreath, even made a joke or two. But once inside the house he gave way to terror. Memories of gunfire and mayhem escaped from the psychic attic in which Jack had locked them and came tumbling down the stairs of his conscious mind: blood, noise, flying glass, flame, Greta's dance with death. After many frantic phone calls he finally reached Morgan at an abortion rights meeting. She listened in silence to what he had to tell her.

After a moment she said, "Get a grip on yourself, Jack."

In a trembling voice Jack replied, "Get a grip on myself? Thanks a lot. I mean, that's really a big help."

"Jack, what makes you think that wreath came from the Mafia?"

"Who else would it have come from? Lilies, Morgan. *Lilies.* It's got Mob written all over it."

"Jack, stop," Morgan said. "Corso is in traction, for God's sake. He's the one who's scared shitless."

Jack's heart rate slowed. He took several deep breaths, pumping oxygen into his system as Danny had taught him to do years before. Morgan could hear this over the wire.

Jack said, "I'm alone here, you know."

"Well, Jesus, Jack, what do you want me to do—send a SWAT team of women to join hands around the house?"

Jack hung up and dialed Danny's home number. He had to look it up because he had never called it before; it was part of Cindy's deal with Danny that she would never even have to talk to Jack or Morgan over the phone. Cindy answered.

Jack said, "Danny Miller, please."

Of course Cindy recognized his voice. There was a silence. After a moment, Danny came on the line. In his mind's eye Jack saw Cindy, cold and angry, handing the phone to Danny without a word. Jack told Danny what had happened.

Danny laughed. Then he said, "Be right over."

When Morgan got home, she found Jack and Danny in the kitchen, playing gin rummy. All the doors were locked, all the shades were drawn. The horseshoe of lilies was propped up in the kitchen sink, as if it were a joke, but at the same time it blocked the kitchen window, the only window in the house without a shade.

Morgan said, "Hi. Who's winning?"

"Jack," said Danny, a mild slur in his voice. Half a dozen empty beer cans were strewed on the tabletop.

Morgan said, "Do you need a ride home, Danny?"

Jack said, "I'll ride along."

Morgan and Danny exchanged a look. Danny said, "I'll be fine."

He heaved himself to his feet, and with the smile—half affection and half exasperation—that he reserved for Jack in his friend's weak moments, he gave Jack's shoulder a little shake of reassurance.

8 After Fats Corso's Cadillac blew up in the early morning and Crime Fighter Jack Adams was so blatantly threatened with bodily harm by the Man in the Shadows, the county prosecutor at last impaneled a special grand jury to look into the many possibilities of indicting Corso. This prosecutor was F. Merriwether Street, the tall, plodding man who had been Jack's adversary in the Phil Gallagher trial. Street's decision to go to a grand jury was, in theory, a secret, but Jack learned of it from his sources in the Gruesome. Street had sewn up the Republican nomination for Ohio attorney general, and the grand jury was his way of grabbing the credit for busting the rackets. He had won office the first time on Nixon's coattails, and to everyone's astonishment had been reelected over a smart, perhaps too smart, liberal.

Street was planning to announce the grand jury on a Monday in late November. On the Sunday before that, Jack ran into Street in the stadium men's room line at halftime of the Michigan game; Michigan was winning again. This was a matter of indifference to the inner Jack, but outwardly he was as glum as everyone else in the shuffling queue of cursing, disgusted Ohioans. Street was standing behind Jack, so several minutes passed before Jack turned around and saw the prosecutor staring down on him from his six foot six inches. His look was cold and contemptuous, as if he had recently blackballed Jack's application for membership in the country club and there was no possible way of Jack ever finding this out. Street was deeply conscious that he and Jack were from opposite ends of the social spectrum. He had gone to Harvard as an undergraduate, then to law school at Ohio State, as had his father and grandfather, who were, respectively, founding partner and managing partner of Street, Frew, Street & Merriwether, a most prestigious local law firm. He was a member of Porcellian. He did not consider that people like Jack and Morgan, who held graduate degrees from Harvard, had gone to the real Harvard.

Jack said, "Hi, Merriwether. What took you so long?"

A cold droplet of silence. Street said, "To do what?"

"Move on Corso."

A long cold stare from Street. "I have no idea what you're talking about," he said.

Jack said, "The special grand jury. Smart move."

"I can't discuss that, Adams. Or didn't they explain that at Harvard Law School?"

Jack smiled. "I guess I was asleep that day," he said. "Help me out, Merriwether. What made you decide to get into the game in the fourth quarter?"

Apart from an intensified coldness of manner, Street did not reply.

Jack said, "I thought maybe the car bomb got you excited."

Street spoke at last. "Why should it?" he said. "Going back to the thirties, there are 167 unsolved bombings in this county."

Jack, who knew that newspaper editors love a good number even better than a demagogue does, felt that he had struck gold. He said, "No kidding? Is that an actual statistic?"

Street compressed his lips in a parody of a smile and responded with the briefest of nods.

Jack said, "That's amazing."

The line had shuffled forward while they spoke, opening a gap between Jack and the man in front of him. "Close it up!" someone shouted. Jack paid no attention; he did not understand the military expression, or so Street thought. Street had served during the Vietnam War as a navy lawyer at the Pentagon while Jack was hiding out from the draft. He knew all about Jack, or thought he did. "Close it up!" the same man shouted again. Street made a shooing gesture with his long fingers and Jack moved up.

Turning around again, Jack said, "By the way, Merriwether, you got away after the Gallagher trial before I could tell you this, but I thought you did a good job."

"Did you now?" said Street.

Jack said, "Yeah, I did. But I always wondered: Why did you bring charges in the first place?"

"Because," Street replied, "Gallagher was guilty."

Jack said, "Oh. If that's what you think, no wonder you're pissed off at me."

"That doesn't exactly describe my feelings," Street said. "Your defense was a travesty. A travesty, Adams."

"Wow," Jack said, "what a burst of eloquence. Are you always such a good loser?"

On the field below, bugles and drums played a Broadway melody in triple time. The tinny music, distorted and seemingly far away because of the stadium acoustics, wafted to their ears. Street turned his head and gazed at the concrete wall of the men's room, as if able to see through it and perceive the musical rednecks in their gaudy uniforms and the bare-legged small-town girls waving banners and twirling batons as they dashed up and down the muddy playing field.

"Not to change the subject," Jack said, "but I hear my partner's wife is going to be working for you in your campaign."

Jack had heard no such thing, and as far as the world knew Street was not running for anything. But Cindy Miller, who worked in obscurity for Street, Frew, Street & Merriwether, was a Republican activist, so Jack had taken a wild guess. The look on F. Merriwether Street's long-jawed narrow face, which ordinarily was about as expressive as a locust's, told him that he had hit the mark. Two closely held secrets betrayed in a single day! Street's lips twitched again, and then without answering he left the line.

Watching him go, clumsy and easy to read as he waded through the crowd, grinning broadly and shaking hands with half-drunken members of the Great Unwashed whose fingers he would not have touched except in hopes of a vote, Jack thought, *I can beat this guy anytime I want to.*

9 A day or two after the game, having done some research of his own, Jack mentioned to his favorite reporter that there had been 167 gangland bombings in and around Columbus, all unsolved.

"How do you know?" the reporter asked.

"Merriwether Street told me," Jack said. "He counted them up, and I guess it occurred to him that maybe the Mafia had something to do with this mysterious string of explosions. Like, it wasn't the Luftwaffe after all."

Jack's devastating wisecrack and the 167 unsolved gangland bombings dominated the next morning's stories announcing the special grand jury. Later in the day, F. Merriwether Street's secretary called Cindy Miller and informed her that she would not be needed in the campaign after all.

Over pizza that evening, Jack told Morgan that he had decided to run in the Democratic primary for the office of Ohio attorney general. The post was now held by a Republican who could not run again. If Jack could win the primary, F. Merriwether Street would be his likely opponent in the fall election.

"That's a big if," Morgan said.

But she knew in her bones that Jack could win. Her job was to make sure he understood he had done so with a little help from his friends.

10 Three weeks before the Democratic primary, Jack was five points behind the leader, a prosecutor from Cleveland who had the support of the party organization. Jack's campaign had already spent a hundred thousand dollars of our money (in well-worn small bills). Another thirty thousand dollars or so was raised from bona fide donors, mostly Morgan's uncombed and unreformed radicals, who otherwise kept themselves out of sight. Nevertheless they were optimistic that one of their own was going to win real power. Jack had fought his way upward in the polls, and the media were saying that he had the momentum.

Then, at a Gruesome affair, the governor took Jack aside for a private word. With an arm around Jack's shoulders he told him how impressed everyone was with the race he had run.

"You've done an amazing job of building your name and building a base, starting from zero," the governor said. "You're going to fall a little short this time, Jack. But everybody in the party knows who you are now, and your day will come."

Jack said, "But I'm going to win, Governor."

The governor tightened his half-hug. "Not this time, Jack," he said.

"What are you saying to me?"

"It's time to step back, Jack."

"Step back? What's that supposed to mean?"

The governor gave his shoulders a fatherly squeeze. "Sometimes, Jack," he said, "you get a better view of the future if you step back a little. You've got a brilliant future. Brilliant. But this is now."

Jack understood. "You want the guy from Cleveland to win."

"It would disappoint a lot of people if he didn't, Jack."

"It would? Why is that?"

"Jack, Jack. He's Polish. Our party is home to the Polish. You know what they say: Home is where they've got to take you in. Pukaszewski's got a right."

"What if I win anyway?"

"It would be hard for the party to accept that, I'm afraid. Or forget it."

"Even if I can't help it?"

"What do you mean by that, Jack?"

"I don't see how I can guarantee I won't win unless I take my name off the ballot. And it's too late for that."

The governor dropped his embracing arm. "Jack, Jack, Jack," he said, sadly shaking his head. "We've got to be able to count on you."

Jack knew what he was expected to say. He said, "I hear what you're saying."

Jack's words were not exactly a promise and the governor knew it. Jack thanked him humbly for his interest and advice and went straight home to Morgan.

"They want me to go into the tank," he said.

After listening to his story, Morgan said, "If you win, the party will never give you another chance."

"That's what they told John F. Kennedy when he tried for the vice presidential nomination at the '56 convention, and they said the same when he went for the presidency in '60. But when he won the big one, they forgot they ever said it. They *denied* they ever said it."

218 ★ CHARLES McCARRY

"So what does that say about you?"

"That I need the same things Kennedy had: ruthlessness and money," he said. "Especially money. We need more money."

"We've already spent more than we can explain. It's risky. And money may not be enough."

Jack said, "Money is always enough if there's enough money."

"What about the ruthlessness?"

Jack said, "You get the money. I'll take care of the ruthlessness."

11 When Morgan told me all this at an unscheduled motel rendezvous (arranged by a system of clandestine signals so clever that it would take a page of type to describe them), I said, "I think Jack has just coined his motto."

"What's that?"

Laughing, I said, " 'Money is always enough if there's enough money.' Maybe he really is a Kennedy."

I heard no answering laughter. Morgan, a bloodstream Camelot romantic, did not like jokes about the Kennedys, even coming from a Russian. Coldly, she said, "Maybe. What about the money?"

"What is he going to do with it, exactly?"

"Go on television. A blitzkrieg of ads for the final days of the campaign: Jack the giant killer."

"Won't that annoy the governor?"

"Yes. Jack doesn't care. The moment has come, I think, to save Jack from himself. But when?" Morgan said. "It has to be soon."

"Today is Tuesday. Friday."

"No. Saturday is a lousy news day. Sunday night. The story will open the week and just keep going."

"Very well. You know what to do? There can be no rehearsals."

"I know what to do," Morgan said.

"Just don't warn Jack. His fear has to be real or the camera will see he's faking."

"No need to worry about that," Morgan said. "Jack will win the Emmy for most convincing coward."

Naturally, I had brought some money with me—the eleventh-hour cry for help had been anticipated. This time I gave it to Morgan in a picnic cooler under a bed of congealed ice cubes. She kissed me. Oh, Daddy!

219 ★ LUCKY BASTARD

Actually, I felt quite paternal, as I so often did where Morgan was concerned. Like a father, I wanted her to be happy. Like many a handler before me, including Judas Iscariot, I was beginning to love the agent more than I loved the operation, a bad sign that I did not recognize at the time, or until long afterward.

12 On Sunday night—actually at three o'clock Monday morning—Jack woke up, gasping for breath, to find Morgan in bed with him. He always went to bed first, and he knew he had been asleep for some time. He was naked between the sheets, as was his habit. He started to speak, a delighted "Hey!" Morgan had awakened him by pinching his nostrils shut, and now she placed a hand over his mouth. With her other hand she showed him, in the feeble streetlight falling through his bedroom window, a bundle of clothes.

"Pajamas," she said. "Get up. Put them on, quick. Then get back in bed."

"Put them *on*?"

Morgan nodded emphatically, showing him a finger on her own lips before removing her hand from his. He did as he was told. Back in bed, Morgan, her long body also encased in pajamas, lay on her back beside him and took his hand. He tried to guide it. Morgan resisted, shaking her head.

"Cut it out," she whispered. "There's somebody in the house."

Jack sat bolt upright. " '*Somebody in the house*' ?" he whispered.

"Jack, shut up. Lie down. It's okay."

"It's *okay*?"

He could hear the intruders now, moving about in the darkness, opening and closing doors. "Call the cops!" He fumbled with the telephone on his bedside table, dropping the receiver. When he recovered it there was no dial tone. "Oh my God!" he groaned. "They've cut the lines!"

Having been reminded so recently of the horseshoe of lilies—Jack's friends in the media had referred to the famous death threat in the Sunday paper—he was even more conscious of danger than usual. Somewhere inside the house someone worked the action of a pump shotgun, a bloodcurdling sound. Jack leaped in fright.

Morgan hissed, "*Lie still.*"

They heard a different mechanical sound, at first unidentifiable.

Jack listened intently and said, "They're pulling down the window shades. We've got to—"

Morgan clapped her hand over his mouth. Suddenly (but how could this be possible?) all the lights in the house went on, even the ones in the bedroom. A gunshot rang out in the living room, and then, in the space of a breath, another. Other guns joined in, dozens of startling explosions, which created an ear-shattering counterpoint of breaking glass, falling objects, pots and pans dancing and colliding. With a sob, Jack leaped out of bed and clawed at the window. Morgan leaped from the bed and tripped him. They fell together. Jack tried to get to his feet.

"Lie still, Jack!" Morgan said, shouting now. "It's your only chance."

Morgan got on top of him and tried to get his head in a scissors grip. He stared up at her with wild eyes. Strong as Morgan was, well trained in the martial arts as she was, she was still a woman and Jack was much stronger than she was even when he wasn't out of his mind with fear. Screaming with primal fright, he lifted her from his body and threw her against the wall. She struck her head and fell in a heap, momentarily stunned.

At this moment a man in a dark suit and fedora burst through the bedroom door, a twelve-gauge pump shotgun in his hands.

The intruder shouted, "Jack, don't fucking move!"

Jack froze. The gunman began shooting. He shot the mirror. He shot the lamp. He shot out the window. He shot the framed pictures on the wall—Jack's mother in her naval uniform, Jack's Harvard pictures. Reloading, he shot everything else in the room that was breakable. He shot the telephone, which broke into hundreds of black acetate shards, one or two of which embedded themselves like shrapnel in Jack's back. Jack saw blood, his own blood, but he did not feel pain. Finally the gunman, pumping one last live shell into the shotgun, pointed it straight at Jack. Two other men in dark suits and fedoras came into the bedroom. They, too, were armed with shotguns.

The original gunman's finger tightened on the trigger. He said, "Watch the birdie, Jack."

The gunman smiled: odd crooked teeth, flashes of aluminum instead of gold. His friends smiled over his shoulders at Jack, big

221 ★ LUCKY BASTARD

taunting wiseguy smiles, like schoolyard bullies. At the last possible instant the gunman swung the muzzle of the shotgun upward and shot out the overhead light. Shards of glass rained down on Jack. Then the gunmen left. A deep silence followed, so deep that Jack wondered if he had been killed and his brain had not yet quite died, so that he could see and remember but all his other senses were going. Then he smelled the stink of cordite that filled the house and heard sirens, and knew that he was alive.

By now Morgan had revived. She sprang to her feet and said, "Get up. Get on your feet, Jack. It's over."

He did as she said. Morgan jumped up on the bed with something in her hand and, grabbing Jack's pajama coat, pulled him closer. After a moment he realized that she was brushing his hair. In the dark.

When the police arrived minutes later, only seconds ahead of a squadron of television and radio vans and newspaper photographers, they found a bloodied but well-combed Jack Adams supporting his half-conscious wife in the wreckage of their bedroom. Every object in the modest little house had been destroyed by blasts of double-ought buckshot fired at point-blank range. Glass littered the floors, pictures had been blasted off the wall. Pots and pans, clothes, books, everything was riddled by shot. Every lamp and lightbulb in the house had been shot away, so all this was revealed in the shadow-free blue-white glare of klieg lights. As cameras whirred.

The police found more than one hundred empty shotgun shells in the house.

Thirteen days later, Jack won the election by two percentage points.

Three

1 On the day after the primary, Jack and Danny lunched on pizza in the conference room of Miller & Adams, which had been converted to Jack's campaign headquarters.

Glowing with happiness, Jack said, "Okay, let's talk about the general election."

Danny did not reply.

Jack said, "Onward and upward to final victory, just like in high school. Dan, what would I do without you?"

Danny said, "You're about to find out. I'm going to have to withdraw as campaign manager."

Jack had just taken a bite of pizza. He spat it into his hand and said, "What?"

"Cindy," Danny said. "She says she'll walk if I'm part of making you attorney general."

"What does she think you've been doing for the last six months?"

"She thought you were going to lose. I guess she didn't count on the Mafia pushing you over the top with a skeet-shooting contest."

Jack said, "Mafia, my ass. You did it, just like in high school."

"That was then. This is now, and you don't need anybody," Danny said. "You're going to wipe up the floor with F. Merriwether Street. And that's the problem. Cindy was supposed to run the women's side of Merriwether's campaign. But thanks to you, he dumped her."

"What does that have to do with me? Or you?"

"Come on, Jack. You're responsible for everything bad that's ever happened in her life, so why shouldn't you be responsible for this?"

"Okay, she's been dumped by that asshole. Why does that mean you have to dump me?"

"Because Cindy says she'll leave me if I choose you over her one more time. She means it. I can't live without her. End of story."

"Is this permanent?"

"No, just this once," Danny said. "She works for Street's father, for Christ's sake. She's the apple of old Street's eye. I can't do it to her."

"Danny, this is a blow. What am I going to do?"

"Win. Run against anybody but Merriwether Street and I'll be right beside you. But I can't help you this time."

Jack said, "Dan, how can you do this to me after all these years? I need you."

"Not as much as I need Cindy."

"That bitch!" Morgan said when she heard the news. "*She* needs Danny more than you do. That's what this is really all about. She cuts his meat, buttons his buttons, polishes his shoes, says his prayers with him, kisses his fucking wounds—"

Jack was genuinely shocked by this last phrase. He said, "Morgan, for God's *sake*—"

"No wonder she's turned into a Republican. She's anti-*abortion*, for Christ's sake. You know what she said at a rally of her stupid fat women? She said, 'These left-wing harpies who are pushing for abortion are the same ones who used to spit on American soldiers and call them baby-killers.' Now, that's *vile*!"

Morgan's face was a mask of anger and contempt, as it always was when someone on the other side touched a nerve. Jack himself believed it possible that a comparison of mug shots of Movement chicks spitting on returning soldiers in the seventies and of present-day prochoice militants might turn up some matching faces. This did not seem to be the moment to voice this thought, so he said, with a glint of humor, "I had no idea Cindy was so eloquent."

"Eloquent? Dangerous!" Morgan mimed a pompom girl leading a cheer. " '*He is peaches, he is cream, he is the captain of our team. Adolf! Hitler!* 'ray! 'ray! 'ray!' Maybe somebody should fuck Danny's mind straight for him."

Though Jack was used to Morgan's outbursts, he was staggered by the spitting rage she was in now. He said, "Like who?"

She batted her eyes in a parody of pompom girl flirtation. "Why do you ask?"

Jack said, "Morgan, don't even think about it. I mean that."

Morgan said, "Oh really? You're a good one to talk, Greasy Gus."

2   Even without Danny at his side, Jack was elected in November. He ran a colorful, witty campaign that made F. Meriwether Street look even more clumsy and dull than he actually was. Street, who sang bass in his church choir, always led a rousing chorus of "God Bless America" to end his rallies. Morgan retched.

Jack said, "Forget it. He's asking them to vote for America, not him."

"Then we need a song that tells people to vote for you."

Jack laughed. "What about 'Jack, Jack, Jack, Coo-coo-too-goo-rooga'? It was my high school campaign song. Danny thought it up."

Morgan said, "You mean, 'Gentleman Jack, the hot dog man, he can make love like no one can'?"

"Get some new words."

"You're crazy."

"No. It's a catchy tune." He grinned. "And the subliminals are good. Or don't you remember?"

"Fuck you."

But Morgan asked one of her people, a professor of creative writing, to come up with new words for the lively, salacious old song. Two days later the woman, holding her nose, handed her the new lyrics:

> *Jack, Jack, Jack! He's our candidate!*
> *Jack, Jack, Jack! Let us demonstrate*
> *That Jack, Jack, Jack does not hesitate*
> *To win! Win! Win!*
> *Let's hear it for Jack, the man who wins!*
> *Let's hear it for Jack as the future begins!*
> *Let's do it for Jack, we wish he was twins!*
> *Ohio needs Jack, and everyone wins!*
> *Jack, Jack, Jack!*

The song caught on at once. Morgan taught the anthem to Jack's ever-growing crowds, and in no time everyone could sing the words and dance to them as he strode into a rally. "Jack, Jack, Jack!" became the "Ruffles and Flourishes" of Jack's political career.

Jack became the youngest attorney general in the history of the state. Just as he had predicted, the governor and nearly everyone in the party apparatus outside Cleveland forgot that they had ever wanted him to lose. A star had been born. Everyone wanted to be one of the original band of brothers and sisters. Jack welcomed all comers, and especially all wise men bearing gifts.

"It was the song that did it," Danny said. "Voters like an alpha male."

"What's an alpha male?" Jack asked.

"The head chimp who gets to bang all the females while nobody else gets any."

"Jeez, is that what they elected me to do?"

"Not yet," Danny said. "But when you run for president, all you have to do is change the words a little."

Jack threw an arm around his friend. "The song is you," he said. "Don't forget that. I'll tell you what really made the difference, and that's what you did with Fats Corso."

"Shhh," Danny said. "Cindy might be listening."

Thanks to Danny's work behind the scenes, Corso had played a role in Jack's victory. Not long after Jack won the primary, Fats Corso came to see Danny. F. Merriwether Street's grand jury was winding up its investigation, and the media had just reported that Jack and Morgan had been called as witnesses in connection with the shotgun attack on their bungalow.

Soon after dark the doorbell had rung. Cindy went to the door and found Corso on the front step. He was on crutches, but otherwise he was his unmistakable self: silk suit, white shirt, white-on-white tie, white fedora. He was alone. He swept off his fedora and said, "Very sorry to disturb, but I'd like a word with Attorney Miller."

"Which one?" Cindy said.

Corso flushed. "No offense," he said. "But your husband is the one I want to talk to."

"Please come in."

Corso seemed surprised by the invitation, but he followed, fedora in hand. In the living room, sitting on the sofa, his damaged leg stretched out before him in its cast, Corso accepted the weak American coffee that Cindy offered. With a last warning look at Danny, she withdrew.

In his hoarse voice Corso said, "Attorney Miller, from what I understand, you're not only Jack Adams's partner but his best friend, maybe his only one."

"We go back a long way," Danny said. "What can I do for you?"

Corso said, "Give him a message from me. The shotguns? I didn't do it. It wasn't me. It wasn't nobody connected to me."

"Then who did do it?"

"If I knew the answer to that question I'd tell you, but I've got no clue. I've asked all around. It was nobody I know. And I don't have no enemies who hate me enough to do something like this to me."

Fats Corso's sincerity was transparent. Still, Danny said, "With all due respect, Mr. Corso, I think Jack is going to find this hard to believe."

Fats waved a hand, pinky ring flashing. He said, "Listen to me. Nobody I know in this town or any other town where I know people had a thing to do with shooting up Jack Adams's house. Me and my friends don't do things like that, violate a man's home. It's against the rules. You understand what I'm saying to you? *Nobody* knows who done it."

Danny said, "Mr. Corso, let me be frank. As far as I know, you're the only enemy Jack has got in the world."

"Attorney Miller, I wish I knew how I got to be his enemy, because I didn't do the other, with the cop and the girl, neither. She's a crazy kid, a born hooker just like her mother. She just wanted to hump a cop, so she knocked on the window of the first parked cruiser she saw. She told me that herself. It never crossed my mind to set Gallagher up. You think I didn't know what would happen if I tried? I don't care how many cops Gallagher—who's a fucking liar by the way—said was on the pad, the cops would never stand for something like that. And now look. As God is my witness, on the grave of my mother, that's the truth as I know it."

Danny said, "Mr. Corso, thanks for stopping by. I'll give him the message."

Corso slumped in undisguised despair. He said, "Let me explain something to you, counselor. I'm no kingpin. I run a few girls, control the numbers, own the cigarette machines and the jukeboxes, make a few loans, use a little muscle. Years ago you could make a living doing what I do. Not anymore. Nobody needs girls. Every college broad does things for free that you used to could only do in Tijuana. Now these crazies who marched against the war when you were over there fighting are getting elected to office—no offense, I name no names, but I'm trying to be honest with you—and they're talking about setting up a state lottery. If they actually do this, which I used to think could never happen in a state like Ohio with all those Protestant churches, there goes the numbers game. So why me? It makes no sense. I can't figure it out."

"I'll tell Jack what you said," Danny replied.

As soon as Corso's white Cadillac, a replica of his former vehicle minus the remote starter, was out of sight, Danny got into his own car and drove to the downtown hotel where Jack and Morgan were staying.

Jack was exuberant. "Old Merriwether will never try Corso while the campaign is going on. If we can pressure Fats into copping a plea, admitting he shot up my house, I win."

Danny said, "Jack, he says he didn't do it."

"What difference does that make? This is his way out."

"You believe him?"

"Of course not. I just want to get some benefit from the situation. Plus screw Merriwether." Jack's mind was racing. He said, "Okay. Call Fats. Tell him to pick a felony, any felony, and plead guilty. He can't possibly be sentenced until after the election. I'll see that he doesn't get too much time and doesn't go to a bad place. He can make his own living arrangements inside. I won't oppose parole. And I'll never bother him again. All he has to do is admit before the world he tried to intimidate me and failed."

"He may be reluctant to do that, Jack."

"Talk to him. Tell him I *know* he did it, and I'll have to tell the grand jury that."

Later that week Morgan, then Jack, appeared before the grand jury and identified three of Corso's most trusted musclemen as the thugs who had blown the Adamses' simple little young-marrieds' house to smithereens. Their testimony was immediately leaked to the media. The newspapers ran a story identifying one of the accused underlings as Frank "Bang-Bang" Russo, so called because his weapon of choice was a pump-action shotgun loaded with double-ought buckshot.

Indictments were returned, and a short time afterward F. Merriwether Street announced that he had accepted a plea bargain from Fats Corso. Jack kept his part of the deal. Corso was given ten to twenty years in prison. Although no one in the media made a point of this—even at this early stage in his career, Jack was far too valuable a source ever to be embarrassed—Corso had every prospect of parole within three years.

"Justice has been done," Jack told the media. "The important thing is, Fats Corso's empire of crime has been smashed. Now we'll move on and make sure he has a lot of old friends to keep him company in prison."

One of the unexpected consequences of the Corso affair was the humanization of Morgan Adams. She won the admiration of all, and perhaps even some votes for her husband, for the way in which she handled the night of terror through which she and Jack had lived together. During the campaign she went everywhere with Jack. Although she was still something of a frump by middle-class standards, she seemed softer, more feminine, less shrewish than before. Nicer to Jack. Always beside him on the hustings, she gazed at him with adoration as he spoke; they held hands in public, even hugged. Everyone noticed it.

On an interview show in Cleveland, Morgan was asked by the host, a locally famous, elderly spinster journalist from another era, if she and Jack were planning a family.

"Oh my goodness, Dorothy, we don't have time to *plan*," Morgan answered. "But I hope every single night that it will just happen."

"Did you say, 'every single night'?" the old lady asked.

Morgan clapped a hand over her mouth in the closest thing she could manage to girlish confusion. "Oh dear!" she cried. "What have I said?"

"Don't worry, Morgan," said the old lady. "Believe me, you've done your husband no harm with the voters."

3 As attorney general, Jack traveled to every corner of Ohio, speaking at bar association meetings, police conventions, Kiwanis and Rotary and Knights of Columbus luncheons, union conventions, high school assemblies, college audiences—any platform would do, as long as it gave him exposure to an audience, a chance to charm civic leaders, and a cameo appearance on the local news. At first his public affairs assistant, a hefty and very plain middle-aged woman handpicked by Morgan (as was all the rest of his female staff), spent nearly every minute of every day offering his services as a public speaker. But soon his reputation as a spellbinding performer and charming dinner guest spread throughout the state, and he began to receive more invitations than he could accept. A Columbus station offered him a weekly call-in show, then a novelty in broadcasting. Jack loved to talk to strangers, loved to give advice, and his delight in being on the air was obvious to all. The bizarre personal lives of the callers soon attracted a large audience, and the show's time slot was switched to late afternoon so that commuters could listen to it on their way home from work. Jack's program was soon syndicated all over Ohio, and later in much of the Midwest.

Meanwhile, as he had promised, Jack pounded on his signature issue: organized crime. Soon his remorseless pursuit of mafiosi encompassed the entire state. A coordinated police raid in fifteen cities, organized by Jack, swooped down on mobsters. Arrests were made, indictments were brought, a few more minor Mafia soldiers, and even a capo or two, were imprisoned.

For all his passion to stamp out crime and evil, Jack almost never mentioned illegal drugs, even though these were available to almost every schoolchild in the state. In part this was because illegal drugs were the eucharist of his core constituency, the radical left, which regarded any attack on mind-altering substances as a fascist attack on their constitutional rights of privacy and free expression. Mostly, however, Jack left drugs alone because Peter had given strict and specific orders that Jack was to stay away from this issue.

Morgan asked for Peter's rationale. I told her, accurately as far as it went, that our chief believed that the traffic in drugs was an important weapon against capitalism—perhaps even the decisive weapon. Drugs weakened the workforce, undermined the moral order, demonstrated the inefficiency and corruptibility of the police apparatus, and drained money out of the economy. These funds—stolen, in effect, from the U.S. Treasury—went straight back to the suffering masses of the Third World, in many cases in the form of arms and ammunition for wars of liberation and terrorism. Money spent for drugs by Americans should be regarded as taxes voluntarily paid to the world revolution.

Needless to say, all this made perfect sense to Morgan, as it did to most of her friends when she passed it on as revealed truth. And in fact, the issue of "taxation" was, as we know, Peter's chief reason for wishing to leave the drug runners in peace. It gave him a way to pay for operations without necessarily letting the Moscow bureaucracy know what those operations were all about. Or what his own true purposes were. As we will see, he also had other reasons that only his own exquisite mind could have conceived. These reasons, imaginative and farseeing even by Peter's standards, he did not confide to me, even when they directly affected the operations with which he entrusted me.

Jack followed orders and laid off drugs without demur and, when questioned about the omission, nimbly defended it in his most sincere altar-boy manner. "Drugs are part of a pattern of crime that includes every other kind of vice and viciousness," he would say to skeptics who pointed out his silence on an issue that was becoming more serious by the day. "Our objective must be to attack and defeat crime as a whole—cut the head off the snake and kill it, not chop off little chunks of the tail until we get to the head. Because if we do that we'll never get there. It can grow a new tail faster than we can snip it off."

Audiences, especially young ones and progressive ones, applauded this vivid metaphor, although—or maybe because—it was, like all metaphors, a way of describing something by calling it something that it was not.

If Jack was careful about coming out too openly for the issues closest to the interests and collective emotions of his most loyal friends, the radicals—well, they understood that he could not reveal his true opinions in a bourgeois democracy and hope to be elected to the higher offices where he would really be able to do them some good. So they bided their time.

By the end of his first term Jack was so popular a public figure, and had been so effective in cutting the state's revenues without resorting to such irksome democratic procedures as legislative debate and decision, that he had begun to frighten friends of the governor—contributors to the party, pillars of the establishment who were made nervous by an activist as the chief law enforcement officer of the state. The governor drew him aside and asked whether he might be available, at the end of his term, for the relatively powerless and harmless post of lieutenant governor.

"You're asking me to step back again?" Jack said.

"No," said the governor, who had learned his lesson on that one. "I'm inviting you to move up. Succeed me. Be the next governor of this state."

Jack saw through this clumsy ploy. But on the other hand, the governorship was exactly the launching platform he needed for his run for the presidency. He said yes to the governor without even consulting us. For once, Morgan approved of his impetuosity. She thought that the attorney generalship was dangerous. Jack was exposing himself too recklessly, making too many enemies, inviting too much curiosity. The lieutenant governorship was a good place to hide in plain sight, and that was the essence of the plan for Jack. Besides, approving of Jack's faits accomplis was becoming routine.

4 Morgan had decided that it was time for her and Jack to have a child. Jack himself believed this to be a good idea, and he and Peter had agreed at the outset that fatherhood must someday be arranged for him. American politicians were expected to have children, to be photographed with their little ones, to speak of the future in terms of the safety and well-being and happiness of their own flesh and blood. If Jack was going to move on the governorship, then he must have children too. "One touch of snot makes the whole world kin," said Morgan, who was in an antic mood. Briefly, looking into her slightly flushed features, which at moments of extreme cunning swelled in a subtle, almost coital way, I wondered if she was not merely suggesting a plausible reason to resume with Jack the active sex life that I believed she strongly missed.

But no. Her plan was far more complex, conspiratorial, and perverse than that—so much so that I knew, the moment I heard it, that it would be irresistible to Peter.

Morgan's entire contribution to the project would be the donation of ova. One of her clients and fellow militants, a medical researcher at Ohio State, was working in an experimental program of in vitro fertilization. An egg was removed from the prospective mother's womb, then mixed with sperm in a petri dish. The resulting embryo was then implanted in the uterus of the mother, who carried it to term and delivered the baby in the usual way. This method of sexless conception, commonplace today, was in its early laboratory stages then, and it was regarded—at least by Morgan and her feminist friends—as a revolutionary advance in female empowerment because it offered women the possibility of conception without admitting actual living sperm into their bodies.

What appealed to Morgan was this: The donor of the ovum did not even have to gestate her own child. The embryo could be implanted in any woman healthy enough to carry the fetus to term and then be delivered of a living baby. The newborn would be handed over immediately to the biological mother, who for the previous nine months had gone on with the more important activities of her life without the inconveniences and discomforts of pregnancy.

"So what we need," Morgan told me, "is a healthy young woman who will carry the child, under discipline of course—"

I was amused. "Of course. What sort of discipline?"

"She'll have to eat a proper diet and avoid drugs, alcohol, tobacco, and sex for nine months. And be willing to bear the child without meeting its actual parents or, above all, knowing who they are. And then she must disappear forever."

I said, "What do you mean by disappear?"

"Go away," Morgan said. "Far away, back to where she came from. Go on with her life."

I said nothing.

Morgan went on, "Secrecy is assured at our end. My friend, who is a physician and therefore bound by an unbreachable oath of secrecy in regard to her patients, will retrieve the ovum and mix in the other ingredient. She herself will implant them in the childbearer—"

I guffawed.

She interrupted herself. "What's so funny?"

I shook my head, wiped my eyes. The lunacy of it. The *solemnity* of it, the invention of an arcane vocabulary understood only by the priestesses of the cult, the treatment of the essentially monstrous as a god-pleasing action—it was all so familiar, yet also so novel. Then I stopped. These little games, these tangled webs, are terribly amusing in the abstract. But oh so different in their human reality, and so incalculable in their consequences.

"Nothing," I said. "Sometimes you forget that I am merely a peasant, a stranger in this strange land. Go on. I am most interested."

"You, a peasant? You're ridiculing me."

"No. Far from it. Continue."

Morgan examined me in moody, disappointed silence. The worst thing a handler can do is step out of character, reveal that the person the agent knows—infinitely patient, infinitely sympathetic, infinitely stern in the name of the agent's own happiness and success—may not be the whole person.

Fearing that she might not tell me the rest (and then what would I tell Peter?), I said, "Morgan, this is one of your most intriguing ideas. Really. Go on."

Somewhat less confidently, but with her usual concision and nicety of detail, she told me the rest of the plan. It was complex but feasible, as almost any lunacy is feasible if tightly controlled from start to finish.

I said, "One question. The world will assume that you, not the anonymous girl, bore the child?"

"Yes. That's the whole point."

"How are you going to fake a pregnancy?"

"Quite simple. Put on a little weight, not too much. Get my exercise. Not show too much—lots of women don't. I know one in New York whose best friends never guessed. Near the end, wear a preggie."

"A what?" I inquired again.

"A preggie. It's a cushion you tuck in your pants. It makes you look pregnant. Actually, a series of cushions, you keep adding padding. It's a sort of post-Pill fad. Everybody fucks, nobody conceives, it's a way to experience the thing, get the look, without actually going through it."

"American women actually wear these things?"

"Some do. It's like meditation or deep analysis or projecting your consciousness onto Mars. Imagining is being."

"Are you actually going to imagine you're pregnant or just wear the pillow?"

"What do you think? I'm a Marxist-Leninist, for God's sake, Dmitri."

"I will consult Peter."

"Good," Morgan said. "I've prepared a budget and a rough operational plan."

To repeat, no project could have been better calculated to appeal to Peter's sense of the outrageous. He provided a nice English-speaking Circassian girl, a Swallow of course, who resembled Morgan enough to deceive the casual eye as long as the two were never seen together. We also provided a midwife to keep an eye on her, a stalwart American Party member long under discipline.

In due course, just as Morgan had described, the Circassian girl was impregnated with one of Morgan's ova, fertilized by one of Jack's sperm. The very first implantation was a success, an omen. After the Circassian missed her second period, the pregnancy was confirmed by a busy Columbus obstetrician, who cared for her—she was using Morgan's original name, Eleanor M. Weatherby—until the end of the eighth month, when she informed him over the phone that she intended to have the child at home. He refused to cooperate. She then went to a female obstetrician who specialized in home deliveries and who had no interest in politics below the abstract level and therefore had no idea who the Adamses were. When the Circassian's labor pains began late one night, she was rushed by the midwife to the Adamses' bungalow. Jack called the doctor, who arrived minutes later.

Jack, attired in surgical gown and mask, assisted at the delivery, holding the Circassian Swallow's hand, helping her breathe and whispering encouragement in her ear as she gasped out the Russian names for the Trinity and howled in the agony that God had promised Eve after the incident of the apple. A child was born.

A son. Followed an instant later by an identical twin who looked as much like Jack as the first comer did. When their eyes were cleaned out, these two little Jacks gazed curiously into the over-flowing eyes of their masked and sobbing father, who had never before understood that such unbounded joy was possible to the human heart.

Against all Morgan's instructions, Jack ripped off his mask, revealing himself to the Swallow as his sons suckled for the first and last time at her breasts. Kneeling by the bed, Jack kissed the girl on the lips as if she were, in fact, a beloved wife to whom he owed the ecstasy that gripped him. In a voice broken by emotion, he murmured over and over again, "Thank you."

5 As soon as the Circassian was spirited away—back to Minsk and the part-time ballet lessons she longed for but was too old, at eighteen, to profit from—Morgan removed her preggie and assumed the public role of mother. She immediately resumed her two-mile daily runs, to the astonishment and admiration of all, and was soon as trim as ever. Home birth was not yet the fad that it later briefly became, and to those who asked her reasons for delivering the twins at home she explained that it had been an act of feminist conviction. "I wanted a natural birth, without drugs, without instruments, without, frankly, some male doctor calling the tune," she would say. "I wanted the children to come into the world in their own home, and for their father's face to be the first face they saw. I hoped that this would bond them together right away. And"—here she would smile fondly if she happened to be talking to a reporter or a constituent—"in Jack's case it sure seems to have worked." After catching several colds and flus from the boys, Morgan took care to stay at a safe distance from their sneezes and runny noses. Jack seemed to be immune to them.

"The Adams vigor," I said when Morgan informed me of his strange immunity.

"Not funny," said Morgan, before coughing deeply into a Kleenex. She had never expected to enjoy motherhood, but like most women who experience it for the first time, even at arm's length like Morgan, nothing had prepared her for its sleepless reality or for the pitiless demands of helpless creatures. Drawing liberally on her trust fund, she hired a live-in, round-the-clock nanny, a squat, slightly hirsute Guatemalan woman who spoke no English. When this woman found the twins were too much for her, Morgan hired her equally unattractive sister as assistant nanny. She called them "the Hermanas," the sisters. After they were hired, Morgan seldom saw the twins awake, except on public occasions.

Morgan had been right about one thing. The twins were a public relations bonanza—wild cards to fill an inside straight, as Danny called them, just two more examples of their father's unpredictable and altogether astonishing luck. To Jack, they were the final proof of his secret genes. Like most male members of what he believed to be their line of descent, the boys were thick-haired exuberant roughhousers and photogenic smilers who attracted cameramen like flies. Jack named them, in order of birth, John Fitzgerald, Jr., and John Morgan; to avoid confusion they were called Fitz and Skipper. It was Morgan's idea to name them both for their father; she reckoned that this doubling of doubles would intrigue the tabloids.

Jack's love for the boys was as real as it was instantaneous. Even Morgan believed that they had truly awakened his heart. She herself had no particular feeling for her sons, and came into physical contact with them only at political rallies or when having her picture taken with them. The twins, who ignored her as she ignored them, seemed to sense that they had some sort of pre-agreed nonaggression pact with their mother. They never fussed when she plopped them down on her lap or offered them a non-gender-specific toy while the kliegs and strobes bathed them in their pitiless glare. (She stopped offering them dolls after, at age one, they dismembered a Barbie on camera, one pulling off the golden head, the other the lissome legs.)

Jack, on the other hand, could not get enough of his kids. He fed them their bottles, changed their diapers, rolled on the floor growling with both of them guffawing in his arms, bought them bicycles and footballs and bats long before they could possibly use them. Even when they were infants he took them everywhere it was possible to take them. He bought them a double pram and, later on, when they could sit up and wave at the crowd like proper little Kennedys, a double stroller. On sunny mornings he would push them as far as Morgan's office, conversing delightedly with his tiny passengers as he went. The twins were as taken with him as he was with them, and on these outings they would gaze upward at their father, fascinated by the chortling happy noises and the grinning faces he made for them. Fitz and Skipper really were identical—so alike that Morgan habitually called them by the wrong names.

Photos of the Adamses peppered the newspapers and local television. Even *People* ran a picture—Jack holding the handsome boys on his knees, all three males smiling identical grins, and Morgan standing behind, a bespectacled Madonna with her own secret smile, steadying fingertips on her proud husband's shoulders. "3 Jacks, Queen High," read the *Time*-style caption.

6 Despite this image of perfect happiness, Morgan continued to suspect Jack of bedding nearly every woman he met. She accused him of having affairs with female lawyers he met in the course of his duties, of using his radio show and campaign speeches as means of lining up quickies with his listeners, and especially of using the miniskirted reporter who still waylaid him on his morning walks as what she called his back-up fuck: "What do you do, give her an interview if nothing else is available and hump her on the desk?" Jack denied all, especially the reporter. "I'd screw a cobra quicker than a journalist," he said. His denials availed him nothing. Morgan was convinced that no one with Jack's sex drive could go without coitus and look as happy as he did. She knew he was doing it; the unanswered question, the one that drove her into her strange brain-numbing rages, was with whom?

When Jack stayed out late, which was often, Morgan questioned him in furious whispers in the kitchen or the living room. She examined his underwear, sniffing it for traces of female musk. Sometimes she smelled *him* when he came home late, sniffing his torso like a dog. She went through his pockets. She never found any conclusive evidence, but she knew—*knew*—that Jack was not living without sex.

Morgan's reports to me regarding her suspicions of Jack were always presented as operational considerations, never in personal terms. Our discussions on this subject were calm, even tinged with a certain humor; nothing is quite so funny as a bedroom farce as long as it's not one's own true love who is slipping through the wrong doors. But underneath Morgan's worldly nonchalance I sensed the inevitable tension. She may have couched her anxieties in terms of the dangers posed to the operation by Jack's peccadilloes, and she was right to fear blackmail and even accusations of rape, given Jack's favorite technique and the many new definitions of this crime that were then being formulated by feminist thinkers. But something primal was involved. I had thought so for a long time; I had discussed the matter with Peter. He had always refused to alter the rules of the operation. He was possessed by the notion that Morgan would channel her sexual energy into operational effectiveness, and that any relief of her pent-up desires would somehow diminish her efficiency as an agent. If it worked for nuns, why not for a bride of Lenin? It would have been futile to point out that it is one thing for a young virgin to renounce the flesh and join a community of penitents and quite another for an experienced woman at the height of her sexuality to be forbidden carnal pleasure while living in the same house as a man who is obsessed with sex. As usual, the idea was all to Peter, the reality nothing; no wonder he commanded such worship from his young idealists. Knowing him as I did, I wondered if he did not have some plan to relieve her stress himself, on some future occasion he had marked on some astrological calendar in his mind.

In any case, my fatherly sympathy for Morgan was such, and her fundamental argument about the danger of Jack's sex drive compromising the operation was so undeniably correct, that I agreed at last to test her suspicions by putting a tail on the suspect. Limited surveillance, I told her, for a limited purpose for a limited time. I thought it unlikely we would uncover anything more than an occasional quickie, very likely arranged pretty much as Morgan had imagined. I isolated Morgan from the investigation; she would hear the results after we obtained them. If Jack had been smart enough and resourceful enough over a period of years to keep a keen operative like her from finding out anything for certain about his sex life, he would be a wary subject. For all her advanced training and impressive skills, he would have spotted her behind him in a minute, and I assumed he had long since alerted whatever sentries he had posted to be on the lookout for her or anyone who even looked like a snooper in her employ. On the theory that Jack had been too terrified the last time he glimpsed their faces to remember them now, I used two of the three thugs who had shot up the Adamses' bungalow to such splendid effect three years before.

What my team found, not by actually following Jack, with all the risks that involved, but by identifying the members of the Gruesome whom he called most often on the phone and following *them*, was this: A sort of Gruesome-within-the-Gruesome existed. A dozen of its members, driven by stranger appetites than their fellows, had banded together to set up what amounted to a safe house in one of those huge multipurpose complexes beloved of American developers. Pooling money, each according to his means, they had leased the penthouse. This penthouse had an elevator of its own that connected it to a vast underground garage that was shared by several other apartment and office buildings and a shopping mall. It was possible, therefore, to enter any of those buildings on foot or in a car, or to stroll through the mall and duck into any of half a dozen staircases, and then walk to the elevator, call it by punching in a code on a keypad, and ascend unnoticed to the top. It was an arrangement any intelligence service would have been proud of but few would have possessed the wit to conceive or the funds to support on an ongoing basis.

There was good reason for secrecy. What these Super Gruesomes did in the penthouse was drink good liquor, snort cocaine, and watch pornography on a huge back-projection television screen. Sometimes, usually on a member's birthday, there were orgies featuring women who shared their tastes, including some very young girls. Such females abounded, and the rule of the house was that no female could be invited more than once. No wonder Jack loved the place and spent about half his salary in its support.

After defining the target, my men installed the usual devices, and we soon had a rich archive of videotapes, still photographs, and audiotapes. From this trove of real-life pornography the technicians winnowed a selection of Jack's performances, and at our next operational meeting, in a motel in Parkersburg, West Virginia, I showed Morgan a montage. Even for surveillance tape, even for amateur pornography, it was remarkably boring footage, because only the girls changed. Jack's technique, described earlier, was always exactly the same. Enter Jack and partner. A snuggle, a murmur or two. Jack pounces. The girl's surprised outcry, part grunt, part gasp, part shriek, part giggle. The marathon coupling, always the same positions in the same sequences, the girl moaning, shouting. Because Jack apparently preferred to fornicate in the dark, these images were in infrared, in which he and his partners were perfectly recognizable but surreal, like transparent lovers risen from the tomb to repeat as ether what had delighted them as flesh.

Morgan watched, rigid with fascination. She controlled her breathing with difficulty. As girl succeeded girl—Jack appeared to find a new and very willing partner almost every day—I expected her to say, Enough. But she watched the screen fixedly—compulsively might be the better word—until the show was over. Then, feigning amusement with an almost complete lack of success, she said, "Jack missed his calling. The son of a bitch should have been a porn star."

Clearly she was in a state of desire—this was obvious to several of my own dulled senses. But something deeper was going on. She was jealous. She twitched with it. She was sick with anger. Like any normal American wife, she regarded her husband as her property and looked on other women, all of them, as a threat to her rights over him. That she was also his handler, that she had been entrusted and given authority over him by the revolution, only intensified her boiling emotions.

At last she cleared her throat violently and then said in a normal, perfectly steady voice, "It's a hopeless case. He's in the grip of a psychotic compulsion. It's folly to think we can control it. Do you agree?"

I did not agree. What I had seen on the surveillance tape was quite understandable human behavior, no more perverse in its way than a prude insisting on the missionary position. Sex creates patterns by providing a pleasure worth repeating. Carefully, I said, "I agree that he will do it again, many times."

"Would you say this is a bad situation?"

I nodded. What was she leading up to?

"In that case," Morgan said, "I have a suggestion."

I waited encouragingly. Morgan crossed her trousered legs, hugged herself, leaned toward me, dropped her voice. "Do you remember," she asked, "what Peter told Jack in Palma about János Kádár?"

I most certainly did. No doubt it was a vivid memory to Jack, too. I said, "Yes. What about it?"

"That may be the only solution for Jack."

In my long and in many respects unusual life I have often had the wind knocked out of me. But never quite so violently as on this occasion.

I said, "Comrade Captain, you amaze me." My tone was harsh, angry. Castrate him? I could have killed her. She took my reaction as delighted surprise. She was oblivious to my real mood. While I recovered my self-control she went on, enumerating the advantages of turning Jack into a eunuch. It occurred to me she was insane—not in her whole being, but in this narrow little strip of it that burned with her hatred, not only of Jack, but—

I interrupted. "Morgan, the answer is no."

She was flabbergasted. "But—"

"Morgan," I said. "No."

"But why? It's so obvious!"

What would convince her? I said, "Because he's not Kádár and we are not in Hungary and it is not 1955 and I am not Beria."

"That doesn't answer the question."

By now I was calmer; I said, "Let me ask you a question: Is it not the first principle of this operation that Jack, our asset, can come to power—supreme power—on the basis of his personality?"

"Yes."

"His unique and sparkling personality?"

I was not smiling. Neither was Morgan, suddenly a darling daughter who was taking my refusal hard. She said, "If you say so."

"Not 'if I say so.' I am asking you if you acknowledge this reality. Answer."

She looked this way and that for some sort of psychic escape hatch but saw none. I was playing the commissar to the hilt. Finally she gave me a tight little nod, lips compressed, eyes defiant. A child betrayed by the person she had trusted most.

"Very well," I said. "What do you think will happen to the sparkle if you cut off his balls?"

She thought and thought. "You have a point," she said at last.

I merely nodded. Within me, anger still boiled. I had not felt such emotion in years. Perhaps I was as irrational on this subject as she was on another. But how could she *imagine*?

She was chastened by my disapproval, but by no means struck dumb. "What *are* we going to do about this?" she asked.

"That is not your concern. It will be handled."

She flinched. Even before this meeting—though I confess I never expected the dialogue to take the turn it took—I had decided to take certain steps to resolve the situation, Peter or no Peter. My solution was unorthodox, but justified by circumstances. It was a matter of saving the operation by saving Morgan from herself, because the problem was not Jack. It was Morgan. It was essential that the tension be broken.

I left her without bestowing the usual comradely kisses on her cheeks.

7   In all the years that I had managed his life, Jack Adams had never seen me, as he might have put it, one on one. In theory he did not even know that I existed. Nevertheless, taking into account that evening in the Italian restaurant in Manhattan and Jack's famous gift for remembering faces, I wore a disguise when we met for the first time. Jack was quite visibly surprised when, at four-thirty in the afternoon, his usual hour of assignation, he stepped onto the elevator to the Gruesome penthouse and found a stocky man wearing a highly realistic gorilla mask already aboard. He recoiled momentarily, as who would not, but after I gave him a friendly waggle of the fingers he grinned and stepped inside. Who could this frolicsome creature be but a fellow Gruesome on his way up to the penthouse for a bit of fun?

The elevator rose. Jack, eyeing me in amusement, said, "Ed?"

I shook my head. Jack grinned. I said, "Welcome to the country of the blind."

Jack fell back against the wall of the car. His face turned white. A tremor swept downward as if a plug had been pulled in his nervous system, releasing a pent-up torrent of dread. In rapid sequence his eyes fluttered, his head shook, his breath became shallow, his shoulders hunched, his hands fluttered, his knees trembled, his shoes scraped on the carpeted floor in a pantomime of instinctive flight. I had never seen anything like it. I stopped the elevator.

"Be calm," I said. "I am your friend."

Jack was anything but calm. However, he seemed to be recovering himself, so I waited, breathing moistly inside the ill-fitting mask and observing him through the tiny eyeholes. It was like being inside a primitive pinhole camera: The image was too large for the point of light in which it was captured.

Finally Jack said, "Give me a name."

I said, "I've already given you words you obviously recognize."

"I still want a name. Who sent you?"

"Peter," I said. This was not strictly true, because this meeting was completely unauthorized, but under the circumstances, perfect veracity was not a consideration.

Jack shook his head. He had a grip on himself now; there was a glint of humor in his eye. "I wish you people would call first," he said.

I told him about the surveillance. On the basis of what I knew about his response to threats, real or imagined, I expected hysteria. However, to my relief Jack took my revelation calmly, even showing a kind of admiration as I described the techniques used and the results obtained. So intense was his interest that I would not have been surprised if he asked to see the pictures we had taken of him and his girlfriends. But he asked no questions. Nor did he seem to be particularly surprised. Given the shocks we had delivered in the past, he must by this time have taken it for granted that Peter and his thugs were everywhere, could do anything, could suborn anyone. How much more efficient than Big Brother was Peter, who understood that he did not have to watch everybody all the time as long as all his assets knew that he could watch them whenever he wished. Paranoia was cheaper than manpower.

"Okay," Jack said. "You've got me. I have committed fornication. Now what?"

His bravado amazed me. He was negotiating.

That being the case, I offered a concession. "We have failed you," I said. "You were promised safe sex—"

"I remember," Jack said.

Inside the mask, I smiled. I went on: "We did not deliver. I apologize. But what you are doing to remedy the failure is unsafe. Moreover, it is disturbing the harmony of your relationship with your wife."

"My wife? Let me tell you something, my friend—do you have a name?"

"No. Go on."

"Okay. You're the ones who've got a problem, not me. She's fucking *obsessed*. This is a woman who loves it, does it like a champ, and she's supposed to live with her memories for the rest of her life? I've got to tell you, it shakes my confidence in you guys that you—"

"So what are you proposing?" I interrupted. "A resumption of marital relations?"

"No. It's too late for that, and if we started fucking she'd only be worse. But an open marriage, that's another matter."

This term was just coming into fashion. I did not quite understand what he meant.

Jack said, "Do everybody a favor. *Order* her to get laid and leave me alone. It won't cure the problem. She wants total control of every atom of my being. Especially my cock."

Jack had no idea how right he was, or by what means Morgan had proposed arranging that control. "You make an interesting point," I said. "But it's not your wife we're concerned about. It's you."

"Oh? Why's that?"

"Because you don't seem to understand the meaning of discretion."

"Really?" Jack said. "How long did it take you to catch me?"

I said, "After we set out to do so, three days, to be precise. And what we did, others can do. Believe me."

"So what? Everybody does it."

"Not everybody does it in the next room to cocaine and marijuana and pornography and underage girls doing the hootchy-cootchy for dirty old men—"

He grinned. "You *do* have the place bugged—"

"—and in the company of people who have a lot to gain from bribing the attorney general with sex and drugs—"

Jack gave me the full Hyannis Port smile. "The flesh is weak."

"That's why they invented blackmail."

"Then give me an alternative," Jack said. "Your problem is, you can't keep up with the requirements, and even if you could, what you've got ain't what I want. Believe me."

Bear in mind, as you listen to Jack, that he was locked in an elevator with a man in a Halloween mask whom he did not know and who might, as far as he knew, turn out to be a mafioso who would murder him or kidnap him. He may have been a physical coward, but he feared no man—and only one woman—when it came to matching wits.

I said, "Your basic requirement, based on our observations, seems to be roughly four women a week."

"You must have been following me around during a slow week. Ten is more like it. A dozen is better."

"You seem to have no trouble getting partners. Does someone procure them for you? Tell the truth. This is important."

"No. They call in to my radio show during commercials and we chat off the air. I meet them at political rallies, ball games, everywhere. Some are referrals."

"Referrals?"

"They tell their girlfriends. Mostly they're married. They're curious. They want what I want, a little nookie with no risk and then goodbye. They have their orgasms, take a shower, and go home and cook supper. And then maybe they have another one to sleep on with good old Harry, who wonders what got into Bobbie Sue."

"So you don't really need this hideout."

"If you want discretion, I need something like it," Jack said. "It's part of the reason the women show up. They think it's safe. If they think they're going to get caught, they won't take the chance. Why should they, for a two-hour jump?"

"Are you meeting somebody today?"

"Why else would I be here?" Jack looked at his watch. "She's probably downstairs now."

"All right," I said. "I won't keep you. But make this the last time you use this elevator. Do you understand?"

I used Peter's favorite question and voiced it in Peter's diction.

The stimulus worked. Suddenly Jack remembered where he was, who I was, what he was. He nodded obediently.

"Out loud," I said.

"Yes. I understand."

"Good," I said. "Within a month you will receive, at your office, an envelope delivered by messenger. Inside the envelope will be a key and an address. From time to time you'll receive other packages with the same contents. When you do, drop the old key down a sewer—just like you did in Heidelberg, Jack—and start using the new address. Never install a telephone or cable television in any of these places or bring any sort of an electronic device into them. Do you understand all that?"

This time he spoke right up. "I understand."

"Good. Because the next time someone has to meet you in an elevator the encounter may not end quite so pleasantly."

Silence. Solemnity, a rare state in Jack. I turned the key. The elevator rose.

We arrived at the penthouse. Jack said, "Don't forget the other side of the equation. I feel for her."

I nodded.

Jack said, "Just a suggestion. Take that thing off on the way down."

He got off the elevator. I went down. The young woman waiting at the bottom was dressed as if for dinner at Côte Basque. I held the door open for her. With the incredible efficiency for which the KGB was famous, I had stuffed the gorilla mask beneath my coat. When I lifted my arm to hold the door, it fell out. She paused, looked down, stepped over it, and got right on the elevator.

As the door closed she smiled a sweet Ohio smile. Brave girl. Pretty ankles, sleepy eyes, wonderful scent. Lucky Jack.

8 A week later, Morgan opened the door of her motel room in response to my usual signal—a knock, a rattle of the doorknob, two more knocks.

It was not Dmitri who stood in the doorway, but the Georgian who had been her lover in Cuba. He had nearly knocked me down in his anxiety to find out if Morgan still had her old power to reinvent herself in bed.

I watched the reunion through the windshield of my parked car, and judging by the expression on Morgan's face when she saw the surprise I had provided—and, of course, understood why—the Georgian needn't have worried.

5

★ ★

Morgan's Room

One

★ ★

1 No member of Jack's own party wanted to run against him in the primary election in April, and once again he was fortunate in his opponent for the office of lieutenant governor—the Republican nominee was his old, all-thumbs adversary, F. Merriwether Street. But it was a Republican year, the final year of a disastrous Democratic presidency, and Jack's party did not provide the money or the organizational support he needed. In fact, frightened as it was by the growing realization that the Right was on the march again, it made no pretense of backing Jack. The fate of the party did not hang on his being elected lieutenant governor, and the regulars didn't much like him anyway. Many feared him as a threat to their own future ambitions and the Cleveland machine positively hated him, so cash flowed to other candidates who were more important, more conventional, and more deserving. Street, handsomely financed by his family and the rest of the Republican establishment, surprised everyone by running a very strong race, never once putting his foot in his mouth. Hoping to change that, Jack demanded a debate, the losing candidate's traditional last resort. Street ignored him.

Jack fell precipitously in the polls. Rumors of his scandalous private life ran through the state. Republican operatives floated scatological Jack jokes. There were allegations—all true, alas—of a secret love nest, of cocaine, of underage girls.

None of this worried Jack. Rumors of his enviable sex life never made the newspapers because the reporters assigned to investigate them were loath to discredit the media hero they had created—and, just as important, even more reluctant to help his Republican opponent. And even though this harmless little exercise in hypocrisy helped her cause, it gave Morgan another reason to despise the press. Weaklings. Whores. If Jack could use them so easily, so could his enemies.

Jack understood this and of his own volition gave up women for the remainder of the campaign. Although he had lost nothing of his seemingly inborn conviction that he could lie his way out of anything, he understood that not even the most ingenious lie could save him if an enemy obtained pictures of him or planted an agent provocateuse on him. He did not subject his partners to background checks before he invited them to his lair, and the game of friendly rape his women came to play could easily be portrayed as a brutal crime. He knew this would finish him, that no one could protect him in such a case. The badger game, in which the errant wife is surprised in the presence of witnesses by an irate husband and a cameraman, has served politics well. Jack did not throw the key to his secret apartment down a sewer, but knowing himself at least as well as Morgan thought she knew him, he gave it to Danny Miller for safekeeping.

"Don't give this back to me before Election Day no matter what I say," Jack said.

Danny fingered the envelope and felt the shape of the key inside. There was no need to tell him what lock it fitted.

Danny said, "This is a truly noble sacrifice."

Jack grinned and made an ancient masculine hand movement. "Anything for the cause," he said.

"Sit down, I've got something to show you," Danny said. He switched on the television set and put a videotape into the VCR. F. Merriwether Street popped onto the screen. He was giving a stump speech.

"Jesus," said Jack, "the eloquence."

Danny said, "Pay attention."

Street was on the attack. "Ohio is snakebit by drugs," he cried. "They're in every school, in too many homes, they are ruining young lives every single day. And, my friends, this happened while my opponent was the chief law enforcement officer of our state. As attorney general he did not prosecute one single significant drug case in four long years. I wonder why. We all wonder why."

Danny said, "You can't let this go on."

"I'll have to think about it."

"What's to think about, Jack? It's like motherhood, for Christ's sake. Make some busts, make a speech. Take the issue away from this jerk."

"I said I'd think about it."

"I heard you. What the fuck is the matter with you on this one, Jack?"

Jack's hands were tied, of course. He pleaded with Morgan to let him denounce the drug trade, and Morgan pleaded with me, but Peter's guideline held firm.

"I'm sorry," I said. "He has to stay away from this issue."

"It's killing him."

"Then Jack will have to find some other issue. A diversion."

"Diversions cost money, Dmitri. And we're broke."

This was true. Ironically, there was no shortage of money. Peter's Caribbean accounts were overflowing. The problem was explaining where it came from. How to hide the funds, how to launder them? Those were the questions; they are always the questions.

Meanwhile, Jack was running out of time. A month before the election, eight points behind in the latest poll, he pleaded in private with the governor for more money, more exposure, more appearances together. The governor put an arm around his young running mate and with a sad shake of the head said, "Jack, your showing is a real disappointment to us, too."

"Those fuckers *want* me to lose," Jack told Danny. "They set me up with this worthless office to get rid of me. I knew what they were doing. I should have gone for the governorship."

"You wouldn't have made it."

"Maybe not, but I could have made it close and then come back. No one would have expected me to win. Just like nobody expected me to lose for this chickenshit office. Except my own party."

"You are so right," said Danny. "I just got off the phone. The word is: no help. You're on your own. Without the party organization, we can't get out the vote for you."

Jack was undaunted. "Then we'll go around the bastards."

"That may not work either. The governor's losing a point a week in the polls. They won't come right out and say it, but they think it's all over for everybody. It's that asshole in the White House, dragging everybody in the party down with him. It will take an act of God for either one of you to win."

"No, just money," Jack said.

"We've got less than two thousand bucks in the kitty."

"I don't give a shit about that. Find out how much it will cost for a week of thirty-second television spots on every TV channel and radio station in Ohio. I'll have Morgan call New York and find out about production costs."

"Jack—"

"Danny, just do it. Now."

Danny picked up the phone. While he made his calls, Jack scribbled on a yellow legal pad, outlining the ads he had in mind. They were mostly images, few words. Subliminals were what he wanted. He knew every inch of footage that had ever been taken of him by the media. Danny finished his telephoning. He made some entries on the old-fashioned hand-cranked adding machine that he kept on his desk, then tore off the tape and handed it to Jack.

"That's about eighty grand more than we've got," he said.

Jack said, "A bargain. Book the time. I want a spot an hour for the last five days, heavy on the football games."

"Jack, they'll want the money up front."

"I'll sell the house," Jack said.

Morgan walked in.

Jack said, "I'll raffle Morgan."

"Very funny," Morgan said. "What's this all about?"

"Money," Jack said. "We need a hundred grand. Now. Morgan, find a buyer for the house."

"The house?" Morgan said. "You're out of your mind."

"It'll be a national landmark someday," Danny said. "On this spot President Adams, unarmed and alone, defeated the Mafia sharp-shooters and went on to save the world for the workers."

"Jack," Morgan said, "get serious."

"Morgan, honey, sell the house. Do you understand what I'm saying to you?"

"No."

"Then I'll spell it out: Merriwether is rich. We're poor. He can spend millions and not miss it. We're willing to lose everything.

Why? Because we have made a sacred promise to the people and we'd rather live in a cardboard box than break that promise."

Morgan looked at him with respect, and something that went beyond respect. "I understand," she said.

"Good. Bring me the money."

The next evening, in a motel near Beaver, Pennsylvania, a Mr. O. N. Laster of Saddle Brook, New Jersey, signed an agreement to purchase the Adamses' bungalow. He handed over to Mrs. Adams, the sole owner, a cashier's check for $59,500 as payment in full for the property.

After Mr. Laster departed—an exit easily arranged inasmuch as he did not exist—I gave Morgan a crate of rare books. Thanks to Morgan's Harvard training in cutthroat bargaining, the books, which included autographed first editions of a work by Henry James and *The Great Gatsby,* brought an aggregate of $68,764, or about 15 percent more than I would have dared to ask for the items. Morgan told interviewers that the books had been a bequest from her grandfather, and though they were the material things she treasured most in the world, she knew that Papa, as she had called that wonderful old man, would have understood that her husband and what he represented to Ohio and America had to come first.

Five days before the election, the spots went on the air. One set of ads showed a dizzying montage of still and moving pictures of F. Merriwether Street in the company of Richard Nixon, closing with a remarkable video sequence of Nixon shooting a sidelong glance at Merriwether, followed immediately by another in which the two men stood side by side in front of a crowd with their backs to the camera and their arms around each other. Because Nixon was so much shorter than Street, his groping hand appeared, briefly, to be fondling Street's buttocks. This was followed by a clip of Nixon's famous "I am not a crook" utterance and finally by an extreme close-up of F. Merriwether Street's habitually puzzled face. As Jack's witty columnist friend wrote, Street looked in that photo like an especially stupid horse that had just awakened to find itself in bed with the severed head of a Hollywood producer.

The other ads focused on Jack: A series were tributes to Jack from wounded Ohioans to whom he had ministered as an army medic during the Vietnam War, shots of Jack pushing the twins in their stroller, an interview with a worshipful Teresa Gallagher, shots of Jack comforting his terrified wife in the ruins of their modest bungalow, footage of Fats Corso scuttling off to jail in manacles. One or the other of these spots ran at least once an hour on every local television channel in Ohio.

The ads were brilliantly ruthless examples of the genre, and thanks to the last-minute surge in the polls that they created, Jack won election to lieutenant governor by 1,936 votes. By no coincidence, the governor, who had been pronounced dead by the media, won by an almost identical plurality of 1,894 votes. His margin might have been greater, but after Jack's closing blitz a lot of voters were under the impression that he was running for governor, and he got about two thousand write-in votes for that office in addition to the total he received for lieutenant governor.

At the victory celebration the governor embraced Jack, called out his name to the exultant crowd, and cried, "Meet a future governor of our great state! Lucky Jack Adams!"

When the governor turned to Morgan, she handed the twin she was holding—Skipper, she thought it was—to Jack and threw her arms around the governor, bestowing a big daughterly kiss onto the empty air beside his cheek.

While the crowd cheered Jack and his twins, who were waving to one and all, Morgan whispered a message into the governor's ear: "Lucky my ass, you double-crossing son of a bitch."

The governor blinked, smiled, and lifted one of the boys out of Jack's arms and held him aloft in triumph. "Cry, Skipper!" Morgan whispered.

This twin's name was Fitz, but frightened out of his wits by his mother's fierce expression, he uttered a mighty yell of distress and, to the crowd's delight, held out his chubby arms to his daddy.

2 Street, Frew, Street & Merriwether, the venerable law firm for which Cindy Miller worked, had devised a peculiar system for choosing partners from within itself. After a promising associate was marked for possible promotion, he was summoned into the presence of the managing partner and offered candidate membership in the Handful, so called because the firm never had more than five senior partners, and because the candidate would be observed and judged by the stern standards of the firm for the next five years. At the end of that period he would either be offered a partnership, or not. The candidate would know which way the decision had gone when, arriving at work on the fifth anniversary of the offer, he opened the door of his office to find either a burst of applause from the assembled senior partners or an empty office. In the latter case, the failed candidate was expected to depart at once. Personal belongings would be packed and shipped at the firm's expense, along with a final paycheck. This system had produced several nervous breakdowns, but the survivors usually did well for Street, Frew, Street & Merriwether and for themselves.

The fifth anniversary of Cindy's candidacy happened to fall in the week after the election in which Jack Adams had defeated F. Merriwether Street for lieutenant governor of Ohio. When she went into work that morning—arriving precisely fifteen minutes early as was the tradition—she found an empty office. Even though she had brought hundreds of thousands of dollars in business into the firm, had won difficult cases in court and settled even knottier ones by negotiation, no appeal was possible, or even thinkable. She left her rest-room key on her desk.

Danny had driven Cindy into work that morning and parked around the corner. His heart fell, then swelled with anger at the Streets, Merriwethers, and Frews of this world as he saw her approaching in the rearview mirror, head up, golden hair bouncing, skirt swinging as she walked at her usual firm, rapid pace. He saw her smile, then smile again and yet again as a stream of people said hi to her. A man in a five-hundred-dollar suit turned to watch her with a rueful smile as she walked by, the American object of desire itself.

"Bastards," Danny said.

"They are what they are," Cindy said.

"Cin, I'm so sorry."

"For what?"

"For sticking with Jack. That's the reason for this. We both know that."

"You're right," Cindy said. "What else would you expect the Merriwethers and the Streets to do to a woman whose husband did what you did to the scion of their fine old family?"

"I don't know what to say."

"I do," Cindy said. Cindy was dry-eyed. Her voice was even. What had happened was exactly what she had expected, and in her tidy way she had already made provisions for a new future. She grasped Danny's ruined right thigh and said, "Cheer up. You just got yourself a new partner."

Danny frowned in puzzlement. "I thought we always were partners," Danny said.

"I mean law partner. I want to join your firm."

Cindy had not mentioned this before. Danny said, "No shit? Are you serious?"

"Absolutely. We can start today."

"What about Jack?"

Cindy said, "When was the last time he came into the office? As a lawyer, not as a candidate?"

"Not since he was elected attorney general. As long as he's a public official he can't mess around with the firm. You know that."

"Which means he'll never come back, because he's going to spend the rest of his life being elected to higher and higher office. Isn't that the plan?"

Danny shrugged. "Unless he loses one."

"Fat chance."

"Cindy, he may not come in to practice law, but he comes in almost every day to talk politics or drop off the kids."

Cindy paused, eyes wide. "He drops off the kids?"

"Only for an hour or two. The receptionist watches them."

"What about Morgan?"

"He never brings them in when she's there."

"Ah. He's using them for cover while he gets laid."

"Probably."

"That will stop," Cindy said. "No kids in the office. And no politics. You've got to split the political operation off from the practice. You can keep the space you've got now as campaign headquarters or whatever you want to call it. Meet him there."

"Isolate the virus?"

"You said it, not me."

"Cindy, why this?"

"I'm unemployed."

"You can get a job with any firm in town."

"No thanks. You can't handle the firm alone. You're going broke.

259 ★ LUCKY BASTARD

You need a litigator and a partner with contacts with the people who run this town. I need a job. Unless you don't want me."

"I want you. You're the best lawyer in Columbus. But is this realistic?"

Cindy took Danny's hand. She said, "Danny, I don't need any lessons in reality. Let's go look at the new offices. We can walk."

"New offices?"

She looked over her shoulder at him, smiling, and crooked a finger: Follow me. To Danny she did not look a day older than she had looked in the corridors of Tannery Falls High. She had rented the offices the week before, in a glass building next door to the Merriwether Building. The brass plate on the mahogany door read: MILLER, ADAMS & MILLER.

"Jack between us," Cindy said. "Just like always."

She turned the key and opened the door onto a handsome suite of offices. Light fell through a glass ceiling onto mahogany and leather, onto Bokhara carpets and aromatic leather-bound books.

Danny whistled. "Can we afford this?"

"If we don't let Jack sign checks, yes, I think so," Cindy replied.

In her office, next to Danny's corner office, she unlocked a drawer and removed the papers she had drawn up for the partnership.

"I've already signed," she said. "Sign them yourself and get Jack's signature and we're in business."

3 To everyone's surprise, Morgan accepted the new partnership with enthusiasm. She saw advantages in removing Cindy from the encampment of the enemy and placing her, as it were, in protective custody. The closer her physical presence, the easier she was to watch and control. Yes, control: Morgan did, after all, have the power to disclose Cindy's innermost secret—or to put her in a position where she would be forced either to confess it to Danny, thus making wreckage of his life, or to do what her blackmailer asked. Any such blackmail would be more likely to succeed if Cindy had no power base of her own. As Morgan saw it, Cindy's loss of a gilded future at Street, Frew, Street & Merriwether was in every way our gain.

Also, from the start, Morgan had disliked having Danny in the same office with her and Jack. Danny's presence was the reason why she and Jack conversed in whispers when they discussed operational matters. Whispering annoyed them both—Jack because he disliked the hiss of Morgan's displeasure in his ear, Morgan because Jack made her want to shout and she was seldom able to do so.

To make possible more outspoken communications she converted Jack's old office into a soundproof room, telling the office staff that Jack needed a place to think, practice and play back his speeches, and, especially, hold strategy meetings out of earshot of the right-wing spies who stalked all persons of conscience who were fighting for social justice. The secretaries and the receptionist were themselves persons of conscience who had lived since Movement days with the suspicion that their telephones were being tapped and their food and drink were being poisoned by fascists, so this explanation made perfect sense to them.

The staff called it Morgan's room. It was equipped with a television set, a coffeepot of its own, a small refrigerator and microwave oven for heating pizza, a reading chair and lamp, a sofa bed. It could only be entered through a heavy steel door with a keypad lock to which Morgan alone had the combination. Not even Jack—especially not Jack—was entrusted with the entry code.

The room was also equipped with a hidden safe and certain other clandestine features. These were installed at night by her friend the Georgian sexual mechanic. He did this without my knowledge or approval. As provided by the approved procedure, he and Morgan now met at least once a month, usually in a motel after she met me. Unbeknownst to me, they also met from time to time on an impulse. These heated assignations had reawakened the Georgian's sexual obsession. In or out of bed, he would—as I soon learned—do anything for Morgan.

It was the Georgian, as you will remember, who headed the team that bugged the Gruesomes' penthouse. For what I thought were sound operational reasons, I had refused to let Morgan keep the tapes of Jack in action. It was, however, a simple matter for the Georgian to make copies and hand them over to her. Given his virtually matchless experience of women and what they are capable of doing in the name of love, this was an act of almost unbelievable folly. You would have thought him the last person in the world to fall into this particular trap. But as the history of the world had taught us long before these two lovers met, no one falls so deeply, madly, truly in love as a whore.

In any case, Morgan stored the tapes in the safe in her sound-proof room and sometimes went there at night to study them. Her power over Jack was slipping from her fingers. I had taken away her control of his sex life. As lieutenant governor, Jack had shaken loose from other bonds. He kept later hours, presiding over the state senate during crucial night sessions and traveling around Ohio to speak at political dinners and other name-building events. After "selling" the bungalow (which was subsequently resold at a loss by its purchaser), the Adamses purchased a new, larger house in an upscale part of town. Jack now had a car of his own, in which Morgan frequently discovered, in wee-hour searches, such traces of female occupancy as long hair of many colors, lipstick-smudged cigarette butts, combs, barrettes, lingerie, the lingering aroma of perfume and bodily secretions, and telltale stains on the upholstery—even, once, a diaphragm. All this forensic evidence of Jack's incurable treachery she kept in her hidden safe, sealed in a Tupperware container.

She sat up late and alone watching tapes of Jack & friends, especially the infrared sequences, in which specters seemed to be making love. Watching them was a disembodying experience, somewhere between seeing in the dark and a bad dream, and she never tired of it. In time it occurred to her that it might be useful to know who else had used the penthouse for adulterous assignations. She began in her usual studious, systematic way to review the other tapes. She found them laughable: pudgy members of the Gruesome engaged in the sort of sex she had left behind even before she was the age of some of their partners, mostly high school girls who paid for their cocaine with inert coitus or reluctant and ludicrously inept fellatio.

And then at the end of a long evening, at the very end of one tape, she saw something that interested her very much: the governor of the state, sucking on a Popsicle with a look of dopey ecstasy that no known flavor of confectionery ice could possibly produce. The camera, remotely controlled by the Georgian or one of his colleagues from a rented room on the floor below, pulls back to show a girl, her back to the camera, kneeling in front of the governor. The girl is a thin blonde with buds for breasts who looks no more than twelve. She licks a Popsicle. The governor asks if she'll share it with him. "No, but I'll give you my sweater!" He holds the Popsicle while she strips off her sweater. This is repeated, while she disrobes item by item, saying, "Don't you dare lick my Popsicle!" At last she is stark naked: prominent ribs, a row of knobs down her spine. He refuses to give back her Popsicle. She whimpers, pleading, "But I *have* to have something to lick." To which the governor replies (I am not making this up), "How about Uncle Wiggly?" She falls to her knees.

Showing me this footage, Morgan said, "Can you imagine?"

"There seems to be no need to imagine anything. Including who gave this to you."

Morgan made no apologies. She said, "You do understand what you have just seen and what it means, do you not?"

I thought I did, but I said, "You tell me."

A completely spontaneous smile, luminous with delight—such a rare event—spread over her face. Giggling, she said, "The Good Humor Man has just made our boy governor of Ohio. And therefore, sooner than we ever hoped, president of the United States."

Peter agreed. He demanded immediate action to exploit this break. This was no work for Morgan. We delivered a copy of the tape to the governor along with several stop-action pictures of the Popsicle so that he would not delay watching it. A day or two later one of our people called him on his car phone.

"Yes."

"This is the photographer."

"What do you want?"

"Take the elevator to the penthouse at five forty-three tomorrow morning."

"Impossible."

"In that case, watch the Public Access Channel at six-thirty."

"Listen, you—"

"The elevator, five forty-three."

Click.

At the appointed hour the Georgian and another man, both wearing gorilla masks, met the governor in the same elevator car in which Jack and I had had our chat about the perils of indulging in sex and drugs in the presence of witnesses. The governor was staggered by the price his blackmailers named.

"Resign?" he said, baffled. "What can I do for you if I do that?"

"We've already told you what you can do for us," said the smaller gorilla, who sounded like a Princeton man who had something disagreeable in his mouth and was looking for a place to spit. "You can accept it or see the tape on television."

"They'd never run it."

"No? Then this is your last day of happiness. Every newspaper and TV station will have a copy by the end of the day."

The governor said, "You're crazy."

"It's up to you. You can resign and walk away or refuse and take the consequences. Either way, you'll be out in a week. We're offering you a chance to go back to the practice of law. But if you prefer twenty years in prison for statutory rape, we won't stand in your way."

The smaller gorilla handed the governor his playmate's birth certificate. "That makes her thirteen," the gorilla said. "She's an eighth grader. Her father is a fireman. Both her parents are devout Baptists. The girl sings in the choir. She's a hopeless cocaine addict, thanks to you. Think about it."

The birth certificate dropped from the governor's long manicured fingers and fluttered to the floor.

"For Christ's sake," he said. "Give me a break."

"Okay, you've got forty-eight hours," said the Georgian. "Today is Tuesday. Resign not later than Thursday."

"That's too soon. It can't be done."

"The stuff goes out in the last mail on Thursday."

On Wednesday night the governor went on television, confessed that owing to the stresses of public life he had developed a dependence on prescription drugs and alcohol that clouded his judgment and endangered his life. His four teenage daughters sat beside him on the sofa as, holding his wife's hand, he formally resigned his office. He asked for the prayers of all Ohioans that the course of treatment on which he was about to enter in a private hospital would restore him, whole and healthy again, to his wife and their wonderful family.

Jack took the oath of office immediately, and a week later he and

Morgan moved into the Governor's Mansion and into an office that had previously been held by seven future presidents of the United States.

4   Jack regarded the governorship as a wonderful opportunity to campaign on a continual basis. He had no real interest in actually governing. Running for office was what exhilarated him, and every victory was important only as a prelude to the next victory.

He continued to denounce crime, to hammer the special interests without interfering with them in any significant way, to champion the downtrodden and walk among them whenever a camera was present. It was a rare month on Ohio television when Jack, often accompanied by the twins, did not visit a distressed welfare mother and promise succor, or visit a school to teach a class to the learning disabled, or throw his arms around the close relatives of a murder victim. He was often on the telephone, consoling widows and orphans, congratulating athletes and scholars, commending policemen on useful arrests and prosecutors on convictions. Ohioans from every walk of life found themselves invited to the governor's mansion for breakfast or lunch or dinner, or just for a chat with Jack Adams. His sincerity was genuine, if not very long in duration—but then, it had to last only long enough for a shutter to whir.

"He's a political mosquito flying around looking for warm bodies," said Cindy, watching him work a disaster scene on the evening news. "A drop of blood here, another case of political malaria there. Thanks for the blood, have a microbe! Today Chillicothe, tomorrow the world."

As to the daily business of his administration, Governor Adams of Ohio, like President Charles de Gaulle of France, did not concern himself with the details of government, but only with its grand strategy and enduring principles and interests.

This approach drove Morgan crazy. What she wanted from Jack was substance, by which she meant a frontal attack on the Establishment, a fearless advocacy of the many causes in which she and her clients so passionately believed. In Morgan's room, shouting now instead of whispering, she pleaded with him to take a stand on all the inflammatory issues of the day.

"Issues make enemies," Jack said. "Tell your friends—"

"*My* friends? Who do you think are the street fighters of your movement?"

"I know. Believe me, I know. But they're already with me. What I need to do is attract the people who aren't yet with me. I can't get them to join me and trust me by doing things and saying things that piss them off."

"What about waking them up?"

"They wake up every morning and look for work. This is the Rust Belt, Morg. People are scared by unemployment, scared by change that has ruined their lives. And you want me to tell them they ain't seen nothin' yet?"

"There's good change and bad change. This is the Rust Belt because capitalism has failed them, screwed them, and left them high and dry. *Capitalism*, Jack."

"Sure it has. But they want it to come home again. You think they look at those abandoned mills and factories and say, 'Hooray, the bosses are gone'? What they say is 'All is forgiven. Bring back the jobs.' "

"That's exactly what has to change—the mind of the people."

"Well, it won't happen except out of the barrel of a gun. My grandfather was thrown into the street and do you know what he said about the rich? 'No poor man ever gave me a job.'"

"I want to vomit," Morgan said. "Jack, listen to me. You have to stand for something."

"I do. Every day. Reelection."

"Goddamnit, Jack, get serious."

"About what? The endangered snail darter?"

"Jesus! You really don't understand, do you? The purpose of the environmental movement is not to save the fucking environment. Its purpose is to demonstrate the crimes and failures of capitalism. Just like every other component of the cause. Hammer away, hammer away, hammer away. Take the Establishment apart chip by chip. First we discredit them, then we remove them, then we apply the remedies."

"I thought my job was to get elected. I thought that was the Prime Directive."

"It is. But not as a goddamned Republican. You can't even give a straight answer on abortion. It's embarrassing, Jack."

"Morgan, I know you don't feel like I do about this, but I look at Fitz and Skipper and I—"

"And you what? I don't want to hear it. You don't understand. You have to send a signal to the faithful. Reassure them."

"That's why I have you," Jack said. "If I wasn't the real thing deep down inside, would I be married to somebody like you? That's the message. Tell them you know what's really in my heart. Tell them to be patient."

"For how long?"

He gave her the smile. "Until tomorrow comes, as they know it will."

"Today pinpricks, tomorrow hammer blows. Is that it?"

"Pinpricks in the darkness are just another name for stars," Jack replied.

Morgan gagged theatrically, then threw her own yellow pad at him. "Here! Write that down too!"

But she could not help admiring him. He was so quick, so glib, so Machiavellian—a prince in the only sense of the word that had any meaning or value.

Tiresome as they were to Jack, these discussions of principle were important to Morgan because they reminded Jack that he was supposed to have a conscience. Even if he refused to act on them, it was her task to remind him constantly of the principles that drove the operation. Otherwise, she knew, he would forget them, as he forgot women, forgot favors, forgot friends, forgot promises. Jack lived in the moment, for the moment, in a psychic world that had no past, only a future in which, she suspected, he believed that he could escape from the consequences of youthful follies whose visible symbol was Morgan herself. He could live with her because he had to, for as long as he had to. But he wanted power as a means of escape from the past. Escape from Peter. Escape from the revolution. Escape from Morgan. That was what she believed.

Fourteen months after succeeding to the governorship through the dirty tricks of the people in gorilla masks, Jack was reelected in a landslide while Republicans were sweeping into almost every other high office in the land. We gave him half a million dollars toward the cost of his campaign, but it wasn't the money that made the difference, it was Jack, Jack, Jack. At least five national media outlets asked the question, "Next Stop, the Presidency?"

Deep within himself, Jack was sure that the answer was yes. Everything favored him.

5 "Everything?" Peter asked Morgan over a bucket of the Colonel's crispy fried chicken in King of Prussia, Pennsylvania. (This hamlet was out of the way, but Peter loved the name when he saw it on the map). "Even," Peter said, "the hatred of his own party's inner circle?"

"Especially that," Morgan said.

She explained Jack's reasoning: The new president in Washington, a charming fascist—who would have thought that such a creature existed?—had just won in a landslide of his own. Like Jack himself, and like JFK, this born winner was an outsider who only a short time before had been given no chance to rise to the top. Yet now his overpowering strengths—

"Which are the strengths of trivia," Peter said.

"Precisely," Morgan replied. "That's the great American secret."

Now even the new president's mortal enemies in the media conceded among themselves that he would probably be unbeatable if he ran for reelection. The economy, a shambles when he took office, was on the upswing. The president's sunny disposition drove his policy. With tireless good nature he repeated over and over again the five or six simplistic principles that seemed to comprise his entire intellectual repertoire. Somehow, bewildering as it was to Morgan, this had produced the dawn of an era of good feeling. Anyone who ran against this lovable optimist would be seen as a doomsayer and would go down in defeat. Therefore, no candidate with the instinct of self-preservation would want the nomination four years hence. Jack's party would be looking for a sacrificial lamb, someone on the outer edge of the party who could lose and then be tossed on the ash heap of history.

Jack saw this as his great opportunity. The party leaders might not support him, but they would not oppose him if he ran. And if he won the primaries and went into the convention with enough votes, they could not stop him.

"All this to lose the election?" I said.

"Maybe," Morgan said. "But to lose honorably, to go down fighting, to make an indelible impression. Jack is young. Four years after he loses he'll still be young enough to run again, and win."

"He's going to come out of the closet, be a radical?" I asked.

"Jack?" Morgan replied. "Don't make me laugh. He'll make a point of being as much like his opponent as possible. It worked for JFK. Nixon was supposed to be the ruthless one, but it was Kennedy who called for nuking China if it took one step across an imaginary line in the Pescadores, Kennedy who claimed there was a missile gap, Kennedy who may have stolen the election—"

"You're quoting Jack?"

"Yes. But it's all true. You can get away with anything in this country if you make the right noises."

"Point taken," Peter said. "Question: Is this a rational judgment or does Jack see this progression of future events as his destiny?"

This was the fundamental question. Jack's delusion that he was a secret carrier of the Kennedy genes had been powerfully reinforced by his unbroken series of political successes.

"He believes in his bones," Morgan answered, "that he can do this because he was born to do it. Every stroke of luck is a sign in the sky to him—Daddy on the heliograph from heaven. He never says this in so many words, but I see it in his eyes. He thinks he has already pulled Excalibur out of the stone, and all he has to do now is sit down at the Round Table."

Peter was smiling, bemused and proud. He had made all this happen with a wave of his magic wand. You could see the thought dancing like a jester in his head. I thought, *And escape from this Merlin. That is his real plan.* I kept the thought to myself; this was not the moment to speak it aloud.

Morgan said, "There is one small problem. It will cost at least twenty million dollars to put this plan into effect. Jack believes he is holding a promissory note from you for that or any other amount he may need."

"Ah, he wants a trust fund, just like a real Kennedy!" Peter waved a careless hand. "Why not?"

Always the worrier, I said, "Explaining where it came from will be the problem."

Peter said, quite distinctly, "Then make it cease to be a problem, Comrade Colonel."

By calling me by my rank, a recent one, he was pointing out that (1), I had just been promoted because I was supposed to be able to solve such routine problems as this, and (2), If there was a problem, it was *my* problem.

Peter had already put all annoying details behind him. "This chicken would be a sensation in Moscow," he said, actually licking his fingers. "These outlets, so cheery with their stripes and cupolas, remind one of St. Basil's, don't you agree, Dmitri?"

"Absolutely," I said. His obedient servant. But I wondered how we were going to move all that money by dark of night.

6   As a warranty of good things to come, Peter authorized the immediate delivery of $250,000 in cash to cover the incidental expenses of Jack's politicking. I made a trip to a Caribbean island to draw the funds from a bank in which Peter deposited some of his fees from his allies in the cocaine trade. Morgan—happy in the knowledge that the drug offensive against the United States was war on capitalism by other means, sweet revenge for the plutocratic opium trade to China of another era—transported the money back to Columbus in the trunk of the used BMW that had replaced her beloved VW bus. The money—all in well-worn tens, twenties, and Peter's signature fifties—made an impressive sight when Morgan untied the strings of the banker's boxes and heaped it on the table in her soundproof safe room. She had summoned Jack by telephone from the governor's mansion, expecting him to explode with joy when he beheld this hillock of greenbacks. His reaction was not quite what she had expected. Because she had been with me, and then with her Georgian (bank boxes under the bed), and then alone in her car on the highway, she had missed the evening news. Jack had not. The lead story described a CIA man who had been arrested, far too late, by the FBI and charged with

passing secrets to us. According to the networks, this spy had been paid almost three million dollars in cash for his treason. Jack was infuriated.

"The Russians pay some fucking file clerk in the CIA three million bucks for a grocery bag full of Xeroxes," he said, "and Peter expects me to become president of the United States on a lousy two hundred and fifty thou?"

He was shouting. He was speaking Peter's name aloud. He was abandoning the pretense that he was a free agent who sometimes got a little help from benevolent friends. All this was a startling turnabout. This red-faced, screaming dervish was not the Jack whom Morgan knew. She was nonplused. She thought she had better defend the cover story lest it unravel altogether.

She said, "Jack, shut up. The comparison is ludicrous. The KGB has nothing to do with Peter."

"Right," said Jack. "And you and I are America's happiest married couple."

Morgan felt a stab of panic. She felt like a guilty wife whose husband reveals that he has known all along about her lover. Or so she said later, after she had had time to classify the anxiety that burst so unexpectedly to the surface. Did Jack *know*? What did he know? How could he know it? Was he going to drag it all into the open? Ruin everything? *Embarrass* her?

With a calmness that surprised them both, she asked, "What's that supposed to mean?"

"It means I'm tired of playing games and even tireder of being poor," Jack replied, also calmer now but still angry; like a husband who is prepared to forgive for the last time, he was laying down the law. "But listen to me, Morgan. I want this problem solved or I'm gone."

"Gone? Where to? Are you crazy?"

Jack laughed, a harsh bark she had not heard before. He said, "You heard me. What are they going to do, hunt me down to the ends of the Earth and shoot me? Have they got somebody else who has a chance at the White House? I got where I am on my own. You think I can't get to the presidency, or somewhere else where I can make life hell for them, on my own?"

"On your own, my ass. If you think that, you *are* crazy."

"Try me. I don't need these fuckers, and I don't care how many pictures of my slippery dick they've got. I'll tell the world they're the CIA trying to frame me because of their ties to the Mafia and the child porn trade. Who do you think will be believed?"

Morgan knew he was serious. She knew he was right about the media's reaction to the outrageous lie he had just invented on the spur of the moment. What a talent! She said, "I can't believe this."

"You'd better believe it. Morgan, this is my message to Peter and his freedom-loving friends: Get the fucking money or get another boy!"

With a sudden, violent gesture straight out of the movies—Steve McQueen in a rage—Jack swept some of Peter's money off the table. Packets of banknotes flew across the room and bounced off the cork-lined walls.

After a disapproving silence Morgan said, "Is that all?"

Jack kicked the money. "Is *that* all? I want more. And I want it now."

"Oh? What amount do you have in mind?"

"The whole twenty million we need to make this run. Up front. Now. They're serious? Fine. So am I."

"Why now?"

"Jesus, Morg, you're the one who went to the Business School. If we hold it for four years and you invest it, how much will it earn?"

"At fifteen percent, twelve million."

"That's why. Three million a year. Twenty million up front or forget it." He pronounced the amount slowly, with exaggeration: *Twen-ty mil-yun.* He said, "And that's a down payment on the hundred, hundred and fifty million we'll need for the fall campaign, beginning with the New Hampshire primary three years from now."

"You're not planning to raise any money of your own, or get any from the party?"

"You know I can't count on that. The party hates me."

"If you're nominated, they'll have to help you."

Jack ignored her; they both knew better. He said, "I was promised money, all the money I needed. You are my witness. Nobody said anything about my raising money. I don't have time to raise money and get elected at the same time. I want what I was promised. If I get it, Peter gets what he wants."

"And if you don't get it?"

"I'll walk."

"Jack, be realistic," Morgan said.

"Morgan, don't fucking *reason* with me."

"I'll fucking shoot you if I have to, Jack. So shut up and listen. Leaving aside what can happen to you if you try, as you so quaintly put it, to walk, do you have any idea what problems are involved in cleaning up money whose origins you can't explain? I go out of my mind as it is. How am I supposed to explain to Danny, let alone the feds, where I got twenty million dollars in tens and twenties? There's got to be paper, transactions, explanations. Appearances must be kept up. Otherwise you're naked to your enemies and you go to prison. For Christ's sake, Jack, the Republicans are running the Justice Department. F. Merriwether Street is the U.S. attorney for this district of Ohio. We can't just keep twenty million in a desk drawer. It has to be explainable, it has to come through banks—"

"Then buy a fucking bank," Jack said. "There must be one for sale somewhere in Ohio. God knows enough of them are failing or on the verge of it."

"A bank?" Morgan was astonished all over again by the mysterious workings of Jack's mind. She said, "Who's going to run it?"

Jack replied, "You. Out of the back room, just like you run everything else. Danny can be chairman of the board."

Morgan said, "Jesus, Jack."

Jack mocked her, " 'Jesus, Jack'—"

"No, I mean it, God bless your Byzantine mind. You're a genius. That's the solution." Morgan was beaming, the proud mother now. "It's so obvious. A bank!" She slapped her forehead. "Why didn't I think of it?"

"I'll tell everybody you did," Jack said. "All your idea, my pleasure, I hope you get a promotion. Just do it. I'm tired of being a poor boy."

All of a sudden he was not smiling, not trying to charm her, not retreating. He was commanding her, confronting her. Morgan saw a different man, as if the hidden Jack had suddenly appeared like some inner Danny to defend the old, timid Jack from a bully.

Jack himself had not changed so much that he didn't instantaneously note the slightest flicker of interest in any female eye, even Morgan's. Now he noted the transformation in the female before him. He had not had a woman that day, which was already deep into its evening. Suddenly he remembered Morgan's sweet cock-eyed breasts, remembered their sweat-soaked spring afternoons in Cambridge all those years ago. Was it possible?

As if in encouragement—surrender?—Morgan smiled at him. This was an actual female smile, misty with the hope of love. For a moment she was lovely. Lovely. He had always thought she could be beautiful if she let her hair grow, got rid of her scratched and smudged granny glasses, wore clothes that let you imagine her body. Morgan saw what was on his mind, just as so many normal women had done in the past. Morgan smelled Jack's peculiar musk. Her lower body moved of its own accord. She turned this sexual twitch into another kind of gesture, bringing herself up short. But Jack was not fooled.

Morgan realized, shocked by her own thought, that she was actually hoping that Jack would make a move. Jack saw this; she saw him see it. And then (Morgan apprehending this thought, too), he said to himself, *Nah.*

In an instant his mind was elsewhere. Morgan was back in real time and space; she and Jack were once again what they really were, handler and asset, their wedding bands a pair of symbolic handcuffs. He looked at his watch.

"Gotta go," he said. "I have a ten o'clock interview with a TV reporter."

Morgan said, "Really? How tall is this TV reporter?"

"About five-four," Jack replied.

"You're disgusting."

Jack smiled and the gates of Camelot opened. He said, "Do you really think so, Morg?"

7 Like most truly dangerous ideas, Jack's was elementary. Its power consisted in the fact that nobody had ever had it before. Peter was as entranced by the notion of owning his own bank as

Morgan had been. It was the solution to all our money problems. He immediately gave his approval.

"It was so obvious!" said Peter. "Dmitri, why don't you ever have ideas like this?"

He left the details to Morgan and me, with one proviso: "Keep the asset completely separate, completely clean," he said. "I want fire walls, mazes, labyrinths between him and the money."

"But the whole idea is to get the money to him," said I, never one to ignore the obvious.

"Yes, Dmitri, it is," Peter replied in his most tired voice. "But the controlling idea, in this as in everything concerning this uniquely valuable asset, is to find a way to get the money to him without letting him touch it, see it, or even smell it. He should not even carry a wallet!"

Certainly. Understood. What could be simpler?

"I am serious about the wallet," Peter said. "Others should pay. Great men should not come in contact with coins and banknotes."

Morgan, at least, was undaunted. With Danny as her lawyer, she set up a dummy corporation and over a period of months used the $250,000 that she had picked up off the floor after Jack's tantrum to purchase enough stock in a struggling suburban bank to take it over. She changed the institution's humdrum name to the Columbus Bank of the Western Reserve, thus suggesting that this wholly owned subsidiary of the Soviet Ministry of State Security was somehow a sister institution of the U.S. Federal Reserve system. She fired the staff and hired new people through a headhunter. She wrote a new charter and reorganized the bank's structure along sound, cutthroat, Harvard B-School principles. All negotiations for this complex transaction were handled, for a handsome fee, by Danny. When total control had been achieved, which happened swiftly, she appointed Danny as the bank's general counsel at an annual retainer of $100,000 plus stock options.

"General counsel?" Jack said. "No, chairman."

"Too risky," said Morgan.

"Danny? Risky? He's the only one I can trust."

"Remember who he's married to, Jack."

"That's never been a problem in the past."

"True, but we're talking about the future here, and we have not yet come to the end of time. Or to the end of Cindy's story."

Jack had not understood his position. Because the bank had been his idea, he was territorial about it. He pressed. "It's got to be Danny."

"No," Morgan said. "I have another candidate."

"Morgan—"

"If you're Danny's friend, you don't want him to be the front man on this. So listen, will you?"

"All right. Who do you have in mind?"

Morgan told him.

Jack whistled. "That's a stroke of fucking genius," he said. "But who's going to talk to him? I can't. You shouldn't."

"Danny will do it," Morgan said. "He's our back-room guy. Are you beginning to see the reasons, the pattern, the thinking behind this?"

Suddenly serious, Jack said, "Yeah, I think so."

"Then relax. This bank is a great idea, but it's just a place to keep money, and money is a danger to you. Next to your cock, the biggest danger. You can't have anything to do with the bank. You know nothing about it. You never talk about it with anyone but me, your spouse, because I'm the only person in the world who can't be compelled to testify against you in a court of law. Don't ask Danny anything. Agreed?"

Deadpan, understanding that he was dealing with Morgan the controller, Jack said, "I'll try to remember that."

8 That evening, after Cindy had gone home, Morgan's candidate for chairman of the board met Danny Miller for a drink— ginger ale, in this case—in the room set aside for such meetings in the office suite of Miller, Adams & Miller. It was the governor. Danny had not seen him since his disgrace and fall.

Danny was deeply affected by the hopeless look of the man, whose features seemed to have been moved in some subtle way from one place to another on his weak, sallow face. His eyes wandered. His expensive clothes, now marginally out of style, did not fit him as before.

Danny said, "Governor, I'm sorry as hell for your troubles. So is Jack."

Since returning from the rehabilitation center, the governor had struggled to reestablish his career as a lawyer, but it had been an uphill struggle. Few clients were willing to entrust their affairs to a self-confessed alcoholic with a pill habit. Besides that, no one except his mother would have believed that the reasons stated for the governor's resignation were the real reasons. The world of acquaintances the governor had created as a politician evaporated the day he left office. He brought very little business into his old law firm and little weight to its councils. And that was not all. While he was in the hospital his wife had found the Popsicle tape after prying open the locked desk drawer in which he had deposited it. She had immediately installed locks on the doors of his daughters' bedrooms and soon afterward filed for divorce. He was broke, lost, confused.

"That's nice to know," said the governor. "Why am I here?"

"Because I need your help. Needless to say I haven't discussed this meeting with Jack, and I never will. He knows nothing about it, and never will. But I know he's been concerned about you, that he's wondered how to put your talents to work again."

"That's Jack all over," the governor said. "So what's this all about, and what does Jack really want from me?"

Even Danny's kindness had its limits. And he knew bravado when he saw it, and knew that the governor was in no position to refuse any reasonable offer. He said, "Governor, if you don't want to have this conversation we don't have to have it."

The governor was startled by this change in tone; after years of being deferred to, jollied, never jostled, he was frequently startled by what people now felt free to say to him. He said, "Sorry, Dan. Go ahead. You know I'm interested in anything you have to say."

"I hope so, because this means a lot to me and my client."

"If Jack's not a party to this, what client are we talking about?"

"The Columbus Bank of the Western Reserve," Danny replied.

The governor raised his eyebrows: The *what*?

Danny said, "I am instructed to offer you the post of chairman of the board of directors, effective immediately."

The governor blinked. "This is flattering. But I'm not sure, Dan."

"The honorarium would be fifty thousand a year, plus stock options and expenses," Danny said. "You won't find your duties much of a distraction. Two meetings a month. Some representation work. We'd hope that you'd bring in the right kind of customers."

The old man's face was a study—the governor was still in his early fifties, but "old man" was the term for him. Thanks to Morgan's credit investigations, Danny knew he was hundreds of thousands in debt and had hardly enough income to cover his mortgage. He was on the brink of bankruptcy, and if he was smart he would file before his wife's divorce settlement came through. The governor said, "Dan, why are you doing this?"

"Because you're the man the bank needs." Danny really believed this; yet he could see that the governor himself had trouble believing it. Danny said, "Governor, to be frank, you're still a name to conjure with in this state, even nationally. We need your reputation behind us."

That was certainly true, though once again Danny had no idea how right he was.

The governor nodded and cleared his throat at length; hardly anyone called him "Governor" anymore. He asked for one last assurance. "Jack's really not involved in this?"

Danny said, "In no way."

"Can you make it seventy-five?"

"Not now. But salary is not the bottom line."

"Then I accept."

"I'm glad. Jack will be glad—" The governor interrupted Danny with a look of deep skepticism. Danny continued, "—when he reads it in the paper. He really does wish you well."

"That's good to know," said the governor. "When do I start?"

"As soon as you sign this contract," Danny said, handing it over.

The governor took out his Mont Blanc Meisterstuck fountain pen and signed all three copies of the twenty-page document without reading it.

This was a man, Danny thought, who no longer cared what happened to him. The governor handed the papers to Danny.

He said, "You and Jack don't match, you know. I've never understood the connection. None of my business, of course."

"That's okay," Danny said. "A lot of people say the same thing. Always have. But I know Jack better than anyone."

"Then you must know something the rest of us don't," the governor said.

Two

★ ★

1 Peter's sarcasm about my creativity notwithstanding, I did occasionally have useful ideas, and one night in Snowshoe, Pennsylvania, I broached a subject never before discussed between us. Morgan had just left us. That night, a wintry one, Morgan had been wearing her usual baggy trousers, sweatshirt, parka, and army boots. Her hair (have I mentioned that it was streaked with gray?) was tied in a bandanna, her granny glasses were covered with thumbprints and flecks of paint from the propaganda posters she had been silk-screening as a corporal act of solidarity with one of her feminist groups. *Abortion Now! Save the Whales! U.S. out of [fill in the blank]!* Gray hair or no, she was fresh and, by American standards, youthful. In certain lights, after certain turnings of the head, as when she smiled at one of Peter's quips, she was mysteriously lovely.

She had had such a moment on this particular evening, and Peter had taken note. I had seen the look in his eyes, the thought in his mind: What could I have made of this girl's beauty if her mind had not been more useful to me? What might I make of her now?

After she left us, but before her image faded from Peter's memory—usually a process of milliseconds—I said, "Morgan does not look much like the first lady of Ohio."

Peter was reading a report on his new bank. My words produced an uninterested lifting of the eyes, a shrug. What else was new?

I persisted. "At one point, Comrade General, you suggested that the time would come when Morgan would have to become a more traditional American political wife."

Needless to say, he had never said any such thing, and probably

realized this. Nevertheless he said, "Yes?" Just as if he really had
made such a foresighted suggestion at an earlier time and was just
too tired to remember it.

I said, "I wonder if the time has now come."

Peter, his eyes still fixed on the page, said, "Why now, after all
these years?"

"Because we are moving into a new stage. Togetherness is important to Americans."

Until now, the cover story for Morgan's apartness, designed to
protect Jack from being contaminated should her cover ever be
blown, had been that the Adamses were a loving and devoted but
very private couple, and that Morgan insisted on leading her own
professional life, quite independent of her husband's political career.

"And now what will she do?" Peter asked. "Gaze adoringly as he
delivers speeches? Entertain political ladies to tea?"

"She already does that when he's out campaigning. What I have
in mind is a physical transformation. This is called a makeover."

I saw that Peter was confused by the word, a most satisfactory result. He said, "Come to the point."

"New hair, new clothes, cosmetics. Manners. She must leave the
costume of revolution behind her."

"Why?" said Peter. "Isn't her dowdiness an advantage—handsome governor loves plain-Jane wife?"

"In Ohio, perhaps. But when he runs for president he'll need a
princess by his side. Not a maid of Stalingrad."

A bad joke. But Peter said, "Very well. Make her over. Tell her it
is my desire, my order." He smiled, actually amused. "I wish I could
be a fly on the wall when you give her the news."

I raised the matter with Morgan the next time we met, about
three weeks later when a convention on women's rights brought
her to Manhattan. We dined late, at an expensive East Side Japanese restaurant. At the time sushi was a bourgeois fad and we were
surrounded by an after-theater crowd who joked knowledgeably
with aloof sushi-makers and kimonoed waitresses about *negi toro*
and *hamachi* and *uni,* as if they were chatting about nose and finish
with a sommelier. This made me gruff. We ordered tempura, the
only cooked dish on the menu. I ate the shrimp, Morgan the veg-

etables. Then I passed on Peter's instructions to Morgan. After absorbing the words she went as still as a doe.

"What exactly are you talking about?" she said.

I explained: a change in appearance as well as a change in role. New style, new personality, a certain new demureness, contact lenses instead of glasses. Dyed hair. Maquillage. Her jaw dropped.

"Carmine fingernails," I said, attempting to lighten the moment.

She threw down her chopsticks and made a wordless sound of disgust.

A flash of revolutionary temper, strangled shout: "Dmitri, I'll be god—"

I said, "Argument is futile. This is Peter's wish."

Of course she did not stop arguing. As if I were a lover who had gotten her into bed by spouting Engels and then asked her to convert to Republicanism (not a bad analogy, in her mind), Morgan told me furiously that she was what she was, take it or leave it. She would lose all credibility with her clientele, with the Movement, they would denounce her as a sellout—

"Believe me," I said, "they will not. In their secret hearts they all want to be starlets."

"That's insulting."

"Nonsense. Think of it as a disguise, an extension of your tradecraft, another way to blind the enemy."

"Jesus, but you're diabolical. Everything is a revolutionary act."

"If coldly considered, yes."

I handed Morgan a business card for a charm farm in Florida.

She said, "The Aphrodite? The *Aphrodite*? In Palm Beach, for Christ's sake? I can't go to Florida. I've got a million—"

I said, "They are expecting you tomorrow. It will take a week for them to transform you, so be sure to call your husband."

"And tell him what?"

I leaned toward her. "That you will have a surprise for him."

"Don't wink at me, Dmitri," she said. "I hate it."

But even at that early stage, one could see that she was not nearly so reluctant as she made out. She was human, after all, and female. Perhaps her Leonardo awaited her in Palm Beach, ready, like the original, to lead the dull young wife out of the mortal flesh and onto the canvas as the immortal Gioconda.

I said, "One little smile?"

Morgan obliged, tight-lipped and empty-eyed, as if she had read my thought. "Do you want a photograph of the results?" she asked.

"I will have a personal report from a certain Georgian who will be in Palm Beach on business."

She smiled. "You think of everything."

In cold revolutionary terms, yes. And as might have been expected, he fell in love with this redesigned Morgan all over again, just as he had done with all her previous personae.

2 A week later, when Morgan came home to the governor's mansion, she found Jack playing cars on the floor with the twins. He did not recognize her at first; neither did Fitz and Skipper, who seldom saw her anyway.

Then Jack said, "Shazam! It's Mommy, guys!"

"No it's not," said Fitz, kicking her on the ankle.

Morgan had been transformed—flowing coiffure, face elaborately made up, sleek designer suit, long depilitated legs seldom before glimpsed by the eyes of man, pedicured feet in sling-back high heels. Her large eyes, always before swimming behind thick lenses, were now exposed, moist and dreamy and slightly out of focus, a most attractive effect, beneath new contact lenses that made them subtly greener than they really were. Perfume wafted from her hair, from the creases of her flesh.

"Good God, how did you get past security?" Jack said.

Morgan said, "They recognized my voice when I raised it. But I'm supposed to work on that, be more kittenish."

"But why?"

"Orders from Peter. It's a disguise, to get you more votes. How do you like it?"

Morgan tossed her luxuriant hair, dark blond but crackling with auburn lights. Jack laughed aloud.

"Yeah, baby," he said. "That's *stimulating*."

"Forget it, baby," Morgan replied.

To Morgan's friends on the Left who were distressed by this abrupt transformation, she told the simple truth: This Morgan was an impersonation, a necessary tactic, a way like any other to wage revolution. The reassurance was not really necessary. As I had predicted, they loved the way she was now—the Red Avenger as Barbie. Such a delicious joke!

For many years, as you know, Jack had been telling true believers to ignore appearances and believe in him as an act of faith. As he explained, "As long as these people think you're lying for a good cause, *their* cause, you can get away with anything." For Jack Adams, bastard son—in his mind at least—of JFK, a reincarnated Caligula who convinced the world that he was really young King Arthur, this was blood wisdom.

Caligula's court, the media, which the old Morgan had avoided like poison while they largely ignored her, was intrigued by the new one and, to her surprise, she by it. This new Morgan was tremendously telegenic. She began to appear with some frequency, then almost compulsively, on talk shows. So charming was her on-camera conversation, so quick her wit, so visible her sympathy for every kind of human being, that there was talk of giving her her own talk show.

Something else happened. For the first time in years Morgan felt men's eyes on her, and after years of feigning frigidity she was surprised to find that she enjoyed the heat of their regard, that she liked returning an age-old, slow measured glance that rebuffed and invited at the same time. Even Danny Miller, most faithful of husbands, gave her the occasional appreciative look. They were seeing a good deal more of each other now as a result of their common involvement in the Columbus Bank of the Western Reserve, which was prospering as a result of Morgan's amazingly good advice as a management consultant. Morgan flirted a little with Danny—nothing much: a flash of thigh, a smile, a physical delight in his jokes. Afterward, lying abed, she felt that he might have made a move, if he were anyone but Danny and she were anyone but Jack's wife.

And then what? Alone in the dark, she imagined it in detail.

3 Though there was no way to be certain, short of submerging him in a diving bell, we had the impression that Jack was living a more orderly sex life. He no longer had his call-in show, and

his mobility and privacy had been greatly diminished by the con-
strictions of high office. Now that he was the governor, he was accompanied at all times by bodyguards. As a precaution against his
turning them, JFK-style, into companions of the bedchamber, Morgan took over the job of interviewing and hiring them. Every one
she selected was a devout, born-again Christian family man who
abhorred sin. This was Jack's first close-up experience with prudery,
but being Jack, he found a way around the problem by arranging
daytime rendezvous with seemingly respectable females in the privacy of his office, by combining nighttime political events with
quick encounters in parking lots, or by slipping out of the house in
the early hours of the morning to jog and then meeting women in
the offices of Miller, Adams & Miller before the doors opened.

Also, quite early in the game he hit on the happy idea of hiring
female bodyguards. To prepare the ground for this new personnel
policy, he planted stories in the press demanding women's rights in
law enforcement and responded to these stories by announcing that
he would set an example by hiring women as guardians of the governor's person. Applications poured in. On Jack's instructions to the
mail room, the ones with photos attached were routed directly to
him. Most of those hired were young, pretty, and eager for promotion. He also had the power to appoint a large number of state officials, and the markedly higher standard of pulchritude among
secretaries, clerks, tax collectors, and even judges soon became a
running joke in press rooms and political back rooms.

"What exactly do you think you're doing?" Morgan asked Jack.

"I thought you wanted me to appoint women to office," he said.

"Women, yes," said Morgan. "A harem, no."

"Morgan, what a strange and suspicious mind you have. I am
compelled by laws lobbied by your own clients to appoint women
to every feasible post."

"What are you going to do when one of them sells her story to
the tabloids? THE GOVERNOR SUCKED MY GUN. I WAS A SEX SLAVE IN A STATE
TROOPER UNIFORM. Not that they spend much time in their cute little
outfits, if I know you. And I do."

"Look at the files," Jack said. "Every one of these women is a
good Christian girl."

"And you know them all in the biblical sense."

This development did little to calm the turbulent waters within Morgan. She was, at thirty-seven, a woman at the apex of her sexual life cycle. Her newly revealed beauty had made a sex object of her while doing her no sexual good. She had not had a rendezvous with the Georgian since the makeover in Palm Beach. But beyond that she was outraged because Jack had outwitted and outmaneuvered her yet again. Her tantrums over the risks Jack was taking with the operation—*her* operation—became more frequent and more violent as the intensity of her jealousy increased in lockstep with her frustration. Jack saw this, she knew he did; he understood it. He did nothing to allay it because, by the ground rules laid down by Peter, it had nothing to do with him.

On a spring night, after a bank board meeting, Morgan came back to the mansion to find Jack, as usual, absent. She was unable to sleep and unable to do anything for herself that would be an aid to sleep. She decided to go down to the office to do some work in her safe room.

The door was rigged so that all the lights went on when the latch was lifted. Stepping over the threshold she found herself in the presence of a naked Jack, who was entwined on the library table with a ripe young bodyguard. The woman's shiny pistol harness lay on a bank box full of laundered currency, beneath her gray trooper's Stetson with its big chrome badge. Her permapolished boots were crossed in the small of Jack's back. She had one leg out of her whipcord trousers, and true to Jack's ritualized methods, she still wore her skewed panties. They were white, sleazy, lacy. She screamed when the lights came on. Jack continued as if hypnotized, undaunted by the light or maybe unaware of it in his single-mindedness. The girl gazed at Morgan with frantically rolling eyes—stupid with fright. Morgan had seen the same look in the eyes of rutting dogs.

All this was happening, remember, in Morgan's room—the holy of holies, the refuge, the safe place, the inner sanctum to which only she knew the entry code. A sense of angry violation seethed in Morgan's breast. *How did he get in?*

The girl trooper was trying to push Jack off. He seemed unaware of her resistance. In a piercing voice, staring wildly into Morgan's furious face, she cried, "Jack! Jack!"

Jack did not seem to hear her. She tried to slither from beneath him, scooting backward across the tabletop. With astonishing agility, refusing to withdraw, he pursued her across the table, pumping rhythmically. Morgan, fascinated—it was like *being* Jack to observe him in this state—saw that his eyes were tightly closed and realized that he really did not know that the lights were on, that he really could not hear voices, that all his senses were concentrated on the single part of his body that he was thrusting into the wild-eyed girl. She was now backed into the wall, forced into a sitting position, unable to move. Her eyes stared, but into space; she groaned. Morgan realized that in spite of all the distractions, she was having an orgasm.

Morgan was seized by rage as if by an enormous primeval animal that shook her, suffocating her, blurring her vision. She snatched up the trooper's revolver. It was a .357 Magnum Colt Python with a six-inch barrel, a most intimidating weapon. Shrieking in primal fury, she fired all six rounds in the cylinder, rapid-fire, into the wall above the girl's tousled head. Morgan was an excellent pistol shot, highly trained. The bullets landed very close, in a tight pattern.

The girl screamed in terror. Jack finished. This seemed to restore his hearing. Still on his hands and knees, still one flesh with his lover, he looked over his shoulder and said, "Jesus Jumping Christ, Morgan."

Morgan broke open the revolver, ejected the shells, plucked a fresh load from the pouch on the trooper's harness, and snapped the cylinder shut. White-faced, teeth clenched, wild-eyed with an anger that she all too plainly did not wish to control, she cocked the weapon, *click-click,* and pointed it at the girl. She was now sitting on Jack's lap, her body between him and the gun. She struggled to escape, but Jack's arms were locked tightly around her waist.

Frozen by terror, the girl said, "No, no, please."

Morgan said, "Get off my husband's cock and get your white-trash ass out of here before I blow another hole in it."

"Oh Mary, Mother of God!" cried the girl. She struggled to escape from the death grip in which Jack held her, but he would not let go, and they both tumbled off the table. The girl leaped to her feet, took one running step, became entangled in her whipcord breeches, and went sprawling. Morgan kicked her hard on the seat of her twisted panties. She crawled rapidly through the door, sobbing.

Morgan closed the door behind her. Hand steady as a rock, she pointed the revolver at Jack's still-glistening member.

"I'm only going to ask this question once," she said. "How did you get in here?"

Jack's teeth chattered. "Seven-three-eight-three-seven," he responded.

"I know *what* you know. *How* did you know?"

"Just guessed."

"Don't fuck with me, Jack. How did you know the combination?"

"Well, Jesus, Morg, it didn't take a rocket scientist. What's your biggest secret? The numbers on the keypad spell 'Peter' backwards and forwards."

Morgan threw the cocked revolver at him. A fully loaded Colt Python weighs almost four pounds. It hit him on the scalp, opening a tiny but gushing wound, and went off at the precise same moment, sending one more high-velocity, metal-jacketed round slamming into the wall.

In the tiny moment of consciousness left to him, Jack thought he had been shot. Was this his fate, to be murdered by a madwoman he had been forbidden to fuck? To be blown away by a jealous wife who was no wife?

4 When Jack awoke, he found Danny Miller standing over him, his arms around Morgan, who was hysterical.

Danny said, "Hi. How do you feel?"

Jack touched his scalp and looked at his hand. "Jesus, the blood," he said.

"Just a scalp wound."

Danny was calm, reassuring, smiling over Morgan's shuddering shoulder. He handed Jack a set of car keys.

"Take my car. I'll catch a ride with Morgan."

After Jack left, Danny attempted to comfort Morgan. She was crying again, sobbing, beating her fists against the soft panels of the soundproof walls. She wore a pleated knee-length skirt that swung prettily with the movements of her body. Danny gazed at her mismatched legs—so like his own, except that each of Morgan's was perfect in its own way. He was aware, too, of the beauty of the rest of her body, and of her ravaged but lovely face. The transformation of the frigid drab he had known for years into this wildly sobbing homicidal beauty was profoundly disorienting.

Feeling his eyes on her, Morgan turned to him, looked long into his eyes, and then uttered a loud sob and held out her arms. The heartbroken sound she was uttering seemed to come not from the Morgan who stood before him but from some much earlier and much smaller and much younger and vulnerable Morgan. A Morgan who could hide nothing from him.

Moments later, with the feral scent of Jack and the trooper still faintly present in the stale air of the sealed room, the inevitable happened. Then again, and again. Morgan poured a dozen years of frustration, anger, and lust for revenge—not to mention her Swallow wisdom—into a frenzied marathon of sex that lasted until dawn. By then Danny was in the grip of what he knew was a sexual obsession from which the richly aromatic, nude, and purring Morgan, regarding him with an air of satisfied ownership, would never let him escape. As for Morgan, she found that she was strangely excited by Danny's wounds, aroused by the pornographic rush of making love to a man who had lost his perfect body in battle against the Viet Cong. It gave her a wonderful sense of power, as if he were her prisoner.

5 Danny and Morgan became lovers—or partners in lust, depending on your point of view—on the night Cindy's mother died of pancreatic cancer in Tannery Falls. It was a hard death; Cindy held her mother's hand until the life went out of it. Then she closed the corpse's eyelids, and tried to reach Danny from the bedside phone. It was two-thirty in the morning. She got the answering machine, her own businesslike voice. She tried the office and got no answer. She went to the nurse's station and told them that her mother was gone. Two nurses rushed down the hall, as if in their familiarity with death they might yet catch the old lady before her boat left shore. At four in the morning, having signed all the necessary papers and talked to the undertaker, she got into her car and started to drive to Columbus, pressing redial over and over on the car phone as she sped down the long, straight north-south highway through villages in which the only sign of human life was the blue-white flicker of television screens in bedroom windows. Was Danny dead, too? She saw a vision of him throwing himself between Jack and an assassin's bullet: not the fleeting real-life event itself on a distant stage over the heads of a crowd, but close-up television images in slo-mo. A highway patrol car passed her; she thought of chasing it, blinking her lights, asking the trooper to find out if anything like that had happened. Or if there had been any fatal accidents involving anyone named Miller.

She arrived home at six. Danny came in at six-thirty.

He said, "Your mother is gone?"

Cindy nodded, unable to speak. She embraced him, burying her face in the pocket between his shoulder and his neck, then recoiled.

"You smell like cunt," she said.

Danny told her everything.

Cindy said, "Morgan Adams? You're telling me that you're fucking Morgan Adams?"

"Tonight was the first time," Danny said. "Cindy, I'm so ashamed, so sor—"

She slapped him hard. "Shut up," she said. "I can't talk to you when you smell like this. Go take a shower."

Half an hour later Danny found her at the kitchen table, hands folded, back erect, feet on the floor—exactly, he thought, like the good girl she had been in the fifth grade, waiting for the teacher to come into the classroom, ignoring the hell-raising boys. Danny had shaved; his face shone. His hair was wet. He began to weep.

Cindy said, "I don't think we'll have a funeral. Picture ops for Jack and Morgan at the graveside is a little more than I want to handle."

Danny spoke her name. His voice broke, tears flowed. She said, "Stop that."

Danny went to the kitchen sink and washed his face. Then he said, "What do you want to know?"

"What more is there to know? If you want to let it all hang out so you'll feel better, see a priest. What do you want to do?"

"I want to come back."

"Can you do that?"

"It's what I need to do."

"That's not quite the answer to my question."

Danny said, "Cindy, I promise you. It will never happen again."

Feeling the faint nausea that follows a sleepless night, but blocking everything else from memory except—as she remembered later on—a bright isolated image of Danny dribbling a basketball, faking, shooting, grinning, shining with sweat, and then another image of him as he had been in that locked room at Walter Reed, Cindy sat in silence for a long moment.

Then she said, "All right." She looked at the clock. "I have to be in court in an hour."

And when, the very next day in the deep cottony silence of Morgan's room, Danny told a wise-eyed Morgan about his promise to his wife, she said, "What kind of soap do you use at home?"

"Dove. Why?"

"If Cindy's got such a great sense of smell, we'll have to get you some for the shower here."

Then, though Danny resisted, she seduced him and, in the weeks that followed, seduced him many times more. Danny lived in guilt and a fear of discovery that was worse than any emotion he had ever felt in Vietnam. Cindy never referred to his adultery again.

6 Before she lost the power of speech, Cindy's mother had asked her to have a child: "Oh, Cindy, it was wrong to let you wear that thing. Your father wouldn't listen to me, but God punished us. If you'd had a child, that boy would have gone away. A second you, a beautiful little girl, would have been so wonderful."

Another daughter might have taken the old woman's ramblings for delirium, but Cindy recognized the barely audible monologue for what it had been, a confession of unhappiness so great—unhappiness caused by Cindy—that her mother preferred death to its continuation. Cindy understood how such a state of mind, produced by a single mistake, a single violation of the rules by which she lived, might take control of a woman. Even though she never used contraceptives with Danny after he was drafted, she had conceived no child except the son she aborted.

Danny had offered many times to have himself tested, to do whatever was necessary for them to have a child of their own. Cindy declined. She did not want to know. If Danny proved to be sterile, that would mean that Jack had made her pregnant. She did not want to confirm this darkest suspicion of her life. But now she realized that at long last she had no choice but to face facts, seek medical help, and conceive a child with Danny, no matter by what means and with what consequences.

She and Danny did not resume physical relations—another sign, he thought, that she knew what was going on—but went to a specialist in fertility problems who, after several attempts to artificially impregnate Cindy with Danny's sperm, suggested the last resort of in vitro fertilization. By now this was a common procedure, though it often resulted in multiple births.

Cindy said, "You mean twins?"

"I mean multiple fetuses. But all but one—or two, if you wish— can be terminated."

"A multiple abortion?"

"We avoid that term."

"I know," Cindy said. "No thanks."

After that she dreamed often about the doctor. In her dream the doctor, a stringy humorless woman, was conspiring with Morgan to use Jack's sperm instead of Danny's. She woke up to find herself alone in the bed. Danny was sitting downstairs in the dark, weeping.

She went downstairs as she was, naked. He told her that the affair with Morgan had resumed. She asked for a divorce.

Danny said, "I can't. It would ruin Jack's chances to be president."

"What?"

"It would destroy his candidacy."

"You bet it would," Cindy said. "Let me ask you something. Do you love that freak?" She saw that Danny did not know which Adams she meant. She said, "I mean Morgan."

"No. It's not that at all. But I'm—"

"Besotted by her? Isn't that the word they use in books?"

"Yes. She—"

"Never mind. I'm filing for divorce tomorrow."

"Cindy, please don't."

"Merriwether Street will be my lawyer."

"Cindy, for God's sake!"

"Talk to my lawyer. Now get out of here."

Danny gave her the most devastated look Cindy had ever seen on a human face.

He said, "I wish I had died over there."

"Me too," Cindy said.

Danny turned to go. Limping. As if he were slipping back into the past, she saw him again as he once had been, an angel in bed, a god on the playing field. She saw him wounded, in despair, then rising back up into his sweet nature; she had always been able to imagine the explosion of the phosphorus grenade as if she had been there herself. The first time they had made love, afterward she had smelled him burning. She had never loved him physically, not with the same part of her heart, after he came back to her ruined by fire. She saw the child she had destroyed, and as if from above, just as she supposed Danny would see it on Judgment Day, she saw in all its details the drunken, spiteful sin she had committed with Jack and knew that that was the real cause of everything because it had killed her capacity to love.

For the first time Cindy noticed that he was fully dressed—shirt, tie, suit. He took his house keys from his pocket and laid them on the table.

Cindy said, "Wait. I have no right to do this."

Danny said, "No right?"

Cindy's chin trembled. She shook her head, unable to speak. The dam broke. She wept like an injured child. Danny comforted her, with the same result he had achieved with the last brokenhearted woman he had taken into his arms without a sexual thought in his head.

His body was a stranger to Cindy's. Morgan had changed him. That morning, after Danny left for work, Cindy moved out of their split-level home and into her mother's vast empty house in Tannery Falls. She set up an office in her father's old den, communicating with her secretary by telephone and driving the two hours to

Columbus when she needed to see a client. By prearrangement, Danny was always absent when she visited the offices of Miller, Adams & Miller.

7 Most of what I have just imparted to you was reported to me by Morgan, good soldier that she was. She left some things out (the revolver, her slip of the Marxist tongue in that "white trash" stuff), but by the time she related her version of the Feydeau farce, I had already seen and heard most of what transpired in her secret room, thanks to cameras and listening devices installed without her knowledge by the Georgian.

Some of the rest came to me bit by bit and much later, but it did not require the mental architecture of Teodor Józef Konrad Korzeniowski to deduce the larger picture. Nothing set in motion by the devil in the flesh ever happens for the first time. But oh, the irony, the irony. Morgan had feared that Jack's sex life would ruin our great operation and so prevent the forces of good from taking over the world. And now her own vengeful mindless bitchy fucking had placed it in such jeopardy that I was at a loss for a remedy. I was not even sure who the guilty party might be. Was all this Jack's fault, as Morgan argued? Or was it Peter's for imposing stupid rules, or mine for breaking those rules out of the worst and, in a handler of agents, the least forgivable of motives— human sympathy? What, after all, did I know about sexual madness? I had spent my life going to peep shows.

I said to Morgan, "You have changed the entry code, I assume?"

"Yes."

"To what? 'Stupidity' spelled backwards?"

She flushed: Unsuspected freckles appeared like a faint rash. "No. Our wedding anniversary. Jack will never remember that." She paused as if apologizing for the witticism; this was not the time or place. No doubt this showed in my stern and frozen face. She said, "You are angry with me."

"No. I am thinking of Janós Kádár."

"Why, for God's sake?"

"Because I don't know whether to have you shot or circumcised."

Morgan blinked; a trembling hand flew to her mouth. For all she knew, these really were the alternatives. Sauce for the goose. The revolution punished everyone sooner or later; that was its beauty.

She said, "I will terminate the affair with Danny."

"Why? Do you want to lose control of him, too?"

She did not answer. She was frightened. I was pleased that this was so. In being kind to her I had let out of the cell a bad part of her. It must be put back inside.

"Cindy is your problem, not Danny," I said. "You've made an enemy for life. A highly intelligent enemy. An enemy who has the power to destroy you in an instant. At any moment."

"Then I will deal with the problem."

"How? With castor beans and sulfuric acid?"

A startled look. Was I making a serious proposal? Or, worse, was I ridiculing her greatest triumph as a secret agent?

Morgan did not answer my question, but her eyes did not waver. Her silence said, *If that is what you want, yes, certainly, I will mix some up and pour it in her ear.*

It was not what I wanted. Then or now. I said, "No. Do not even think of doing something that cannot be explained. Do you think she has not written all this down, given the facts in a sealed envelope to this Merriwether Street?"

"Anything is possible," Morgan said, recovering her old self. "But what do you propose? I can hardly ask her to let bygones be bygones."

"You have certain information about her."

"If you mean fornication with Jack, I'd say the shock value of that little episode has been overtaken by events, thanks to me. At this point she'd probably thank me for telling Danny."

"And its disclosure would also injure Jack, perhaps fatally."

"If a little boyish rape is all of a sudden a disqualification for the presidency, yes."

"Then what do *you* propose?"

Morgan told me. She had thought the whole thing out. If anything in this business could be called perfect in its conception, her plan would have merited use of the word. But then, I had thought the same of some of her earlier schemes that had entangled us in unforeseen consequences. Nevertheless, for want of a better idea, I gave my approval.

8 Like a deadfall, Morgan's plan, primitive in its method, required infinitely subtle camouflage to guarantee its success. It evolved slowly, cautiously, over many weeks. Morgan studied Cindy as a savage might have studied a bear, observing its movements, memorizing every detail of its familiar ground. If a leaf was turned, a stone displaced, they must be returned to the precise spot from which they'd been taken. No scent but the bear's could linger. The slightest change in its world would put the bear off, awaken its senses, turn the hunted into the hunter.

Every Tuesday, Cindy drove down to Columbus from Tannery Falls to spend a day in the office. One Tuesday in summer, a slow season for attorneys in a political town, her last appointment of the day was with a man who told her that he had just moved into town. He explained that he was in the computer business, had just sold his company in Indiana, and now wanted to form an Ohio corporation to develop and sell sophisticated software.

"How did you happen to come to me?" Cindy asked.

"I made inquiries. You seem to be the kind of firm I need—small enough to remember who I am when I call, large enough and connected enough to get things done."

A straight answer. No attempt at charm. Articulate. Serious, even brusque. He felt no apparent need to smile unless he was amused. He was well dressed: excellent woolen suit and tie, custom shirt of Sea Island cotton, English shoes. No cologne; Cindy gagged on English Leather. Blond, easy-moving. Handsome in a rough, masculine way. He reminded Cindy of the pre–*Dr. Strangelove* Sterling Hayden. If he noticed Cindy's looks, he gave no sign. He handed her a typed sheet with the particulars of the company he wished to create.

"All right," Cindy said. "We'll draw up the papers."

"I'd like to get it done as soon as possible."

"How about next Tuesday?"

"Should be all right."

"Two o'clock?"

He looked at a pocket diary. "Can't. Would five be possible?"

"No. Is six too late?"

"No." He smiled for the first time—strong, slightly crooked teeth, no fancy orthodontia—and held her eyes for a moment longer than the business at hand required.

Flirtation? Cindy was not sure. She had not looked for the signs of it in years. She did not smile back. "It won't take much of your time."

That evening she went to dinner with some of her Republican friends, a long-standing engagement. They spent the evening ridiculing Jack Adams's presidential aspirations. It was too late afterward to drive back to Tannery Falls—it was dangerous for a woman to be alone in a car on lonely roads after dark—so Cindy spent the night in a hotel.

When she came downstairs in the morning, there was her new client, buying *The Wall Street Journal* at the newsstand. It was natural enough that he should be there—he was looking for a place to live in Ohio, and had flown in from Indianapolis. He saw her through the glass, waved but did not grin, and then came out, making no haste. Instead of walking on, she waited for him; she didn't know why.

He seemed surprised that she was still there. "Hi. Had breakfast yet?"

"No."

"Neither have I. Want some?"

She didn't, really. She was a coffee-and-juice girl, but something stirred and she said, "All right."

He ate an omelet and talked about movies. He had seen all of Ronald Reagan's movies.

"That was a real icebreaker with Nancy," he said.

Cindy was surprised that he would drop a name—that one especially. If she turned out to be a Democrat, he had lost all hope of winning her heart. She said, "You've met Mrs. Reagan?"

"At a fund-raiser. But I don't mind paying to talk about *Kings Row*. It shows what can happen when you date the wrong doctor's daughter."

"Watch it."

"You're one?"

"Yep." Cindy grinned. "But there's good news. I'm a Republican."

He laughed. She liked him. He seemed to be unaware of her beauty. She might have been another male for all the attention he paid to her, even though she attracted her usual looks of longing from strangers. It was the number of hellos she attracted from passersby that interested him.

"Looks like I've got a lawyer who knows her Columbus," he said. "I meant to ask: Who's the other Miller in Miller, Adams and Miller?"

"My husband, Danny."

"The football player?"

"A long time ago, yes. How did you know?"

"He beat us often enough. Amazing athlete. And the Adams is . . ."

"I thought you said you checked around."

"I did. But I was told he was inactive."

"He is."

"Good." He did not elaborate; he had already made it plain that he was a Republican. "I always thought your husband would wind up in the NFL."

"Actually, it would have been baseball. He was drafted by the Indians. But he was wounded in Vietnam."

"Oh shit! Not him."

"What's that mean?"

"The waste. Sorry. Is he all right now?"

Cindy said, "He adjusted. We're not together anymore." It was the first time she had uttered these words. What was there about this man?

He said, "That's funny. Neither are my wife and me. That's why I sold the company."

"Ah."

"If I ask you to dinner, can we not talk about that part of our lives?"

"Yes."

They dined together that night, on bad food at an expensive restaurant. Cindy had a wonderful time. He talked about everything but himself, treated her like the intelligent woman she was, and then said good night in the lobby of the hotel and—she had no reason to think otherwise—went to his own room.

The next Tuesday, after executing the papers Cindy had drawn up, they dined again; same ending. He did not ask for her home number but called her at the office over the next couple of weeks to invite her to lunch, to dinner, to the theater. He revealed that he was a Vietnam veteran—no combat, he'd been a staff officer at Westmoreland's headquarters. He had a very slight speech impediment, neither a lisp nor a stammer; he had trouble with certain diphthongs. He seemed unaware of this; it was quite charming, quite nice.

At last he found an apartment in a huge new condominium. He asked her to stop by and see it, to give him an opinion of the decoration. He had ended up with a lot of dark wood and sectional furniture and lithographs of ships and waterfowl. Was it too Great Western?

"More Hyatt-esque," Cindy said.

They were in the large, lavishly equipped master bathroom, last stop on the tour.

He said, "Would you like to be kissed?"

She was truly startled. "Kissed?" she said. "No, not—"

He interrupted. "Fine."

"Let me finish," Cindy said. "Not in the bathroom."

She took his hand and led him into the bedroom. Moments later they were in bed.

After they'd finished he said, "I didn't think I could do that with anyone again. Be so happy afterward, I mean. May I tell you something?"

"Yes."

"I think you're the most beautiful woman I've ever met. I've wanted to tell you that from the first moment, but I was afraid I'd lose you if I did."

Cindy said, "You're not so bad yourself."

"Stay."

"I can't. I have to go."

"To get away from me or what?"

"Not to get away from you. Believe me."

"Then I'll come with you."

9 He drove her to Tannery Falls. He admired the old Victorian house, noticing all the right details. But Cindy thought something was wrong. The house felt different.

"Different? How?"

"As if someone has been here," she said.

"Let's check it out."

They went from room to room in the darkened mansion, switching on lights as they went. Over the years, bit by bit, Cindy's father had lovingly restored the old place. He had been an aficionado of Victoriana. Every detail was authentic. Cindy's companion expressed the same enthusiasm for carved woodwork, molded plaster, bronze chandeliers, Tiffany windows. He knew the name for everything he saw, even the names of one or two of the obscure artists whose oils and watercolors of inert landscapes and portraits of bewildered nouveau riche husbands and wives her father had bought at estate sales.

Despite Cindy's apprehensions, the house was empty and seemingly undisturbed, except for one tiny thimbleful of plaster dust on the bed in the master bedroom, where Cindy now slept. "Carpenter ants," he said, fingering the dust. "Have it checked out by an exterminator. They can be real trouble."

She touched the light switch. He said, "No. Leave it on. Let's go outside and look."

Lights burned in every window and turret. The whole house was aglow, like a great lantern on the hill above the tawdry village, and strips of golden lamplight fell on the authentic nineteenth-century perennials and flowering shrubs that Dr. Rogers had planted so that something would always be in bloom.

"What a wonderful place to grow up in, to live in," said Cindy's new lover. They kissed. Strange bodies, strange excitement. Fragrance filled the darkness like an invisible frequency of the spectrum.

They went upstairs. That night, and then during a long, intense Saturday and Sunday, he took her several times through the Swallow manual and, because she was so beautiful and so awakened, somewhat beyond the last page. He made everything—acts of love she had never imagined—seem natural. She soon got over her initial shock at her seducer's total lack of inhibitions; like so many before her, like Danny, like Jack, she was transported into unimagined regions of pleasure. Her lover was conservative in only one respect: He would make love only in bed, always the same bed, and always with the lights on.

On Monday morning she drove him into Columbus.

"I'll call," he said, with love in his eyes.

10 But Cindy did not hear from her lover, and when she called the apartment a woman answered. She said she had never heard of the person Cindy was asking for. Cindy, a practiced investigator, quickly discovered that the name, address, phone number, and personal particulars he had given her were fictitious. The Indiana computer tycoon he pretended to be existed in reality, but he was a little tattooed fat man who lived quite happily in Indianapolis with a twenty-year-old boy. Cindy's seducer had taken the unsuspecting fat man's name and curriculum vitae as his own.

Cindy's mysterious and accomplished lover was, of course, Morgan's Georgian. A few days after his disappearance Cindy received a UPS package from a Cleveland department store containing a Gucci purse. Inside the purse, sealed in an envelope, she found a videotape. The tape was labeled *Cindy's Ecstasy*—an unnecessary cruelty, in my opinion. Alone, she watched the tape. Her lover's face had been replaced by an electronic checkerboard, but Cindy's own features, by turns distorted with lust and illuminated by the indescribable happiness she still remembered with the greatest clarity, were recognizable in each and every shot, and her voice, though changed by the heat of her desire as she shrilly begged for more, was also unmistakable.

The last frame of the tape was a title: "Silence Is Golden."

Cindy switched off the television set and called Danny, this time reaching him at home.

"I'm coming back," she said, then hung up.

This was the last result that Morgan expected. But Cindy was as good as her word. That very week she moved back into the house with Danny. She never mentioned his affair with Morgan to him again, and never again slept with him. Like Morgan before her, she became a nun within her own marriage, aware that the man she loved was at the sexual service of another woman.

Morgan said, "She knows. She doesn't care. I don't understand."

We watched Cindy. We had made her dangerous, therefore we had to be on guard. To all outward appearances, Cindy lived for work, often staying until after midnight at the law firm. We supposed she was losing herself in her work, and in a sense this was precisely the case. What Cindy was doing all alone at night was following the money: examining old records, making copies, building a file on the origins and transactions of the Columbus Bank of the Western Reserve. She was methodically investigating Morgan's client list and financial records.

Also, in Tannery Falls, with the help of a man who had served on the draft board and owed her father his life, she looked into the draft records and verified that Danny was, indeed, drafted to take Jack's place. Had he gone into service when originally scheduled, the following month, he would not have been on that jungle trail in Cambodia. Such records exist. One wonders what might happen if they were all made public by order of some supreme court of the wretched and every soldier who lost an arm or a leg or his sanity in Vietnam had the option of knocking on the door of the draft dodger for whom he made this sacrifice. It is a theme for Dostoyevsky.

Night after night, Cindy gathered her information. She deposited the evidence in the huge old safe that was hidden in a wall of the mansion's cellar, along with the videotape of her weekend with the Georgian.

Sometimes when a certain mood came over her she watched the tape, not for any reason of sexual stimulation—she had never liked pornography—but because it helped her to understand life and helped her to do her tedious work of reconstructing the past. It helped her to see, as an objective witness, a different woman from the one in the pictures.

While Cindy was looking back into darkness, we were looking ahead. Glowing horizons were what we saw.

6

★ ★

Lady Luck

One

★ ★

1 Meanwhile, Jack Adams was frantic for money. His campaign had spent the twenty million dollars deposited for his benefit in the Columbus Bank of the Western Reserve—and then some. By Herculean efforts Danny Miller had raised an additional ten million dollars. But by the first day of the presidential election year it was all gone, spent on nationalizing Jack's reputation, on setting up all the many committees and campaign offices and phone banks and staffs of radicals, intellectuals, Young Turks, disaffected labor leaders, old pols, and babes in the wood who were beginning to think that this man whom nobody trusted, this idealist who believed in nothing except his own glittering destiny, might very well end up as president of the United States.

Morgan said, "We need an infusion of cash. Now."

I replied, "I know. But we can't help."

"You can't *help*? Dmitri, what is that supposed to mean?"

I said, "Don't you know? History is over."

Morgan made a disgusted face. "For God's sake!"

But it was true—at least for what people like Morgan and me had always called "history." America had won the Cold War, what a surprise. As Jack said later, in a different context: The beauty of America is that you never know who is going to walk out of the crowd, carrying its fate in his hands.

In Russia's case it was an Afghan religious fanatic with a Stinger antiaircraft missile supplied by the CIA—actually, hundreds of fanatics with hundreds of missiles. In a matter of months, the Red Army's air cover was destroyed and its ground forces were driven out of Afghanistan. The economy of the USSR collapsed, and so did its spirit, such as it was. The Party apparat suddenly understood that it was defenseless against the capitalists unless it wanted to blow up the world. In short, the Soviet Union, and with it the great Soviet intelligence service, was ceasing to exist at the very moment that its fondest dream, a wholly owned and controlled agent in the Oval Office, seemed finally to be within reach.

All this I explained. Morgan said, "You can't be serious."

"But I am," I said. "The KGB is poor in the only meaningful sense of the word. It has no money."

Morgan ignored me. How could she possibly believe such a thing? Besides, she knew that Peter had other sources. She had killed with poison to secure those sources. She said, "Stop being sardonic, Dmitri. Where is the money? Jack asks me that question once an hour."

As a matter of form I replied, "How much do you need?"

"Five million dollars immediately. Much more later."

"Impossible. The bank can't absorb it. It will set off alarms."

"Alarms?" Morgan said. "Let me tell you about alarms. We're already moving money around inside the bank like there's no tomorrow. If we don't put this money back, if we don't cover it—"

"You are *embezzling*?"

"No. Robbing Peter to pay Paul."

I was truly alarmed. "That is madness. Why are you doing it?"

"Because *we need the money*, Dmitri. If Jack loses in New Hampshire, we lose everything. We fail. He'll disappear in a week. It will be all over. I will have wasted my life. You do understand that, Dmitri?"

With a gloved hand, through layers of cloth, I patted her on the back. It was after midnight. We were walking between snowbanks down an empty, winding street in Boston. Jack was in some town hall in rural New Hampshire, debating his five—or was it six?—opponents for the nomination, every one of whom was better qualified for the presidency than he. A howling North Atlantic wind blew in our faces. In her thin designer clothes, Morgan trembled, sucked in her breath. It could not possibly have been colder or lonelier, even in Moscow.

I said, "Are we lost? I see no one, recognize nothing."

"You're not the only one," Morgan said. "But don't worry. We turn left at the end and come out at the Common."

She said, "Dmitri, listen to me. If what you say is true, if it really is all over in Russia, then you and Jack and I are all that remains. Am I wrong?"

"Grandiose," I said, "but correct."

"Then where's Peter? What is he doing? Why isn't he keeping his promises?"

"We are not his only concern."

"Oh really?" Morgan said. "Is there some bigger, more powerful country than the USA he wants to repossess? What's happening here? We must have the money. Immediately."

I thought it very unlikely that they would get it. But I did not want to say so. We stepped into a sort of arcade. I gave her what I had with me in a shoulder bag, my last hundred thousand dollars in safe cash, and advised her to be patient.

She gave me a look of desperation, of a woman betrayed. For a long time, ever since the shooting incident with Jack, our relations had been cool. Now, however, on a sudden mutual impulse we kissed—loud Russian kisses on both cheeks. My spittle glistened, freezing on her cheek, a Siberian tear.

2 When I kissed Morgan goodbye in Boston—with love, I admit it—I expected to see her again in a matter of days. My expectations changed when I arrived home in New York and found a child of the Nomenklatura waiting for me in a car parked outside my apartment building. He told me I had been ordered to Moscow. I was leaving immediately; I was already late. He would drive me to the airport, never mind about luggage. I had not been home in twenty years; I had not seen my Russian passport in longer than that. The young man handed it to me. There I was as I had been, youthful, serious, doing my professional best to look as if the false name below my photograph was the one I had been born with.

At the Moscow airport, to my great anxiety, I was met at the plane by Peter's man Igor. This was an older and wiser Igor than the boy who had shown Jack the sights of Moscow, but just as muscular and just as falsely amiable. In former times he always talked about Swallows—he was Peter's casting director—but now he drove me in silence to a birch forest, where another car awaited. What did this mean? Probably that he no longer worked for Peter but had been sent to collect me because I could be counted on to assume that he did. I expected to change vehicles, to be greeted with comradely smiles in the backseat, then pounded with truncheons, then driven to another place, and there, finally, to confess at length. And then, with luck, to be believed when I said I had confessed everything, and to die. The Red Passion.

Igor stopped the car. He handed me a woman's stocking. "Here," he said. "Put this on your head, to cover your face." He pulled the stocking's mate over his own head. While I did as he said, he pulled a pistol from his breast—a 9 millimeter Walther, nothing but top-of-the-line for Peter's men—and checked the action.

"Get out," Igor said.

I did as he said, turning my back to the Walther, wondering, *Why the stocking? To keep the snow white?*

But there was no bullet. As soon as my feet touched the snow, Peter got out of the parked car—out of the driver's seat: He was alone. He wore his magnificent sable hat and, draped across his shoulders, his Chesterfield coat with sable lining. I walked toward him, but before I could reach him he started to walk off into the forest. I followed. I heard Igor's feet crunching the snow behind me. The path had been *shoveled;* still lost in my train of thought, I was startled awake by this surrealistic detail. I lost a step or two. I had to trot to catch up to Peter. Behind me, Igor trotted too, *crunch-crunch-crunch.*

I caught up. Peter and I were side by side, marching in step. Hands clasped behind his back, Peter said, "It is over. Tomorrow they will summon me to a meeting, examine my accounts, humiliate me, reduce me three ranks to colonel, and retire me beyond the Urals at an annual pension of two thousand dollars a year."

He spoke English. In the same language I said, "I am sorry to hear it. May I know my own fate?"

"It has not been confided to me. You may imagine it. They don't know you're here. They're looking for you in New York, under your cover name."

"That was your man who put me on the plane?"

"Yes. That's why you're here."

Had I only known, I could have slept on the plane.

Peter said, "You are in the last place in the world where they would look for you. So for the moment, and in the circumstances, you are in the safest place in the world—Russia. Can you imagine?"

He was amused. Greatly amused, openly amused.

This was irritating. I said, "And you? What brought about this . . . fall from grace?"

"They are reinventing themselves. They are getting rid of anti-Stalinists before they reinvent Stalin."

"I thought perhaps they wanted to take over Jack for themselves."

"If so, they are cleverer than I think. They think Jack is another of my parlor games. I have quarantined this operation from everyone."

"How, with such a budget?"

Not a flicker, not a glance, not a word of explanation. "Take my word for it," he said. "This operation must continue. It is the hope of the future. You understand?"

"Yes. But it cannot do so without money. Immediate—"

"Stop telling me the obvious," Peter said. "Pay attention to orders." He gave me a severe look.

I said, "Yes, Comrade General."

"We must disengage, maintain the quarantine," Peter said, ticking off items as if leaving an order for breakfast before retiring for the night. "Wait these traitors out. They will fail. And if they don't, we'll deal with them. Listen. Our time together is limited. I have an assignment for you. It is vital."

"At your orders, Comrade General."

He turned to face me for the first time. He was smiling. "Faithful Dmitri Alexeyivich," he said. To me, the vestigial serf, his smile said: In tsarist times men like you were coachmen who froze to death outside while men like me finished dinner and had a virgin for dessert.

"I want you to go back to America," he said.

I was startled. "Why? How?"

"Be quiet. Everything is arranged. Igor will see you across the frontier. You will travel by a circuitous route." He smiled at the hackneyed phrase, transforming real drama into false drama.

"And then what?"

"Dmitri Alexeyivich, listen."

Another rebuke. I lowered my eyes, clasped my hands. We were walking deeper and deeper into the forest on the shoveled path, white birches against white snow, not a footprint except our own. I had been away too long: Russia was far colder than Massachusetts.

Peter talked on, describing my task. He handed me an envelope. "The instructions are inside. Your contact is Escobar. He will require a recognition phrase, a number, and a name. The name is mine, in Spanish, with honorific. Give him my regards."

Peter handed me a tiny slip of paper with a five-digit number written on it. I memorized it.

When I nodded, signifying I had committed it to memory, Peter pointed to his mouth. I rolled the paper into a pill, put it in my own mouth, salivated, and swallowed it. He handed me another. A phrase in Spanish: *Los caballeros quieren beber.* "The horsemen want to drink." I swallowed this too.

After running the errand that required use of these bona fides, I was to return to the United States.

"Make contact with Morgan," Peter said. "Tell her the truth, that the KGB has found me out, that it is hunting down the friends. In its death throes it is trying to destroy me. I must hide. Tell her I am safe, that I am rallying the friends. Then break contact."

"For how long?"

"Forever. Break off. Disappear. Tell them they will be contacted by someone from me. The caller will say, 'I come from the fisherman.'"

He was taking Jack away from me. Morgan, too. My lifework. He made no explanation or apology. A wave of nausea rose within me. I smelled it, tasted it. "Igor has a special telephone for Morgan," Peter said. "She should have it with her at all times."

I said, "Very well, Comrade General. Will I see you again?"

"I think not. But you have done a great thing, Dmitri Alexeyivich, greater than you know, and you will be rewarded. This creature we have created together is very, very valuable. More valuable than even you can guess. We have never had such an asset before, and we will never again have such an opportunity as this. This operation must at all costs be preserved."

Now it was noon. An alabaster sun shed milky light on the white forest. We came to a turning in the path. A man in white, dressed like a ski trooper, waited on the trail. I looked behind us. Another one, dressed in the same way, with his back to us. Beyond him, Igor. I thought perhaps Igor was about to be shot. But no, and suddenly I understood why.

Peter said, "Go, Dmitri Alexeyivich. You do not want to meet these gentlemen."

A nod. Our meeting was over. Also our life together. He walked onward with firm tread toward the man ahead—a large man wearing a white ski mask, and under his white hood a sable hat that was even more luxuriant than Peter's. The man behind—smaller, wearing a sheepskin cap under his hood—walked by me as if I were invisible. Very rhythmically, breathing deeply with every stroke, he was sweeping the path with a broom.

I turned around to watch him. Beyond him, Peter's footprints. He swept them away, then disappeared himself. My footprints, Igor's footprints, did not matter.

In Russian, flattened like his face by the stocking, Igor called out to me. "Let's get the hell out of here."

We took Peter's Mercedes; he would not need it anymore. At first light the next morning we reached the Finnish frontier. For obvious reasons, no advance arrangements had been made. Crossing was a simple matter of dollars for the border guards captain, a Japanese watch for the sergeant, American ballpoint pens for the men, a bottle of French perfume for the female lieutenant. Igor distributed the baksheesh, coin of the revolution. To me he entrusted Morgan's telephone, a clever instrument no larger than a ballet slipper.

3 As Peter had promised, my return trip was circuitous. So that you know how such things are done and what a waste of motion and money tradecraft is, I will tell you I flew from Helsinki to Bahrain to Bombay, then to Singapore, Manila, and finally Quito. I continued by boat down the Amazon to Francisco de Orellana, Peru, and finally by motor canoe to my destination, Leticia, a tiny frontier town in Colombia. The famous pink dolphins sported in the brown river, raiding the nets of fishermen and causing Pepe, my guide and boatman, to laugh in fellow-feeling: *"¡Banditos!"*

In Leticia, in a little pastel concrete box of a bank, its entire front open to the weather but otherwise windowless, I met Escobar. He was a mestizo, neither Spanish nor Indian. Quite short like his YaWa mother, capaciously intelligent like his European father, and quite noticeably subtle, as people who are neither one thing nor the other often are. All this autobiography he recited while we drank a glass of mineral water before getting down to business. This happened subtly, after I answered to his satisfaction the last of a string of polite, impersonal questions he put to me. On my river trip had I eaten the famous Amazonian *tambaquí,* most delicious of all fishes, cooked on charcoal? Yes? Good. Had I seen the pink dolphins? The gray ones? "A poet called them the flying horses of the Amazon," said Escobar. *"Los caballeros quieren beber,"* I replied. Escobar smiled and sent for coffee the other two people who worked in the bank. They scurried away.

Escobar was very serious now. I said, "Don Pedro sends his regards." I recited the magic number. Escobar held out his hand. I placed Peter's letter in it. He examined the seals, opened it, and read.

With a fond but baffled smile—*That Peter!*—Escobar said, "Oh my. Such an amount."

"Is there a problem?"

"Certainly not. Everything is perfectly in order. But you understand that we do not keep such amounts on hand here in our own safe?"

An impressive black-and-gilt safe stood in the corner, large and forbidding to any safecracker born before 1885; the bank's perimeter security system was a steel shutter secured by night with a formidable padlock.

I said, "How long will the business take?"

He tapped the letter. "Several different transfers from several different accounts will be required. One does not wish to do it all at once. Six days?"

"Very well."

He looked at his watch. "Then you should be on your way. It isn't good to be on the Amazon at night, and even with Pepe's Evinrudes, you will just make it to Loreto before dark. Excellent *tam-baquí* in Loreto."

Others were out at night. The country around Leticia was controlled by guerrillas. Peter's friends—just like me, but how would they know that? Escobar looked worriedly at the westering sun. "Have you any dollars with you?"

"A few. Most of my money is in deutsche marks."

"You should take some dollars with you," he said. He crouched in front of the safe and twirled the dial. The door of the safe swung open with a rusty squeal. He handed me six envelopes, already stuffed and sealed.

"Each contains the right amount," he said. "Give one if they simply show you weapons, two if a weapon is fired. Be very careful if they seem very young. The kids are often on drugs. They grew up in the camps. They don't know the meaning of restraint."

I offered him deutsche marks in exchange for the envelopes.

"*¡Señor!*" Escobar spread his hands, looked to heaven. "Permit me, I beg you," he said in Spanish. His body language said, How could a man with my bona fides make such a suggestion?

4   By the time I got back to America—Rye, New Hampshire, a handsome Republican stronghold by the sea—Jack had pulled himself up in the polls. With two weeks to go, he was three points behind the front-runner, a war hero who despised him even more than the other candidates did—especially after Danny found a legless New Hampshire man who had been one of Jack's former patients from Walter Reed and induced him to make a television spot. The media agreed that Jack had the momentum. He became the story, the impossible winner, the underdog. They followed him everywhere. Because Jack was where the cameras were, the other candidates began following him too, hoping for a chance encounter, a spontaneous debate in a diner, exposure.

Morgan and I met at night in the parking lot of a McDonald's at the edge of town. Neither of us had eaten; we never did on meeting days until we could eat together. As usual we ordered a Big Mac meal, and I ate the hamburger while she consumed the large fries. We each drank a chocolate shake. Apple pie for Morgan, who had no weight problem. Such tasty food after bony, fishy *tambaquí* and pulpy Amazonian fruit. Not to mention Aeroflot's menu. I was glad to be back in the enemy camp.

Morgan said, "We got the money."

"I'm glad."

She said, "Now all we have to do is stay out of jail. Are you people out of your minds?"

"Quite possibly. What do you mean?"

She said, "What the fuck am I supposed to do with a single deposit of twenty-seven million dollars? From a bank in Colombia, for Christ's sake. The IRS, the bank examiners, every gumshoe in the world will be electrified by this. How could you do this to us?"

Twenty-seven million dollars? I was amazed. How could Peter possibly pay such a sum from secret funds a day before he was scheduled to be disgraced? I concealed my feelings. Wiping ketchup from my fingers with a sodden paper napkin, I said, "I thought you said you could handle large amounts."

"Five mill, yes. Twenty-seven is a whole different question. Danny is going apeshit. So is the governor. They're lawyers; they want to know where all this money is coming from. How am I supposed to explain this to them, let alone the bank examiners?"

I had no idea. To cover my confusion, I went on wiping my fingers. It was hopeless: There was more ketchup on the napkin than on my skin. I have a weakness for ketchup. Morgan opened her large purse and plucked a Wet One from a plastic container. "Use this, for Christ's sake."

The wonderful American invention made me clean in an instant.

Morgan said, "What the fuck was Peter thinking of?" Tonight she was as profane as the Movement chick she used to be, a bad sign.

"You asked for money in a hurry," I replied. "Peter provided it in a hurry. Is the twenty-seven million going to be enough to get Jack through the primaries?"

"It should be," she said. "If we can get it out of the mattress and onto the street."

"How will you do that?"

"The governor has an idea." She smiled, on-off. "He's very experienced."

I did not like this—an outsider fingering our money. I said, "Explain."

"The governor's idea is to resurrect rejected loan applications," she said. "Change the bank's mind. Loan the failed applicants, mostly shady business people anyway, more than they asked for— much more."

"Why?"

"To shake loose some cash. If, for example, a real estate venture needs five hundred thousand dollars in capital, we loan it a million and a quarter and take back the extra seven-fifty in cash."

I figured in my head. "Using those figures, you'd net only fifteen million. You said Jack needs twenty million. At least."

"The governor thinks we can milk the businesses for another five million or so," she said.

"How?"

"Lean on them."

"You'd still be throwing seven million dollars away."

"What choice do we have? Anyway, it won't amount to that much in the end. These are business ventures that are designed to fail, understand?"

"Perfectly."

"So after the campaign, they'll all go quietly bankrupt, a process that takes months, and vanish from sight as if they never existed."

"What happens to the bank?"

"It fails. Vanishes out of our lives. Everything is sterilized."

I said, "You actually think you can get away with this?"

"Why not?" Morgan replied. "Jack's name doesn't appear on a single piece of paper connected to the bank."

"What about you?"

"My name will come up, but only as an adviser, not as a responsible officer of the bank. I have possession of all that paper, and it will vanish with the bank."

I said, "Did the governor really think this up?"

Morgan smiled a mysterious smile. "By now he thinks he did. That's why you sent me to the B School, Daddy."

"Could I stop this if I wanted to?"

"No."

"Then I hope you're as smart as Harvard thought you were. Next subject."

"Thank God."

With money out of the way, Morgan was, as always, calmer. Alas, this would not last. "Morgan," I said, "I have something to tell you." Then I delivered Peter's message, verbatim.

Morgan said, "This is our last meeting? What do you mean by that?"

"That we will not meet again."

She was stricken. "You're joking."

"No."

"You're going to leave me? Now? In the middle of everything? One step from the end? What are you *talking* about?"

She was shrieking with anger and pain. I could not have upset her more by announcing my own death. She beat me with her fists. An old couple, walking to their car, heard her through the closed windows and stared. The blue-haired wife clucked. More of those foulmouthed Democrats. She peered into the car. Morgan was not yet as famous as Jackie, but her picture had been in the media. Like an embarrassed husband I pulled her head onto my shoulder and said, "Morgan, calm yourself."

Bony skull, elbow in the ribs; there was nothing soft about her.

"Listen," I said.

I delivered Peter's message, nothing more.

Morgan was stunned. "What do you mean, the KGB is after Peter, after you? You *are* the KGB."

"No longer. Everything is changing."

"Are they after me?"

"No. They don't know about you. Or Jack."

She stared. No doubt she had imagined that the chaps in Moscow gossiped about her, wondered how a mere American, a female, a romantic, a walk-in, could do such brilliant work. She said, "They don't know about us? What are you telling me?"

"That Peter took precautions. That he knew this day might come. That he protected you."

She fell into a silence. Then, at last: "Where is he?"

"I have no idea," I replied. "And soon you will have no idea where I am."

"I'll be alone?"

"For the time being."

"How long is this 'time being' of yours?"

"As far as I am concerned, forever. But—"

"No!" She pounded the instrument panel, a single hard blow with both fists.

I said, "Comrade Major, you know the rules. It is for your own protection. It is temporary. I am not the only fish in Peter's sea."

I handed her a cell phone, an early model, bulky by later standards. "Keep this with you at all times. It's your only link."

She stared at the phone as if it were an urn that contained her own ashes.

"The call from Peter will come on this phone. After the nomination. The voice will not necessarily be Peter's." I told her the code phrase.

She said, " 'I come from the fisherman'? I'm supposed to wait for a fucking phone call? That's *it*? Jesus!" Stricken to the heart, wide-eyed, she stared at me in shattered disbelief. "Fucked again," she said. "Thanks a lot, Dmitri."

She rolled down her window and gulped air. Stern and fatherly for the last time—what would she do in the future when she needed this?—I said, "Close the window, Morgan. Stop mutilating yourself."

"*Mutilating myself?*" She held up the cell phone. "This is my reward for twenty years of masturbation? Do you know what you're telling me, Dmitri? You're telling me that the world is coming to an end."

"Yes, but not history. You know it's true. But that was the reason for you, the reason for Jack. To keep history from coming to an end. To keep life alive."

"What the fuck is that supposed to mean?" Her voice broke.

I said, "Peter is loading the revolution onto Noah's ark."

"Jack is his Noah, for Christ's sake? You want me to believe that?"

"In a word, yes. We will start it up again. This time in America. This time correctly. That was always the idea."

Tears now. "You really believe that?"

"Yes," I said. "Because otherwise, as you said in Boston, we have wasted our lives."

She was silent. Then she broke into sobs, covering her face, turning on the radio loud, as if it would be fatal if her grief were overheard. She had not felt the same just moments before, when she was shouting instead of weeping—anger was supposed to be audible, otherwise what was the use of it?

I handed her my handkerchief. "I'm sorry," she said, dabbing her eyes. "This is very hard."

"Yes. But necessary. This operation must not fall into the wrong hands. They are changing in Moscow, accommodating themselves to defeat. We must not."

"Suppose they come to me?"

"They may try. Anything is possible. Unless they speak the phrase I have just given you, they are not from Peter. If they are impostors, call the FBI."

"You're joking."

"Far from it. What would the wife of any other candidate do if the KGB showed up on her doorstep? Believe me, if you put the feds on them they will go away and stay away."

We had finished our dinner. As was our invariable custom after one of these picnics, we put the garbage in order, separating it according to fingerprints—the flimsy Big Mac package for me, the more substantial french fries container for Morgan. No sleuth would ever know, by lifting prints from grease and ketchup, that we had shared a final meal before I vanished into the desert and she became first lady.

At last I said—actually said—"This is goodbye." I said it in Russian.

In Russian, Morgan replied, "This is unbearable. Peter can't ask this of us."

"He can ask anything and we must do it."

She seized me—the last thing I expected—and pulled me to her. She kissed me on the lips, a sweet, lingering, undaughterly kiss. I tasted the salt of her tears. Also the french fries, the flavor of childhood. She held me, convulsive with sorrow. I felt the heat of her body through her thin American clothes; she wasn't dressed warmly enough. This worried me, as it had worried me in Boston.

Sexually I felt nothing. How could I when she had been entrusted to me? But in my soul I realized—even though I already knew it—that I loved her. That she loved me. That if we had met as professor and student instead of handler and agent I would have divorced a wife as I could not divorce the mad and inescapable thing I was actually married to. Never before had I allowed myself such a thought. I was shaken by it now. At firsthand, at last, I felt what I had spent my life observing others feel: loss, regret, guilt, the misery of acts never completed. I felt jealousy of my successor. I was angry at him, the son of a bitch.

Without another word, I got out of the car with my paper sack full of Russian fingerprints, walked across the snowy pavement, and deposited my trash in the can. Morgan's headlights flashed twice. She stopped beside me and, for perhaps ten seconds, looked at me longingly—yes, that is the word—before driving away.

In the blinking of an eye, her car vanished. I wept. Yes. Because I understood, and so did she. We were not saying goodbye to each other. We were, each in our own way, saying goodbye to Russia. Like a couple of old Bolsheviks who had outlived their passion, we had been erased from the official photograph.

5 Driving down Interstate 91 through a snowstorm, I pondered the question of the twenty-seven million dollars. The amount staggered me. How could Peter—on the day before he was going to be disgraced, perhaps even tortured, almost certainly shot— disburse such an enormous sum to an asset? It was contrary to all procedures to do what he had done. This suggested two possibilities: (1), he had, improbably, forged the director's signature, stolen twenty-seven million dollars in secret funds and somehow transferred the loot to Escobar's tiny bank in remotest Amazonia; or (2), the sum in question was not the KGB's money.

If the answer was (2), whose money was it?

The truth seemed obvious. I had always assumed, and Peter had encouraged me to assume, that funds for Jack came from his share of the drug trade. But I had also assumed that he ran this money through the KGB mill before distributing it to his operatives. This was only an assumption. Certainly Peter had never told me any such thing. Now it seemed possible that this was not the case, that he had simply deposited all those tainted millions in the most unlikely bank in the world and then spent it, raw and unlaundered, on operations that had not been approved by Moscow and therefore were not controlled by Moscow.

It made the blood run cold. Why? Why would even Peter take such a chance, commit such a folly? If they came to suspect him, they would kill him. But not before he told them everything. And then they would kill me, and everyone else, too.

As if Morgan's kiss had infected me with her naïveté, I was stunned by the realization that I was now alone, utterly alone. Falling snow whirled hypnotically in the headlights of my rented Buick. Driving with the utmost caution, peering into the cone of fragmented light, I fell into something resembling a trance. Faces and figures from the distant past drifted across the bleak landscape of my memory, as across an endless expanse of snow. A dog I had known in childhood, which had somehow escaped being eaten, found me on this vast and empty steppe—just the two of us suspended in a prison of space, a black-and-tan dog with wagging tail, a boy of ten who was walking across Siberia, both with empty stomachs. Why did we walk together instead of one killing and eating the other? We must not have been in Russia after all.

The dog and I entered a birch forest. The dog scented something and ran away. I came upon a man in white, sweeping a path in the snow. It was the man in ski trooper camouflage who had swept away Peter's footprints. I remembered the broom—a big, efficient broom with a varnished wooden stick and wonderfully supple straw. It made the snow fly, it left the path as smooth as powder; it had a life, a purpose, of its own. Like the man who had made this broom, the man who wielded it respected it. This was no Soviet broom. It was an American broom.

Peter! I woke with a spasm of nerves and muscles. My car swerved, nearly hitting another that had been passing me at God knows what speed; the other fellow must have been drunk to be going so fast in such weather. He wore hunter's clothes—camouflage in bright red, how odd. He blew his horn, slammed on his brakes, and barely avoided death for both of us. He shook his fist at me and sped away.

I stopped at the next rest area. Trembling, I closed my eyes and concentrated. The scene in the birch forest returned to me in all its shades of white and I realized who it was that Peter was meeting that day, and why the man was sweeping away Peter's footprints, and why Peter had let me witness all this. Who but a CIA station chief, overdressed egomaniacs every one, would wear such a hat as the big man wore to a secret meeting in a forest? Peter was defecting. The men in white were not his captors. They were his liberators, and they were from the CIA. Peter had let me see this man, wanted me to know who and what he was. But why? Why? Peter would not defect merely to save his own life. He had a greater purpose. He wanted me to know this. But why did I need to know? What was the plan?

In our last moment together he had said to me about Jack, "We have never had such an asset before, and we will never again have such an opportunity as this. This operation must at all costs be preserved."

Now I understood his meaning. It was an order to me not to interfere no matter how great the threat seemed. There was no threat, no KGB, no CIA. Only Peter. Nothing had changed. He, Peter, carried the next revolution, the true revolution, out of Russia with him. His plan was to tell the CIA every detail of everything he knew about KGB operations—with one exception. About Jack he would tell them nothing. Because Jack was the only thing that mattered. Madness? That is certainly one word for what Peter represented.

By now Moscow knew that he was gone, and where to. Soon they would have more evidence of his treachery than they knew what to do with. Moles would confess, networks would cease to function, the whole worldwide apparatus would be infected with the virus that Peter had become. He was the ultimate defector; he knew so much and had learned it by such devious means over such a long period of time that no one could be sure what he knew and what he did not know. The KGB would never be able to trust anyone again. It would cease to function. The apparatchiks would have to start over, reinvent themselves.

Peter was doing all this to preserve Jack Adams.

The KGB would never know that Peter had kept one vital fragment of knowledge—the very existence of Jack—back from the CIA. Result? Jack and Morgan were untouchable from the KGB's point of view. Moscow must assume that Jack Adams had been named by Peter with all the hundreds of other assets with which Soviet intelligence had salted the American body politic.

But would the CIA report this fact, as a fact, to the White House? Think about this for a moment. How can they be sure that Peter is telling them the truth? And if he is, is it in their interest, is it in America's interest, to bring the issue to a head in the middle of an election campaign? The moment they did, the outraged American president would phone the new Russian president and demand satisfaction—such as a public apology for the plot and the dismissal and disgrace of the entire top leadership of the KGB, or whatever it was calling itself by then. Jack's opponents in his own party would join in the attack, along with the entire U.S. Congress and perhaps even the media. His enemies in the party were legion; few ever believed that he actually was a Democrat or a Republican or anything else that American politics could put a name to. Asses—famous asses, liberal asses, exquisitely tender asses—would be on the line all over America.

Besides, there was political reality to consider. Jack Adams was about to win his first primary. Who knew? He might after all become president. If that happened, no matter what the proofs of treason against him, Jack would be invulnerable. Who would dare to accuse him, the president of the United States, elected by the infallible will of the American people in the highest rite of democracy, of being the agent of a foreign intelligence service? The only possible accuser, the CIA, would destroy itself with such an allegation. Of all possible witnesses, it had the least chance of being believed by the media, the priesthood in charge of ritual executions in the United States. Besides, being a clandestine service, the CIA would prefer blackmail of the guilty president to exposure, would it not? Certainly that would be the KGB's choice of options in such a delicious situation.

So what now? It would take Peter at least four months to tell his CIA debriefers all that he knew—except, not to labor the point, the most important thing he knew. At the end of the debriefing, he would be fitted out by the CIA with a new identity, with a new face if he wanted one, with a house, a car, a generous stipend. A telephone number to call if he needed anything. And then the CIA would go away and leave him alone. Yes, incredible as it seems, that is what they would do. Why not? The whole world was having its memory edited. The USSR itself was vanishing. In a year it would be gone like God's great rival Baal after his statues were overturned by the Israelites and his temple walls tumbled, his bloody altars demolished. No mystery, no god; no god, no future.

Unless you believed in resurrection. Peter might fool the CIA, but not me, the last Soviet man.

6 Methodical fellow that I am, I had taken certain precautions against the day when the revolution decided to eat me. Your lip curls, your eye rolls, you mutter, *Preposterous!* Let me brighten your day with some statistics. Forty-eight million people of all nations were killed in World War II, about half of those in the USSR. At least twenty million perished in the Soviet terror, and perhaps sixty million more in China, Cambodia, Vietnam, and other outposts of the faith. I was looking for two of the vanished, my mother and father, when I met the black-and-tan dog on the steppe. All this—the snow, the dog, my parents, the emptiness—was real, no vision. I learned a lesson. In my parents' memory I had planned for the future. Remember, my cover in America was investor, rare-book dealer. I had been entrusted with large sums of money. In my suitcase, in the trunk of the car I was driving, I had just over one million dollars in cash. In investment accounts under two false identities, I had another couple of million. In warehouses in three different American cities I had stored valuable books and even more valuable manuscripts. *Ah-ha!*, you mutter. *A thief as well as a slanderer.* No, not one kopeck. All this wealth was interest earned on seed money provided by my masters. They got their original investment back; I kept what it had produced by breeding their cash with more vigorous American stock. Also in the suitcase, I had complete sets of documentation for two fallback identities—passports, driver's licenses, Social Security cards, credit cards.

I drove back to New York, arriving at four in the morning. I parked the Buick near the Port Authority Bus Terminal with the keys in the ignition. Then I took the subway to Penn Station, a train to Baltimore, and finally a plane to Miami, changing in Winston-Salem, where I went into town and placed some things in a safe deposit box.

In Miami Beach I rented a modest furnished apartment and moved in. Over the weeks that followed I watched the news for traces of Peter and had some minor plastic surgery done: a higher bridge for my Slavic nose, a few millimeters off my Asiatic cheekbones, an eye job to get rid of the epicanthic fold. While waiting for my face to heal, I went on the Ultra Slim Fast diet—if it worked for Tommy Lasorda, why not for a mujik like me?—and shed thirty pounds. In a new voice, with new facial expressions, I carried on imaginary conversations in front of a video camera and then studied my performance on-screen. Gradually I exchanged old mannerisms for new ones and adopted a new way of walking—a sauntering, hands-in-pockets American shamble with a touch of sea legs.

In the mirror I still looked very much the same, but in matters of disguise, major changes are not necessary. A loss in weight and the mere act of exchanging suit and tie for shorts, sandals, and a Florida shirt would have been enough to render me unrecognizable to all but the keenest of eyes. Just the same, a little extra never hurts. I did not imagine that I could deceive Peter's eyes if ever they fell on me again. I merely wanted to pass unnoticed through the circle of disciples that would certainly surround him.

7 Jack won the New Hampshire primary, then Iowa. Three of the six original candidates withdrew from the race, including the one the party leaders had favored. All threw their support to the candidate who was Jack's closest competitor in the polls. No matter. The media, in their deep affinity for the unlikely and the implausible and in their historic affection for the right kind of scoundrel, had chosen Jack as the winner. His face was on every front page, every television screen. The camera, famous for capturing the great and holding them hostage, surrendered like a smitten trollop to Jack and made the world see him as more lovable, wiser, and more human than he actually was.

But that was what Jack was all about. He made liars of us all by recruiting us to defend a faith worth lying for.

By some bizarre alchemy that no one except Jack himself pretended to understand, film and videotape concealed his true character rather than driving the real Jack out of hiding for all to see. When I say that Jack alone understood this phenomenon, I mean that he believed that he had inherited his strange power over the lens from his real father, JFK, that it was in his blood, or was perhaps part of some pact the Kennedys had made with whatever invisible power controls such matters. Had he been Nixon's love child his image would have seemed to squirm and sweat no matter how much the human being that embodies it stood tall and smiled. Danny called this the Dorian Gray factor. In his sound bites, Jack was modesty itself, a man who was as mystified by the workings of the Lord as the next most humble citizen in the land. Actually he knew in his bones that he was under the protection of quite a different supernatural power. Jack smiled and spoke softly to turn away wrath; he hoped that he was worthy of the trust that was being invested in his ideas, his vision. He stood up for his ideas without really having any ideas. He defended grand concepts and proposed trivial solutions to meaningless problems. He was hailed by pundits as a thinker. Naturally he made enemies.

On the day before the next important primary after Iowa—who can remember them all?—a leading tabloid ran the full, delicious story of the girl bodyguard: smoking pistol, outraged wife, and all. She posed in a bikini, wearing her trooper Stetson and pistol harness. The story was a one-week sensation. Holding hands with Morgan and the twins—they were on their way to church—Jack told a television crew that he honestly could not remember this unfortunate young woman. His advisers told him she had indeed served on his staff of bodyguards for less than two weeks, and had been dismissed for losing her weapon and other items of equipment. With a smile of Christian forgiveness, Jack told the world he hoped with all his heart that this deluded young person would get the help she needed. He made his statement to the cameras while standing in front of a tumbledown little AME Zion chapel, Bible in hand. No one who saw Morgan's upturned face, beaming at Jack as he spoke, could doubt that she believed every word her husband said.

326 ★ CHARLES McCARRY

Jack won the primary, though more narrowly than forecast. His desperate opponents were encouraged by this faint evidence that he might be vulnerable on the character issue. Soon they had more reason to hope that the public was getting wise to this man they could not defeat. Half a dozen women who claimed to have performed sexual services for Jack, willingly and otherwise, came forward with their stories. Jack denied nothing. He merely repeated, in every case, what he had said in the first case: He honestly didn't remember the lady. His puzzlement gave way at length to anger—suppressed but all too evident to his friend the minicam—that his family should be put through this tawdry exercise in dirty politics. Finally, on a syndicated confession program watched by millions of women all over the world, Jack's beautiful and obviously loyal and adoring wife, flanked by their darling twin sons, broke the dignified silence with which she had previously treated these allegations.

"Morgan," asked the host, the most influential woman in America, "how do you feel in your inner self when you hear these stories?"

A blush, a sigh. A search for words while staring straight into America's eyes. "To be honest, I just feel sorry for these women," Morgan replied. "All they have is their fantasies. I have Jack Adams, and I'm the luckiest woman in the world."

"Morgan, when you hear these terrible stories that you can't believe, do you ever ask yourself *Why?*"

A pause; how painful this was. "Of course I do, and I think I know—" Morgan broke off. "I'd better not say it. Jack Adams wouldn't want me to."

"The audience wants you to say it, Morgan."

Cries of *Say it, Morgan! Go for it!*

At last Morgan said, "All right. Sorry, Jack. But what I think, after a whole lot of prayer and meditation, is this: My husband came from nowhere with a new idea for America, and nobody much gave him a chance of succeeding. But the people like what they see when they look at Jack Adams, and I think that scares some people. Now I'd really better stop before—"

Go on! Say it, girl! Morgan! Morgan! A brief spontaneous chorus of Jack's song: "Jack, Jack, Jack!"

"All right," said Morgan, "I will say it. I think that these accusations—and they hurt so much—I think they may, just possibly, be *forming a pattern,* and that this just might have something to do with the fact that my husband, Jack Adams, is the outsider in this race, the only candidate without powerful friends, without very much money, just an ordinary American orphan from a little village in Ohio. And as I said, I think that frightens certain people, and that they're all connected to each other, and that they are out to destroy Jack because he is right about America and they are wrong, and he is good and they are evil. That's what I really think, that it's some sort of plot. And oh, how I hope I'm wrong!"

Wise and sympathetic, the host said, "I don't think so, Morgan."

Neither did the audience.

Jack's campaign really took off after Morgan's brave outburst. The media played Morgan's accusations big. The Unconscious Underground picked it up at once, as if it were a thought that occurred simultaneously in twenty million minds. It explained Jack. It explained everything. It got everyone off the hook. No matter what befell, it immunized Jack against exposure, even against prosecution and conviction, because it cast doubt on all future accusations against him. It wasn't only the elite who loved Jack. The common people showed that they did, too. Jack won primary after primary. Like all great natural politicians, Jack Adams was ordinary, but ordinary in a way that magnified the virtues of all the people who instinctively perceived that he was a whole lot like them. This benevolent deception of the people delighted the intelligentsia. This was what made the media love him: He was their fantasy candidate. How they would have loved Peter, too, if only they had known him.

Two

1 The race for the nomination came down to the final primary. Jack won by a tiny plurality, but he was still fifty delegates short of the number needed to be nominated on the first ballot at his party's convention, a month hence. He was, of course, broke. His campaign had spent Peter's twenty-seven million dollars, or whatever laundered portion of it Morgan had been able to salvage from the shambles that was the Columbus Bank of the Western Reserve. In its insatiable hunger for money, the campaign had also consumed every penny the faithful had raised from other sources, and it was in debt for millions more.

Back in Columbus, in Morgan's soundproof room, Jack said, "What do we do now?"

"Win," Morgan said.

Jack was tired, querulous. The onslaught of unbelievers had taken its toll on him. "How, without money?" he cried. "The bastards won't give me any because they think I can't win, because they don't want me to win."

He was talking about the leaders of his own party. Despite his victories, they still did not want him. Jack had won the popularity contest, yes—but barely. They still did not believe that he could win the election against a popular incumbent president who had no negatives except for a mild downturn in the economy after ten years of prosperity.

"They're killing me," Jack said. "Killing me, Morg!"

Morgan ignored the hated nickname. "They can't kill you," she retorted. "Remember who you are."

Morgan meant one thing by this—that he was a child of history, of which Peter was principal agent. Jack understood another, that he was a child of a handsome prince and a beautiful maiden thrown together by fate. Just the same, her words cheered him up. He needed cheering. For the first time, and at what the world saw as his moment of triumph, he himself was not sure. The Republicans were already taking an interest in him; they were turning over rocks. Every insider already knew that the stories about Jack's sex life were true—and if these tales of serial rape were fact, what else might he turn out to be? As for his own party's leaders, they did not suspect the real truth about Jack—who would?—but they sensed that something was wrong with this boy. Something hidden. Something dark. If it came out, it could destroy not just Jack but the party itself, which was already bleeding from a thousand self-inflicted wounds. Jack was a time bomb; he worried them deeply. If he was elected, they would have to defend him to save themselves, and God knew what the price might turn out to be.

Jack was worried too. Morgan's plan to pour money into businesses designed to fail had worked admirably. Nearly every one of these bogus enterprises was by now on the brink of failure or bankruptcy. However, the scam had drained the Columbus Bank of the Western Reserve of nearly all its assets. The bank through which most of Jack's campaign funds had flowed was about to fail. The examiners were about to arrive.

"Then what?" Jack asked again.

Morgan said, "This is exactly what we anticipated and planned for. The examiners will close the bank down. Fine. That was always the plan. The bank has served its purpose. It's time to get rid of it before it can become an embarrassment."

"It's already an embarrassment."

"To the governor, to some of our friends who will stand up for you no matter what. Not to you. There's not a single conversation, not a single fingerprint, to link you to that institution."

"Jesus, Morg! It was my idea."

"Nobody knows that but me, and I'm not going to tell. The governor is the one who's got things to worry about."

"You think he's going to take the fall? You don't know him."

"What fall? Bad judgment? Everybody already knows he has that. So he fucked up a bank just like he fucked up the state and his own life. If he keeps his mouth shut, he's home free. He'll toe the mark. He's got two million five in a bank in the Cayman Islands."

"That son of a bitch! I don't even own a wallet. And even if I did, I'd have nothing but air to put in it. We're going to lose this thing."

"Jack, don't worry. Peter has always come through. He'll come through again. Just raise as much money as you can to fill the gap."

"I told you, it's hopeless. I get nowhere. Danny says he's getting nowhere. The word is out. The fix is in. They're setting me up to lose. They fucking hate me, Morgan."

"All that will change when you don't lose."

"Then get me the money I need to win this thing," Jack said. "The only thing they understand is money. You tell Peter that."

Jack had no idea that I had disappeared, that Peter had vanished, that Morgan did not know if he would ever come back, that they were alone. She had thought it best not to worry him. Like me, she was what she was. Nothing could change that. In her heart she believed they would be rescued by the revolution, by history. By Peter. She tousled Jack's hair, actually touched him. He looked surprised. What had he done to earn this sympathy?

"Don't worry," Morgan said. "We ain't dead yet."

2 Back in Columbus, Danny found Cindy at the kitchen table, hair combed, dressed for the day, drinking coffee and reading the newspapers. It was early in the morning, about six-thirty; he had been with Morgan all night. Cindy wore yellow vinyl dish-washing gloves to keep the ink off her hands. He had forgotten, actually forgotten, that she always did this. Once he had loved her for her Minnie Mouse gloves. The stab of guilt he always felt when he saw her after an absence was sharper than usual.

Danny said, "Can we talk?"

"That depends on what you want to talk about," Cindy replied.

"It's about the firm," Danny said. "Actually, about the bank. But there's a connection."

Cindy folded her paper and took off her gloves but said nothing.

Danny said, "A lot has gone wrong."

"How much?"

"A lot. We'll have to fold it. The bank."

"It's going to fail?"

"That's right."

"What about the depositors?"

"There's the FDIC. But some of them will lose a lot."

Knowing the answer, Cindy said, "Danny, what exactly do you stand to lose?"

"I'm not sure. My name is on a lot of paper."

"But not Jack's name, not Morgan's?"

"Jack was never involved in any way. Morgan was never an officer of the bank, only its consultant on management methods, never on substance. She was careful to make that point every time."

"You mean she's covered her ass and hung yours out to dry."

"Whatever, she's clean. I'm one of the responsible officers."

"What did you do on your own?"

"Nothing. It was always Morgan. Her advice, her orders."

"But never her signature?"

"Rarely. And when it was, she kept that paper."

"Where?"

"In Morgan's room."

"What's that?"

"A room in the old offices. It's soundproofed, locked with a keypad. Only Morgan has the combination."

"She didn't trust you with that, just with criminal responsibility for her malfeasance?"

Danny did not reply.

Cindy said, "Do you want me to be your lawyer?"

"Yes."

"Is that Morgan's idea, too? Double indemnity—I can't testify because I'm your wife, technically. And I can't disclose anything you tell me because I'm your law—"

"It wasn't Morgan's idea. I haven't discussed it with her."

Cindy had known that this moment would come. She was ready for it. "All right," she said. "Let's get started."

Cindy asked Danny a series of questions. He was amazed at how sharp she was, how clearly she saw patterns that had been designed to be undetectable. Of course, he did not know what a lot she already knew about the inner workings of the bank. By the end of her interrogation she also knew everything that Danny knew.

"Danny," she said, "you're in very deep trouble."

"I know," he said. "What am I going to do?"

"There's only one thing to do. Go to Merriwether Street—"

"You're out of your mind."

"—right now, at his house, before he leaves for the office. Tell him everything and make the best deal you can. Say nothing about this to that woman who's been fucking you, and not one word to Jack."

Danny was staggered. What he had wanted was delay, not an explosion. He said, "Go to the U.S. attorney a month before the convention that's going to nominate Jack? How can I do that?"

"You have to do it."

"I can't. I'm Jack's attorney. I'm Morgan's attorney. Everything they've ever told me is protected by attorney-client privilege."

"And I'm *your* attorney, Danny."

"And Jack's law partner. Your lips are sealed, too."

"Like hell they are. There's no partner-partner immunity. They've set you up, Danny. They've systematically plundered the bank to get Jack the nomination, and now they don't need it or you anymore, and you're the designated fall guy. That was the idea from the start."

"No."

"No? Okay, say it's just bad luck. What does that change? You'll be indicted, Jack will say how much he loves you and feels for you and what a hero you've always been to him and always will be, sob. Morgan will simper for the cameras. And then you'll go to jail and they'll go to the White House."

Danny exploded. "Merriwether Street is a Republican, for Christ's sake! He'll use this to destroy Jack!"

Of course he is, Cindy thought. *Of course he will. That's the whole point.* She said, "Nobody can destroy Jack. He's a fucking hydra, every head with a great big smile. Lop one off, he grows another one. But you're human, Danny, and you've got only one head to lose."

Danny recoiled. "I can't do this," he said.

"You've got to do it or go to prison for twenty years." She stood up. "Let's go. We don't have much time."

But Danny could not move. His brain refused to send the necessary signals to his body. "I can't," he said. "Not to Jack; not to Morgan. She and I have already betrayed Jack. I can't do it again. I can't do it to the country."

"You can't do it to the *country*?" Cindy said. "Think what you'll be doing to the country if you don't do this, Danny! They won't be satisfied until they ruin the country. They *hate* America, Danny. They always have. They wanted the other side to win in Vietnam, the side that tried to burn you alive. They didn't give a shit what happened to you then, and if you think they care now, you're a bigger chump than even they think you are."

Danny shook his head in denial. "You can't," he said, "reduce this whole situation to the wounds I got in Vietnam."

"Like hell I can't," Cindy said. "They might as well have set you on fire with their own hands."

But Danny would not be convinced. "They're not that way at all, Cindy," he said. "You're wrong about them. You have every right to be angry. I know what you think and feel, but Jack would never do such a thing to me. Never."

"Oh no? Danny, take my hands. I have something to tell you."

"Do I want to hear it?"

"No. Give me your hands."

They clasped hands across the tabletop. In minute detail, Cindy told Danny what had happened on the night he left for Vietnam: what she had felt, what she had done, why she had done it.

Then she told him he had been drafted in Jack's place: "It's documented, Danny. You got your future burned up for him because you were where he was supposed to be. And he was so grateful that he got me drunk and raped me so I had to kill my baby just in case it belonged to Jack."

"Kill your baby?" Danny cried, horrified. "What in the name of God are you talking about?"

"I had an abortion."

"An abortion? Wasn't it my baby, too?"

"I don't know. I'll never know. If I had been sure it was yours, I would have had it, Dan. It was a boy. And if it was yours, then Jack Adams murdered it just as surely as if he had smothered it with a pillow."

Danny was white-faced. He said, "Why?"

"Because I couldn't have anything left behind by that son of a bitch growing inside of me."

"Cin!"

His eyes overflowed. He reached out for her. She moved away, holding up a hand as if it were a crucifix and he had come from Satan.

She said, "If you won't do this, Dan, if you won't save yourself, I will. I'll divorce you and testify against all three of you. I'll see you in prison before I'll see those two going scot-free so they can fuck the United States of America like they've fucked the two of us and ruined our lives. You'll have to kill me to stop me, Dan. Take your choice."

Danny said, "You think I could do you harm?"

Cindy laughed, and it sounded to Danny like someone he did not know had made the sound. "Oh, Danny."

He looked at her as his wife for what he was sure would be the last time. He said, "I can't do it. I'm sorry."

"What a surprise," Cindy said. She walked out the door and got into her car.

3 Cindy arrived at F. Merriwether Street's large old-money Tudor house in time to watch him back his battered Oldsmobile out of the driveway. She followed and, at the next stop sign, pulled up beside him and signaled him to pull over.

It was a mellow, sun-splashed morning. Standing on the sidewalk in a shower of pollen, he sneezed spasmodically as he listened with mouth agape to what Cindy had to tell him.

The Columbus Bank of the Western Reserve had loaned twenty-seven million dollars to twenty-two different new enterprises that had all failed or gone bankrupt? And the loans were inflated?

Cindy said, "That's correct."

"Where did this all this money come from in the first place?" Street asked.

"From the Banco Amazones in Leticia, Colombia."

"Who put the money into the bank?"

"I don't know. Danny doesn't know, either."

"It's pretty obvious what the possibilities are," Street said. "They've been laundering drug money to finance Jack's campaign. Tell me if I'm wrong."

Cindy was silent.

Street said, "They must be crazy. Twenty million dollars in one whack?"

"Twenty-*seven* million."

"The only questions," Street said, "are, one, Which drug cartel provided the cash? and, two, What do they want in return?"

"I don't know who they are, or what they want," Cindy replied. "But now I'll tell you, before I tell you one more thing, what I want."

"I'm listening."

"Clemency for Danny Miller."

"You want a lot."

"Nailing Danny means nothing," Cindy said. "Jack and Morgan would love it if you did get him. Plus the ex-governor. That's the way they set it up. Don't take the bait. You've got to promise me to get the real criminals and treat Danny as the patsy he is, or—"

"Or what? Do you realize what you've just told me?"

"Do you realize what I've just given you?"

Yes, he realized. If F. Merriwether Street, rock-ribbed Republican, cracked this case and sent the nominee of the opposition party to prison, not only would he assure his own political future by winning the presidential election for his own party almost single-handed, he would also destroy his old tormentor, Jack Adams, and paint Jack's party with Jack's crime. Nearly dead of its own follies anyway, that party would vanish into the political wilderness for years to come, perhaps forever.

Street's face twisted. "Damn!" he said. He whirled, turning his back to Cindy, and sneezed. Finally, he faced her and said, "I'll have to think about it."

"Fine, you've got sixty seconds," Cindy said. "Danny gets a deal or I walk away and you've got nothing. No documentation. No witness. No case."

"You have documentation?"

"I am in a strong position," Cindy said. "What's your answer?"

Street said, "He'll have to serve some time."

"All right, but the absolute minimum. And not in a bad place."

"He'll have to testify."

"I don't think he'll do that."

"Then it's no deal."

"You won't need him. The governor will sing. And yes, there is a paper trail."

"You mean it when you say you're in a strong position on that?"

"Trust me."

"What's that supposed to mean?"

"I'll tell you that when we have a deal."

Street said, "You've got the goods, haven't you, Cindy?"

She did not answer. She did not have to. Street knew that she had the goods, and that she was using them to buy back Danny's life.

He said, "Deal."

4 One fine day, the Soviet intelligence service announced to the world that Peter had destroyed it. Not in so many words, of course; voluntary confession in the bright light of day never was its style. But what it did do amounted to full disclosure: It had a clearance sale and closed up shop. The KGB, already calling itself by another name, began to sell off the booty it had accumulated during three quarters of a century of Bolshevik rule. Everything disposable that would bring hard currency went on the block: dachas, apartments in Moscow, works of art from secret vaults, every weapon in the Soviet arsenal—including the complete list of components of nuclear devices.

Above all, gossip went on sale—suddenly, inexplicably, the deep dark secrets of the late world revolution became available to anyone who believed sufficiently in their genuineness to buy them, cash on the barrelhead. This was the signal I had been waiting for. It could mean only one thing: These treasures, this archive of the most extensive espionage enterprise in the history of the world, this chimera that had cost trillions of rubles and consumed millions of lives and kept the USSR in the Dark Ages, was no longer of any value to its owners. The only value the files had ever had was their secrecy. And Peter had already sold that to the CIA. The KGB was counterattacking. Thanks to Peter, the last traitor to the cause, the CIA knew all of its secrets? Fine, so would the whole world. Moscow would turn treasure into junk.

Eager buyers flocked to Russia; nearly all went away with a macabre souvenir of the late lamented Socialist motherland. It was like *Zorba the Greek,* the scene in which the old prostitute dies and while her corpse cools on the bed the villagers come into her house and strip the sheets and loot her house of all her pathetic treasures. Russian communism had become the dead whore of history—just as Peter had known it would.

Only Peter had had the vision to steal the old harlot's most valuable asset while she was still alive. He must act soon—sell short. But how, and to whom, and for how much?

I began to look for him in earnest.

5 Action proceeds from character. Peter had always believed that he could control any situation, dominate any human being or combination of people and events. He would not change now, no matter what outward changes the forgers and plastic surgeons of the CIA may have wrought. Next to intrigue he loved comfort, and next to comfort he loved beauty. As soon as his business with the CIA was over, Peter would go to a warm climate—not some backwater, but a place where the action was, a mecca for the young, the beautiful, and the lost who were the raw material of his art.

That was why I was in Miami Beach. With its Art Deco revival, the very name of which suggested decadence—drugs, sex, mindlessness—it was the Now Place. It was Peter's kind of place, readymade for his purposes, the spa of the rebellious children of the American Nomenklatura. And unlike Los Angeles, another likely destination, it was not a media center. Peter could not live without a circle of disciples—boys and girls, beautiful and willing to belong to him in mind and body. He did not have time to wait for them to come to him; he did not have the power in the USA, as he had had in the USSR, to send out scouts to bring them to him. He would go to where they already were and announce his presence with the party of the year. Then he would gather the sheaves. He was a born guru. Whatever he called himself, whatever he preached, wherever he was, disciples would gather.

Identify the disciples and find Peter. Find out by watching them what Peter had in mind for Jack Adams. Those were my objectives. I was driven by a compulsion; I will not hide this from you. I no longer trusted the only Russian I had ever trusted, and I wanted to know the reason why.

Every day or two I took a bus from Surfside, my blighted neighborhood, down Collins Avenue to South Beach and wandered along the oceanfront among the disciples-in-waiting. What a wonderful beach, what an amazing place; it was like reading Dante in blinding sunlight. How beautiful are American faces and bodies, how empty these souls, how arrogant American shame in its disguise as exhibitionism.

I did not imagine that I would bump into Peter himself. Instead, I was looking for a sign of him, something I could follow to his lair. Sooner than I had hoped, I found it. I had had no idea that the sign would be such an unmistakable one: Igor. He was standing by the pool behind the Delano Hotel, talking to a tall girl in a bikini. Her skin, all but six square inches of it on display, was the color of honey, her hair a blue-black cape. Her eyes, which passed over me in contempt, were very large and blue, and had the epicanthic fold. Half Chinese, half Caucasian, with breasts grown in America and nowhere else in the known universe.

I followed Igor and this goddess home, to a houseboat moored in the Intracoastal Waterway just a few blocks away. A week later I moved into an apartment in a high-rise that had an unobstructed view from its balcony of the houseboat, and a day or two after that, while sipping a glass of tea, I saw Peter. He emerged from the houseboat with the honey-colored girl by his side and got into a seventy-five-thousand-dollar BMW. She held the door for him.

I studied them through binoculars. Same Peter. Tall, elegant, nonchalant. He belonged in Miami Beach as he belonged everywhere. No plastic surgery, not even a change in hair color. What was the point? The damage was done, and who in Moscow knew what might happen if they laid a finger on him and offended their new friends, the CIA? The apparatchiks were trying to forget him and get on with their new lives and marriages, not turn him into a ghost that would haunt them forever.

6 At the party convention, Jack was nominated for the presidency on the first ballot after he offered second place on the ticket to the only one of his rivals cynical enough to accept it and throw his delegates to Jack. This man, a wealthy U.S. senator, accepted because, like most of his powerful friends in politics and journalism, he did not imagine that Jack could win or survive long in office if he did. In the latter case, he, the senator, would be president.

"The vice presidency is like the last cookie on the plate," the senator's wife told Morgan in an extra-plummy Seven Sisters voice. "Nobody wants it, but somebody always takes it."

Morgan turned away without reply; she was not one to laugh at the class enemy's jokes. Public appearances were another matter, so the two women, both young, slim, and comely, held hands on the convention stage—even danced a few steps of the exuberant dance that now went with the tune of "Jack, Jack, Jack!"

All this ersatz excitement notwithstanding, the incumbent president looked unbeatable; his campaign was rolling in money. The popularity polls gave him a huge lead. Jack's percentage of the vote was estimated at 35 percent or less.

In private, in Morgan's room, Jack was desperate. Even though his campaign would now receive tens of millions of dollars in federal funds and his party would be obliged for appearances' sake to supply additional millions, Jack was in desperate financial straits. His own treasury was empty and he was millions of dollars in debt. Even with the nomination sewed up, frantic efforts to raise additional funds continued to fall short. Few big donors wanted to gamble large contributions on a sure loser—especially one like Jack, who was as slippery as a trout when it came to signing political IOUs. The smart money flowed to the Republican president and to candidates for Congress, not to this compulsively talkative outsider who had systematically concealed his true beliefs—assuming he had any—from voters and party leaders alike. All the world knew Jack's face and voice; nobody knew Jack, even though he seemed to be willing to answer any question put to him, no matter how personal.

Every day when they saw each other for the first time, Jack raised his eyebrows to Morgan, asking the silent question: *Had Peter come back, bringing with him the millions he had promised?* And every day Morgan shook her head no. Not yet.

Then, to everyone's astonishment except his own, Jack's luck took a hand. The incumbent president had been seen by the conservatives in his party as not being conservative enough. A rump group of extreme right-wing voters—the same people who, as Dixiecrats, had in former times deserted the Democratic Party in periodic fits of racist pique—now deserted the Republicans and formed a third party. Few took this movement seriously. However, there was an almost immediate groundswell of support for the simplistic ideas of the third party's nominee, a self-made billionaire who seemed to be in urgent need of psychiatric intervention. Jack called him "the Nutcase." The Left loathed and feared this man and his movement. But Jack immediately understood that the mad tycoon was a good omen—that his, Jack's, sardonic father in heaven had taken a hand in events.

"This means we're going to be elected," he told his dispirited staff. "We can do it with forty percent of the vote if the Nutcase takes away enough votes from the president to deny him the electoral votes of states that he needs to win."

Few thought that Jack really believed this, but he did. Like JFK in 1960, he would concede certain states where his opponent was strong and concentrate his campaign in battleground states where a few thousand popular votes could decide the outcome. He knew he had found the door to the presidency; he was sure of this. But to unlock it he needed at least thirty million dollars more to spend on attack ads in battleground states in the last, vital days of the campaign.

By now Morgan had absolute trust in Jack's political instincts, if in nothing else about him. She saw the same opportunity Jack saw. She was frantic. Only a call from Peter could save them now. She carried the cell phone I had given her at our final meeting in the McDonald's parking lot. She kept it on her person in waking hours; it recharged on her bedside table when she slept.

It never rang. When would the promised messenger come, speaking the code words that meant rescue and power and possession of the U.S. government and the beginning of the end of evil in the world?

As the hourglass of the campaign ran out, Jack asked Morgan that question every single day.

"Soon," she said.

"It had better be damn soon," Jack replied.

7 On the morning after the nomination, in a rumpled bed in a hotel in California, Danny told Morgan about his conversation with Cindy. He had her full attention immediately.

She said, "Why didn't you tell me this right away?"

"I wasn't sure what she was going to do."

"But she's gone to Merriwether Street?"

"I'm not sure. I think she may have."

"Street is the biggest dumb shit in the country."

"Close. But he's also the U.S. attorney."

"That's right. And he hates Jack. And if he fucks around with us, he'll lose."

Was Morgan as unworried as she seemed, as arrogant? Danny said, "Don't be too sure of that, Morgan. I don't know whether this has occurred to you and Jack, but practically everyone you know has become a felon in the process of trying to help you. The bank alone—"

Morgan did not want to hear this. "The bank is cool," she said. "It's going to fail. The governor made some bad calls. It's a judgment issue. He'll walk away. Not our fault."

"How can you be so sure?"

"Danny, trust me. Are *you* going to rat on Jack?"

"No, but—"

"Okay, that's the key," Morgan said. "Go back to Columbus. Talk to Merriwether Street. Warn him to be careful. Tell him about your fight with Cindy."

Danny said, "It wasn't a fight."

"Of course it was a fight. She's got some wild idea that you and I are lovers, and this is the way she's getting her revenge. Merriwether will never believe that Danny Miller, all-American, is capable of adultery. Especially if you're married to Cindy. Have you ever noticed the way he looks at her?"

Danny felt a pang of jealousy. "A lot of people look at Cindy."

"Danny, do as I ask. Please."

"I can't do that to Cindy."

"Do what to Cindy? Save her from making a fool of herself in front of the whole world, of making an enemy of everyone who'll want to get next to Jack when he's president?"

"She doesn't see it that way."

Morgan said, "Then she's got a real problem with her future, because that's the way it's going to be. Jack will be the most powerful man in the world and she'll be an ex–prom queen."

"Morgan, come off it," Danny said. "Jack's not going to hurt Cindy."

"Not personally. If you care about her you'll save her from herself. Merriwether Street is a right-wing prick who will do anything to get Jack. You really want him to use your wife to destroy your best friend and get yourself locked up for thirty years?"

Danny was silent. Morgan said, "I remind you that Jack is running for president. That he's the good guy and the other side are the bad guys. Think, Danny."

"I don't know what to tell Street that would penetrate his skull."

"I just got through telling you. Cindy is making the whole thing up out of jealousy."

"That's untrue. It's simplistic."

"Simple is good. Simple *works*. Tell him."

"What am I supposed to tell him after I've told him Cindy is crazy?"

"The truth. The bank is going to fail because it made some bad loans. You tried to give the governor a break, a new opportunity in life, but it just didn't work out. He fucked up because he's a born fuckup. We're the real losers. We can live with that. Bad luck. End of story."

"It won't fly," Danny said. "Let me talk to Jack."

8 Back in Columbus, zealously but secretly, F. Merriwether Street had been pursuing his case against the Adamses. But because he did not yet have solid proof, and because he feared that left-wingers in the Department of Justice would tip off their masters in the party, if not Jack and Morgan, and also because he wanted all the credit for himself, he had not told Washington what he was doing. He had not even told his staff or his father or his uncle. Only he and Cindy, poring over documents in the cellar of the Victorian mansion in Tannery Falls night after night, were in on the secret. Their meetings resembled lovers' assignations: cryptic phone calls,

343 ★ LUCKY BASTARD

separate cars, lies, and an intimacy that was deepened by the thrill of the forbidden and the fear of discovery. Street had always known that Cindy was beautiful and desirable; as a result of their furtive hours together, these qualities were no longer an abstraction. There she was, within reach. Nothing happened between them, of course; nothing could.

Nevertheless, their relationship troubled Merriwether Street's conscience. He was a puritan, the heir to old money and old obligations. He believed strongly in the public trust as the highest expression of a Christian life next to fidelity in marriage and stern but loving fatherhood. He was a model of probity, a man who kept a tight rein on his appetites. He loved his wife and had never betrayed her with another woman and never would. In fact he had never had another woman even before marriage. He was a dutiful father, but in that respect as in so many others he was Jack's opposite.

With every passing day, Street was more and more certain that Jack and Morgan were criminals, that the bank was only the tip of the vast iceberg of their evil works, that it was not important in itself but for whatever larger criminal conspiracy it had been designed to cover up. At the same time he worried incessantly that Jack and Morgan, in their ruthlessness, would trump him again, that in spite of all he knew, in spite of his honor and sense of duty, they would win again and he would be the one who was destroyed.

That did not deter him from his duty. While Jack's triumphant homecoming parade was still in progress, Danny called on Street in his office in the federal courthouse. On the other side of the building, which faced the parade route, drums and bugles blared wind-snatched bars of "Jack, Jack, Jack!" as the bands marched past the reviewing stand where Jack and Morgan were waving merrily and the twins, in matching sailor suits, were snapping off salutes.

Street listened without expression to Danny's story. Then he asked a single question: Where did the twenty-seven-million-dollar deposit—the working capital that brought down the bank—come from?

Danny did not answer.

Street said, "You don't know or you won't say?"

"It's irrelevant. And anyway, it's a confidential matter protected by lawyer-client privilege. I am here as the bank's lawyer."

"We'll see about that."

Danny said, "Good luck. But you're barking up the wrong tree."

For a while Street sat in heavy silence as if listening intently to Jack's exuberant song. People were dancing in the streets. Mass foreplay. He had to admit that pinkos had more fun. Finally he said, "Okay, Miller, have it your way. You have the right to remain silent. And maybe that's what you should do. But I know what kind of money that twenty-seven million was, and how it smelled. And you can tell your friends in the drug business that they're going to go down, and that you and your co-conspirators are going to go down with them. That's a promise."

Danny said, "My friends in the drug business? What are you talking about?"

He was surprised and deeply disturbed by Street's words. Drug money? This had never occurred to him.

Later, when he delivered his report to Morgan, she snorted in amusement. "My God, that's wonderful! He really thinks it was drug money?"

"I certainly got that impression."

"Wonderful! Wonderful!" Morgan was laughing, positively bursting with merriment. She had been desperate for a diversion, something that would steer the world away from the truth about Jack's sources of finance. Folding the bank was good. But drug money! Only a Republican could have imagined that he could penetrate Peter's smoke screens, avoid Peter's booby traps, and break through to the drug cartels, which would turn out to be a happy band of eager witnesses. F. Merriwether Street was off on a wild-goose chase that could last for years and was guaranteed to come to nothing!

"Drug money!" Morgan said. "Manna from heaven."

Danny said, "I'm glad you're pleased. But he's coming after us. What now?"

"Ignore the blockhead. Full speed ahead on closing the bank. File bankruptcy, whatever. You handle the details. The governor signs everything. And whenever Merriwether Street mentions drug money, look very, very nervous."

Danny said, "Morgan, I *am* nervous."

"We can fix that, baby."

She kissed him, long and wet. "My God, it's been so long!"

It had been three days. They were in Morgan's room. It was four o'clock in the afternoon. Morgan picked up the phone and said, "Muriel, I don't want to be disturbed for any reason. That goes for the watchdogs." She meant the Secret Service agents who now went everywhere with her, who stood guard outside the door. She was undressing as she spoke.

After Danny left, Morgan opened her safe. After pulling on a pair of surgical gloves stored inside, she extracted a videotape. It was sealed in a padded envelope. She turned on her computer and, still wearing the gloves, typed F. Merriwether Street's name and home address on a label and printed it out. She affixed the label to the envelope along with a priority mail stamp.

Then, without a glance at the waiting Secret Service agents, she strode into the outer office and out the front door. The agents leaped to their feet and followed.

At the curb, where her limousine waited, she dropped the envelope into a mailbox.

One of the agents said, "We'd have been glad to take care of that for you, ma'am."

Morgan smiled, cold-eyed, with all thirty-two of her perfect teeth. "I like to do things for myself," she replied.

The agent opened the car door for her. She said, sharply, "You don't listen, do you? Don't ever do that again. I can open my own fucking doors."

9 F. Merriwether Street was revolted by the tape. As a puritan he was also fascinated by it. It confirmed so many of the things that he had always known, in the abstract, to be true of human females. It was plain from Cindy's reactions that what was happening to her was new, shocking, totally unexpected. Yet she loved it; she could not help herself. This man had her running on all fours. There was no mistaking that what she felt was, in fact, ecstasy. But what must she have felt afterward?

Only by sealing the tape as evidence and locking it in a safe was Street able to resist the urge to look at it again. At the same time, he recognized it as a blatant attempt to impeach his witness and intimidate him. And he knew where it had come from. That had been the whole point of sending it to him. It was a warning.

He immediately called Cindy. She calmly acknowledged that the tape was genuine and described the circumstances in which it was made.

"You were set up for blackmail against a contingency exactly like this one," Street said.

"A reasonable person could so conclude," Cindy replied.

"By whom?"

"Who else could it be?"

"As far as I'm concerned, this just reinforces the case. Do you want to go on?"

"Yes."

"I can't burn the tape. I may have to produce it on discovery."

"I know that."

"Cindy, I have to ask you this. Is the tape everything they have on you?"

"Everything I know about, everything that's true," Cindy said. "But that doesn't mean there won't be more things coming in the mail. They're going to do everything they can to distort this investigation and lead it down blind alleys. Accuse the accuser, that's their first law."

Street didn't quite know what she meant by that, and even when her prediction came true he did not see the connection.

Three

★ ★

1 The honey-colored half-Chinese girl was Peter's first disciple. Soon she became the bait of the fisherman. She was good—so good that I suspected prior training. She brought others to him. Only the brightest and most beautiful were invited to remain. There were parties on the houseboat, parties on the beach. As expected, Peter was staying in character, building a cadre. I watched, but with circumspection. Even assisted by amateurs, Peter was a formidable counterespionage service all by himself. The fact that he had trained me was both an advantage and a danger: He knew what to look for because he knew what I would be looking for. One evening by accident I found myself dining across the room from Peter in a trendy restaurant. I was alone; he was with the honey-colored girl and two or three other beauties of both sexes. Waiters (only slightly less beautiful) hovered. Peter was already a celebrity; I was a regular whom the headwaiter was happy to meet for the first time each time I tipped him twenty dollars for a good table. As wine was poured for him to taste, Peter's eyes rested on me for a moment. Without recognition? Perhaps.

A day or two later, while I read a newspaper and drank coffee at the News Café, the honey-colored girl swept down on me. She wore her usual street costume, string bikini and Rollerblades. The only part of her body completely concealed were her eyes, behind huge sunglasses. She leaned over my table, displaying even the nipples of her admirable breasts, and with a catlike smile said, in excellent Mandarin, "Love your face. Is it new?" She dipped a fingertip in my coffee and drew it lingeringly along one of the surgical scars behind my ears. Then she skated away, naked buttocks working for the tantalization of the invisible man who was myself, grinning and sticking out her tongue. Was this a message from Peter or cocaine? I assumed the former; it is always best to assume the worst.

I watched my back. I never saw anyone behind me, but I began to hear familiar phenomena on my telephone—the sudden fading in volume that is sometimes, though not always, a sign that the phone is being tapped. When outdoors I began to wear an amplifier, also disguised as a Walkman, which permitted me to hear small sounds from a considerable distance. One day while sitting on my balcony, and then the next day as I walked along the beach, I heard what I was listening for, the snicker and hiss of a shutter on a camera with a long lens. I was being photographed. Or was I?

I no longer appeared on my balcony in person, but set up a video camera inside an innocent-looking table and watched the door of Peter's houseboat on the screen in my bedroom, while in the other room the television played soaps and movie reruns: Ingrid Bergman as a psychiatrist, Richard Burton as the disillusioned unwitting pawn of a diabolically clever British intelligence service; oh my. Early one morning, just at dawn, an hour at which I was especially vigilant because first light has always been Peter's favorite moment to do the unexpected, a Lincoln Town Car with a liveried chauffeur arrived outside the houseboat. From the bedroom window I focused my most powerful optic, a night-vision telescope, on the interior of the car, and in the backseat I saw the wavering wormlike green figure of a small, slender person. Not a woman, judging by the body language. An Oriental, I decided. The person looked out the window—not in anxiety but in impatience. A Chinese. I recognized the face but could not put a name to it or remember how I knew it. I photographed it.

Peter emerged from the houseboat, carrying a hanger bag. He got into the Lincoln. It drove off immediately. I was already dressed, Florida fashion, in shorts and T-shirt and tennis shoes. I went down in the elevator, got into my car, and drove at high speed straight to the Miami airport.

I caught a glimpse of Peter on the curb. He sauntered inside. I double-parked and dashed into the terminal in pursuit. Just inside the door I found Peter waiting for me to catch up. He smiled, winked broadly, sauntered away. I was in the trap. Beyond his tall and elegant figure—he wore white duck trousers that day and a pale blue blazer—I spotted three young Americans in dark suits hurrying toward me through the crowd. The two flankers split off left and right to envelop me, the center man made eye contact and came right at me. Almost surely CIA agents. I thought, *He has told them I'm a KGB assassin.*

The thought of escape did not even cross my mind. I knew they would not kill me unless I pulled a gun. The CIA has no power of arrest—what a country!—and I had no intention of letting myself be kidnapped without a struggle. There was nothing to do but walk straight toward them, as if I were the honest American citizen my documentation said I was.

They, too, kept coming. Now I saw who they really were: not CIA men, but three of Peter's disciples. There was cause for anxiety after all. There is no telling what an amateur will do. I looked to either side for a way out. While my attention was distracted, a girl carrying a suitcase materialized in front of me. She dropped her bag— that's how I knew she was there, I heard it hit the floor. Long legs apart, she bent over from the waist as if to pick it up.

All this I saw in a flash a fraction of a second before I bumped into her. She shrieked, whirled, and slapped me hard on the face. In a voice churned by outrage and disgust she shouted, in a British accent, "*Oh, you filthy swine!* Police! Someone bring the police!"

It was Peter's honey-colored girl, now dressed—demurely, for her—in miniskirt and blouse instead of string bikini and Rollerblades. An airport cop arrived in seconds. The girl filed a complaint of sexual battery against me, charging that I had thrust my hand between her legs and fondled her as she leaned over in all innocence to pick up her suitcase. Her startling beauty was more than enough to make the cops believe almost anything she said. The technique was so quintessentially Peter: a distraction inside a diversion wrapped up in a double cross, and the whole package tied up with a merry laugh.

It took seven hours to be booked, briefly incarcerated, and then released on cash bond—I never leave home without my traveler's checks. By then one of my two remaining false American identities, invented over years of careful planning, had been destroyed forever. No matter. My work in Miami Beach was done. I stopped at my apartment long enough to sweep it of all evidences of my presence—not a fingerprint survived. I packed a bag and bundled up my surveillance equipment and loaded it into the trunk of the car.

On a laptop computer I called up the flights that left Miami in the hours following my arrest. I looked for matching connections for all passengers on all those planes. Within minutes I had made a match: two men, a Mr. N. Carlisle and a Mr. J. Yung, who had departed Miami at nine o'clock in the morning on the same flight for London, and then in London boarded a PIA flight for Karachi, with ongoing connections to Shanghai.

A few hours later I was in the air myself. I had friends in Shanghai. But then, so did Peter.

2 My Shanghai friend and I found each other in the throngs along the Bund, the famous promenade beside the Huang Po River. We used the old signals—a certain pin in her hair, a certain book in my hand. I asked for directions to the Chinese Seaman's Club.

"It is by a little bridge over a tributary of the river," she replied. "Follow me."

On the bridge, she stared into my altered face.

In Uighur, the language we had always spoken to each other, she said, "You have been to a doctor."

"Not you, my friend."

"Only Dr. Time."

And Dr. History. Twenty years before she had been a beauty, but what I saw now was a skull in which two well-remembered, fiercely intelligent eyes burned. No other traces remained of the girl she had been before the Red Guards did what they had done to her.

Nothing of importance had changed. This woman was a pure-hearted Communist who knew that I was one, too. She also knew that she was alive because of me and might have died because of Peter, and that I had come for help—help for the revolution, to which we were both pledged and bound together. No explanations or appeals to the past were necessary. This was why she had wanted to go on living; it was why I had helped her to stay alive. In the old days she had been a junior officer in the Chinese foreign intelligence service. After the death of Mao and the rise of new Party leadership she was rehabilitated. She now held a high position in Chinese counterintelligence. That meant that what she was not trusted to know she found out by her own means.

I told her what I wanted to know.

She said, "Tomorrow, take the tour bus that arrives on the Bund at four in the afternoon."

The crowd at the bus stop was enormous—a sea of black eyes staring at the foreigners. I did not see my friend at once, but when I stepped off the bus I felt a sharp pain in my hip, and there she was, hatpin in hand, utterly expressionless. I stared into her eyes and waited for the poison to work. Nothing happened; I did not die. This was her message: She was still my friend, the pin was not tipped with poison.

She led me—I followed at a discreet distance, eyes fixed on the ornament in her hair as she slipped ahead of me through the tangled crowd. She stepped aboard a sampan moored in the yellow water of the Huang Po. I followed. This was risky—a white man and a Chinese woman alone. It was impossible even for my friend to know which molecules of the great crowd-beast were watching for just such a lapse in tradecraft. She seemed unconcerned.

In plain speech, using no pseudonyms or circumlocutions, she said, "Peter is in Shanghai. He is meeting in a safe house with a man called Ji De Lu. You know who that is?"

"No."

"He is the famous Mr. Gee."

"Ah."

Of course. Until the most recent rearrangement of power, Mr. Gee had been a member of the counterintelligence directorate of the Chinese intelligence service. Under Mao Zedong he had been the head of the secret police in Shanghai, and therefore my friend's persecutor. He had controlled the Red Guards in this city. He was a brute, a coarse-faced Manchu, a torturer. He may even have raped my friend himself. But now he was a member of the new class, a maker of money. He had become very, very rich off joint contracts with American and other foreign manufacturers looking for cheap labor. Mr. Gee was able to provide the labor because he controlled manufacturing in China's archipelago of labor camps—ten million political prisoners who worked without wages.

I said, "He is now a capitalist?"

"Mr. Gee keeps up with the times."

"Does this mean that his connection with Chinese intelligence no longer exists?"

"He has the same important friends as always, only they are richer now. It is he who brought Peter to us."

What? "Please explain," I said.

She said, "You do not know?"

"No."

"That's odd. Moscow knows."

"I haven't been in Moscow for years. Peter has kept me away."

"I see," said my friend. "Then I will tell you. After Afghanistan, but before the Berlin Wall came down, when Gorbachev was destroying the Communist Party of the USSR, Peter came to Mr. Gee and made an offer. They are old friends; it goes back to Vietnam—the anti-imperialist drugs operations."

"And?"

"Peter sold us his memoirs."

I felt quite short of breath. I said, "When, exactly?"

"Two years ago."

That was a year before he defected, if that was still the operative word, to the CIA. I said, "What was his price?"

"Thirty million American dollars is the figure I've heard."

Now I knew where the twenty-seven million dollars in Escobar's Banco Amazones had come from. Peter had kept three million in pocket change to tide him over while he waited for the real return on his investment.

I said, "Is he here to sell more memoirs?"

"He is negotiating," my friend said. "But I am told that it is not information Peter is selling this time, but a more valuable item. They say that the price for this item is one hundred million American dollars, plus a percentage of future profits."

I said, "Future profits? What does that mean?"

My friend paused, considering her words. Big rusty vessels churned the Huang Po, whose stagnant waters looked and smelled like the disgorged contents of China's bowels.

My friend said, "It is expected that business opportunities in America and other advantages will result from this deal," she said. "For example, most-favored-nation status for China and official U.S. silence on Chinese human-rights questions. Also, Mr. Gee and partners would like their own port on the West Coast of the United States."

"Their own port?"

"Yes. Exclusive rights to the docks and private storage of goods with no interference by U.S. customs. They speak also of a Chinese port at either end of the Panama Canal. Certain joint economic ventures. A certain consideration in matters of licensing military technology. Peter is asking two percent of profits from all such enterprises. He has been offered one percent."

"That's it? That's all there is to the deal?"

She hesitated. I was afraid she might say no more, and I knew in my bones that there was more.

Finally she said, "Perhaps not. There is a curious condition in the basic agreement. Thirty million dollars, broken down into smaller sums, will be paid at once, before the end of this week. But not to Peter. To a second party. Some of this money has already been transferred to many banks in the United States. The balance of seventy million will be paid directly to Peter, but not until the first Wednesday after the first Monday in November."

The day after Election Day. The "item" Peter had just sold to Mr. Gee was Jack. The seventy million dollars payable to Peter in November was a finder's fee. The thirty million dollars now fluttering into the vaults of a hundred American banks was the money Jack had been waiting for. The money he needed to win.

Peter had optioned Jack Adams's contract with us to the new Chinese capitalists, who now owned all rights to the next president of the United States.

The blood drained from my face. "Dmitri," my friend said, "what's the matter?"

3 That week, the Adams campaign was in California. As soon as I stepped off my plane, I called Morgan's personal cell phone. She answered on the first ring.

In a voice deeper than my natural tone I said, "I come from the fisherman."

She said, "It's about time. Fly to Monterey. Four-thirty at the aquarium. By the shark's tank. I will speak to you."

I recognized her at once, and like my friend in Shanghai she had no difficulty seeing past my new face. She herself was in disguise—her old false tummy and her counterculture clothes. She wore the thick glasses she had discarded years before and joke-store fake crooked teeth snapped over her own perfect smile.

"Nice try with the basso profundo, but I knew who you were," she said. "I didn't think the call would come from you."

"You're in for a lot of surprises," I said.

I told her what I had learned in Shanghai.

I had thought that I knew her so well that nothing she did could surprise me. I was wrong. When I told her about the money, a magnified tear squeezed from the corner of her magnified eye. She said, "Thank God. God bless Peter. So *that* was what he meant!"

"Meant by what?"

"By Peter's message."

"Peter has been in touch?"

"In a roundabout way. He sent Jack a girl. Actually, she called me on the cell phone. She spoke the recognition phrase."

"Describe this woman."

"Black hair, tawny skin, long legs, big tits, high IQ. Mixed ancestry. Your basic bunny."

The honey-colored girl. I said, "And what was Peter's message?"

"That Jack was to keep himself only unto this bimbo until further notice. No other playmates. So far Jack doesn't mind that part; you should see the girl. She's his closest adviser."

"Tell me more."

"*Lovely* name: Trixie Wang. Poli-sci at Berkeley, master's from Yale in Chinese."

"Did she bring a message?"

"Peter wants Jack to play a round of golf with an important contributor. A Chinese gentleman."

"Is his name by any chance Mr. Gee?"

"Yes. My, what a lot you know, Uncle Wiggly."

"When does the golf game take place?"

"Why do you want to know?"

"Someone has to warn Jack."

Morgan said, "Warn him of what? That Peter has come through again, that all his problems are solved?"

I explained who Mr. Gee was, and what he stood for.

Morgan shrugged. "So he has good cover. He's still a friend of Peter's."

"Morgan, he is no friend of ours."

"Then why is Peter sending him to us?"

Peter, Peter. The bond was very strong. Could I make her understand? I tried. I said, "Morgan, remember what this operation you have given your life to is really about. It's about saving the revolution, not betraying it."

"Of course it is. And saving it is what's happening."

"No. Something else is happening. Our objective was to start over with a clean slate in a fresh country—the right country this time. To make the revolution work by purifying it. This man Gee represents corruption."

Morgan frowned. "How so?"

"He is a capitalist."

"He can't be. Peter said he would never abandon us, and he hasn't. The Soviet Union is gone, Dmitri. So Peter is bringing help from China. From the last good country on Earth, the last Marxist country in the world. He's saving the operation, saving our lives, keeping his promises. Saving the revolution, for pity's sake. Why are you saying these things against him?"

"Because you don't know Peter."

"Ha!"

"Morgan, listen to me. Peter doesn't give a shit for communism. He wants money and secret thrills and he wants to die a long time from now with the knowledge that he double-crossed the whole world and got away with it. That's all he ever wanted." I spoke from the heart. As always, this was a mistake.

Morgan said, "Oh, really?" She took off her glasses and from eyes swimming with myopia gave me a look of deep, inexpressible disgust, as though she had been told what to expect and had fought belief but now understood that I had never been the honest Communist spy I represented myself to be but a secret fascist from the start. Now I had unmasked myself. In the tick of the clock everything had changed. She hated me.

"Are you sure it's Peter you're talking about and not whatever kind of slime you've become since the last time I saw you?" she said. "You've changed your face. What else have you changed?"

I said, "I'm not the one who has changed, Morgan. I want to talk to Jack."

"So do a lot of other people. But they can't get near him, and neither can you." Her eyes were watering—from anger, not sorrow. "The bimbo brought me something in secret writing," she said. "Shades of the Comintern. I had almost forgotten how to develop it."

Morgan showed me the message, ghostly letters written in invisible ink on a slightly charred notebook page. The words were written in English, in Peter's unmistakable flowing hand: *Warning: D. is no longer a friend. Burn this.*

I said, "If you believe this, why did you meet me?"

"Because I couldn't believe it. But now I do. Dmitri, Jesus. You, of all people."

"Morgan, tell me for your own sake. Where is the golf game?"

Morgan smiled very sweetly with her false hillbilly teeth, then produced a cigarette lighter and set Peter's message alight. She let it fall from her hand and it fluttered, burning, to the ground.

I sensed movement just outside my field of vision. This was a signal. I looked behind Morgan and saw Igor. In the tiny lenses of her glasses I could see the Georgian's reflection. I put my wallet into her hand. She stared at it, uncomprehending. I seized her and threw her to the ground.

"Thief!" I shouted.

A woman screamed. "She's pregnant!"

People turned to look. A security guard arrived.

"Fucking bitch stole my wallet," I said.

"A pregnant woman?" the cop said.

"She's about as pregnant as you are," I said. "Look at her. It's a pillow. It's part of the scam."

Morgan was tugging frantically at her preggie, which had slid around to the side.

I said, "She's got two confederates." I described Igor and the Georgian. By now they had vanished.

Morgan denied everything, but there my wallet was, and there, twisted onto her hip, was her preggie. The security man unlimbered his handset, to call the police.

"Wait," I said. "Forget the cops. All I want is my wallet."

"You don't want to file charges?"

"I'm on vacation. She's fucked up my good time enough already. Just get her out of sight."

He handed me my wallet. I counted the money and the credit cards. "All there."

"Let her go," I said. And to Morgan: "You need help, sister. Here's a number you can call." I tucked a card in the pocket of her jacket.

The guard walked her to the door, never dreaming whose elbow he was holding. "Never come back," he said. I was sure she never would.

4 Time was running out for Jack; Election Day was just five weeks ahead. Broke as he was, behind in the polls as he was, he knew that he could win, that he could come from behind in the last two weeks exactly as JFK had done if he could do what Kennedy had done: pick up just a few thousand additional votes in a few key precincts in swing states. He knew precisely which precincts to target and precisely what the voters in those precincts wanted to hear and were willing to believe.

What Jack needed was a breakthrough issue—something to get the media's mind off drugs and the character issue. A new ex-mistress popped up on supermarket tabloid racks more or less weekly. All were good-looking and, in Jack's opinion, did him as much good as harm with the voters, especially among women. The polls confirmed this; with each revelation his popularity took a little hop upward, as if in reward for potency. One of the wilder papers had even run a story—much milder than the reality—on the Gruesome penthouse. Jack was under daily attack from the Right on his drugs record. He wanted to counterattack with an issue that would startle and surprise the country and get the columnists talking about something else.

"What we need is a hidden danger," Jack said to Danny. "A plot. A dragon to slay."

Danny said, "You want to slay this dragon or just beat the shit out of it until November and then let it slink away?"

"Depends on how big a dragon it turns out to be."

"Like a missile gap?"

"It's been done," Jack said.

"So has 'What this country needs is a good five-cent cigar.' "

Jack slapped his own forehead. "Thank you, Lord, that's it!" With a whoop that brought the Secret Service running, Jack leaped to his feet, overturning a chair with a crash. "Daniel, you're a genius. *Tobacco.*"

This fit right in with his overall strategy for victory. Attacking the tobacco barons had worked for him before. The polls told him he had no realistic chance to carry the tobacco states or any other major southern state except Florida, one of the keystones of his plan.

Jack hugged Danny. He counted off the elements of the story on his fingers. "You leak it, Dan," he said. "I'll take it from there."

After one of its writers met in private with Danny, a news-magazine ran a story claiming that Jack, if elected, was planning to dismantle the federal anti-drug effort, which he had already re-peatedly described as expensive and ineffective, and concentrate in-stead on banning the sale of tobacco in the United States.

The rest of the media, stunned by what they saw as the complete irrelevance of this idea, expected Jack to deny the story and back away, but he did not. Instead, the very day after the story broke, he wrapped his arms around the issue and, speaking to a cheering crowd on a college campus, hit the tobacco industry hard.

"My fellow Americans, the tobacco kingpins are the secret weapon of the talk-big, think-small, do-nothing government they want to keep in office," Jack cried. "America can lick drugs, but let's start with the drug we grow at home and subsidize with billions in taxpayers' hard-earned money. Tobacco! Tobacco kills more Amer-icans than any other substance, ruins more lives, costs the taxpay-ers more, and makes the rich richer and the poor sicker. Tobacco! That's the real threat to our families and our freedom. This admin-istration is spending twenty billion dollars a year on secret drug po-lice. They're everywhere, watching anybody they don't like, breaking down doors, shooting instead of asking questions. Ask yourself: Why? What's the connection? We're going to start asking questions the day we're elected. We're going after the evil forces that are behind this plot against America's health, against America's children. And we're going to put this conspiracy out of business."

This diatribe made no sense. But it worked. The new polls came out. Jack had dropped off the charts in the Carolinas and Tennessee and Kentucky, but overall he had gained five points on the president in a single week while the third-party candidate neither gained nor lost ground. Some money began to dribble into Jack's campaign from individual donors. It was nowhere near enough, but he was staying afloat.

Four

1 On the second Friday in October, the news of the failure of the Columbus Bank of the Western Reserve broke in the Columbus press. It became national news the following day when the governor was found dead in his car, late at night on a street near the bank. As nearly as police could reconstruct events, the governor had stopped for a red light and suffered a seizure. When his foot slipped off the brake, the car rolled onward for a few yards, climbed the curb, and came to rest against a tree. An autopsy revealed that he had suffered a massive coronary thrombosis, together with many other, apparently simultaneous thromboses elsewhere in his circulatory system. Multiple thromboses were an extremely rare event for which there was no accepted medical explanation. There was no trace of alcohol or drugs in the dead man, apart from the residue of the widely prescribed medication he took daily to control long-standing high blood pressure. Although the coroner had no way of knowing—because its very existence was, at that time, a deep secret—this was a typical autopsy report in a death caused by ricin, the favorite poison of the KGB.

Morgan, a pioneer in the home manufacture and use of this surprising derivative of the otherwise harmless castor bean, was in California when the governor's blood vessels burst like a string of firecrackers and his heart stopped. But I had seen Igor and the Georgian in her company, and who knew where they were at the fatal moment? I wondered if the governor had perhaps stopped at his red light, felt a pinprick, looked into the mirror, and . . .

No matter. The point was that the governor's dramatic death was a grand diversion, a tabloid windfall. The respectable media got involved a day later when the FBI entered the bank with a search warrant and discovered that most of the bank's crucial files had disappeared.

The diversion soon turned into a nightmare. The media reported that the bank's depositors and investors, mostly poor, had lost their life's savings. By the end of the day, reporters had discovered that the bank's legal work was handled by the Columbus firm of Miller, Adams & Miller. The story broke on the evening news of one network only. It was a bare-facts report, but it mentioned Jack's name and made note of the fact that the general counsel of the Columbus Bank of the Western Reserve was none other than Danny Miller, who was not only Jack's law partner but his oldest friend and the manager of his struggling presidential campaign. By midnight, six separate contributors had called to cancel a total of four million dollars in desperately needed contributions.

"Jesus Christ!" Jack screamed, pacing the spongy carpet of a presidential suite in Detroit. "We've already spent the money on TV spots. We've sent rubber checks to half the stations in America. Danny, do something!"

"Like what?" Danny asked. "Put up our houses as collateral? We're broke, Jack."

"Then find other contributors."

"These were the last six in America. The seventh dwarf isn't answering the phone."

"I'm glad you think this is funny," Jack said. "Because this fucking bank was never supposed to touch my name, the money was supposed to be cleaned up, there wasn't supposed to be any fucking failure until after the campaign, it was all supposed to be neat and tidy. And now it's all over the fucking—"

Danny said, "Wait a minute. What did you just say?"

Jack remembered, too late, that Danny was not in on the secret of the bank's true origins and sources of cash.

"Nothing," Jack said. "Just raving. It all looks so goddamned bad, Danny. And the fucking money has stopped. And the fucking Morg is flipping her wig on me. Forget I opened my mouth." He grinned, a sickly substitute for his usual supernova when caught in a lie. "It's the stress."

Danny gave his friend a long, searching look. "Jack," he said at last, "what have you been up to with the bank?"

"I never had anything to do with the bank, Dan. It was you and Morgan."

"Jack, tell me."

Jack had never been able to lie to Danny. It had never been necessary, because Danny had always accepted him for what he was, a fellow who lived in a trance of untruth because he had no choice in the matter. Jack was a liar in the way that Danny had been a world-class athlete, because the great hidden river of their genetic heritage had spit them out that way on the shores of American life.

"Tell you what?" Jack said.

"The truth. For example, where did that twenty-seven million come from? And the mysterious millions before that?"

Danny was sitting down, yellow legal pad in his lap. He sat because his wounded leg could not long bear the weight of his body. He held the pad because it was his habit to write down everything Jack said to him or said to others in his presence—not as evidence, but so that Jack would have a reliable record of his words in case he needed to remember them. Even Jack's capacious memory could not contain and classify all the fibs and evasions, half-truths and exaggerations, and outright lies that he told on any given day. Danny had been scribbling as they talked. Jack reached down and took the pad out of his hand.

"Danny," he said, "I think you should go. Now."

"Go?" Danny said. "What do you mean, go?"

"I don't mean resign," Jack said. "Take leave to defend yourself, to save what you can of the bank. Somebody's got to look out for the little people who are going to lose their savings because the governor fucked up the way he did. That person should be you."

"Why me?" Danny said.

"So you can help out the poor folks," Jack replied. "They need you more than I do. Both of us see that, Danny, and the media will see it too."

"When do I go?" Danny asked.

"The sooner the better," Jack said.

This was pure Jack—self-delusion, diversion, deception, escape, legal defense all combining like chemical components to produce a lightning flash of brilliance. For the first time in their long, long life together, Danny did not laugh explosively at the wonder of it all. He simply stared in disbelief. Jack was doing to Danny what Danny had helped Jack do to so many others since they were boys, and for the first time Danny understood that this moment had always been inevitable. And that it was not the first time it had occurred.

He said, "Jack, different subject."

Jack was surprised, but he nodded amiably. *Why, sure, old buddy.*

Danny said, "Did you really fuck Cindy in that strip mine the night I left for 'Nam?"

As if hit by a sucker punch, Jack said, *"Woof!"* And then he smiled—his real, original smile this time. "Cindy? Not that I remember, Dan. And, baby, I would remember."

Danny smiled, too, and for a long moment held his friend's eyes with his own. Then he said, "That's good enough for me, Jack. I'll take care of the other thing."

He took his pad from Jack's hand, tore off the top ten pages, and, holding the paper in his teeth and tearing with his one good hand, ripped them to shreds. He threw the pieces into the air and limped out of the room. Some of the pieces stuck to Jack like yellow snow as they fluttered downward to the floor.

Danny went straight to the pressroom and did exactly as Jack had suggested. He added one detail: Jack and Morgan Adams had lost their life's savings in the bank failure, every penny of the little bit of money they had been able to put aside from Jack's meager salary for the twins' college tuition.

In Columbus, the U.S. attorney, F. Merriwether Street, impaneled a grand jury and called the bank's surviving officers and directors and its counsel, Danny Miller, as witnesses.

Within the hour, as he left the hotel for a rally in Cadillac Square, Jack made his first and last public statement on the issue. In response to a shouted question about Danny, Jack halted in midstride and walked back to the cameras. Looking straight into the lenses, he said, "I'm terribly sorry for the folks who have lost money, like my wife and I have. Everything will come out in time, and that's the way it should be. And though I haven't talked to him about this, I know it's the way Danny Miller wants it, because in my heart I believe he has nothing to hide. Danny Miller and I have been friends since before we could walk. He's my law partner, my best friend, and the most honest and honorable man I've ever known. He's a war hero who sacrificed a brilliant career as an athlete for his country. He could have been in all the halls of fame, but he isn't and he won't be because he did his duty to America and bled for every one of us. And I say this to you: If I have to choose between the presidency and my friend, I know that God will give me the strength to choose my friend. That's all I have to say on this subject and all I'll ever have to say."

2 Every network news show ran Jack's entire statement, which by coincidence timed out at the exact length of the average stand-up report by a correspondent. A media chorus began to talk and write about Jack's pluck, about his loyalty to old friends, about his poverty compared to the wealth of his opponents, both of whom were multimillionaires whose fat-cat friends were pouring millions into their campaigns. The miracle, wrote the pundits, was not that Jack, a penniless nobody from nowhere who had nothing but brains, guts, personality, and a smart and beautiful and utterly devoted wife, was losing. The miracle was that he was still in the race. And not only still in the race, but making one hell of a stretch run.

When the next polls came out, Jack had gained more points and was almost even with the president. The media started doing the same arithmetic Jack had done months before, and press and television began to say, "By God, he might win!"

Jack knew that he would win. Money was trickling into his campaign from many quarters—big sums, medium sums, small sums. He was already taping his attack ads for the final week of the campaign. For that he needed huge sums.

3 "This Mr. Gee wants to talk to you absolutely alone," Morgan had said.

"Who is he?"

"A very important contributor."

"How important?"

Morgan had very little patience left. She said, "Jack, do you really want me to spell it out?"

Jack gave her his full attention. "It's happened," he said.

Morgan nodded. "Why the surprise?"

"Jeez, Morg, I dunno. Maybe it's the exquisite timing of the thing. What does Mr. Gee—that's his name?—want to talk about?"

Morgan said, "The future, I suppose. Just keep the caddies at a distance."

"Why?"

"Do you have any idea what he wants in return for his largesse?"

"No."

"Then don't talk in the golf cart," Morgan said. "Or anywhere near it or the golf bags."

"You mean they might be bugged?"

Morgan simply stared. Would he never learn to be serious?

Jack said, "What about the clubs? Are they clean?"

Morgan said, "Just be yourself, Jack, and it won't make much difference what anybody has on tape."

At the Pebble Beach golf course, one of the most beautiful in the world, Mr. Gee waited near the first tee. Unlike most of the unctuous Orientals who had given money to the Jack Adams campaign, Mr. Gee was dour and ponderous. He was very tall and rawboned for a man of his race. He reminded Jack of a Chinese F. Merriwether Street. Mr. Gee watched impassively as this comical thought brought a furtive smile to Jack's lips.

To the Secret Service men Jack said, "I'll drive the cart. Stay well behind. Kibitzers make him nervous."

"How many holes, sir?"

"Nine, max," Jack said. "Then I get an urgent phone call. Got it?"

"Yes, sir."

Jack, who had been too poor as a boy to learn bourgeois games, had taken up golf as a member of the Gruesome and, to his own great surprise, had found that he had a talent for it. If he was not quite a handicap player, he was a long way from being a duffer, especially when it came to the short game. For the first two holes Mr. Gee said nothing. He was an involved, determined player who hit tremendous drives off the tee but had less luck with short irons and putter. These were the best parts of Jack's game, and he sank a picture-perfect chip shot on the second hole.

"Hot damn," Jack said with boyish enthusiasm. "Want to bet twenty on who's closest to the hole?"

Mr. Gee hit his own shot. It went clear over the green and

plopped into a sand trap. He smiled and said, "Welcome to the country of the blind."

The ball that Jack had just taken out of the cup dropped from his hand and rolled across the green. Hoarsely, he said, "What did you say?"

Mr. Gee said, "Peter said you were easily startled. Keep walking. We'll leave the cart to your servants. I have something to explain to you."

In fluent but heavily accented singsong English, Mr. Gee explained that the twenty-seven-million-dollar lump sum Jack had received in the spring came from him and some associates in China. "Through Peter, of course," he said. "We regret that the transfer was so clumsily handled. It had nothing to do with us. There were special circumstances having to do with the chaos in Russia at the time."

"What did Russia have to do with it?"

Mr. Gee ignored the question. "The clumsiness will not happen again. At this moment, the sum of thirty million dollars is being made available to you. It is in the process of being broken down into more manageable increments and emanating from many different American banks. This process should be complete within one week." He smiled again. "But I think you already know that."

"Very generous," Jack said, as if acknowledging a detail—as, in a way, he was. "Please make sure it comes from many different donors."

For the first time, Mr. Gee smiled. "There are many, many Chinese in the world. A restaurant in every American town. Do not worry."

"Fortune cookies, eh?" Jack said.

Mr. Gee smiled; dark wayward teeth. "That's a good one."

"The restaurateurs"—Jack put an incorrect *n* in the word—"all have my sincere thanks. What do you want in return?"

Such crudeness. Mr. Gee sighed. They were approaching the fourth tee, with the Secret Service men trailing along in the golf carts. "Ah, Jack, what *do* we want?" he said. "That we should be friends—friends in Peter's sense of the word."

"No problem, but be specific. What do you expect from me?"

"Not military secrets. We know you are not a spy. What we want is the advantages of your friendship. In return for our wholehearted support until, as they say, the end of time. Of course."

Jack said, "You're being too subtle for me, Mr. Gee. What's your first name?"

"I'm just Mr. Gee, Jack. We don't really have first names. It's too early for a shopping list." Mr. Gee searched Jack's incredulous face. "But, Jack, I must know—is all this agreeable to you?"

"You say Peter set this up. But how do I know you're telling the truth?"

As if he had been waiting for this question, Mr. Gee handed Jack a cellular phone. "This is a scrambler phone, brand-new type, absolutely secure, Jack, very latest software from the mysterious East." He smiled, tight-lipped. "So you may say whatever you like. The correct number has already been punched in. Please press SEND."

Jack did as he was told, and Peter came on the line in the middle of the first ring. "Hi, Jack," he said. "What can I do for you?" Jack was hearing this voice for the first time in fifteen years, but its sound was unmistakable.

Jack said, "I hardly know where to begin."

"Let me start things off then," said Peter. He confirmed the financial terms of the deal in exactly the same terms as Mr. Gee had. "This will make it possible for you to achieve your goal, don't you agree?"

"Maybe," Jack said. "But the question is, what happens then?"

"They will want what any investor wants. A fair return. Certain advantages. Certain opportunities. An assurance that your military technology will never be better than theirs."

"How can I guarantee that, for Christ's sake?"

"Use your imagination. Let's just say they look forward to a mutually satisfactory working relationship."

"Peter, you're making me very nervous."

"I'm sure I am. But I am also saving your sweet American ass, probably from prison and the disgrace of the family name. And if I may remind you, the two of us, plus that other person you know, are also saving, in the only way possible, the thing we set out to do together all those years ago: making the United States into a just society and the hope of the world."

"Right." Jack's tone was flat.

Peter said, "You can, of course, refuse."

"And if I do?"

"Well, you might not be elected president, though knowing you I wouldn't bet on it. You're the real thing, Jack. Remember where you heard it first."

"That's your threat?"

"Who am I to threaten anybody?" Peter asked. "But Mr. Gee and his associates are realists—it's a national characteristic—so they demanded insurance. They feel that you owe them. I'm afraid I had to give them the photos we looked at together in Moscow all those years ago. You do remember?"

"Yes."

"And some other material. So being elected might not be much of a guarantee that you would ever serve."

"Assuming you can find somebody to believe a mad Russian."

"You'd be surprised, Jack. In certain American circles I am regarded as a very reliable witness. Think it over. Remember who your friends are and who your friends have always been. Then do what's best for Jack. Follow your star. That's all I ask."

Jack said, "Same deal as always, right?"

He handed the phone back to Mr. Gee. The two men gazed long into each other's eyes.

Mr. Gee said, "Before I hang up, I think it would be nice to tell Peter your decision."

Jack nodded, one quick jerk of the head. "I'm so glad," said Mr. Gee. He spoke a single word into the phone, then clicked off. "What can you tell me about the next hole?" he asked.

Jack did not hear him.

"Two iron?" Mr. Gee asked, examining his ball, which had landed near a tree.

"Three wood, maybe," Jack replied. This was mischievous advice, but Mr. Gee pulled the club from his bag.

He hit the three wood. The ball dropped toward the green, landed at its far edge, bounced high, and trickled over the lip of the green into another trap.

"Shit!" said Mr. Gee.

"Bad dream," Jack said. "Guess you were right about the two

iron." He hit a perfect shot with that club—onto the green, six feet from the cup. They walked on.

"One more thing," Mr. Gee said. "On October twenty-ninth, something will happen in China. This will have a bad effect on the U.S. economy. Only temporary. But this event will make the president look stupid and put you over the top in the election, only five days later. Correct?"

Jack said, "What do you mean, something will happen in China?"

"Better you do not know the details. It will be a nice surprise. But take nothing for granted. Campaign hard. Spend all the money. Go for it."

"I'll do that little thing," Jack said.

Mr. Gee shook Jack's hand. "True friends," he said.

"To the end," said Jack, remembering his perfect shot with the two iron. He grinned at Mr. Gee. *Star Wars*, he mused. He let his innermost thought show: *I can always drop one on Beijing if I have to.* He smiled at Mr. Gee.

"You look like your real father when you smile," Mr. Gee said. "However, don't think like him, okay? He was a *very* impetuous man."

4 Ten days remained in the campaign. Using Mr. Gee's money and the last reserves of his own energy, Jack launched his trademark end game: the last-minute blitz of television commercials and a flying, fifteen-state speaking tour. The country resounded to the strains of "Jack, Jack, Jack!" Jack Adams girls danced at the rallies. The commentators spoke of a rising fever of enthusiasm in the land. Maybe it was too little, too late, they said, but you had to hand it to Jack Adams: He never gave up.

Jack's numbers went up, but not quite enough. At midweek he was a little more than one point behind the president in the polls. Jack was saying nothing new, doing nothing different. He had just stepped up the intensity.

Morgan told him he was off-message. He was not hitting the issues. The core constituency was disturbed. Jack had heard all this before, and always at the wrong moment—the last moment, when none of that shit mattered.

"Morg," he said, "I just can't give twelve speeches a day and argue with you, too. My throat feels like I've been gargling paint remover."

But she kept after him, ticking off a long list of ideas he had not mentioned in weeks, positions he had abandoned, verbiage he had pruned from his political vocabulary.

"It's a fucking sellout," she said. "The troops are mad as hell."

Jack said, "Morgan, lighten up. I'm just trying to get elected."

"By sounding like Barry Goldwater?"

"Duplicity in the name of victory is no crime."

"Duplicity is one thing," Morgan said. "Treason to the Left is another. You're not supposed to bamboozle the good people. You can't be elected without your own constituency."

"They're *your* department," Jack said. "Always have been. Go talk to them."

Morgan's temper kindled. Jack was patronizing her. "No," she said. "That's not the way it's going to be."

Jack simply stared at her.

Morgan said, "You agree? I can't leave without an answer."

Jack said, "You want an answer? Okay, here it is. You're out, Morgan."

She blinked theatrically—something else Jack had seen too many times. "Out?" she said. "Out of what?"

"Out of here," Jack said. "Out of the campaign. Out of my hair, you pain in the ass."

"Who the fuck says so?"

"Morgan," Jack said, "go away."

"You don't tell *me* what to do. As far as I know, the rules haven't changed."

"Right," Jack said. "As far as *you* know."

"What's that supposed to mean?"

A cellular phone rang in the far corner of the vast hotel suite. Trixie Wang stepped from behind a Chinese screen with the phone in her hand. "It's for you," she said to Morgan.

Morgan lifted the phone to her ear and heard Peter's voice. "Hi," he said, as if they had spoken only the day before. "I have some new instructions for you."

"Over the *phone*?"

"It's okay. Special phone."

In a few sentences, Peter told Morgan that from now on she would have no contact with him, or with anyone representing him. Peter was taking away Morgan's power over Jack on the very day before Jack took power. She realized that I had told her the truth about Peter's purposes and Jack's future.

Too late.

Barely able to breathe, Morgan said, "Peter, what are you telling me?"

"That phase one is over," Peter replied. "You've done wonderful work. It's time to say thanks and make an honest woman of you."

"I don't understand."

"I want you to step back. Retire. First lady is a full-time job. From now on, being first lady is your only job."

"First lady?" Morgan said. Her voice trembled. Her face twisted like a child's. Listening, watching, Jack had never thought such reactions possible. Fighting for self-control, she said, "Peter, please don't do this to me."

Peter said, "Comrade Colonel, an operational decision has been made. The case has been given to another handler. You have a new assignment. There is no appeal. Do as you are ordered. Goodbye."

Having ruined her life by informing her of a promotion in an organization that no longer existed, Peter hung up. For several heartbeats, Morgan listened to the dial tone. Then she handed the phone back to Trixie, who regarded her with a blank face. The inscrutable East. Then Morgan realized the truth. *Trixie had taken over.* She was the new Morgan. The truth, the monstrous reality of it, penetrated Morgan's consciousness with the force of a bullet shattering bone. She put her face in her hands and wept like a woman.

Not for long, of course. After a moment her old friend anger came to her rescue. Her eyes, still wet, rested on Trixie Wang, a woman twenty years younger than she, a stupid woman with a stupid name who looked like a stupid centerfold. *Trixie enjoys clandestine meetings on Air Force One and kinky sex.*

Morgan said, "One question. Are you two fucking?"

"Like mad," Trixie replied. "It soothes the savage beast. Peter never makes the same mistake twice."

Jack shrugged, goodbye.

5 On October 29, the government of the People's Republic of China announced that the strong U.S. dollar, cynically foisted on the Third World by an arrogant and reckless administration, had created the conditions for a massive economic crash in East Asia. To avoid chaos and great human suffering, China had decided to intervene decisively.

Ji De Lu, the hitherto obscure party official who had been chosen to make this momentous announcement, explained that China had accumulated massive gold reserves through Western central bank sales. This had happened slowly, over a period of years, and now China's gold reserves were the largest in the world.

But there was more. Beneath the desert of Xinjiang province, in the bed of an extinct underground river, Chinese engineers had made a major new find of gold. This discovery, kept secret for ten years for reasons of national security, was now being announced to the world. The new gold mine, called the Victory of Socialism Mine, was the richest in the world, and it was now fully developed. Through intensive use of the most modern methods (read "slave labor"), the Victory of Socialism Mine was producing more gold than all the mines of the former Soviet Union and Africa combined.

"Therefore," said the man Jack knew as Mr. Gee, "the government of the People's Republic of China today announces the full convertibility of the Chinese renminbi, backed by gold at the ratio of one ounce of gold per twenty-four hundred renminbi, or three hundred United States dollars per ounce. We invite all neighbors of China on the rim of Asia to join with the Chinese people and their government in a Pacific Prosperity Zone, in which all their currencies will be pegged to the renminbi."

Within hours, all Southeast Asian countries, plus India and the Philippines, had accepted Mr. Gee's invitation and linked their currency to the new gold-backed renminbi. Despite heavy American pressure, Japan tied the yen to the Chinese currency.

This series of events, coming one after the other with sickening rapidity, meant that roughly half the world's population had gone onto the gold standard over a single weekend.

World currency and capital markets and the New York stock market crashed. It was the worst decline since 1929.

On Tuesday, Jack Adams was elected president of the United States with a plurality of one twentieth of 1 percent of all popular votes cast, and with the slimmest possible margin in the Electoral College.

He and Morgan listened to the returns in Tannery Falls. After the president conceded defeat in the wee hours of the morning, the first couple–elect appeared before a rally of thousands of dancing, singing supporters. Jack, who had lost his voice in the final hours of the campaign, was unable to say a word. While he held their sleepy twin sons in his arms, Morgan stepped up to the microphone. "I can't say it as eloquently as my husband," she said, "but at this great moment for our country and for all humanity, I can say what Jack Adams in his humility might not say—that the man and the hour have met at last, and that America and the world are going to be different and better and more just and generous because of it. God bless Jack Adams."

Smiling more luminously than ever, Jack handed his wife one of the twins, and while she gazed at him with what looked for all the world like adoration, he managed to croak out a single phrase: "God bless America."

The crowd sang his name. The twins saluted.

A network commentator, one of the crustiest veterans of his craft, had the last word. "And so Jack Adams begins and ends with 'God bless America,' " he said. "That may be a cliché, but clichés are clichés for a reason, and after all maybe there's a certain poignant symbolism in all this. We can be sure it was a cliché from the heart. As most people know by now, Jack Adams is all heart. He wears it on his sleeve, he carves it on every rhetorical tree he passes. He's not ashamed of heart, and neither should we be. Looking at Jack Adams, looking at Tannery Falls, Ohio, where he was born and raised, it's just plain impossible not to believe another cliché—the one that says any American boy, no matter how humble his beginnings, can be president. We'd better believe it, because tonight he walks tall even if he cannot talk. Good night, Peter."

The old journalist was addressing a different Peter, but somewhere the real Peter was smiling as broadly as his asset.

Five

1 Now I had no one to turn to but Cindy. The day after the election I called her at Miller, Adams & Miller and asked for an appointment to discuss a delicate legal matter. Her voice was familiar to me from the tapes but clearer, more musical, over the phone.

"I'm not taking on new clients at the moment," Cindy said. "But I'd be happy to refer you to another lawyer."

I said, "Ms. Miller, I want to talk to you because I think I may be able to help your husband."

A silence. "Oh? In what way?"

"You put me in a difficult position. But this is not a crank call. I mention the name Banco Amazones. I mention the sum of twenty-seven million dollars. I'll talk to you in person about this. Not over the phone."

"Five-thirty today," Cindy said crisply. "You know where we are?"

"Yes."

I was punctual, a matter of training and long practice. The many photographs I had seen of Cindy and the many reports I had read did not prepare me for the reality. There is no beauty like American beauty. Whatever Europeans may say and write in their envy and rancor, there is more to this than diet and dentistry. You look at a former beauty who is Russian or French or English and you see an exile fleeing from lost looks. Life is over and pleasure an impossibility—she is Helen of Troy after Paris's family lost everything. But American beauty is a palimpsest. The girl Cindy had been was visible in every lineament and gesture of the woman she had become. She could not possibly have been lovelier at eighteen than she was at forty: slim, with skin that glowed, eyes that shone with health, and the hands of a young girl. There was a little blue vein at her temple, faint wrinkles at the eyes. The physical being was not all. Her intelligence and honesty enveloped her like an electrical field. No wonder Morgan had hated her; no wonder fucking a creature like Jack had left this goddess dazed by shame.

I am a far less impressive specimen. Besides, I could have come from Morgan. As an assassin. Partial as her knowledge was, such a thing was not beyond Cindy's imagining. Naturally Cindy was suspicious, wary. She did not hide this. She met me herself at the outer door of the office; her secretary had left. We were alone. Nevertheless she seemed perfectly at ease, perfectly unafraid. With another woman I might have suspected a trap: a body wire, a camera in the clock, FBI agents in the next room.

It didn't matter. She led me into the book-lined conference room—neutral ground. We sat across the table from each other. She offered nothing to drink, no small talk.

She said, "Shall we get right down to it?"

"Yes," I replied. "You will find what I am going to tell you strange. Even unbelievable. I ask you to keep an open mind, to hear me out to the end. Please do not interrupt. When I have finished, I will be glad to answer any question you care to put to me. Is that agreeable?"

"All right," Cindy said. "But on the condition that I may ask you to leave at any point and you will do so."

"Agreed."

I then told her, in short form, everything that I have told you in this memoir. As we went along, I showed her the corroborating evidence I had brought in a large sample case: The Heidelberg photos of Jack, from the first chilly coupling in the rain to the bank robbery. Tapes both audio and video of everything that had ever transpired in Morgan's room, including her assignations with Danny. Tapes of our motel meetings, and of Morgan's trysts with the Georgian. When she saw this man's face, Cindy gasped, her only lapse from detached professional behavior. I presented various other proofs: Photocopies of twenty years of reports by Morgan, receipts for operating funds signed and thumbprinted by both Jack and Morgan. Videos of Jack and Mr. Gee together, taken from far away and therefore silent, but with a transcript provided by a lip-reader.

Through it all, as she watched me undress the monster, she remained a lawyer: unruffled, calm, detached. At the end of it, she did nothing that could be regarded as punctuation, let alone response. No exchange of glances, no outlet of breath, not the slightest shake of the head to indicate incredulity or the beginning of a beautiful friendship.

With steady gaze she said, "Why are you doing this?"

The whole point was to tell her the truth and hope that she could understand it. I said, "Because they have betrayed communism."

"By selling out to the Chinese?"

"Yes."

"The Chinese aren't Communists?"

"Not these Chinese."

Cindy examined me for many moments. Again, no flicker of expression.

At last Cindy said, "All right. Let's go."

"Where?"

"To the U.S. attorney. Isn't that what you have in mind?"

"Yes. He has a motive to believe all this."

"Good point," Cindy said. "But if I were you, I'd think twice before telling Merriwether Street that you're giving up Jack Adams to the legal system in order to save communism."

2 Although it was nine in the evening, F. Merriwether Street was still at his office, pondering the outcome of the election. It had been a heavy blow to him. He had seen Jack win before with smoke and mirrors. But now the American people in their mystical wisdom had lifted up this sociopath, this liar, this rapist, this hollow man beloved by lunatics and traitors, and made him the most powerful human being in the world. The outcome contradicted everything he had ever believed about the nature of democracy. Jack Adams had perceived what F. Merriwether Street was not even willing to consider, that you did not *have* to fool all of the people all of the time. If you were lucky, you only had to fool 40 percent of the ones who voted. And you only had to do so once.

Street was not the only workaholic still at his post in the federal courthouse. I shivered to walk again down dim odorless corridors past numbered squares of frosted glass lighted from behind. Who worked behind these opaque windowpanes, at what tasks, with what human consequences? F. Merriwether Street, a minor functionary in a minor city, must have had hundreds of underlings, more than the arch-prosecutor Vyshinsky had needed to carry out the Great Purge for Stalin. Vyshinsky had taught us what could be done with an apparatus like this one. That Americans had made this particular bureaucracy was irrelevant. It was what it was: a blind thing, designed to suspect, to investigate, to operate in secret, to seize, to prosecute, to punish. To divert its attention from criminals to enemies of the leader required only the simplest change in instructions.

After a long walk we came to F. Merriwether Street's large and imposing office. It was decorated with steel engravings of warships, with photographs of Street with every Republican president of his lifetime. He was a child in some of these pictures. The presidents had been friends of his father, his grandfathers. I did not expect to find a happy man behind the U.S. attorney's massive oak desk. I expected agitation, anger; I found numbness.

Street gave me hardly a glance. Without waiting for Cindy to introduce me, he said, "So he won."

Cindy said, "He sure did."

"And dumped Danny. Threw him to the wolves."

"Yes."

"It's all over. Jack's home free. Danny will be indicted, you know. They'll get him after I go. They'll destroy him to protect Jack. They have to. I've lost the power to help you."

"We'll see about that," Cindy said. "Merriwether, this man has something to tell you."

"About what?"

"About Jack. About Morgan."

"Why tell me?" Street asked. "I'm a lame duck. No matter what your friend has or thinks he has—and I don't want to see it no matter what it is—I'll be out on the street in three months, and one of Morgan's twisted pinkos will be sitting in this chair. So thank you very much. Save your time."

"This is now. You're still in that chair. You should take a look at what we have."

"Why?"

"You'll have to see it to believe it."

"Ah, a copy of the contract with Mephistopheles?"

A joke? No, not from Merriwether Street.

Cindy said, "As a matter of fact, that's exactly what it is."

"Really?" said Street. "Then he's brought it to the one place where it's certain to be destroyed if it gets into the files. I won't touch it." He looked at me for the first time. "Take it away, sir— whatever it is, whoever you are."

His speech was slurred, his manner derisive. His eyes were red. Had he been weeping, actually weeping? He was not drunk; clearly not. But I was beginning to suspect tranquilizers. He had a certain self-mocking recklessness that comes with the loss of illusions. There was about him the aroma of a priest who has just lost his faith.

Cindy said, "Merriwether, listen to me. This man is a colonel in the Soviet KGB. He was Jack's case officer for twenty years. Morgan's, too. That's the evidence you won't look at."

"Jack is a traitor?"

"As defined by the Constitution," Cindy replied. She then showed him everything, item by item, whether he wanted to see it or not.

At the end, F. Merriwether Street raised bushy eyebrows, not in incredulity but as if to say, *Of course.* This was no surprise to him. Nevertheless, he shook his great equine head, emphatically. "Sorry," he said. "It's still out of the question."

"Out of the question?" Cindy said. "Please explain why."

"Gladly," Street said. "I'm sure that what you tell me is true. It explains everything. Jack was born to sell out America."

"That's exactly right," Cindy said. "So why is it out of the question to expose him?"

Street pointed a huge forefinger. "I'll tell you why. No prosecutor ever born in the United States of America would act on this information. No one could. You want me to accuse the president-elect of the United States of being a lifelong secret agent of a foreign power? With a turncoat KGB man as my main witness? And adult videos as evidence? Are you crazy?"

Cindy said, "But Jack and Morgan *are* lifelong traitors. And they've just changed masters in return for a thirty-million-dollar bribe and a plot to destroy the American dollar. That's no adult video. There's a paper trail. There has to be. They've sold the country to the Chinese Communists. We've got the transaction on tape. For God's sake, Merriweather, don't you see what's at stake?"

"God moves in mysterious ways," Street replied.

Cindy said, "What does God have to do with it?"

"I believe that democracy is God's work," Street said. "Jack Adams may be exactly what you say he is. But he was elected president by the people, and the people is always right. It's up to them to decide his fate."

Cindy said, "Merriwether, I want to be sure I understand. You believe it's your patriotic duty to let a traitor, an agent in the pay of a hostile foreign power, become president of the United States even though you have the power to prevent that from happening. Is that what you just told me?"

"You could put it that way," Street replied. He smiled beatifically, eyes only, like a stunned peasant in the background of an Adoration tableau.

Cindy said, "Do you want to know what I really think? I think you're afraid that all this is just another one of Jack's tricks, and afraid of looking like a fool again."

"I can't help what you think," he said. "Of course you could always take what you have to the media. Maybe they'd like an opportunity to catch Jack Adams by the toe."

Cindy said, "You must be joking."

He shrugged. "I think God is the one who's joking," he said.

3 Riding down in the elevator with a stunned and silent Cindy, I felt utterly alone. A matter of choice, I must confess. I felt the cell phone in my pocket. My mind fluttered back to Shanghai—to the old Shanghai of the maid and the civil servant, and to the new one in which they had met as grown-ups. I saw my friend's face again, so greatly changed by suffering and time. Yet after the first moment it seemed unchanged to me, like the face of a beloved wife one has awakened to every day for the lifetime we had, in fact, been apart. Suppose, instead of asking the questions I had asked this woman, I had said, "Will we ever be together again?"

But I did not ask this question, nor would she have known the answer if I had. There was no answer; it had died, like so many youthful secrets before it, in one of Mr. Gee's many interrogation rooms. It was my friend's young beauty, gone but still present, that I saw in Cindy's perfect face.

She said, "Poor Merriwether. The moral is pure Marxist prophecy. In the end the capitalists did sell you people the rope to hang us with."

I said, "Do you actually think so?"

Her voice was toneless. "Okay, you supply the moral."

I said, "Okay. 'It ain't over till it's over.' Yogi Berra."

"Oh, for Christ's sake," Cindy said.

But it was a straw to grasp at, so she listened to what I had to say next. In the open air—standing in perfect safety on the sidewalk in front of a building full of federal agents—I told her, in minute detail, about Morgan's brilliant operation against the Latin American guerrilla leader a quarter of a century before.

She listened in calm and unsurprised silence, then said, "You can provide what I would need?"

"Yes, but I'd have to consult a technician," I said. "It will take roughly twenty-four hours."

4 On Friday, Jack received Cindy at midnight, in his hideaway office in the governor's mansion.

"This is a surprise," he said. He took her coat, a mink.

Cindy said, "I wasn't sure you'd be interested."

"I've always been interested. But why, after all these years?"

Cindy said, "Let's just say power corrupts. You're the alpha male now. Availability is a given."

Jack was grinning. "I like the way you think."

Cindy said, "And then, too, I think we owe Morgan and Danny one for the road."

"Those two really surprised me."

"Me, too," Cindy said. "But revenge isn't my only motive. I was more or less unconscious the last time—"

"You mean all that noise was just delirium?"

"That's what I want to check out," Cindy said.

Jack, never one to delay sweet moments, lifted the short skirt of her clinging dress. She was naked beneath it. He put his hands on the skin of her waist and said, "Hey, you're serious."

With one hand he dropped his pants, with the other reached into his coat pocket. He slid his hands to her buttocks, thrust his knee between hers, and started to lift.

Cindy felt the Vaseline on his right hand. She resisted. "None of that," she said. "Last time it was really, really uncomfortable. This time we take off our clothes and do it in bed."

"I'm putty in your hands," Jack said.

"I hope not," Cindy replied, grasping his slippery member.

He pulled up his pants, tucked himself in with some difficulty, and led her upstairs. He had dismissed the Secret Service agents— by now he had made confederates of a few, and embarrassed accomplices of the rest. The mansion seemed to be deserted. At the top of the stairs, Cindy stripped off her dress and shook out her hair. She was wearing nothing but high-heel pumps and a ring on her left hand.

In the governor's bedroom, in the great canopied bed, Cindy took the tube of Vaseline from his hand and said, "Let me." She was quick about it. As before there was no foreplay, which may have accounted in part for Jack's exceptional endurance. And as before, Cindy's autonomic nervous system took control and delivered pleasures she did not want but could not prevent.

"Wow!" said Jack when it was over. "I think we just set a record."

"A personal best, anyway," Cindy said.

Jack's face wore a look of real tenderness. He said, "You're not going to believe this, but I've never fucked in this bed before."

"Right now I'd believe anything you said, big boy," Cindy said. "Turn over."

"What for?"

"Trust me."

In good-natured surrender, Jack rolled over onto his stomach. "God," he said. "The wasted years."

Cindy said, "Where's the Vaseline?"

"Wait a minute!"

"Scaredy-cat. Relax."

Kneeling between his outspread legs, she rubbed his back, deep massage as she had learned when the VA doctors believed that massage might bring back Danny's muscles.

Cindy could not open the hollow ring she wore with greasy fingers, so she wrenched it open with her teeth. She inserted the ricin suppository it had contained.

Feeling her finger, Jack said, "*H—*"

Before he could pronounce the *ey* in *Hey* or Cindy could withdraw her finger, he convulsed, then lay still, eyes wide open and empty.

Cindy closed the ring, put the top back on the Vaseline tube, then put on her dress. There was no need to wipe fingerprints; the Vaseline had prevented her from leaving any.

Carrying her shoes in her hand, Cindy walked down the hall to the head of the stairs. She had left her fur coat in Jack's office, a mistake. As she placed her hand on the banister, she heard a hiss. Cindy turned her face to the sound and saw Morgan standing in shadow on the other side of the stairwell. Morgan wore a floor-length navy-blue dressing gown; her loose hair hung down her back. When she recognized Cindy, her face twisted into a rictus of utter surprise.

The encounter was a shock to Cindy, too. She did not know what to expect—gunshots, perhaps. She started to speak. Morgan shook her head violently and pointed downward. Cindy looked over the stairwell and saw a bodyguard seated in the foyer below.

Cindy's mink coat, vile Republican object that it was, hung suspended by its collar loop from Morgan's forefinger. Cindy took it, as from a hook, and put it on. The women did not speak or look into each other's eyes. Cindy followed Morgan down the hallway, then down a back stairway to a back door that opened onto the private parking lot, where a car was waiting.

Upstairs again, Morgan found Jack as Cindy had left him. She saw at once what had happened. As the inventor of the suppository, Morgan knew that all traces of the poison would disappear from the victim's system in less than two hours. It was 2:12 A.M. She removed her dressing gown, took the ribbon from her hair, and got into bed with her husband. When the clock read 4:30, she ran naked into the hall and shrieked down the staircase for help. The Secret Service agents on duty came at once, and when they saw the president-elect they threw aside their drawn weapons and tried to revive him. But of course it was too late.

5 Four days later, the veiled widow walked behind the caisson to Arlington Cemetery. On either side of her marched the twin sons who looked so much like their father. It was unclear whether Jack, as the only president-elect to die before inauguration, was entitled to a president's funeral or to burial in Arlington among the nation's bravest dead. But that was what he got. Although there was a difference in the manner of death—the world believed that Jack Adams had met an enviable but risible end in the arms of his loving wife—the ceremony bore an eerie resemblance to an earlier presidential funeral. Morgan's dress and behavior—the black veil, the admirable self-control—added to this effect. So did the presence of the children.

As "Taps" sounded among the gravestones, Morgan lost her composure for a brief moment and let out a great but silent sob. And then she gazed icily into the cameras as if directly, contemptuously, into the eyes of all the sluts who had ever slept with her husband. Her whole being seemed to say, with almost superhuman vehemence, "You had your moments, but this is the final moment, and I am the one in black."

Fitz and Skipper had been given strict instructions not to salute when "Taps" was played, and so they did not. This was a disappointment to many.

Epilogue

★ ★

As perhaps you have guessed, I have always loved the movies. In my new life, I go more than ever. I like the darkness, the pictures flickering on the wall of the cave, the churchly oneness of the audience, the luxury of surrendering to the implausible.

Usually I avoid foreign movies, but in my travels—there is safety in movement, so I am continually in passage these days—I saw a German film in which some of the actors played the parts of angels. They were assigned to watch over certain human beings, to whom the angels were, of course, invisible. The angels were quite unhappy. They were former human beings themselves, and they longed to go back to being what they once had been.

The wonderful thing was, return was possible. Angels who did their duty by their human wards could earn redemption and return to the world somewhat in the way that good Christians go to heaven. Such second-comers to earthly existence were able to see angels, though they did not always know right away that they *were* angels, because, as I have explained, they looked just like the other actors in the film. The only returned angel in the movie was played by an American. All the rest were Germans.

I am haunted by this movie. It gave me the idea that I had been Jack Adams's angel, invisible to him but always by his side, speaking to him through other, seemingly real beings whom he could see and hear and touch. As a child, to keep me good after my parents were murdered, I was told that the dead know everything, so perhaps Jack can see me now.

No one else seems to be able to do so when I make my little visits. Not Cindy when she met Danny at the gates of his prison with a picnic basket full of Ohio treats. Not Morgan when she takes her boys to visit their father's grave at Arlington, and their grandfather's fabled grave nearby. Not Arthur from his resting place.

I watch, I remember, I go away. I drive a hundred miles and check into a motel. I stand in line with children and order a Big Mac supermeal. I buy a movie ticket. A flower. No one lifts his eyes.

Except, now and then, another member of our order of angels. We are a multitude, of course. We recognize each other, we exchange glances. But we do not speak, we do not tarry. We have anniversaries to observe, watches to keep, hopes for the world.

To the Reader

Lucky Bastard is a work of the imagination in which no character is based on anyone who ever lived and no reference is intended to anything that ever happened in the real world. To the reader whose own imagination perceives linkages that I did not intend, I can only suggest that Dmitri's confessions make the same essential point as the memoirs, biographies, and investigations of some of the great figures of the twentieth century, namely that in our time history became fiction and fiction history. It is no simple matter to reclaim the one from the other.

In the realm of the unequivocal, I am indebted to the late Emily Sears Lodge for the description of the vice presidential nomination; to Allen Weinstein's *Perjury* for details of Alger Hiss's life; to Loren McIntyre for introducing me to Amazonia; to Arthur Zich for snapshots of Shanghai; and to George Foot for the renminbi scenario. Nancy McCarry was, as always, my first and best reader.

C. McC.

About the Author

CHARLES MCCARRY, who grew up on a
farm in Massachusetts, has been a soldier,
a journalist, a speechwriter and
screenwriter, an intelligence officer, and
an editor. He established his reputation as
a novelist in 1975 with the publication of
The Tears of Autumn, a worldwide
bestseller. *Lucky Bastard* is the ninth novel
among his seventeen books.

About the Type

This book was set in Meridien, a classic roman typeface designed in 1957 by the Swiss-born Adrian Frutiger for the French typefoundry Deberny et Peignot. Frutiger also designed the famous and much-used typeface Univers.